Leather + Lace

A.B. GAYLE

Dreamspinner Press

Published by
Dreamspinner Press
5032 Capital Circle SW
Ste 2, PMB# 279
Tallahassee, FL 32305-7886
USA
http://www.dreamspinnerpress.com/

Leather+Lace

Cover Art by Anne Cain
annecain.art@gmail.com

ISBN: 978-1-62380-418-3
Digital ISBN: 978-1-62380-419-0

Printed in the United States of America
First Edition
March 2013

Author's Note

The plus symbol in the title is not just "and." It indicates that the final result is the sum of the two. Both aspects contribute to something new.

While the characters in this book are different, they exist in the same world and time frame as the series opener, *Red+Blue*, and one minor character links in.

Fans of *Caught* will also be pleased to see Nat and Danny making an appearance as they join the Opposites Attract universe.

Acknowledgments

I'VE always been fascinated by the concept of BDSM. Not so much the mechanics, but the mind-set and why people would become involved. Lately, kink is drifting into more mainstream literature, coming out of the closet, as it were, with scenes depicted as glamorous and exciting. But one day, I had a conversation with a writer who had lived the scene and been badly scarred both mentally and physically. His experiences made me think about the flip side, when the rules of safe, sane, and consensual are ignored.

I also find the concept of drag fascinating. We have some great drag artists in Sydney. For the most part, they tend to be the over-the-top caricatures, real ball-busting females, but others can be glamorous even if, in real life, there is nothing femme about them.

So, being me, I was intrigued as to what would happen if the two met and mixed. One who, by convention, flouts rules, and the other who continually expounds them.

Books like John Preston's *Mr. Benson* and david stein's *Carried Away*, with their concept of putting yourself totally into another man's hands, gave me the extreme fantasy sparked by their own experiences. To ensure I understood the reality, I read every book I could find on the Old Guard and the traditions of BDSM by writers like Guy Baldwin, Joseph Bean, Don Bastian, and Thom Magister. There are also great online sites such as Fetlife, where people speak of their lives with sometimes unflinching honesty. I also contacted david stein, who cleared up a few misconceptions.

Rush Derr IV needs a special thanks for sharing his experience of years spent performing drag in the States and Canada.

Others helped enormously, starting with readers and fellow writers Stevie Carroll, M.J. Sánchez, and Melanie Tushmore, who followed its progress in NaNoWriMo. A special shout-out to Melanie for her feedback on bikes.

Once the first draft was complete, it was the turn of my faithful duo, Don Schecter and Kate, who steered me through the process of converting the raw version into something worth publishing. They were assisted this time by a new critique partner, Jess, who not only helped with the text but gave a further polish to the bikes.

Writing about a scene you don't participate in is not easy. I'm indebted to Sascha Illyvich for his course on writing BDSM and Dusk Peterson, who provided lots of advice and leads on real life Master/slave relationships. From them I learned there is no single way to do things. In the end, I hope I captured both the best aspects of what BDSM and slavery can mean while also showing what can happen if care is not taken to do it correctly. According to two real-life slaves, Jason and Christopher, who read the finished text, I did.

I would also like to acknowledge the assistance of fellow writers Barry Lowe, Eden Winters, Charles Edward, Kayla Jameth, and my Goodreads buddies, Vivian de la Cruz and Jo. After finding a couple of things others had missed, they assured me the story had been beta'ed into submission and was ready to send off to Dreamspinner Press.

Here I'd like to thank Elizabeth North, Ginnifer Eastwick and her great team of editors, and the art department, represented by Paul Richmond and Anne Cain.

Finally, but definitely not least, I need to thank Stevie Nicks for not only giving me the inspiration for the title but providing me with a worthy artist any drag performer would be privileged to emulate. Her songs captivated me just as much as they did my hero.

—A.B. Gayle

Understanding the nature of a rip helps you deal with them.

Rips are powerful currents that can easily trap and carry the unwary swimmer out of their depth. Once past the line of breaking waves, the power of the rip diminishes.

If caught in a rip, don't panic and direct all your energy toward keeping your head above water.

Signal for help as soon as possible.

If none is available, once you are out of danger, swim parallel to the shore, then surf back in or let the natural momentum of the water carry you in.

Remember, swim in patrolled areas and keep between the flags.

CHAPTER
+++
ONE

Stand Back

"SEE, Marty, we told you Stevie Nicks was here."

Stevie Tricks to you, dahling. As if the real deal would ever stoop to something this trashy!

"But he's a guy."

She's a guy, I said to myself, but I didn't give a fuck what anyone called me, as long as it wasn't *boy*. Pushing the distraction aside, I concentrated on sucking the cock in my mouth. *Next time Fred says he needs me to participate in a charitable fundraiser, I should ask for more details.* This wasn't the first time I'd made that vow this evening, and judging by the number of new arrivals, it wouldn't be the last.

It was all Fred's fault. Since leaving for England four years ago, I hadn't been in contact with any of my Aussie friends, preferring to keep my whereabouts a secret to avoid any nasty confrontations with my ex... but I hadn't been able to resist sending Fred a good-luck e-mail when I discovered he had taken over the Hotel Paradiso. He'd need it.

"God, mate, long time no talk," he replied. "What the fuck are you doing in London?"

I gave him a brief rundown, leaving out all the bad bits—the therapy, the sleepless nights—and concentrated on the fact that I now made a living day-trading derivatives, and in my spare time, amused myself by performing in drag at the local nightspots.

After hearing I wasn't looking forward to another freezing winter, Fred messaged, "Get your ass back here. I could use your sweet mouth in our opening-night extravaganza." He went on to list the other people who would be appearing: two porn stars sponsored by a gay magazine, and Master D, a recent winner of one of the big Mr. Leather competitions in the US Midwest, who would be giving a whip and flogging exhibition.

Fred's proposal gave me the perfect opportunity to check out the scene without being seen, if you catch my drift, and discover if Julius was still obsessed with leather. If he was, he wouldn't miss the opportunity to watch a demonstration by a Leather Master, especially one from the States. If he wasn't here, maybe he'd finished with all that *I'm the Master, you're my slave* bullshit, and it was finally safe to go back to the house and retrieve the rest of my possessions.

In return for participating, I made Fred promise he wouldn't tell *anyone*. He agreed. Two days later, I packed my bags, caught the next flight home, and booked into a hotel in Darling Harbour. I contacted Fred shortly afterward but didn't disclose my address. Maybe I was being paranoid, but I wasn't a hundred percent sure where his loyalties lay. He'd known Julius before he met me.

"Great, mate. Come to the Paradiso. I need a photo for the flyer."

Fred nearly had a coronary when I sashayed into the bar in an exact replica of a frock Stevie had worn in one of her videos. He'd never seen me in drag before. "But why Stevie Nicks?" he asked.

I shrugged. "Try having a Fleetwood Mac fan for a mother and being named after Stevie and Lindsey Buckingham." Being shorter than average helped, and once that curly wig was on my head, the concept kinda stuck. Who would have thought I'd ever be grateful for the pretty-boy face that prompted a few kids to shove me into the lockers at school?

After Fred stopped laughing, he asked me to perform a couple of numbers as well as participate in the *Blowjobs for Bucks* segment.

I tried to pump him for information about Julius, but as soon as I mentioned my ex's name, Fred shook his head and stammered something about how it wasn't his place to tell me. However, he did

2

say that the American leather man wanted to speak to me later. Just what I needed. Not.

The cock in my mouth swelled and jerked, filling the condom I'd smoothed on ten minutes earlier. *Good. Another one bites the dust.*

"Thanks, that was great."

I gingerly rotated my jaw, easing out the kinks, and gave him a quick smile.

Don't know why he sounded so surprised. If there was one thing I was good at, it was giving blowjobs. Hence Fred's invite.

I groaned as the familiar ache in my knees returned. I should have worn kneepads. A trickle of sweat made its way down from under the wig. Damn. I'd have to apply fresh makeup before my act began. Resting back on my heels, I took my time applying another coat of lipstick as I checked out the latest arrivals.

These must be the heteros Fred warned me about: members of a local rugby club stopping in as part of a buck's party.

The intended groom was young and blond with an innocence about him the others probably lost when they were fifteen—no, make that ten—years old. Judging by the appalled expression on his face, he'd been shown a promotional flyer and someone's thumb had concealed my tricked-up surname. *Seriously cute.* Shame he was straight.

For once, my years of slave training proved useful. Gathering up the folds of my lace dress, I rose gracefully to my feet and flicked the long drop-cuffs out of the way. "What's the matter, hon? Surely you're not afraid of little ol' me?" The recent wear and tear on my throat made me sound as husky as the real Stevie.

Poor kid. The tension in his body didn't ease. You'd think he'd been told to walk down Oxford Street in his birthday suit.

"It's only a blowjob," someone in the background suggested.

"Go on, Marty. You're not married yet."

I studied the last speaker. Ugly fucker, but damn, didn't they grow them big nowadays. Imagine that hulk tackling you at full speed. I beckoned him forward with a lace-clad finger. "Come here, you big hunk. Show Marty there's nothing to be afraid of." It's a wonder my fake eyelashes didn't fall off, I fluttered them so hard.

"Yeah, you go first, Rob." Marty wasn't the only one egging him on.

Rob didn't seem too fazed by the suggestion. Interesting. I was vaguely aware of the required fee for service changing hands, but my concentration was more drawn to the long, fat, uncut cock being slowly unveiled. *Ooh, nice one.*

Too bad tonight's sponsorship agreement forced us to use flavored condoms. They smelled divine, and the chocolate added a touch of decadence to the proceedings, but after a few decent sucks, the revolting taste made me want to puke. This time, I chose the banana variety. Suitably phallic. Right then, I would have killed for a real one.

Sighing, I sank down to the floor again. Bloody condoms. Even come would be better than nothing. I had a serious case of the munchies.

When everything was in readiness, I caught the big guy's eye. "Crouch," I murmured and winked at him. Well, now I was kneeling again, his cock *was* a tad too high.

Rob eventually worked out what I wanted and spread his stance, bringing his groin down to my level.

In a louder voice, so all the room could hear, I said, "Touch." Leaning forward, I brushed my lips briefly against his sheathed member, pulled back, and uttered, "Pause."

The onlookers caught on to my use of the standard referee's commands for packing a scrum. A thunderous roar of "Engage" erupted as I engulfed his length in my mouth, dispelling any lingering tension.

In fact, things became boisterous as I worked my way through the team. The onlookers kept checking to see if I was binding properly and asking whether the ball was in play yet. Raucous laughter spilled over to the rest of the pub, drawing in more takers. Marty, the young groom-to-be, kept encouraging his friends to have their turn first.

Good thinking, kid. If you don't fancy getting a BJ from a male, there are enough willing dicks here to keep me busy.

Sighing, I settled down to my task again.

The sharp click of heeled boots on the hard wooden floor and the resulting deathly hush made me pause in midsuck as someone came up to stand behind me. The scent of sweat, sex, musk, and flavored condoms vanished. In their place was… *Leather.*

The guy whose cock I was sucking tensed, but he didn't pull away. Had the vice squad arrived to put an end to our gay little orgy? No, this was more like a confrontation with an opposing rugby team. Anticipation.

Tap, tap, tap.

A crop or whip handle rapped impatiently against a boot. I didn't need to see to know. I'd heard the sound often enough. Blindfolded. My insides twisted into a knot.

"Carry on."

I let out a sigh at the hint of an American accent. Thank God, it wasn't my ex-Master.

The sick churning in my gut surprised me. I'd thought I'd be fine when confronted by reminders of my past, but if I fell to pieces like this with a perfect stranger, how would I have reacted if it *had* been Julius? Then the words themselves sank in. *Who does this fucktard think he is? I don't need his permission.* There had been no friendliness in his voice either, more disdain.

The guy I was servicing grabbed hold of my head.

Oops, maybe I'd clenched my jaw a tad too tight.

"Let go."

A quick slap, with what turned out to be the base of a coiled whip, swept the offending hand away. Whips. Leather. Rules. No, I'd put an end to all that shit. Left Julius and taken back control of my life.

The smell grew stronger as his gloved hand settled on my shoulder. Not enough pressure to hurt, purely to remind *me* of his presence, letting others know who was in charge. Him.

My skin burned at the point of contact, and I shuddered. *This is a test*, I told myself. If I was going to confront Julius, I had to be able to deal with things like this.

Burying the deeply programmed instinct to adopt the familiar position, with my elbows clasped behind my back and my head bowed,

I grasped the cock of my current client and, aided by some jacking off—cheating, I know—finally made the guy ejaculate.

He nodded his thanks, and we exchanged grins. After he left, I leaned back and rested on my booted heels, fanning the lace skirt around me, trying to get back into character. From the corner of my eye, I could see black motorcycle boots, their surface so shiny they almost begged to be licked. But I didn't do that anymore. Did I?

Who the hell does this leather-clad prick think he is? I'd been coping fine until he arrived. Sure, at times the rugby players had been a tad rough and made me gag as they thrust down my throat. "Carried away in the heat of the moment," they apologized afterward, but I wasn't a total novice at breath play. Far from it. So why did this dickhead think he had the right to come along and spoil everything by reminding me of all the reasons I hated men who wore leather?

Marty had finally reached the front of the line. His attention flicked from my face to the guy behind me. Poor kid still didn't appear eager to participate, and I didn't want to continue with the dickhead watching. No doubt he would judge my performance and find fault.

Resting my lace-gloved hand in Marty's, I daintily rose to my feet. "Thanks, honey." I drew in close to the groom-to-be's side, fitting easily under his arm. *And he's one of the small ones?* I squeezed his hand before turning to glare at my unwanted protector.

From the way he had commanded everyone's attention, I expected some big hulk, but the cocky bastard staring back at me was roughly my size.

I relaxed, safe in the protection of Marty's loose embrace, and returned the stranger's scrutiny. This must be Master D. A walking, talking cliché if there ever was one. He looked like he'd stepped off a Tom of Finland calendar: droopy moustache, leather jacket emphasizing his broad shoulders, with more soft leather stretched tight across his hips. Every muscle was on display—plus the fact he dressed left. My gaze tracked lower. I was right—you could see your reflection in his boots. *Which sucker did he bully into cleaning them?* I wondered.

Julius would have given his back teeth to have looked as authentic as this guy. He didn't just wear the leather. He was the embodiment of Leather. Maybe I should ask if he had a hanky handy?

My chin could certainly do with a wipe. *Careful, Steve*, I admonished myself. *You know where sass always got you.*

Thankful for my heels and platform soles, I drew myself up to my full five-foot-seven. The guy's gaze hadn't wavered. It was as if we were carrying on a silent conversation the other people present had no knowledge of.

The disdain I'd detected in his voice was reflected in his eyes, their narrowed edges revealing his message: *Remember who is the Master here.*

No. Not anymore. This man had no power over me. I had to stop thinking so submissively. I was his equal. But if he wanted to hook up with me after the show, like Fred had suggested, the man was dreamin'.

CHAPTER
+++
TWO

Rooms on Fire

I NEEDED to escape. Fast. With a flirty shake of my long curly wig, I smiled sweetly at Marty. "You know what, honey. You were so generous in letting all your mates have their turn first, I'm not sure I'd do you justice. My lips feel like fucking footballs." I was about to suggest one of the porn stars take my place when the arm around me tightened. The poor kid was definitely uncomfortable. If his mates wanted him to get laid, why bring him to a gay bar? Why not take him to one of the local strip joints—the traditional buck's night of choice? There were certainly enough in the vicinity.

"Stevie's got another hole you could fuck." I couldn't tell which of his so-called friends made the suggestion, but the accompanying snickers showed that most of them agreed.

Damn. They weren't going to give up easily.

Marty's arm tightened even more. Most people would have assumed he was hugging me because he was excited about the prospect, but the stiffness of his body betrayed him.

"What a good idea," I said enthusiastically, turning in his embrace. "Let's go upstairs so you can have your wicked way with me." Grabbing his hand, I headed for the exit, only to be stopped in my tracks before I'd gone two paces.

The brandished handle of the single-tail scarcely brushed my stomach, but I flinched as if I'd been caressed by the business end.

"Where are you going?" the leather man demanded. "I need to speak to you."

"You heard them." Without letting go of the young man's damp hand, I tilted my head at his smirking companions. "Marty was promised a session with me, and I plan to give him one, but I doubt we'd be allowed to fuck here, so I'm *finding a room*, as the saying goes."

Stroking the edge of the leather man's carefully shaved jaw with my free hand, I murmured seductively, "Wanna join us, sweetie pie?"

His only response was a slight shake of his head. "The live segment will be kicking off in half an hour."

"Thirty minutes? Plenty of time."

Accompanied by shouts of encouragement from his teammates, I dragged the reluctant rugby player up the two flights of narrow stairs. Once inside the bedroom, I pulled off my wig and placed it on its stand. Marty's look of astonishment was priceless. "What's wrong?" I wet a wash cloth with cold water and rubbed it over my shaven scalp. Ah, that was better. I'd forgotten how hot Sydney summers could be. "You knew I was a bloke."

Marty cleared his throat and shifted his attention to the floor, clearly embarrassed by the whole episode. "Yeah, but knowing and seeing are two different things."

I snorted. "Don't get your knickers in a twist, honey. You don't have to do anything you don't want to." On other occasions, I might have taken his comical expression of relief as an insult, but after two hours of sucking cocks with my own wedged back in my crack, I didn't give a flying fuck. "Why don't you ring your fiancée and have a chat while I get rid of this revolting taste." I grabbed a glass of water, rinsed, and spat.

"You want me to ring Sara?"

I burst out laughing at the irony. "Sara? You've got a fiancée named Sara? The poet in my heart?" I dabbed my mouth dry. "Yeah, give her a call. I wanna chat."

Marty plonked himself on the bed. After staring at my reflection for a few minutes as I started creaming off my makeup, he dutifully extracted his iPhone. A young female responded immediately.

"No, I'm fine," Marty said sheepishly in response to her greeting. "The guys brought me up to the Cross, and I'm in a hotel room with a Stevie Nicks impersonator, and 'he'—I mean 'she'—wants to talk to you." Marty handed me the cell, looking for all the world like he wished the bed would open up and swallow him.

"Hi, sweetheart," I said in my normal voice, that wasn't very different from Stevie's. "I wanted to set your mind at rest. Marty is still as pure as the driven snow."

"Yeah, right," she drawled and gave a low, throaty chuckle. "Hey, Marty said you do Stevie Nicks impersonations. My mother was a big fan of hers, hence the name."

Another one! "Was?"

"She died when I was ten."

"Oh. Sorry to hear that." Sara sounded cool, confident. Marty had good taste when it came to women. "You should meet my sister, Rhiannon," I added.

She laughed, and we chatted for a while about what it was like being named after a song. Then I remembered what her fiancée and I were supposed to be doing. "Hey, Sara, it's been great chatting, but Marty's mates think he's in here shagging me. Why don't you two lovebirds bill and coo while I finish getting ready? Remind him to make suitable sound effects every now and then. No doubt they're checking up on him." I passed the phone back to Marty and called out, "Oh, no. It's too big." A faint giggle sounded on the other side of the door.

Marty finally figured out he didn't have to shag me. A cheeky grin crossed his face as he added, "Yeah. Take it all, you bitch."

I smothered a laugh and turned back to the mirror. Damn. Giving blowjobs did terrible things to pancake makeup. While I continued fixing the damage, Marty got into the swing of things, bouncing up and down on the bed, making it bang against the wall. Every now and then I screamed, "Fuck, yeah, you stud." At least one of us was having fun. After meeting the leather man, I'd lost some of my enthusiasm, but the show must go on. Professional trouper and all that shit.

I checked the time. Only ten minutes to go. Better hurry. As soon as I was dressed, I grabbed the phone and said my good-byes to Sara.

10

"Best wishes for the wedding, hon, and don't forget to teach Marty the lyrics of 'Sara' so he can sing it for you on your special night."

She chuckled. "He sounds like a frog warbling. Why don't you do it instead?"

"What? Do a proxy serenade outside your window like Steve Martin does in *Roxanne*? Nah, Marty will manage just fine without me."

Sara giggled. "No, I mean at the reception. Mum would have got a real kick out of the thought of Stevie Nicks singing at my wedding."

"Sure." She was joking, right? A siren sounded downstairs. *My cue.* I handed Marty the phone, grabbed my gear, and headed to the door.

Outside, four hunky firemen stood waiting. Before I could say a word, Jeff, their leader, tossed me over his shoulder in the classic fireman's hold. Stupid idiot. My wig nearly fell off. I banged my fists on his back and squealed convincingly as he carted me downstairs. By the time Stevie's song came out of the sound system, I was standing center stage with my tambourine and scarf-decorated microphone in hand.

Clad only in dungarees with their sweat-slicked skin glowing under the spotlights, Jeff and his friends certainly looked hot enough to set the "Rooms on Fire." The crowd got into the spirit of things, joining in when the chorus started.

I did my best Stevie impression, lip-syncing the words I knew so well, flicking my skirt out and twirling around in her inimitable style. At the end, as I graciously acknowledged the applause, I noticed one person wasn't clapping.

Master D.

He'd finally wised up to the fact it was summer and removed his jacket and shirt, revealing a broad, hairy chest crisscrossed by traditional studded leather straps. No leather bands on his arms, though. Instead, he had a double twist of barbed wire tattooed around his right biceps and a broken chain around the other. He was glowering at me as if he'd trodden in a steaming pile of dog shit. Hmm, not a fan of Stevie Nicks—or of Stevie Tricks, at any rate.

The DJ launched into our next number, "Stand Back." Pretending it was all part of the act, I sauntered across, gave Master D my most seductive smile, and hooked my gloved finger under his harness so I could drag him up on stage. He resisted for a second and then followed my lead.

As he stood in the middle of the row of dancers, doing a brilliant impression of an immovable rock, I twirled around him, singing about it being all right to stand in line.

Pity he didn't get the hint and strip like the other guys. Their line work was inspirational.

Maybe I shouldn't have enjoyed pissing him off so much, but I couldn't help it. I must have sucked one condom too many, and a Trojan virus had wormed its way into my brain, destroying any fears I had about confronting masterful men in leather.

The audience thought it was a hoot, but whenever I glanced at Fred, he was shaking his head and rolling his eyes at me. Not a single muscle twitched in Master D's face.

What's wrong with this guy? Doesn't he have a sense of humor?

Before the song finished, I had spun around so much I had to grab his arm for support. Given his lack of reaction, I might as well have clung onto a statue. His eyes reacted, though, sending me an unspoken promise of retribution.

Had it been Julius, I knew exactly what the result would have been. The hairbrush. I closed my eyes as memories returned, making my heart tap out a staccato rhythm.

The roar of the crowd snapped me back to the moment. Wearing nothing but glittering jockstraps, Jeff and his buddies had lined up for their bows. I took a deep breath and transferred my hand to the leather man's chest, threading my fingers through the soft fuzz. "You should donate some of this hair to my poor dancers, honey. What do you think, guys?" Another roar. Luckily, the audience's alcohol consumption made even my lame jokes funny. With his S and M demonstration to follow, the leather man probably hadn't touched a drop all night. A muscle started ticking in his jaw. Nope, not used to people making fun of him.

"Come on, another round of applause for Jeff and his Buff Brigade."

The dancers pranced off stage to much hooting and hollering from the patrons. While the cheers and queries about whether their hoses were big enough reverberated around the room, I checked out the audience. The crowd was better than expected but not exactly packed to the rafters.

Earlier in the day, I'd asked Fred what he wanted me to do. He merely shrugged and said, "Entertain people. The usual stuff." He didn't have a clue about how to put on live shows, but if this venture was to be a success, he needed regular nights of performers.

After giving Fred a cheery I Got Everything Under Control nod, I turned to the gathered throng and cooed into the microphone like a white-winged dove, "Thanks for inviting me to your beautiful city. I'm soooo excited to be here." I ignored all the catcalls of "We want the real one." If I'd been impersonating Stevie overseas, I would have stayed in character, but Australian audiences weren't such purists; they wanted to be entertained. Well, entertain them, I would. In my most sultry drawl, I continued, "When Fred sent the invitation to participate in this fabulous event, he assured me everyone who was anybody would be *coming* tonight.... Don't worry. If you haven't yet, I'm sure you will by the end of the evening." I paused long enough for them to get the joke before continuing, "We have *loads* of great entertainment lined up for you." At my cue, the DJ did a prepared drum roll. "All the way from the great US of A...." Another drum roll. "Hotel Paradiso is proud to present someone who is sure to whip you into a frenzy."

The man in question inclined his head politely. But he looked nervous. Strange. If he'd won a leather title, he must be used to being up on stage, performing.

I breathed huskily into the microphone. "Welcome to Australia, *Mister* D.... Oops." I raised my gloved hands to my lips. "*Master* D." I gave a fake laugh. "Sorry, I keep getting confused. After all, you did win the title of *Mister* Leather." I winked at the crowd. "Shame you didn't wear your sash, honey."

That gave me another excuse to stroke his hairy chest. For some reason, the urge to touch the leather man refused to go away. Under my palm, his breathing steadied, and the man's previous calm reasserted itself. Reluctantly, I dragged my hand away and gave a nervous laugh before addressing the audience again.

"As you know, I'm something of a connoisseur of clothes." Now that I wasn't touching him, my own confidence returned. Twirling around, I showed off my red gown. "Love your leather, *dahling*, but how many cows *did* you have to kill to get that outfit?" I placed the microphone near his mouth, but he just started tapping his whip on his boot again. Ooh, goodie, I was starting to ruffle his feathers. These guys could dish it out, but they didn't like being on the receiving end. I'd noticed that with Julius.

"Tell me, Master D, since you're wearing all this leather, you must ride a bike. Correct?"

"Yes."

I never realized you could talk without opening your mouth. This guy proved me wrong. At least the sound coming through the speakers sounded like grudging agreement.

"What sort?"

"Harley."

"A *Harley*." I might have known. A walking cliché if I ever saw one. "Careful. Around here, the cops assume everyone riding a Harley is a member of an outlaw bikie-gang, up to all sorts of illegal activities. I assume you're on the straight and narrow."

One of the guys near the front of the stage muttered something.

I went across and placed the microphone near his mouth. "What did you say, hon?"

"I doubt he's straight."

I adopted the classic *Oh. My. God.* pose, palm on chest. "Do you mean he's *gay*?"

I went back to the leather man. "Is that true?"

His lips curled back, exposing tightly clenched teeth. No, not the final stages of rigor mortis; that grimace was meant to be a smile. He muttered an almost inaudible, "Yes."

Now it was the turn of Fred's DJ, with the unpronounceable name full of hyphens and consonants, to say something. I sashayed over to hear what he had to contribute. Pity, I would have liked to hang around and see if I could actually make the leather man explode.

"This *is* a gay bar, Stevie."

"You're *kidding* me." I moved my palm up to my throat and looked around. "No wonder there are so many handsome men here." I fanned my face and panted softly. "But wait. Didn't I see some rugby players before? They're not gay, even if they do insist on grabbing each other's balls." Loud cheers exploded from both the players and the rest of the assembled crowd. "Hi, Marty." I waved and blew a kiss to the blushing groom-to-be. The DJ muttered something. This time, I merely pretended to hear what he said. "They came to see me? How sweet." I fluttered my eyelashes at them. "Well, they certainly came. I can vouch for that." More laughter.

"Now if you're good, I'll sing you one of my favorite Stevie numbers, 'Beauty and the Beast'. Are you good?" I placed the microphone up in the air and wasn't surprised when a number of "Shit, yeahs" came back. "But this one's a ballad, and you really need someone to sing love songs to, don't you?" Usually I chose one of the uglier members of the audience. I crossed the stage a couple of times, as if searching for a likely candidate. Then I hit myself upside the head. "Silly me, I have the perfect target, I mean *person* here. All he has to do is stay still."

I stalked up to Master D and stroked the side of his face again.

This time his eyes met mine, and I noticed a dangerous gleam in them, but I didn't have a tiger tattooed on my back for nothing. "You *can* stand still, can't you, honey?" I patted his thighs and noticed they quivered slightly under my touch. "Oh, I think I need a spreader bar." I gestured to Fred, but he just shook his head, wrote something on a piece of paper, and held it out to me. As I went to collect it, I made a big deal about who Fred was and what a great job he was doing. Perhaps he was going to give me an update on how much they had already raised to "Save the Centipede" or whatever tonight's charity was in aid of.

After a quick glance at the note, I nearly burst out laughing.

Pretending I was shortsighted, I brought the paper close to my eyes. "This says…." Fred groaned. He didn't want me to read the bloody thing, but there were years of built-up issues at stake here. "Don't piss on Master D."

I returned to center stage, shaking my head. "Well, of course I can't piss on the guy in leather. You need a wet room for that." Waving the note in front of the leather man's face, I said, "Your eyesight is probably better than mine. What does this say?"

After perusing the message, he said, "Don't piss *off* Master D."

I really should find out how he managed his talking-with-his-mouth-closed trick. It was neat. The audience burst out laughing.

"Oh dear, too late." I gave an exaggerated shrug in Fred's direction and signaled to the DJ to start the music. To his credit, the leather man didn't move an inch, but his gaze locked onto mine when I sang about an untamed lover who lived in pleasure and pain. The words were certainly apt. No one would ever tame him.

In the end, I had to give him ten out of ten for tenacity, the sort I knew too well. Having to stay still and quiet while someone likened him to a beast must have been humiliating. *Welcome to my world, buster.* Thank God we would be parting ways as soon as the evening was over. "You're too kind," I said after the applause died down. "Now it's Master D's turn to show us what he can do with the long thing dangling below his waist." Judging by the resulting comments, those without a dirty mind were in the minority. "Come on, guys, give him a big hand."

One wannabe comedian in the audience yelled, "How about a fist in the ass."

I laughed and noticed a faint twitch at the corner of Master D's jaw. "Ah, not yet. He's not stretched properly."

Holding out my arm, I backed away, giving him the spotlight. "Come on, honey, now it's time to crack that whip." Before I left, I did a not-too-subtle stage whisper. "Have you ever noticed that cracks lead directly to assholes?" With that parting shot, I took my final bows and exited. Some guys dressed in leather rolled a Saint Andrew's Cross onto the stage, one I knew intimately.

I made it back to the bedroom before the next whip crack sounded.

Running helped.

CHAPTER
✚✚✚
THREE

Two Kinds of Love

INSIDE, I stared at the photo taped to the dressing table mirror. *God, Steve, who was being the beast there?* Stevie Nicks was beautiful, inside and out. If I was going to impersonate her, I had to nix the attitude, or I'd turn into one of those drag queens who got off on being bitchy.

Okay, the leather and whip brought back lots of memories, good and bad, but the guy downstairs wasn't Julius. He didn't deserve to be the butt of my jokes. The trouble was, touching him called to something deep inside, lighting a spark that had been dormant since I left Australia. But you don't poke the dragon to see if he will spit flame.

I sat on the bed and buried my head in my hands. Julius always accused me of loving to flirt with danger, but my behavior downstairs had been beyond the realms of stupidity. What the fuck was I trying to prove, treating the American like that? Maybe I *should* meet him afterward and apologize. Reassure him it was just part of the show.

The sound of an anguished groan penetrated the wooden barrier behind me. The lack of an accompanying whip crack suggested the leather man had used a different instrument. The first two had probably been a promise of things to come. He had to warm the guy up with a flogger before he got into the heavy stuff. No doubt we were in for a long session.

A soft swish proved me right. I shuddered. Now *that* was a sound that always revved my engines. A shiver ran up my spine as I recalled exquisite pain. Talk about love/hate relationships. Already, I could feel blood rushing southward.

Another swish sounded.

Damn. I needed a distraction.

Fred wanted me to mingle with the guests. Shouldn't be too hard. All I had to do was ignore the noise and pull a shutter over the memories, using the techniques my therapist had taught me.

I eased my way out of the expensive gown and donned my third outfit for the evening: a long, flowing black-chiffon number from Marks and Sparks.

Downstairs, the rugby crowd had migrated into the other bar area, along with the porn stars who had been sharing my *Blowjobs for Bucks* segment. I wandered over, pausing every now and then for a quick chat and photo op with other attendees.

I'd expected the footballers to disappear as soon as they'd pulled the "BJ from Stevie Nicks" joke, but they looked settled in for the night. Rob was the center of attention. A regular life-of-the-party. "You'd be a natural," he said, patting an obviously uncomfortable Marty on the shoulder.

I insinuated myself between the two men and drawled, "A natural at what, dahling?"

"Doing gay-for-pay porn."

"Marty?" I scanned the young man from tip to toe and gave him a wink. "Yeah, I could imagine he'd be popular." I turned to his tormentor and ran my hand down his front, fondling his package before letting go. "But what about you, handsome? Nothing like a brawny, well-hung top to get all the guys *and* chicks swooning."

He flinched at my caress.

"Oh, Rob would never do anything like that." Marty's hasty interjection didn't seem to sit well with his friend. Judging by his subsequent glare, he would have decked me if I wasn't half his size. And a lady. Or dressed like one at any rate.

I gave a sarcastic smile in return.

18

Marty gave me a big grin, his embarrassment forgotten. "Hey, I really liked your act. I sent a couple of photos to Sara. She's sorry she didn't get to see the whole performance." He started to rise from his stool. "Would you like a seat?"

Gee, he was a cutie. I could see what both Sara and his possessive teammate saw in him. I smiled sweetly and replied, "Don't move, sugar. I'll sit on you instead."

One of his companions chimed in. "Give him a lap dance, Stevie."

Marty blushed and angled out his leg so I could perch on top. A few cameras flashed, but they didn't worry me. A photo with Stevie Tricks on his lap wouldn't do his reputation any harm. Better than being caught with his cock down my throat.

The slaps of the flogger became quicker, and the grunts grew louder.

"How could anyone want to be whipped?" I didn't catch who asked the question, but the disgust in his voice shone through loud and clear.

While guys with no experience offered up explanation after explanation, I tossed the question around in my mind. I remembered having difficulty when Rhiannon asked me the same thing. But how can you explain a kink? Describe that exquisite agony as you're forced to drop thoughts of everything else and focus on the one thing that is real? The thing that makes *you* feel real. Everything else pales into insignificance. Becomes manageable. That part of sadomasochism actually made sense. The rest? Doing it to please my Master? Nah.

A curious stillness fell at the cessation of sound. Was the demonstration over, or was the leather man merely switching implements?

The guy being flogged wouldn't have been a complete novice, probably one of Master D's leather friends. But how would he cope with the whip?

Just the sight of the single-tail had set my nerves on fire. As if on cue, a sharp crack sounded, followed by a lingering wail.

Everyone around me flinched.

I didn't. My leg jerked in anticipation. Goose bumps crawled over my skin as I recalled exactly what the man on the cross would be thinking. *How hard will the next strike be? Where? Will I be able to breathe through the pain? Convert the fire into ecstasy?*

When the sound of the blow came, the subsequent cry was louder, harsher, before dwindling into anguished sobs and then silence.

My catty inner voice noted, *Hmph, only two?* As soon as the thought crossed my mind, I felt ill. *Stop it, Steven Lindsey Stanhope, you are* not *going down that road ever again.*

"Glad that's over," another muttered. "All that S and M shit put me off my beer."

"Woops." Marty gestured to the barman. "I'm sorry, Stevie, I should have offered you a drink. What can I get you? Beer? Wine?"

I'd had a few sips of water while in my room but didn't want to drink too much. Unleashing my tackle to piss and then having to re-tuck again was a pain in the ass. "A glass of red would be fine." I could sit on that for a while.

The talk and laughter grew louder as Fred's DJ started pumping out some ubiquitous house music. There was a general exodus from the bar into the dance area, although none of our group left. Shortly after, a similar influx of leather men strolled into the room. Fred approached, a huge smile creasing his craggy face. I was pleased to see Master D was not with him. Anyway, if the guy was any good, he'd be spending time with the guy he'd whipped, tending to the results of his flogging, easing him down gently. Taking care of him.

"Thanks for coming, mate." Fred gave Rob a hug before disappearing behind the bar. So they were friends. Curiouser and curiouser. From my position on Marty's lap, I was content to stare at the carpet and listen to their banter.

Rob's possessiveness toward Marty became more apparent as the evening progressed… to me at least. Whenever I glanced up, I detected a hint of jealousy in his eyes. Turned out he would be best man at the wedding in a few weeks' time. Had I made him jealous by vanishing upstairs with Marty? Not that anything went on in the bedroom. *What a waste.* I sighed and smoothed the black chiffon over my padded hips.

20

Movement made me lift my gaze from the carpet again. Master D.

Fred poured him a schooner of beer. I was surprised to detect a fleeting grimace of weariness cross the leather man's face as he accepted it. He smiled at my companions, pointedly ignoring me.

One of the members of the rugby team asked, "What does the D stand for, mate? I can't keep calling you Master D all the time."

I pricked up my ears, waiting for the answer. I'd gone through the whole gamut of alternatives in my mind, Deryck, Demetrios—there was a slight hint of a Mediterranean background in his olive skin—Damon, Dale, and even Dagwood. None seemed to fit.

"If 'Sir' doesn't rock your boat, just call me Donato or Don."

Don the Dom, how appropriate. I snickered to myself and took another sip of wine.

The conversation around me drifted to different topics. From what I could gather, the leather man came from the Chicago area, but back in the Second World War days, his Aussie grandmother had met and married a Yank serviceman who had been spending his R&R up at the Cross. Now he was in Australia, he wanted to meet her younger sister, a spinster living in Fairlight.

"Hey, Donato, it's a shame you didn't get a chance to sample the wares." Rob glanced sideways at me. "It wouldn't take long. Stevie's a real pro."

"No!" I waved my hand around, trying to appear nonchalant, even though my heart rate jumped twenty percent. "Dawson's much better than I am." I'd nicknamed one of the porn stars Dawson the Dyson because he'd been like a bloody Hoover, cycling his tricks through like a bottling plant. Cock in mouth, quick suck, full condom, next please.

"How quick are we talking here?" The leather man eyed Rob speculatively. "Five minutes, ten?"

"Ten at the max," one of his teammates suggested.

From memory, *he* hadn't lasted long.

"Hey, I got an idea," Rob interjected. "If the person giving you the blowjob can't get you off in the required time, you get to fuck them."

The leather man nodded. "Okay." A few bystanders had gathered around, attracted by the laughter each suggestion generated. "But we better extend the time limit to make it fair. What about half an hour?"

Dawson seemed to be looking forward to the proposal, probably figuring he'd won either way.

"Sounds reasonable." Fred rubbed his hands in glee. "And to make it more interesting, seeing as we're short of the fund-raising target, why don't we bet on the result to make up the shortfall?"

"I'm in," an enthusiastic voice behind me chimed in.

"Good idea." Both leather men and rugby players signaled their assent.

I groaned and shook my head. What was it with Aussies? They would wager on two flies crawling up a wall.

"Bet on the fact that Master D can last for thirty minutes?" Rob sounded intrigued.

The man in question smiled and shrugged. "Yeah, why not? Everyone here puts their money down. If I can resist coming before the time is up, the pot goes into tonight's kitty. If I lose, I'll match the amount myself."

"You're on, mate." Rob checked to see he had his friends' nods of agreement. "Draw up a betting book, Fred."

"Stupid idiots," I muttered. "You might as well just hand over the money."

"Do you think you could do any better, Stevie?" The leather man had one of those voices where the softer he spoke, the more you paid attention.

I squirmed uncomfortably on Marty's lap.

The piercing gaze flicked over to Marty as if asking him the same question.

"Yeah, Stevie's great."

I felt like hitting Marty upside the head. People who played with their balls all day were dumb but surely not that dumb. Couldn't he see the guy was stringing him along? I knew exactly how long a man used to denying his orgasm could last when he put his mind to it. Before I could tell Marty to keep his helpful comments to himself, Rob chimed in. "Hey, that's not a bad idea. Stevie can do it."

"No. Puhleese. I wouldn't dream of depriving Dawson of the pleasure." I batted my eyelashes and smiled as sweetly as I could.

"But we'd have a better chance if you did it," Rob volunteered. There was a snide undercurrent present, as if he knew exactly what he was doing.

Damn it, he is *pissed off at me for being so friendly with Marty. Talk about payback.*

"We need someone on our side who wants to win. After the razzing you gave him on stage, I'd imagine you'd do anything to avoid being fucked by Master D." The smile Rob gave me made a mockery of his words. He probably grinned like that just before he ground his opposition into the dirt. Damn, he was good. Next time, I wanted him on my team. For now, I had to accept I'd been played for a sucker. Trouble was, I couldn't decide which voodoo doll to stick the pin in— him or the leather man.

"We can't do it here," Fred said. "If the Licensing Board finds out, we're history."

I heaved a sigh of relief. I'd been surprised tonight's entertainment was being conducted so openly. Apparently the phrases "testing a new range of condoms specifically designed for oral use," "infection prevention strategies," and "all for a good cause" had magically morphed into something legal—or at least worthy of a blind eye from the vice squad.

"We'll use the cellar. There's enough room."

Shit. Thanks for nothing, Fred. Great friend you are. What did he care, anyway? Win or lose, he got his money. I turned to the leather man. "Can we dispense with the latex?" The prospect of sucking one of those bloody things non-stop for half an hour was enough to make me gag. It would be more of a handicap than a help, anyway.

"Okay."

Didn't this Yank ever smile? You'd have thought he was the one getting the rough end of the pineapple.

"My last tests were negative," he added. "What about yours?"

"The same," I admitted grudgingly. Since leaving Julius, I'd been fanatically careful.

Surrounded by guys who towered above me, I felt like a lamb being led to the slaughter as they escorted me downstairs. The whole situation was absurd, yet a weird kind of logic underpinned everything. *Karma for not showing sufficient respect?*

The leather man's crotch was at a perfect height as I knelt at his feet. All night, I'd been fascinated by the bulge in his soft leather pants. I swallowed as he opened the waistband and pulled out a nice fat cock. Tearing my gaze away, I was surprised to find him watching me with a curious expression on his face. I had the weird feeling we'd done this before. But we hadn't, had we? Surely I'd remember someone like him. I swallowed, licked my lips, and reached out, ready to start.

"No hands," he said in that quiet, no-argument tone I was beginning to know well.

What the fuck? His cock was semi-flaccid. If it had been rampant and ready, I would have had no trouble. Damn the man. If he didn't want a blowjob, why the fuck had he agreed to take part in this bet? I reached out again, but he grabbed my wrists and held them out from his sides.

Being trapped by his viselike grip sent a shudder right through me. I couldn't have disguised my reaction even if I'd tried.

He must have noticed. Under my fascinated gaze, his cock slowly started to fill. Of course, being a Master, he needed to feel in control. He needed to *be* in control.

Panic flared for a moment, until my instinct for self-preservation kicked in. With a quick wrench, I twisted my hands to break his hold and collapsed back onto my heels. My fake boobs quivered with pent-up frustration. "You don't get to touch me, either."

A flash of irritation—or was it regret—washed across his face. Around us, the murmurs of the watching crowd built. I gathered all my determination and demanded, as coolly as I could, "Put your hands behind your back, and I'll do the same." It had taken me ages to regain the confidence to make demands again.

With a slight nod of agreement, the leather man adopted classic parade ground posture. At ease. *At ease indeed.* I clasped my wrists behind my back.

Fred approached with a stopwatch in his hands. "Ready?"

I nodded and heard the voice above me say, "Ready."

Although his hands were behind his back, I almost felt one on my head and the other on my shoulder, where it had rested before. I couldn't look at his face. No way did I want to witness the gloating expression I knew he'd have. Any Master with his experience would have superb control of his body's reactions.

The urge to prove him wrong—to meet his challenge—grew. Not only to help my fellow Aussies and take one for the team. I needed to prove something.

His cock had grown even bigger during our short but tense struggle. The flushed head jutted out, tantalizingly close to my lips.

I leaned forward. A subtle shift in his stance meant the tip no more than grazed my lips before slipping away.

"That's cheating." A couple of people in our small audience agreed, others laughed. I leaned forward again, only to be foiled by a movement the other way.

I glared up at Fred. "If I can't get the bloody thing in my mouth, how am I ever going to get him off?"

The leather man gave a smirk and drawled, "You're wasting time."

Laughs and titters in the assembled throng sounded behind me. I took a deep breath and tried to calm my mind. My next lunge forward was met by a well-timed sway backward as he kept the target out of reach.

I persevered, but he continued to thwart my efforts. Any suspicion he was an unwilling participant was disproved by the occasional smearing of precome on my lips. Some of the onlookers' laughter turned cruel. Others were getting anxious. Let's face it; their money was on the line. The crowd might be giggling, but my tormentor wasn't.

How was I going to solve this problem? Earlier, I'd had the eerie feeling there was a conversation going on between us, some unspoken dialogue only the two of us understood. Had Fred said something to him? Divulged the secrets of my past?

A single sentence chiseled at the barrier of my brain, trying to get out, but I clenched my jaw to prevent its escape. Words I knew he wanted me to say. Words I vowed never to utter again: *Please, Sir, may I suck your cock?*

A hush descended over the crowd. That invisible hand was on my shoulder again, followed by a finger under my chin, yet his hands hadn't moved. Neither had mine.

I glared at him and ground out my response through clenched teeth. "When you're fucking well ready to get started, let me know." I turned to Fred. "I thought this was a cock-sucking contest, not bobbing for apples in a bloody barrel." Jeers greeted my jibe, along with support. I didn't face front again until Fred restarted the clock after receiving an acknowledgement of assent from the man in leather.

Glancing up briefly, I caught a hint of grudging respect in his eyes. I gave my lips a final lick. This time, he let his smooth, hard shaft slide in slowly through them.

CHAPTER
+++
FOUR

Blue Denim

WHAT followed could have been a lesson in the art of giving a blowjob, as I used every trick in my arsenal. At first, enthusiasm exceeded skill. A fifteen-year-old would have done better. I glanced up again after a few minutes of fruitless sucking to discover respect had morphed into amusement. The dude thought this was funny, did he?

Instinctively, I sucked harder, drawing him in until his cock rested against the back of my throat. The inevitable gag reflex kicked in, but I managed to control it. Saliva trickled out the side of my mouth, but I didn't give a hoot if it wrecked my makeup. Whichever way the bet went, Stevie wouldn't be hanging around afterward.

Pressing my tongue up, I held him tight, letting my throat do all the work until the world lost its intensity. A misty cloud descended.

I gasped, filling my lungs with air, but I didn't let his hard shaft escape. No more chase-the-possum, thank you very much.

Once more, I glanced up. Wary concern greeted me, as if he wasn't sure I knew what I was doing. No doubt he was usually the one in control. I could imagine his hands on my head, guiding me down and holding me there for as long as he wanted. Never what I wanted.

I wanted him to come. ASAP.

The assembled audience chattered amongst themselves, their conversations creating an unwelcome distraction. I felt like telling them all to shut the fuck up and go away.

Sucking harder on his cock, I gave an impatient toss of my head and clenched my arms tighter behind my back. A frustrated whimper escaped.

"Silence!"

One word, barked out with the authority of a drill sergeant. My eyes closed. Was the man a bloody mind reader as well?

I shifted position slightly to relieve my knees. My shoulders were aching from the strain of holding my arms behind my back. I was out of practice. Using all the techniques I'd learned over the years, I tried to block those distractions from my mind and went back to work. Thank God some people didn't mind being told what to do. The noise level decreased dramatically. Either they'd fallen asleep or left, seeking more interactive entertainment. The floor above reverberated with the thud of people dancing. Musical accompaniment filtered downstairs.

Unconsciously, I had begun to move with the rhythm, performing my own oral dance with his cock, squeezing my lips in time with the up-beat, relaxing them on the down.

His silence wasn't helping. I'd never realized how much the sense of sound during sex added to the scene. Grunts of approval. Whispered words of encouragement. Never endearment. The leather man's silence made the whole procedure clinical. I wasn't surprised he couldn't get off. If our positions had been reversed, I probably couldn't have either. When Julius and I did any of our rare public scenes together, I had always found onlookers a distraction. Ironic, considering how much I enjoyed performing before an audience dressed as Stevie. Perhaps that was the answer. Lose myself and become someone else.

A quick glance assured me I now had his undivided attention, almost as if he had access to the running commentary inside my head and knew exactly what I was thinking. His focus shifted to where my lips were stretched around his engorged shaft, reminding me I had a job to do. *Concentrate.*

Yep. He definitely knew I spoke his language and didn't need words for instruction. *Who had told him?*

Taking a deep breath through my nostrils, I settled back to the task. One by one, I dismissed the outside influences affecting my ability to concentrate: the music, the audience, my physical discomfort. All that mattered was the obstruction in my mouth.

I hated having to admit it, but the man did have a beautiful cock: well-proportioned, straight, not too veiny, with just the right amount of trimmed hair at its base. Some big cocks are often unattractive and disappointingly soft, but despite his size, not once did his hardness falter. Every now and then, a trace of salty-sweet precome trickled from the tip, which I savored before swallowing.

A hum of satisfaction welled up from inside, as I lavished the specimen in my mouth with the attention it deserved. Eventually, I forgot about the man himself. Who was he anyway? Some foreign fucktard. Since first meeting, we'd barely exchanged a civil word.

The appendage had nothing to do with the man. It almost had a life of its own, totally innocent of any part of our interaction. From being a passive participant in the proceedings, it became alive, took shape. Barely perceptibly at first, but then more and more noticeably, his cock joined me in the dance of sex, meeting my thrusting tongue with a thrust of its own. Eager. Responsive. Urgent. At that moment, although Don the Dom might be the embodiment of all I hated, I fell head-over-heels in love with his cock.

A visible tremor passed along his legs, probably too subtle for onlookers to notice, yet clearly discernible to one who was by now so in tune with his movements. I glanced up briefly, but for once his attention was not fixed on me but on the ceiling.

"He's coming."

The raucous remark must have stifled his urge as forcibly as a cock ring shoved firmly against his balls. I caught the leather man's reaction when he glanced down for a second before staring stoically ahead. Confusion? Anger? Hard to tell.

The moment had passed. I could have killed the idiot who made the comment. One more minute, and I would have had him. I know I would have.

Mucus streamed from my nose from gagging so much. My jaw ached from not only this session but all those before. I buried my nose in his pubic hair, letting his cock wedge once more in my throat, using it to stifle the groans of despair welling up inside.

Relishing the opportunity to take a breather, I tried to get myself back under control. After a few seconds, I swallowed my frustration and resumed my task, but the magic had disappeared, and I felt its absence as keenly as if I'd lost a finger or a toe. One of those body parts you take for granted and don't miss until they're gone.

My actions grew jerky, uncoordinated. Nothing like the sensual dance we'd been sharing. Now I was going through the motions like an automaton. A cock-sucking machine. The tension hadn't disappeared from his legs, though. I longed to run my hands up and down those firm muscles. Caress them. However, that would be cheating, right? And I might have done many despicable things in my life, but cheating wasn't one of them.

Fred's call of "Time" brought me back to the moment. I collapsed back on my heels, feeling utterly defeated. Before I could react, spurts of come splashed across my face, startling me and the man who'd loosed them.

"You fucking cunt!" I yelled. There was absolutely no need for him to do the money shot like he was in a porno flick. A flush of pure rage ripped through me. I shook off his proffered hand, ignoring what could have been a belated apology, and scrambled to my feet. My face was a streaky mess of runny makeup, sweat, semen, and, worst of all, tears. To add insult to injury, the ominous sound of ripping seams followed as my boot became entangled in soft material.

Fuck being feminine. Gathering the torn skirt in my clenched fists, I raced up the two flights of stairs and slammed the bedroom door behind me. With only one thought in mind, *escape,* I locked myself in.

Safe in the en-suite bathroom, I studied my reflection in the mirror. Tears of frustration diluted the sticky white fluid as both dribbled down my face. Wasn't breaking off with the only man I ever loved to escape this sort of degradation enough? Did all Doms need to humiliate people just to prove their superiority, or was that his payback for humiliating him on stage? If it was, it's a wonder the guy hadn't pissed on me as well. Julius would have, just to show me my place.

Angrily, I threw the wig into a bin, scrubbed my face clean, then ran a cool wash cloth over my shaved scalp. Usually, removing Stevie's persona was as much an act of homage as applying it, but tonight I didn't give a hoot. I tore off my false eyelashes, taking some of my own in the process. One landed in the sink, the other somewhere down the back of the cabinet. Too bad. I wasn't about to go chase either of them. I replaced the rhinestone earrings with my usual metal studs and stared at the glittering stones as they sat forlornly on the vanity. Fred could sell them for all I cared. I didn't want them anymore.

More ripped seams followed as I doffed the frock then stripped off the various bits of padding and clothing until I was butt naked. After freeing my balls from their hiding place, I gave my cock a quick tug of apology for squashing it for so long. I would have killed for a hot shower, but I didn't have time. As far as I was concerned, the second condition of the bet, fucking me, was null and void. *Mister* D could go to hell in a handbasket if he thought otherwise.

Unfortunately, the leather man probably wouldn't see things my way. But what were my chances of escaping? Hopefully, everyone would still be busy congratulating the bastard, and he'd be preoccupied making sure all bets were paid.

I grabbed my street clothes from the cupboard and slipped into my jeans. As soon as the buckle on my belt was fastened, I tucked a plain white T-shirt into my back pocket instead of putting it on and shoved my feet into a pair of R.M. Williams. After making sure I ditched anything connecting me to Stevie Tricks and left behind nothing belonging to Steven Lindsey Stanhope, I unlocked the door and sauntered outside.

So far, so good. A group of guys were mingling at the bottom of the staircase when I arrived. They didn't give me a second glance as I slipped among them. With my chest bare, I looked like I'd recently come off the dance floor.

Thank fuck for the anonymity of blue denim.

CHAPTER
+++
FIVE

After the Glitter Fades

I'D ASSUMED the group was leaving and figured I could slip outside undetected in their midst, but instead, they fanned out when they reached the bar. *Damn.* But perhaps I still had a chance. The rugby players were no longer hanging around like a bad smell. No Marty to give the game away. A definite plus. He was the only one who'd seen me wigless. Maybe they'd left after losing the bet, seeking safer pastures.

I checked the exit. *Double damn.* Wall-to-wall leather restricted my long walk to freedom. Anxiously, I scanned their faces. Nope. Still no Julius. No one who knew me.

I took another couple of steps and stopped in my tracks. *Fuck.* Perched on a stool at the end of the bar with a clear view of everyone leaving was the biggest fly in the ointment. Had he anticipated my welshing on the deal? The bloody cheek. The fact he would be right was irrelevant. It wasn't as if the money ended up coming out of his pocket. Hadn't I saved him from forking out a whole heap of dough? He should be thanking me, not lying in wait so he could fuck my ass. *Fuck* his *ass might be a better option.*

The big question was: would he connect a short, shaven-headed tattooed man with the Gypsy Queen? Nah, I couldn't take the risk. Reversing direction, I headed back into the interior of the nightclub. Eventually, Don the Dom would give up, and if he still wanted some ass action, no doubt Dawson the Dyson would happily oblige. That's

32

assuming the leather man could get it up again. I grinned inwardly at my malicious thought. Just because I doffed the frock didn't mean I had to stop being bitchy.

For once, I was glad of my lack of inches as I moved amongst the dancers. Being surrounded by tall guys made it much easier to blend in with the crowd. While doing my usual on-the-spot shuffle to the techno music, I texted Fred, saying I had urgent business to attend to and would pick up my gear tomorrow.

Maybe I would, maybe I wouldn't. Drag had served its purpose by giving me the courage to come back and check out the scene incognito. Julius wasn't here, so I could hitch a lift to the house and pick up my bike. If he wasn't home, though, the fucking security gate might be a problem.

A gorgeous guy approached. For a second, I thought I'd been sprung, but then he gave me a shy smile and traced his finger across my shoulder blades, following the ink. "Wow, these are incredible."

"Glad you like them." I smiled up at him. Seriously cute.

His finger ran up along the spine of the flying dragon, down through the jaws of the snarling tiger to the end of its bristling tail. "Must have taken simply ages to do."

"It did." I'd seen the design on a martial arts exponent and adapted the theme, twisting the two animals around so they were grappling as well as snarling: the strength of the tiger versus the supposed wisdom of the dragon. "Have you got any tats?" It took a devotee to know one.

He opened his shirt and pulled it off his shoulders, exposing the top of angel's wings etched across his shoulders. "I don't want to show it off until it's finished." After redoing the buttons, he leaned down and whispered in my ear. "My name's Gabriel, by the way, and I think you're hot."

Archangel Gabriel. With his wavy, snow-white locks, he certainly looked the part. I wondered whether he was as pure as his namesake. From the vibes I was getting, definitely not. He appeared to be in his early twenties, and, judging by the paleness of his skin, he spent most of his day indoors. "Steve," I said, extending my hand in greeting.

Before grasping it, Gabriel stared at my outstretched palm as if unsure what to do. I'd been out of the scene here for so long, I wasn't up to speed with current Aussie cruising protocol. Nowadays, was being told you were hot the latest code for "wanna fuck"?

Side by side, we bopped to the dance music. Dance music, trance music. I suppose you could call it music. Having been brought up by a Fleetwood Mac fanatic, I'd developed a taste for words and melody, not this endless *kathump, kathump*. Hopefully, I could last until closing time and slip out with the mass exodus.

While we danced, Gabriel's fingers lingered over the multicolored artwork on my back. He seemed more enthralled by the design than my body, which suited me fine. He wasn't unattractive, quite the opposite, but my jaded jaw couldn't cope with another BJ tonight. Wrong place, wrong time, buddy. Pity.

The surrounding dancers squashed closer, heralding an influx of people onto the dance floor. I glanced around. Some of the leather set had arrived. Goose bumps broke out. Although I couldn't see him, I was willing to bet my bottom dollar my nemesis was with them. Heads turned in their direction. Keeping my face carefully blank, I casually checked out the newcomers.

"There he is."

Gabriel's words made me stop dancing. My stomach did a belly flop. "Who?" I asked, projecting a casualness totally at odds with the churning in my gut.

"The guy who did the S and M demonstration. Master D."

Judging by the awe in my new friend's voice, you'd think someone adopting the superior role in a relationship was a good thing. I took a deep breath and shrugged. "So?"

"Didn't you catch his act? He was awesome."

I angled my body to the door, lessening the chance of anyone recognizing me. "Nope. Sorry. I arrived late."

"That's probably why I didn't see you earlier." Gabriel gave me a shy smile; then his face grew serious. "Pity. You would have liked it. At least you missed having to watch that terrible Stevie Nicks impersonator. It's a wonder Master D didn't deck him. I would have."

I stepped back and scanned the earnest expression on my companion's face. Was he winding me up? Did he know who he was speaking to? No. His concentration was fixed on my tattoo. I flexed my muscles, making the dragon's tail ripple across my shoulder blades. Good, the group hadn't advanced too far into the room. "So, what was the leather man like?"

"Scary. The poor guy he was flogging couldn't stop screaming."

I would have called them groans myself. Gabriel didn't appear to be as shocked as the words suggested. Interesting. "Are you into all that shit?"

He shuffled his feet and stared at the floor. "Sort of."

Julius would tell him not to do that, to look at the person speaking.

Strange how sometimes looking down was wrong and other times raising your eyes earned a rebuke. I could never be bothered remembering which was which, hence my familiarity with the bloody hairbrush. "What else did I miss? I couldn't get away from work until nine."

"Only some singers and that drag queen."

Gabriel looked directly at me when he made that statement. Nope, the kid was as straight as a die. Honesty-wise, at any rate.

We danced some more. He seemed nice, but why hang around a guy pushing thirty and not someone his own age? The tattoo, no doubt.

After a while, the leather contingent drifted back to the bar, and the temperature in the room reverted to normal.

I should make my move now, while people were milling about. "Do you want to split?" I tried not to sound too eager.

"Yeah, why not."

Following the leather-clad men, I held my breath until we reached the heavy double doors at the entrance. After nodding briefly at the bouncer, I pushed them open. For once in my life, luck seemed to be on my side. Somehow, I'd managed to escape Fred's eagle eye. Keeping Gabriel between me and any source of danger helped. Though, in a perverse way, the fact I hadn't seen the leather man was a worry. I knew guys like him. Persistence was their fucking middle name.

Once safely outside, I said, "Where to now?" I really didn't want to party on, but it seemed rude to use Gabriel simply for cover. "How about we head off to your place?"

His face turned a nice shade of rosy pink. "Um, I still live with my parents."

Midtwenties, gay, and still living at home? "Do they know you're out?"

A spark of spirit flashed. "Out of the closet or out at night?"

"Both." I grinned to show him I was kidding, and his defensiveness disappeared.

"Yeah, but I still can't bring guys home." There was something about Gabriel. A curious mix of vulnerability and defiance. One minute he was giving off that *Take me home and look after me* vibe, and next he was like a two-year-old kid who stubbornly insists on doing everything himself.

The pub door opened. Oops. We should have split while the going was good. A group of leather-clad figures headed toward a row of motorbikes parked diagonally next to the curb. I turned away and held my breath, waiting for a gloved hand to clasp my shoulder. Damn guilty conscience. My mind might have felt justified in leaving, but some small part still wanted to obey. I had to purge that instinct. I was beholden to no one.

"What about your place?" Gabriel asked.

No. The instinctive reaction to keep my whereabouts secret was a hard one to break. I still hadn't told Fred where I was staying. "Another time," I suggested and gave Gabriel an apologetic grin.

The thunderous roar of bike engines split the night air. *Finally.* I shut my eyes and let the rumble caress my soul. My favorite song.

As soon as the noise died down, I held my cell phone out to Gabriel. "Here, enter your contact info. I'll give you a call tomorrow."

"You do the same for me."

After exchanging details, Gabriel leaned over and gave me a quick kiss. My lips still felt like shit, so I didn't respond immediately. My hesitation must have come across as rejection. He pulled back awkwardly.

"I *will* be in touch," I promised.

"Okay. See you." His shy smile brought out the protective instinct in me.

Damn. Not all the bikes had gone. One still remained. I watched warily as Gabriel approached the corner. A man seated sideways on a parked Harley called him over and spoke briefly before they parted company.

Fuck. I knew that figure. Now what? Even if Gabriel told the leather man my name, what did that prove? Gabriel didn't know Steven Stanhope was in fact Stevie Tricks. If I ran off, though, that would be a dead giveaway. The fucking leather man would be after me on his Harley before I made it to the next corner. Besides, I'd look stupid running.

At the top of the hill, the light above the entrance to the underground railway station shone like a beacon, beckoning me to safety. A hundred meters. It may as well have been a thousand.

Damn the man. A shiver ran through me. After working up a sweat on the dance floor, I shouldn't be that cold, surely. Faking a casualness I didn't feel, I strolled along the narrow laneway, pretending to send a text. I thought I had escaped detection until he spoke.

"You shouldn't have run, boy." His deep voice rumbled into the silence.

I didn't have to fake confusion; I *hadn't* run—that was the whole point. "Sorry, mate. Do I know you?" *And if you call me "boy" again, I swear I'll deck you!* Something seemed odd, but I ignored it, trying for a calm I didn't possess.

"You and I have some business to attend to."

"Pardon?" Chills trickled up and down my spine.

"Didn't Fred tell you that I gotta talk to you?"

Was that also code for: I gotta fuck you? What was it with this guy? Anyway, how had he recognized me? Did Fred spill the beans? *Why would he?* "I think you've got your wires crossed, mate. We've never met." I avoided his steady gaze, trying to stop my heart from doing the Watusi.

The leather man slid off the seat and held out his gloved hand in greeting.

I stared at it much like Gabriel had stared at mine earlier. I'd rather grab the hot end of a branding iron.

"Donato Rossi." He rolled the *r*, revealing perfect teeth on the last syllable. "And I believe you are Steven Stanhope."

I'd been so mesmerized by the contrasting expressions on his face, the hard steeliness of his eyes and the white flashing curve of his mouth, that I had grasped his hand before I knew what I was doing. I expected him to do one of those knuckle-crushing jobs, but his grip was merely firm until I tried to pull my hand free. The pressure gradually increased to counter my efforts. All the time, his gaze didn't waver.

"You've been a difficult man to track down, Steven. I thought you might at least honor your bets, but I should have known I wouldn't be able to trust you."

Honor? Trust? Fuck. *What was he going on about?* You'd think I'd broken the Eleventh Commandment. I dragged my gaze from his eyes, about to deny everything again. Then I caught sight of something that drove all thoughts from my head. No wonder I kept having this feeling of déjà vu! The bloody bike was screaming out to me.

Apart from the hundreds of hours I must have spent polishing every square inch until the chrome shone, no way had anyone managed to duplicate the modifications we'd done on Julius's Ultra Classic Glide, stripping off all the unwanted factory parts before dressing the chopper into his ultimate touring machine. While everything else went to the dogs, this shared love was the one thing that had kept us together. Helped me put up with all the other crap. "What the fuck are you doing with Julius's bike?"

With a swift jerk, I yanked my hand from his and stroked the leather upholstery. The fine cracks on the surface were crying out for another application of Dubbin. "Julius always said he'd rather die than sell this." I gave the bike a final pat. It still looked great.

"But he did." A strange expression crossed the American's face. "I'm sorry. I thought you knew."

CHAPTER
+++
SIX

Landslide

THE leather man's baldly stated words lashed me as viciously as his single-tail whip would have. Desperately, I scanned his impassive face, looking for some indication I'd misunderstood. Hoping I had. "Did you just say Julius is dead?"

"Would I lie to you?"

The world wavered for a second, then jolted back onto its axis. "Fuck." My knees gave way. I fell into a defensive crouch, placing my hands on the ground, trying to find strength from somewhere. Anywhere. The concrete seemed as good a place as any. At least it was real. Everything else felt like it belonged to some sort of surreal nightmare.

Tilting my head back, I gulped in a lungful of air. Although I'd removed his collar years ago, it felt like Julius had his fingers twisted under the leather, pulling it tighter, choking me. "No." I bellowed the word as loudly as an enraged bull. *How could Julius be dead?* In all our time together, he never had a day's illness. Damn it. I wish the leather man *had* lied.

Nearby, a window banged and a woman yelled out, "Keep the fucking noise down. People are trying to sleep." Muttered threats to call the cops followed.

It's funny how when someone dies, you remember the good times and ignore the bad. An image surfaced of a photo I'd taken the first time we took the modified Harley out for a spin. Julius, clad in his favorite jeans and leather jacket, sporting reflective Ray-Bans.

After I took the photo, he removed his sunglasses and gave me one of his trademark killer smiles. *"What a waste,"* the girls used to say when they discovered he was gay. Tall, tanned, strong. Confidence oozed out of every pore. Not a single moment of doubt. Ever.

I never understood what he saw in me. Perhaps he just liked basking in the glow of my adoration. Liked being the center of my attention. I idolized him. Simple as that.

I didn't realize I was crying until something was shoved into my hand. "You really didn't know," he muttered.

Angrily, I wiped the crap off my face and stowed the stained handkerchief in my pocket. My gaze might be directed at the man in front of me, but all I kept seeing was Julius.

Stacks of questions spilled onto my tongue, but only two made their way out. "How? When?" In the silence following the woman's complaint, the harshness of my voice reverberated between the tall buildings.

Leaning down, the leather man grasped my wrists, pulling me to my feet. "Come on. We can't talk here. I'm taking you home."

Home? I choked back a shout of laughter. *Home is where the heart is, isn't it?* Mine had been ripped out ages ago. They don't regrow, unfortunately. Part of the reason I came back to Australia. To see if I could find the original. I stood, rigid as a statue, while the leather man slipped a helmet over my head and fastened the strap.

I didn't want to go anywhere with him, but he owed me some answers, not the least of which was what the fuck he was doing riding Julius's bike.

The leather man buckled his own helmet and slung his leg over the seat. "Coming?"

Moving like a zombie, I sat behind him and clung on tight as, with one deft move, he kicked back the strut and took off.

I wasn't exaggerating either. Zombies are dead people who can still move, aren't they? That's exactly how I felt.

The wind flayed my skin, evaporating each trickle of tears from my eyes. Through the blur, one by one, I ticked off the familiar landmarks as we wound our way through the back streets of the Cross before veering off into the Eastern Distributor.

The American handled the Harley like he'd owned it forever, but he couldn't have. I hugged the bike with my knees and buried my face in the expanse of leather stretched across his back, drinking in the familiar smell. Wrong angle, though. Wrong feel. Julius was easily six inches taller, and leaner. A thoroughbred stallion. This man was a bulldog. A scrapper.

How many times had I been in this position? Hundreds? Thousands? At first, we used to ride separately, but as our relationship changed, Julius preferred having me behind him. *Where he could keep me safe*, he explained. Although I missed riding my BMW, I accepted his decision. Meant he loved me, right? Later, I wondered whether it was more of a snobbish reaction to any bike that wasn't a Harley.

As we sped south, the lights in the tunnel flashed like a strobe. Light: Julius... Dark: Dead... Light: Julius... Dark: Dead... Light... Dark... Light....

Fighting back tears, I concentrated on the echoing roar of the engine now magnified by the enclosing walls. Each rev of the throttle pushed the familiar sound deeper into my psyche, soothing my jangled nerves into a semblance of order, channeling them into something approaching sanity.

Eventually, we burst out of the tunnel into light. A different kind of light. High-powered halogens cast an uninterrupted, sulfurous glare, throwing the rest of the world into deep shadows. More landmarks. Golf course. Airport.

After booking my flight home, I had contacted my family, explaining that I was coming back to gain closure.

Of course, my mother and sister were looking forward to seeing me again, but they were the ones who had suggested I go to the UK in the first place. "Make a new life for yourself. As far from that bastard as possible." Not only a safe distance from a possessive ex, but where I wouldn't be tempted to forgive him and go back.

41

"I'll just collect my gear and move on. Put the past behind me," I reassured them.

"Make sure that's all you do," my mother said.

She knew me too well.

When I left England, the prospect of being in just this position had lurked somewhere in the back of my brain. On Julius's bike. With him. As equals. A dream. This was a nightmare.

Rhiannon had especially warned me to be careful. "The man is poisonous," she'd said.

If so, I'd been addicted to his venom. Weird, then, that he was the one who was dead.

I choked back a sob. How on earth could I hate a guy, yet love him so much?

As soon as we pulled up at a traffic light, I dragged the rag out of my pocket and dried my face. Fucking tears. I thought they'd run out years ago. Seemed I was wrong. Twisting the bandana around, I stared at the black material. What was it? Another piece of symbolic shit. A concrete example of all the things that had spoiled something special.

I brought the leather man's hanky up to my nose and blew into it.

Its owner twisted around and yelled, "Hands back where they belong, boy."

Anger flared, drowning all other emotions, blotting out my memories. "I have a name, you fucker. Use it."

The only response was a deafening roar as he gunned the bike and set off.

Bastard. Given no choice in the matter, I automatically shoved the symbolic square into my left pocket and grabbed his waist, resting my head against his back. Some things were so familiar, others so different. For starters, Julius wouldn't have bothered wearing a helmet. Removing his cap would have been an admission that other people's rules were superior to his. Something he would never accept.

He never cared whether I wore mine either. We copped a few fines, but so what? The pigs saw the bike and leather, and that was enough for them. They probably assumed, because of my long hair, I was his bitch. Julius used to get off on their looks of surprise when they filled out their tickets and discovered I was a guy. Who cared what people thought? *Too good to be true*, our friends used to mock, making gagging noises with their fingers in their mouths.

When we got home, if I complained about their teasing, Julius used to say they were jealous and fondle my hair. Before long, the casual touch would grow urgent, and we'd be making love, Julius matching his comments with his thrusts. "We *are* good, baby. Don't you worry about them." That was before "baby" grew into "boy" and our relationship slithered downhill, caught up in the fucking leather landslide.

Damn. I could put up with physical pain. No worries. In fact, I fucking loved it. That was the easy part. This waking nightmare was worse. Much worse.

"Hang on. Not much farther."

My eyes jerked open at the unfamiliar American accent to discover we were stopped at another set of traffic lights. The man in front was studying my face intently. I don't know what he saw, but he cursed when he turned back and started off again. "Fucking hell."

Hell. So that's where we were. Red taillights ahead added to the impression. Earlier, I'd wished the leather man to hell in a handbasket. Looked like he'd taken me there, literally.

Opening the throttle further, he whisked us through the night, the familiar scenery of the F6 providing a welcome distraction until clouds blocked the moon, drenching us in a scudding shower of rain. Pierced by icy needles, I shivered in my wet clothes, wishing I had my leathers with me. Not the sort the man in front wore, but proper, padded racing leathers.

My brain grew fuzzy as we wove like a snake down the highway, passing truck after truck. Their vampire-like drivers sleep by day, coming out at night when normal people are home, safe in bed. As we flew by, gusts of wind buffeted us, followed by the occasional blare of a horn. *"Yeah, we see you, buddy, but never forget who rules the road."*

The traffic thinned, and night settled like a shroud, enfolding us in its embrace. Bereft of thought, my frozen body swayed instinctively with that of my companion. Another dance, this time the bike keeping us together in perfect synchronization.

Dimly, I was aware of a garage door opening and closing, the whining motor stirring me from my daze.

"Damn it, boy. You're frozen stiff."

Boy! I was too tired to object. Every bone in my body ached.

"Come on." Placing his arm around my waist, the leather man helped me off the bike and led me up a flight of steps.

No! Not here!

As soon as I realized where we were, I resisted, but my brain refused to function above that initial start of recognition. I made it to the bathroom before my knees gave way.

The leather man must have anticipated my collapse, as he managed to maneuver me onto the closed seat of the toilet. The sound of running water stirred me a little, but mostly my brain had shut down. Was I trapped in hell again? What were we doing here?

"Steven."

I winced at the harshness of his voice and flinched, expecting an accompanying slap, but nothing.

"Boy." That worked. I glared up at him, ready to spit in his face. "Unless you want a shower with all your clothes on, you have to undress yourself."

In the end, he had to help me because my fingers refused to work properly.

"Hurry up. Your core temperature is way too low." His words may have been impatient, but his voice wasn't. Almost worried.

He only let me stay under the water for a few minutes, rubbing his hands over my skin, trying to restore circulation.

My brain still didn't want to function. From the cold? Or, more likely, a refusal to deal with the reality of Julius's death.

The brisk towel-down helped.

By the time we reached the bedroom door, I'd recovered enough to understand where we were going. I stretched out my arms until they were rigid against the frame, forming a barrier. No way was I going in there. That was Julius's room.

"What's the matter now?" He sounded genuinely confused.

44

I had no fucking clue how the American came to be riding Julius's bike or how he came to be in Julius's home. Our home. But he didn't belong. Neither did I.

"I can't sleep in there." I detected a hint of pity in his gaze before I turned away. I didn't move, waiting for the shove in my back, forcing me inside.

He didn't.

I shivered and stared at the floor. The shower had thawed some of the chill, but my bones still felt like solid chunks of ice.

"Fuck it. I'm too tired to argue. Come with me." Grasping my arm, he pulled me in the opposite direction. "Lucky for you, one of the other beds is still made up."

I stumbled along beside the irate man, not caring where he took me as long as he didn't expect me to sleep in Julius's bed.

In another room, he pulled a light bedspread back and shoved me down. I snuggled into the soft mattress and watched him strip off his own clothes. As soon as he was naked, he lay beside me and pulled the cover over. The warmth from his body helped more than anything. I closed my eyes as he rubbed every part of me with his rough palms.

CHAPTER
+++
SEVEN

Nightbird

I WOKE, lying on my back in a room swathed in darkness. A naked man stretched out on his front alongside me, his leg draped over one of mine.

Shit! I went through my usual morning-after checklist. *Where am I? How did I get here, and who the fuck is this?* I started by breathing in. Pine. Where had I smelled that aftershave before? A pub. Yeah, definitely, a pub. An image of big butch guys and leather men standing at a bar began to form. But this wasn't the pub or my hotel. A red light shone in through the open doorway, casting an eerie glow. There had been red lights last night too. Pinpricks of flames in the blackness. I closed my eyes and took another deep breath.

Perhaps some subtle smell lingers in the air and lodges in your senses, or maybe buildings take on a corporeal form that is recognizable, but without opening my eyes, I could now identify this place, this house. My old home. We were in one of the guest bedrooms, and the red glow came from the electronic displays on the appliances in the kitchen.

My sleeping companion mumbled something and turned to face me. Even in the gloom, I could see his moustache. *Shit.* Master D. The man who raved on about honor.

I tried to escape but was trapped by his outstretched leg. This was the last person I expected to end up in bed with. By rights, he should hate my guts. After all, hadn't I been disrespectful in front of an audience of his peers? Instead, he'd warmed me up and taken the chill from my bones.

When he didn't move, I relaxed and watched, fascinated, as the dark bristles quivered slightly with each breath. Another fucking Master. In his case, a Master of mystery. An enigma. The guy who, for some unexplained reason, now rode Julius's bike.

The one who told me Julius was dead. *No, don't go there. Think of something else.*

Waking up with a stranger in my bed wasn't too unusual. Anonymous, mattress-humping sex was a great way to reassure me that my world didn't begin and end with my ex.

Since removing his collar, I'd been fucked by all sorts of guys. Some I liked, some I didn't. A cock is a cock is a cock, right? In fact, if the guy sleeping next to me still insisted on fucking me because of the stupid bet, I'd probably agree. At least it would reassure me that *I* was alive.

But it wouldn't be *anonymous* sex. Although we'd never met, this guy recognized me and knew my real name. What did he know of my connection with Julius? And if I'd known he was bringing me here, would I have jumped on the bike? I'd assumed when he said *home*, he meant *his* home.

I had to find out what happened. To Julius. To the man I loved. Loved? Had loved. While I slept, my mind remembered I didn't love him anymore. Or wasn't supposed to. During my therapy sessions, I'd been encouraged to consider our relationship objectively, and my therapist told me I wasn't in love with Julius, I was *besotted* by him. According to her, he took advantage of this weakness and bolstered his narcissism by enslaving me in an unhealthy bond of forced inequality.

Yeah, right.

The heavy weight across my body reminded me too much of shackles for comfort. I twisted, trying to dislodge his leg.

"Stop fidgeting, boy."

Boy! That bloody word again. I shoved as hard as I could, but I might as well have been trying to move a ten-ton truck.

The leather man rolled over until he now lay completely on top of me, twisting his leg around mine in a classic wrestling hold. I must have been weaker than I thought. He wasn't that much bigger; I should've been able to shift him. Despite my lack of gym muscles, my natural wiry strength usually served me well when I needed it. Not that I allowed myself to get into vulnerable positions very often.

"Get *orf* me," I said, giving him another shove.

The man above eased back slightly, balancing on his elbows, our legs still entwined.

"Is that all the thanks I get for saving your life?" he murmured drowsily.

"Saving my life? What a load of crap! I was only cold because you insisted on bringing me here. Why did you?"

He didn't respond.

I tried to free my legs. "Which reminds me. What the fuck are you doing in this house? Who gave you the keys?"

"Too tired now. We can talk in the morning, boy,"

"Shit." I grabbed his arms and tried to push him away again. "I am *not* your boy, never have been, never will be. I'm done with all that crap."

"Old habits are hard to break," he muttered and untangled our legs.

He was telling me something I didn't know? "Well, just don't."

Giving a huge sigh, he slid out of bed. The red glow hugged the edge of his figure, making him appear almost demonic.

"Where are you going?" I tried to suppress a sudden flare of panic.

"To my own bed. With a bit of luck, I might get some more sleep before morning."

I felt like screaming *Julius's bed* at him. How come he acted like he owned the place? Nothing made any sense. "What if I get cold again?"

The leather man strode off down the corridor and returned moments later, carrying something bulky. He spread the quilt over me, leaning in close to tuck the bedding under my chin. "Now go to sleep."

48

"Don't I get a good-night kiss?" Strange how, in times of stress, I managed to disguise it with sass. I had a couple of scars to prove it.

"You're lucky you don't get a good-night spanking, boy!"

"I'm not…."

"Yeah, I know." His voice sounded even more tired when he interrupted my tirade. "Go back to sleep." This time his command suggested I better obey or else.

I probably should be glad he went back to his own bed, right? But in a weird way, the weight of his body against mine hadn't upset me as much as I thought it would. I didn't want to be alone in this house ever again. I struggled up onto my elbows, trying to stop the begging words from escaping. *Please, don't go.* How many times had I called that out as footsteps retreated down the corridor? Probably as many times as Julius laughed and said that's what I got for not being a good boy, adding he'd see me in the morning.

He learned quickly that a hundred whacks with the hairbrush might piss me off, but they didn't punish me the way he thought I deserved. Chaining me to the bed by his fucking collar and making me sleep on my own worked. Brilliantly.

Since leaving, if I didn't have a human bed warmer, I usually ended up sleeping with my good ol' buddy, temazepam.

I lay there for a while, straining to hear something, anything.

Tonight, the wind must have been blowing from the west. Otherwise, I'd hear the occasional rumble of a train at the bottom of the escarpment.

Pity the guy in the other room didn't snore. Sleeping apart, I used to find Julius's soft whistles a comfort, though they annoyed the shit out of me when we shared a bed.

But now, the house was quiet. Too quiet. The absence of sound that frays your nerves. In the UK, it wasn't just cheapness that led me to choose lodgings right in the thick of the action. Other people thought I was crazy, staying near pubs where people would hang around long after closing, not realizing how far their drunken conversations carried in the night air.

Weird to think its isolated location was the main reason we had bought this rambling old guest house. Privacy. The ability to do whatever we wanted without any neighbors complaining about the noise. When it was operational, the original owners had promoted the place as a retreat from the cares of the world. I often wondered whether the spirit of the old ashram was upset by the switch from yoga and its *Om*s to BDSM and its groaned *Argh*s.

I turned over and buried my head in the pillow. Thank God the leather man hadn't taken me to my old room. Had Julius left it like it was? Some people keep the rooms of the departed intact as a memorial to their presence. Not likely in my case. Rhiannon had borne the brunt of his rage when he came searching for me. In the end, my mother had been forced to take out a restraining order to prevent him from harassing them. *Deal with his lawyer* was all she would say.

If it hadn't been for Rhi, I would never have left. She was only seventeen when she made the journey from Melbourne all by herself, alarmed at not hearing from her big brother for so long. Without her intervention, I wouldn't have had the courage to break the bonds, both figuratively and literally. Not that I left then, but the seed had been planted. When I finally managed to leave and remove Julius's collar, she merely said, "About bloody time."

Time. Was it my imagination, or was the sky outside lighter? The sooner dawn came, the better. Then I could discover what the bloody hell was going on, collect my bike, and get the fuck out of here.

A mournful cry shattered the silence. "Ko-*el*."

I laughed to myself. Fancy being glad to hear a bloody stormbird. When I hadn't broken any of his rules and was allowed into Julius's bed, I slept so soundly that I never heard them. But, confined to my own room, night after night, all through spring and summer, often as early as two in the morning, the incessant birdcalls would wake me up. There was something about its distinctive sound that haunted me, a reminder I hadn't obeyed some stupid command.

Sleep would be impossible now. Who *was* this guy? Why was he here? *Talk to me in the morning.* As if I could go to sleep with all those questions running through my head. Bloody typical Master. He gave me the command to go to sleep, and somehow, miraculously, I was meant to obey.

I draped the quilt around my naked body. Hopefully, he wasn't asleep yet. At the open doorway to Julius's bedroom, I knocked quietly but didn't step inside. The rain clouds had dispersed, allowing the moon to shine in. Being shorter, the leather man took up less of the bed than Julius did, but he still looked like he belonged there.

His face was in shadow as he turned toward me. "What is it?" He sounded seriously pissed off.

"Have you got any sleeping tablets?"

"Nope. Don't believe in those things."

Bloody typical. I should have known. Masters don't have problems. About anything.

Damn it. I did.

"You're dependent on them," he muttered and shook his head.

"Not completely. I only need them when I think too much."

"Well, stop thinking."

"I can't."

He closed his eyes, obviously wanting to go back to sleep. The covering sheet had slipped down, exposing his bare chest. His black-and-silver pelt glowed in the moonlight. It looked different without the leather harness. *He* looked different. More approachable.

"What do you do when you can't go to sleep?" I asked quietly.

"Jerk off," he muttered without opening his eyes.

"Excuse me?"

"You asked me what I do when I can't get to sleep, and I told you."

No help there. I wandered back to the guest room and lay down. After a quick spit on my palm, I started stroking my dick. The leather man was right. If I got off, I would relax.

Memories of the evening swirled around as my fist flew. Sucking off all the rugby players. Then giving the leather man a blowjob. I licked my lips, recalling the sweetness of his precome and how good my tongue felt wrapped around his cock. The musky smell when I buried my nose in his pubes. The feel of his hard length lodged in my throat. That moment when sucking him off seemed like the most natural thing in the world. The prospect of being fucked because I lost the bet. My hand sped up, and I groaned. I wanted to come, but something held me back. An image of Gabriel intruded. What would have happened if I'd asked him back to my hotel instead of letting him go home alone? For starters, I wouldn't be back here. Not in this house. Our house.

Julius. Once, I would have been pleased to hear he was dead. I told him so often enough. He always laughed and stroked my face while I struggled against my bonds, knowing no matter how much he hurt me beforehand, all it took was one touch, one whispered word of praise—of assurance that he loved me, that I belonged to him and only him, and then he would fuck me like no one else ever had. Before. Or since.

At first, I'd enjoyed being taken care of. Thanks to his wealthy parents, he had experienced all the good things in life, much more than I'd been exposed to, hence he knew the best places to go, the fun things to do. But after a while, that care morphed into a prison just as restrictive as the six-foot wall around the house. Especially when he started laying down the law about when I could and couldn't come.

My hand paused in midstroke. *Julius hadn't given me permission to come.*

"*Julius!*" In frustration, I yelled loud enough to call him back from the dead, half expecting, half hoping for a vengeful spirit to appear and snarl his approval.

Instead, all I got was an irate American leaning over me saying, "What the hell is wrong with you, boy?"

Damn, my cock was so hard it hurt. "Julius didn't give me permission to come." Even to my ears, the whimpered excuse sounded pathetic.

Another blast appeared imminent. Going to sleep was obviously the most important thing on the man's mind, and I kept interrupting him. Instead, he flicked the quilt back, knocked my hand off my cock, and replaced it with his own. Without breaking eye contact, he pumped my shaft. "If I let you come, will you promise to answer all my questions in the morning?"

I swallowed and groaned under his ministrations. He wasn't being gentle, yet I still needed more friction. "As long as you answer mine."

He paused in midstroke. *Slaves don't make demands.* I held my breath, waiting for his response. Part of me was still shit-scared about demanding anything, but I'd had four years of counseling to reassure me I could now ask for whatever I wanted.

"I don't know what the fuck is going through your head, but relax, I'm not going to hit you." Swiping his palm over the tip and using my precome for lubrication, his stroke gentled, became longer, more thorough.

Perfect. I lay back and enjoyed his hand job, moaning slightly. Sex was the perfect way to block out all the crap in my brain. "Were you a dairy maid in a former life?" The way he was milking my cock sure suggested he was.

His stroke faltered again as he gave a small huff of a laugh. "Good to see you're feeling better, boy."

"I am not your boy." When would he get the message?

"I know." He almost sounded sad about the fact.

The leather man's technique might be mechanical, without any degree of affection, but it was certainly effective. What had he done for sex before I arrived? His response earlier that he jerked off before going to sleep suggested he didn't have anyone to share his bed with. The thought of him lying there jacking himself was kinda sad.

Our gazes locked, and, once again, it was as if he could read my mind. "I'm only doing this because I want to get some sleep. If I didn't, you'd come and annoy me again."

His pumping grew harder, faster.

I gasped. "Well, I think I'm coming now."

My back arched, and every muscle quivered as shots of creamy fluid sprayed wildly all over my chest. During the aftershocks, I grabbed the sheet and stared as he casually scooped some come off my chest and ran his tongue over his palm. I moaned. *Talk about hot.*

"Now will you go back to sleep?" He ran a pink tongue over his lips.

For once, words failed me. I merely nodded.

"No asking for a drink of water in a few minutes either."

"No, Pop."

Was that a slight twinkle I saw in his eyes as he pulled the quilt back up and tucked it in again? Before I could say anything embarrassing like *Stay with me*, he turned on his heel and walked away. I eyed the muscles in his butt as he left the room. I'd been so wrapped up in his brilliant hand job I hadn't noticed he was naked and hard. Hmm, he still hadn't collected on his bet. Should I remind him in the morning?

CHAPTER
✝✝✝
EIGHT

Crash Into Me

THE clatter of pots and pans woke me from a mercifully dream-free sleep. I rubbed my chest, where specks of dried come had matted the hairs together. Fuck. One drawback of not manscaping. After a quick shower in the guest room's en-suite, I wiped myself dry and wrapped the towel around my waist. My wet clothes were probably still lying in a heap in the other bathroom. Now the sun was up, the horrors of the previous night had evaporated. Darkness always reminded me too much of being blindfolded and helpless.

The smell of frying bacon wafted in from the kitchen, followed by the crack of shells and sizzle of eggs hitting the pan. "I like mine sunny-side up," I yelled and grinned at the resulting snort from the adjoining room. Okay, the guy wasn't a complete jerk. After all, he did help me get to sleep twice last night. For a certified insomniac, that amounted to two huge ticks in his favor. One essential aroma was missing, though. Coffee.

Pausing at the doorway, I checked out the jeans-clad man as he pushed pieces of bacon around with a plastic spatula. *What the fuck* is *his name?* I couldn't keep thinking of him as the leather man.

A memory returned of the way he'd rolled his R's when he introduced himself last night. Donato Rossi. Don the Dom.

"Morning, Sunshine." I grinned. I couldn't imagine anyone less sunny if I tried. For me, the guy would always be associated with memories of blackness and the horrors of night. But that's typical of Aussie nicknames. Shorty for the tall ones, Blue for the redheads, Snowy for the brunettes. Crazy, huh?

Don seemed to be of the same opinion. After raising one derisory eyebrow at me, he turned back to his cooking. Now he wasn't wearing leather, he looked different. Give him a decent haircut, shave off that ridiculous moustache, and he wouldn't look too bad. No sign of a paunch. In fact, I rather liked the way his butt filled out his faded jeans. Pure muscle with a nice big bulge at the front. My mouth watered. Talk about a Pavlov's dog reaction. "Any chance of a coffee?" I asked, as if this was his house, not mine.

He shrugged. "If you can work the machine, be my guest."

I glanced at the cappuccino maker and snorted. "I suppose you prefer drip coffee."

"Why you Australians like all that frothy stuff on top beats me."

Yeah, the Brits couldn't understand either.

I opened the freezer and stared inside. Great. Coffee beans. They were probably stale, but who cared. A quick check through the cupboards didn't reveal any new ones. It also confirmed another thing I'd been wondering about. The guy hadn't been staying here long. Either that, or he didn't do *shopping*.

I checked the machine and groaned. Whoever used the thing last hadn't cleaned it. That was always my job. I put the packet back in the freezer and straightened.

"Don't leave it there, boy."

Concentrating on what I was doing, I had inadvertently dropped my borrowed towel. Without thinking twice, I butted my chest against his and backed Don into the refrigerator.

He held up his hands in surprise, one still clutching the spatula.

"If you use that insulting term on everyone," I snarled, "it's a wonder you haven't been killed by now." To make sure he got the message, I poked his chest to emphasize each word. "When will you get it into your thick skull that I am not your boy? My name is Steve. If you're pissed off at me, you can call me Steven, and if you really want

56

to get my attention, call me Steven Lindsey Stanhope. But whatever you do, don't call me *boy*. Got it?"

We stared at each other, toe to toe, face to face, our eyes nearly level. *Way to go, Steve. Forget about pissing off the man in leather; now you've pissed off the man with the spatula.* I had a vague recollection of receiving a few swats, courtesy of Julius.

Don gave a little shake of his head, as if bemused by my extreme reaction. "Funny you should see it that way. I see *boy* as a term of affection." A shadow crossed his face. "My apologies, though. I keep forgetting." He looked like he was going to say more; then his gaze flicked away for a second before latching back onto mine. A sly smile replaced his previous sadness. "Lindsey?" Using his groin, he nudged me forward to give himself room.

"Yeah, with an 'e' and Steven with a 'v'. Mum was a Fleetwood Mac fan."

"Well, back off before you start giving me ideas. I'm not sure whether your cock is sending me signals, or do you need to take a piss?"

Surprised, I stared down at my erection and laughed. Before I could move, he grabbed my balls in a grip so tight, my eyes rolled up into my head. "But be more careful next time, Steven Lindsey Stanhope. A few inches to the left, and I would have burned myself on the stove."

Don's hand felt good and bad at the same time, sending a raw pain into my gut, making me all tingly inside.

He released his grip, and I backed away warily, rubbing my balls.

With a derisive glance, he checked out my cock, noting it was still hard. "You better go take care of that yourself. I only do charity cases in the middle of the night."

I grabbed the towel and headed off to the other bathroom. My jeans and shirt still lay in a damp pile on the floor. *Yuck.* Were any of my old clothes still here? I'd only been able to take a few things when I left. Cautiously, I eased open the door of my old bedroom and laughed. So much for Julius leaving my room intact for sentiment's sake. The space was now an office. Nothing of mine remained.

Wondering if my gear had migrated elsewhere, I quickly checked the other bedrooms. We'd bought the place fully furnished, but, even in its prime, the guest house would have been lucky to qualify as three-star. Now only an exercise bike and the old Chuck Norris machine stood forlornly in the next room. Another contained a big flat-screen television and some stereo equipment, all stacked together, obviously not connected. The last bedroom had boxes of what looked like books. The cupboards in the room I'd slept in were also bare. The house had an unlived-in air about it. How long had Julius been gone?

I wandered back to the kitchen. Walking round naked didn't feel strange. Another one of the many rules Julius had imposed. At least I didn't have the fucking chains around my ankles. "You didn't happen to bring a spare frock with you, did you, dahl? Green to match my eyes would be cool."

Without turning around, Don said, "Green? I would have called them more hazel."

Damn. Why did the man have to unsettle me by noticing details like the color of my eyes? I closed them and took a deep breath. When my heart rate turned to normal, I added in a waspish voice, "Either way, you better sack the maid. These are still wet."

Don turned, waving the spatula around. "Don't look at me. After spending most of the night making sure you were okay, I was kept awake by some damn bird and hardly slept a wink. What are those fucking things, anyway?"

I laughed. "Koels? Some people call them stormbirds." Good. I wasn't the only one who found their incessant calls annoying. "They lay their eggs in other birds' nests."

Muttering something about rifles, Don turned back to the stove. I didn't blame him. But speaking of taking over another nest, what was *this* cuckoo doing here? And what other information did he have about Julius? Part of me was desperate to find out. The trouble was, then he would start asking *me* questions. No thanks. Not without clothes on. I rescued my wallet and phone, threw everything else into the dryer, and turned it on.

Back in the kitchen, I rubbed myself up against Don like a cat. "Um. Clothes? Or would you rather I stay naked?" There was something about the guy that made me want to push his buttons. See if

I could make him lose his cool. Discover *his* limits. Except, wouldn't you know it? He just stood there calmly, continuing what he was doing.

After a few minutes, when I realized I was getting hard again, I stopped.

Don gave me a considering look, but he didn't seem too upset. Quite the contrary, judging by the bulge in his jeans. "Here, make yourself useful. And don't let them burn." After popping a couple of slices of bread in the toaster, he headed off to his room. I grabbed a tray from on top of the cupboard, dished out the breakfast, then added the toast as soon as it popped up.

"Here ya go," he said when he returned. A pair of boxers with the Australian flag on them floated in my direction. "Present from my Great Aunt Mildred."

Kinky. Mind you, it looked like he'd never worn them. "Thanks." I drew them up, poking my half-hard dick back inside. Damn thing didn't want to go down. "And here I was hoping you might lend me those leather pants from last night." Long ago, I'd given up wondering why I liked wearing leather, even though I loathed the idea of *Leather*.

"Not in a million years, b…."

I smiled at the exasperated expression on his face, wondering if swallowing too many "oys" before breakfast could give you indigestion. Obviously, he was used to calling whoever he lived with *boy*. I wondered where that guy was.

I picked up the tray and followed Don outside.

Shit. The yard was an absolute mess. Attractive if you went in for clover, yellow dandelions, and onion weed. Julius always insisted I take care of the lawn. While he was at work, I was often tempted to ring a mowing service. Unfortunately, I couldn't because of the locked gate.

I set the breakfast on the wrought-iron picnic table and stared in horrid fascination as Don chose the seat Julius always used. Did he pick that one instinctively, or was there some hidden label: *The seat of choice for your discerning Master?* I eyed the other chair and swallowed. What now? The urge to kneel at his feet nearly overwhelmed me. Talk about old habits being hard to break. Looked like I wasn't as cured as I thought.

"Sit down. Your breakfast is getting cold." Don nodded at the vacant seat and resumed eating as if nothing had happened, but I noticed he flicked me a sideways glance as I sidled in to sit on furniture I'd never been allowed to use before. Not when a fucking Master was around, at any rate.

After a couple of seconds, when the ground didn't rise up and swallow me, I started eating. Even using utensils again had taken some getting used to. I kept waiting for commands. *Eat this. Don't eat that.*

At first, being fed by someone else had been sexy, almost decadent. Then it became irksome. Julius never gave me enough time to chew properly. I wondered sometimes whether he did it deliberately, laughing as I spluttered. But whenever I complained, he just licked all the stray bits of food from around my mouth, and pretty soon we'd be fucking.

Damn. Now the view had gone all blurry. "What happened to Julius?" I flicked my head to dislodge the tears. Over time, I'd become adept at the move. You needed to be when your hands were tied. I rubbed my wrists at the memory before picking up the toast to blot up all the runny yolk. As I brought the concoction up to my mouth, I noticed Don watching me intently. "What? You said you'd answer my questions."

"You really don't know?"

"No, so tell me."

His gaze shifted to the knife in his hand. He was flipping it over and over as if he wanted to throw it at something or someone. Who? *Me?*

"Where to start?" He paused for second and glanced up. "Julius was killed in a motorcycle accident."

"What? A bike accident? How? That doesn't make sense. I had a good look at his Harley last night, and there isn't even a scratch on it."

"He was riding *my* bike."

"Here?"

"No." He gave an impatient wave with the knife toward the ocean. "In the States."

"Huh? When did he go there?"

60

"About two years after you left." He gave me a look of pure disdain. "After you broke your word and ran, boy."

I gripped the edge of the table and started to rise, the fork gripped tightly in my hand.

"Don't try it." He glared at me until I let the fork drop onto the table; then he gave a sigh. "Let me tell my story, will ya? This is hard for me too."

Hard for *him*? I stared back, trying to work out why he was so upset. There were lines between his eyes I hadn't noticed before. What was Julius to him? More than a friend, obviously. A lover? Difficult to imagine the two together, but then again, who would be able to resist Julius? The fucker had an almost irresistible charm. I was living proof of that.

I gave a nod, encouraging him to continue as I resumed eating my breakfast. Now was not the time to compliment him on his cooking.

"He told me he came to Chicago to 'learn from the Masters'."

Merely by the way Don uttered the words, I could hear the capital and quotes around the phrase. To the leather man, that was obviously a perfectly rational thing to do. The news didn't surprise me. Julius had read everything he could find on the Old Guard and wanted to recreate their way of life, following everything they did or said as if it were gospel.

"I met him soon after he arrived, and we became friends after discovering that we both owned Ultra Classics. He was thinking of buying another one and shipping it back here."

"Hey, hang on a minute." I waved my fork to gain his attention. "I know he always wanted to do that, but how could he afford to buy another bike, let alone travel to the States? He never had any money to spare." Lack of money had been another bone of contention between us.

"His grandmother died, and he inherited a portion of her estate."

"Oh, fair enough." His parents were loaded, so there had to have been money somewhere. "Go on." There was something Don wasn't telling me. I could sense it in the way his gaze slipped away from mine every now and then. "When did he die?"

"The fourth of June."

Five months ago. "What happened?" Don was staring at his plate, but I had a feeling he didn't really see it. "Give me details. Was it raining? Loose gravel?"

His eyes flicked up to mine again before staring back at the remains of his breakfast. He took a deep breath before continuing, "The bike skidded on an oil slick and was sideswiped by an SUV in the next lane. His passenger was thrown clear, but unfortunately, Julius and the bike ended up right in front of an oncoming truck." Don's voice took on a dead quality, devoid of any emotion. "He was killed instantly. Decapitated." The last word was added nonchalantly. A trifling detail.

I pushed back the chair and staggered to my feet. So much for breakfast. It made a lovely Technicolor splash on the lawn.

Don hadn't moved. He still gripped the knife, his knuckles showing white against his tan. I fell rather than sat back down, landing so heavily the seat stung my butt through the thin satin boxers. At times, I'd felt like strangling Julius, but I would never have wished that fate on him.

The man beside me stared blankly at his empty plate. Something he'd said struck me as odd. *His passenger was thrown clear.* "Who was on the bike with him?"

"Alex."

Alex? Who the fuck was he? "What happened to him?"

"He received massive head injuries." There was a long pause. "So he died too." A tear formed at the edge of his eye.

"Who was he? A relative?"

Don looked briefly at the knife that he'd been turning over and over in his hands, and then with one swift flick, he threw it at a nearby tree. The point landed fair and square in the middle. The hilt quivered for a few seconds before the whole thing fell to the ground. "Alexander was my slave. My *boy*."

The leather man rose to his feet, gathered up the empty plates, and disappeared into the house. There was a jerkiness to his stride as if, inside, a coiled spring struggled to break free.

CHAPTER
+++
NINE

Talk to Me

SHIT. The taste of bile in my mouth echoed the sick feeling inside. My favorite memory of Julius returned: posing on his bike with his chiseled jaw and classic features just begging to be photographed. The thought of that beautiful head being separated from his broad shoulders brought another heave in my gut. No matter what went wrong between us, Julius hadn't deserved that fate.

I retrieved the knife and followed Don into the kitchen. From my vantage point at the doorway, I studied his profile as he painstakingly washed every scrap of stuck-on yolk from the plates. His face was once again a rigid mask of self-control. *How deep did it go?*

"You lost someone too. I'm sorry," I said quietly, dropping the knife into the sink.

After giving a tight-lipped nod, he went back to his task.

What was Alex like? Probably the perfect slave, desiring only to please his Master. The bitterness of bile surfaced again. I headed for the bathroom. The vanity cabinet yielded a nearly empty bottle of mouthwash. I swilled and spat. Better than nothing.

Blocking out the dreadful details, my brain returned to the numbness of the previous evening. I paused at the doorway to Julius's room and looked in.

There were a few of the American's possessions scattered around. His boots were side by side underneath the bed, and his cap was carefully placed on the bedside table.

Although I knew I'd never see Julius in there again, I still couldn't venture inside. I headed toward the garage to find my bike. The sooner I discovered if it was roadworthy and got the fuck away from another kinky man who believed in collaring people, the better.

At the bottom of the stairs, I turned on the light. I hadn't taken much in last night. Now I knew why the house looked so empty. The garage resembled a second-hand furniture store. Pushed back against the walls were neatly stacked tables and chairs, bed bases, and behind them, all the old wooden wardrobes with their slatted doors. Covers had been placed over some items, but others were clearly visible, including a couple of old Harleys we'd bought, intending to dress up and sell. Judging by the absence of wheels and other bits and pieces strewn around, Julius had been cannibalizing them for parts. He had probably sold the bits on eBay or something. Neither of the bikes would ever see the road again. Nor would Julius.

I closed my eyes and took a deep breath. When I opened them again, I noticed the door in the back wall was completely blocked by junk. Good. The room behind there held too many memories for my sanity.

No sign of my bike. Double damn. He must have sold it.

Frustrated rage filled me as I headed back upstairs. How dare Julius sell my pride and joy! There was nothing wrong with my BMW. The world didn't begin and end with Harleys.

At the top of the staircase, two sets of keys and a well-worn wallet lay on a small table. From the occasional clatter of plates, Don was still busy washing up and couldn't see me from where he was standing. I quickly thumbed open the clip. A quick check of his driving license reassured me that Don hadn't lied about his name: Donato Maximilian Rossi, resident of Chicago, thirty-five. Six years older than me.

I let out my breath sharply when I caught sight of the photo of a smiling young man in the picture holder. He may have been a few years older than Gabriel, but there was an uncanny resemblance between the two men, plus a shared aura of innocence. Angelic. Alex's snow-blond hair brushed the top of the studded leather band encircling his neck.

Rhi's words reverberated in my head. "Why are you wearing a fucking collar? You're not a dog."

Collars. Submission. I needed to get away before I became trapped again. The Harley's keys beckoned me like a siren. The bike was much heavier than mine, but I'd ridden it before and could again at a pinch.

"We were together for ten years." At the sound of its owner's deep voice, his wallet fell from my nerveless fingers.

Don stood in the kitchen doorway, his arms crossed in front of his broad chest, his back rigid. Not a trace of humor or softness in his gaze.

I wiped my hands on my boxers. No, *his* boxers. "I don't get it. What the fuck was your slave doing with Julius?" Embarrassment at being caught rifling through his personal possessions made me snap sharper than usual. But the question had been niggling at the back of my brain. Except when he was at work, Julius never let me out of his sight. He felt he owned me; that was why he'd taken ages to believe I'd really gone.

"He was staying with us." For a second, I thought the leather man was going to say more, but he only picked up his wallet and glanced quickly at the photo inside before tucking it into his pocket. He hadn't checked the money section. A minor consolation. He didn't think I was a thief. Just a slave who removed his Master's collar without permission. Probably a much worse crime in his book.

I brushed past him on my way to the laundry. I needed my own clothes. Now. The thin material of his boxers made me feel exposed. Defenseless.

I retrieved my shirt and jeans from the dryer and picked up my wallet and cell phone. While getting dressed, I checked to see if I had any messages. Two. One from Gabriel, suggesting we get together for lunch. "I have a car if you need wheels."

The other message was from Sara and Marty, inviting me to their wedding at the end of the month. Wow. She hadn't been joking. She really wanted me to perform "Sara" at the reception in memory of her mother, so she had contacted Fred for my number. "Bring a friend," she texted.

Looked like my career in drag wasn't over. The only problem was that all my frocks and makeup were at the Paradiso. Hang on a minute. Gabriel had a car. Could I take advantage of that fact and collect everything today?

I sat on a kitchen stool and started texting, giving him my whereabouts and suggesting he pick me up. Don was staring out the window again. *Lost in contemplation of the scenery or thinking about the tragedy that wrecked his life?* At least I'd had four years to "get over" Julius, and, believe me, the first couple of years weren't pretty. True, there may have been some vague hope we might get together again, but an insistent inner voice always protested at how bad that idea would be. I sighed. *You can't turn back time, as the saying goes.*

Now that I knew the circumstances surrounding Julius's death, there wasn't any reason to stay. I certainly couldn't live in this house again, even if someone paid me to. As soon as possible, I'd put the place on the market. In the meantime, Don could stay here as long as he liked. "Look, I'm sorry about your boy… friend's death." No way could I use that demeaning term. "And, er… thanks for making such an effort to tell me." Maybe he brought back Julius's remains for his family. No doubt, his parents would be heartbroken. They thought the sun shone out of their son's ass. After pressing Send, I added to Don, "I'll get out of your hair now, Sunshine. A friend is coming to collect me."

I glanced up to find him frowning at me.

"You're leaving?"

"Yeah, going back to the city. There doesn't seem to be anything of mine here." He still looked stunned by my announcement.

"So I gather you won't have any objection to selling the house?"

Was the guy a mind reader? I stared out at the uninterrupted view of the Pacific Ocean. On weekends, I used to love watching hang gliders swoop and glide like seagulls after throwing themselves off the cliff at the nearby lookout. How had the real estate blurb described the block? "One hour's drive south of Sydney, surrounded by pristine bushland, the property has a view to die for."

66

In my case, the view wasn't to die for but one to live for. The strange thing was that, even at the worst times—and there had been some humdingers—I had never been tempted to launch myself off the cliff to see how far I could get without the benefit of wings. I let out a huge sigh. Once, I would have been devastated at the thought of leaving, but there was nothing to keep me here now. If anything, there were too many bad memories. "No. The sooner this house goes on the market, the better."

"Good."

My gaze dropped to the weeds in the garden. "Pity the place looks such a mess." Out of habit, I started cleaning the cappuccino machine. Yuck. A scum line. The tank hadn't been emptied when Julius left, and the coffee container looked filthy.

"Actually, there may be something of yours here." Without explaining what he meant, Don disappeared downstairs. What was he up to now? I'd only just learned Julius was dead, and this guy, a virtual stranger, was encouraging me to sell the place. It made sense. But why was he butting in? I didn't need his approval. Typical Master. A real control freak.

As soon as the machine was clean, I added some beans from the packet in the freezer. The aroma created as they were crushed made the house smell scrumptious.

Moments later Don came up the stairs, lugging a big suitcase. "These clothes would have been too small for Julius. Are they yours?"

He dumped the heavy bag on the floor.

I pulled open the zipper. Inside were all the clothes I hadn't managed to stuff into the backpack when I left: a couple of suits, bulky sweaters, heavy winter clothing, and, miracle of miracles, folded at the bottom, my racing leathers. Now if only I had my bike I could go anywhere. "Where did you find this?"

"Down in the garage. I was sorting stuff out prior to putting the house on the market."

What the fuck? "Come again? What gives *you* the right to sell this house… *my* house?"

"Didn't you get the letters from Julius's lawyer? I used the same one he did. I figured he knew how best to contact you."

Damn. They should put stickers on the outside saying *"Please Read. This isn't another reminder from your ex, saying your mortgage repayment is overdue."* I had done my best to keep up with my side of the housing loan commitment, but with the expense of travelling overseas and the cost of my therapy, finding enough money hadn't been easy, especially in the beginning. "Um, no, I don't think I saw that one." After he realized I wasn't coming back with my tail between my legs, Julius sent the reminders via his lawyer to my lawyer, Irving Schofield. Sometimes, a personal note would be included, saying how much he missed me and wished I'd come back, promising things would be different this time. The temptation to read them continued to haunt me, but I knew if I did, I'd give in. So, as soon as I opened the outer envelope and saw the enclosed one from Julius's lawyer, I chucked them in the bin, figuring if it was really important, Irving would let me know himself.

"When you contacted Fred after the lawyer sent you the letter, we assumed that's why you agreed to return."

"Um, no." I wasn't about to admit I'd come back because I had this crazy idea of getting back with Julius. "Why are you sticking your nose into my business, anyway? What right do you have to put my house on the market? You don't own the place."

Planting his butt on one of the kitchen stools, Don avoided looking at me for a second. When he finally met my gaze, his face was flushed. "Er…. Actually, I do. I own exactly half of it, or at least I will, once probate is settled."

Don picked up the knife he'd tossed earlier and turned it over and over in his hands again. I dragged my gaze up to his face and noticed he wasn't looking at what he was doing, more studying me, as if I was some weird insect he'd never seen before. Given the number of unusual species we had in Australia, that gave him a lot to choose from. Damn. His actions had distracted me. Now his comment sank in. "How come you own half? If Julius died, the property should have reverted to me."

"You need to talk to your lawyer, as soon as possible." Don indicated the machine that was now making the appropriate gurgling noises. "I could do with a coffee. Straight black, please."

I made him a cup and frothed up milk for my own, working by instinct, my brain still churning through his astounding announcement.

"I still don't understand how you own half. We bought the property together."

Don gave a small sniff. "If you'd bothered to read the fine print, you would have realized your purchase was tenancy in common, not joint tenancy. They're different."

"I know that, but we didn't have a choice." According to the guy who organized the loan, seeing as we weren't married, we had to set it up that way. Same-sex partnerships were almost unheard of back then. "The bank wanted to treat it like a business venture."

"Yeah, but that means when one partner dies, the property doesn't automatically go to the other person like it does with joint tenancy. It goes to whoever is mentioned in the will."

"But when we took out the loan, we made out wills in favor of each other." *Oh, shit. I should have suspected that, but why to the American?*

Don's cup was empty. Without asking, I handed him a refill. "Did he make out a new will?"

Don stared at the coffee as if trying to find the answer to my question there. By the time he faced me again, his facade of calmness was back, but I caught a trace of something else. *Pity?* Fuck. The last thing I wanted.

"Yes. A few months before he died." A shadow crossed his face. "I think you definitely need to talk to your lawyer."

"Were you lovers or something?"

A flush of redness covered his face, and he shuddered before replying, "No."

"Well, if you weren't lovers, why would he make out the will in your favor? Did he owe you money?"

Don stiffened, looking more like he was on trial for his life rather than sitting in a kitchen, answering my questions. I bet he was usually the one trying to draw the information out of his slave. Getting Alex to spill his guts about how the scene went, exploring every angle, delving for any weakness that had been exposed. Wasn't that how all Masters worked? He wasn't used to people badgering *him*. A bead of sweat appeared on his brow. "Julius didn't make the will out in my favor. Alex was the beneficiary."

"Alex? Your slave?" That still didn't make any fucking sense. Unless…. Unless…. Understanding washed over me like a wave. Of course, how dumb could I get? Obviously, Julius went to the States by himself, but knowing how fucking charismatic the guy could be, he wouldn't have been alone for long. According to my therapist, Julius was a master of manipulation, gathering others around him, then criticizing the ones he didn't like in order to bolster his deep-seated feelings of inadequacy. In Alex, he probably met the perfect submissive. Trained to defer to others. Much easier to appropriate an experienced slave than start again from scratch.

As Don gazed at his empty cup, his face took on that bleak-eyed stare of those thinking of the past. Of lost loves. He looked completely gutted by the tragedy. "He stole Alex from you," I said quietly.

Only a small tic at the edge of his jaw indicated Don heard me. After a few seconds, he gave an almost imperceptible nod.

Typical Julius, taking what he wanted and not thinking about anyone else. I sighed. Alex would have been just the sort of guy he would like. Their hair was the same shade of sun-bleached blond. Once, Julius made me lighten mine with peroxide because he liked things to match. It didn't work. He'd been furious when I'd hacked it all off afterward. "That still doesn't explain how you came to own half this house."

Don gave a soft snort, the sudden gust of air making his moustache quiver. "Actually, it does. Although his injuries were horrific, Alex managed to hang onto life for a few days. When he regained consciousness, he revealed that they'd been in a Master/slave relationship for weeks. Julius promised Alex he would look after him, make Alex his. He even rewrote his will as proof."

Don took another sip of his coffee, obviously upset by the admission. His voice softened to a murmur as he added, "I'm not sure how my boy hung onto life for so long, but I think he wanted to make things right. Beg my forgiveness." Tears welled into his eyes. For a second, I thought he was going to lose control, but he fought them back. "I tried to stop him from speaking because every breath was agony, but he seemed to want to confess. Needed to."

Like Don needed to confess now. Sharing information seemed to be an unusual experience for him. No wonder he seemed so uptight. Devastated might be a better word.

"At least you got a chance to talk to him before he died."

"I suppose you're right."

If he'd been the cuddly type, I would have given him a hug, but I could tell he wasn't looking for sympathy. Perhaps he blamed me in a way. If I'd still been with Julius, none of this would have happened. I didn't interrupt as he silently consumed another cup of coffee. After a while, he seemed to relax. When I felt he'd regained enough composure, I continued. "I get that Alex inherited Julius's share because he wasn't killed immediately, but how come you're involved? Didn't Alex make his will out to Julius in return?"

When he replied, Don had the grace to look a tad embarrassed. "I gather they didn't think it would be necessary. Alex didn't work, and he'd turned all his possessions over to me, so he didn't actually own anything."

I didn't comment, but he must have sensed the disapproval on my face as he hastily added, "If anything happened to me, he was covered by my will, but they can be challenged." He turned to stare out the window. "My family accepted us, but who knows what people will do when you're dead. Once the Illinois Civil Union law passed, I figured if we made our relationship legal, that sort of agreement would totally protect him if I died." A soft sigh escaped as his attention returned to the cup in his hand. Finally, he spoke in words no louder than a whisper. "I never envisaged my boy dying first."

Don still seemed uncomfortable talking about the subject. The man had just admitted he and Alex were virtually married, so his lover's infidelity suddenly took on another dimension. No wonder Don looked gutted before. I shook my head in disgust. *Bloody Julius.*

I sat there for a while, sipping my coffee, trying to take it all in. "What do we do now?"

Don gave a small grimace. "Seeing as neither of us wants to live here, I figure that if we make the house look presentable, by the time probate comes through, we stand a better chance of selling it."

That's probably why the house looked so bare. Don had been clearing out the rooms, getting it ready for painting. "Fair enough. But if we're going to renovate, I want it done properly. None of this slap a coat on and cover all the crap. I want to clean the walls and ceilings, fill in the cracks, get a good surface before we begin."

Don didn't move for a second. Then he gave a small laugh, almost to himself.

"What?" I demanded.

"I figured you'd happily take the easy option." Don shook his head and smiled. "I'm handy with tools if you need any major work done." A twinkle in his eyes suggested I could take his comment either way, making it my turn to be amazed.

I wasn't too sure what to make of the American. His initial antagonism had died down, but sometimes, as we discussed what needed to be done, he still seemed on edge, as if he expected an eruption from me any minute. So far, I'd been able to keep a lid on my feelings. Unfortunately, much as I wanted to hit the road as quickly as possible, I was tied here for a bit longer. Don probably wanted to get back to the States too. In the meantime, he certainly looked like he needed cheering up. Sara's invitation came to mind. I still had to let her know my decision. Nothing like a traditional Aussie hitch, bitch, and all you can eat to distract him.

"Marty and his fiancée, Sara, have asked me to perform as Stevie Tricks at their wedding. They said to bring a guest. Wanna come?"

Don wasn't keen at first, but after I told him what really happened in the hotel bedroom last night and why Marty and I were now best buddies, he reluctantly agreed.

I contacted Sara to thank her, and she promised to post me all the details.

"Send them via the Hotel Paradiso," I suggested. The wedding wasn't for a couple of weeks, and who knew where I'd be staying by then. "And perhaps it's best if I don't come to the actual ceremony, dahl. Don't want my magnificence to draw attention away from the bride."

She laughed. "Good thinking."

CHAPTER
✝✝✝
TEN

Reconsider Me

THE buzzer sounded, signaling someone was at the front gate.

A disembodied voice came through the speaker. "Ah, Steve? This is Gabriel. Have I come to the right place?"

"Yeah, mate." I checked my watch, 10:00 a.m. He must have left immediately. A warm feeling coursed through me. Seemed I hadn't completely lost my touch.

"Gabriel?" Don gave me an inquiring glance.

"The guy I was with last night." The guy he probably saw me kiss, or who at least had kissed me. From a distance, the actions would look the same. I depressed the buzzer on the intercom that would grant him access.

Don pressed the garage remote as we went downstairs.

The door rolled up to reveal a dark-blue Corolla outside the slowly opening security gate. While we waited, Don went over to the double garage's second entrance. "That reminds me," he said, running his hands over the metal surface. "There's something wrong with this one. It won't open."

I laughed. Well, it was a sort of a laugh, more of a snort, really. After checking that Gabriel had negotiated his way safely past the entrance, I crossed to where Don was standing and ran my palm over the dents, feeling the pain again.

"What caused these?" he asked quietly.

Without saying anything, I formed a fist and pummeled the metal. The dull clang brought back a lot of memories. Too many.

"Did you do this?"

"Yeah." I shuddered, remembering Julius's rage when he came downstairs to investigate the racket and discovered this side wouldn't open any more. From memory, that particular day he was mad at me for not shining his boots properly. As punishment, he told me, he was going upstairs to relax while I bloody well finished the job. To make sure I stayed put, he took the remotes with him and removed the cords so I couldn't open the doors manually. Shortly afterward, "Bat Out of Hell" blared out of the speakers.

One of the unusual features of the house was that the main entry point was through the garage. The lock on the door at the top of the stairs added another level of security. Easy to open if you had the key, impossible if you didn't. I couldn't go up, and I couldn't get out. Under cover of Meatloaf's singing, I had vented my frustration on the garage door. With each punch, Rhi's parting words reverberated in my brain: "You need to get out of here. This place is no better than a fucking prison." That's when the image of escaping from what had become my own personal hell took seed.

As it turned out, the pain of my abraded knuckles was nothing compared to what had followed. On my back, I still bore the scars from his viciously wielded whip. That had been my tipping point. After the punishment, Julius locked me in my bedroom with instructions to think about where I'd gone wrong. Then he went for a spin on his bike. Well, I thought about it. Problem was, I came to a different conclusion than he'd been expecting.

While the memories resurfaced, I'd unconsciously been rubbing one clenched fist with the other. Don pried my fingers apart and straightened them out so he could inspect them. Not that any traces remained. Apart from the scars on my back, most of the damage was on the inside and had taken years of counseling to fix.

"Hadn't you guys heard of safe, sane, and consensual?"

"Sane?" I nearly screamed the word at him, jerking my hands from his grip. "How can any of this be considered sane? People voluntarily subjecting themselves to that sort of abuse." I repeated the words by rote, reiterating the mantra my family drummed into me after I left. The therapist I went to agreed as well. "If it hadn't been for the bloody BDSM, none of this would have happened."

"Not all Master and slave relationships are like that." Don seemed about to say more, but the bang of a car door put an end to our conversation.

"Is anybody here?"

Gabriel's head appeared in the open doorway. He smiled when he saw me. Then his expression changed to bewilderment when he caught sight of who I was with. "Master... D?" He looked in amazement from me to the man who had impressed him so much during the S and M demonstration. "How come... I thought.... You said...," he stammered and blushed.

Poor kid. He didn't have a clue, and for that matter, neither did I. I shrugged. "I know. A lot has happened since I saw you last."

His blush grew deeper as he put two and two together and came up with twenty-two. "Long story, kid. I'll tell you over lunch." I patted his back. "I know you two guys sort of met outside the Paradiso, but perhaps it's time for a formal introduction. Donato Rossi. Gabriel Ferguson. Gabriel. Donato."

"Pleased to meet you, Sir." Gabriel wiped his hand on his jeans and extended it toward the motionless man. I snorted to myself. From the awestruck expression on the young man's face, his admiration hadn't decreased one iota in the meantime.

The American seemed just as affected. Maybe he hadn't taken a good look at Gabriel during their brief conversation in the dark laneway. In the light of day, he could see the young man's features more clearly, take in the resemblance I'd seen immediately when I saw Alex's photo. Talk about the dead coming back to life. As far as I could tell, this version was even better. As they shook hands, Don's features softened into a warm smile.

"Are you coming back, Steve?" Don's question sounded innocuous to someone who didn't know what was going on, but a loaded one if you did. "I could do with some help."

"Yeah, I have a few things to attend to first. If Gabriel doesn't mind, we need to go to Darling Harbour, so I can check out of the hotel. Then I need to pick up some things from the Paradiso." Hopefully, Gabriel would be so ecstatic at getting an excuse to see his idol again that he would forgive me for being the drag queen he'd despised last night.

"Sure," the young man said, nodding enthusiastically.

I ran upstairs to grab my boots and belt. When I returned, Gabriel was staring at the garage floor, blushing furiously while Don gazed at him in silence. Well, *he'd* never get into trouble for giving the leather man too much sass.

"See you later, Sunshine." I jumped into the car, taking great relish in slamming the door.

Gabriel didn't follow immediately.

Don smiled, nodded, and jogged back inside.

What the….

Gabriel walked slowly toward me, an expression of excitement muted by the occasional blush. "Um, seeing we're going to Darling Harbour, do you mind if Master D comes too? He hasn't had a chance to visit the aquarium yet." My total lack of comprehension must have registered, as Gabriel explained, somewhat defensively, "Well, he *is* an overseas visitor. I'm simply being hospitable." He blushed again. "He said he had to come into the city anyway so wouldn't mind a lift." Turning his puppy-dog eyes on me, Gabriel added, "He has some things to attend to after lunch, so you and I can spend some time together then."

Aquarium? Lunch? What had happened to our quiet, intimate meal followed by a fuck in my hotel room? It was well past checkout time, so I'd be charged for another day no matter what happened. Don's appearance at the car door cut off any pithy comments I might have made.

At least I got to sit up front.

As we headed off, I tried to relax, but my brain kept racing along at a hundred miles an hour. What the fuck was I going to do now? Don was right about one thing: first thing tomorrow, I had to make an appointment with my lawyer, Irving Schofield. Then the million-dollar question, how soon could I leave? Once the renovations were finished, we could lock the place up and go our separate ways. The real estate agent should have no trouble off-loading a vacant property. The room downstairs would be a problem, though. A huge problem.

With Don's help, fixing the place up shouldn't take too long. At least the animosity between us had decreased. It was hard to pick when the change had occurred. Sharing coffee and the pain of our ex-lovers' accident definitely helped, but there was still a certain wariness present, as if he wasn't used to having a friend.

At times, I caught him checking me out. Did he feel the same vibe I did? In many ways, he was the total opposite to Julius, yet there was something about him that pushed all my buttons. My problem was that, as a Dominant, he still spelled Danger with a capital D.

I tuned back into their conversation as we joined the F6. Maybe Gabriel was nervous, but the way he was giving Don a full-blown résumé about his life, his family, and where he went to school, you'd think he was applying for a job. Apparently, he was doing an IT course at Wollongong Uni and did the trip south regularly. "What a coincidence that you live just off the highway."

I eyed Don in the mirror as he blandly replied he hadn't been living there long.

Don wasn't encouraging the kid's chattiness, only commenting enough to be polite. No doubt he was used to inspiring that kind of nervous reaction in impressionable young males.

From what I could gather, Gabriel's background was typical middle-class Sydney. Catholic school education. Both parents working in good jobs, proud of their tolerance if not of their son.

A couple of times, Don tried to pump me for similar information, but I wasn't born yesterday and managed to fob him off with the bare minimum before getting Gabriel talking about himself again. The less Don knew about me the better.

Unfortunately, being used to ferreting out information, he knew exactly what I was up to. Every chance he got, he twisted the conversation around my way again. After learning that Gabriel was one of five so there hadn't been any pressure in carrying on the family name, Don said, "And what about your family, Steve?"

I snorted. "Seeing as my father left when I was two, my mother doesn't give a fuck if his name does die out." That shut them both up. I didn't bother to tell them she'd eventually hooked up with a nice guy called Tom and had Rhiannon, but her second husband succumbed to an aggressive melanoma a few years later.

Neither of us had much luck with men.

THE aquarium had changed a lot since my last visit. Some of the tanks were now surrounded by molded structures, giving the impression you were looking through mangroves or into the depths of a sunken ship. Colored lights casting shadow patterns on the floor added to the impression you were in a water wonderland.

I crossed my arms and leaned back against one of the displays, watching the tall young man try to shrink himself to match the leather man's height as he pointed out all the things he thought the American might be interested in. I felt like saying: *Stand up straight. Power has nothing to do with size. It's a state of mind.*

"Look, Sir," Gabriel said, indicating a tank containing tropical fish. "The big fish is like a Master, carrying a whip, and the little fish are its slaves."

Sure enough, black-and-white cleaner wrasse were darting around, tending to a large yellow-and-black angelfish. I suppose if you were obsessed with sadism and masochism, the two long feelers extending from the base of the fish might be likened to the tails of a flogger.

Gabriel glanced sideways at Don, whose impassive face made me wonder if he was even listening. Personally, I wished the kid would let the man enjoy his outing and give the subject a rest, especially when he smiled shyly at Don and offered in an awestruck voice, "Beautiful things deserve that degree of subservience."

"Hey," I cut in before I barfed at his display of over-the-top groveling. "Forget about needing other fish to look after you. I'd rather be a lungfish. According to what this says, Gorbachev, here"—the aquarium had given the twenty-year-old fish a name—"may not be the prettiest fish around, but he can adapt to conditions, being able to breathe in both air and water."

Don merely grunted and moved on. He didn't seem too impressed by the boy's blatant attempts to flatter him or my cynicism. "Speaking of adapting…." Don gestured for me to come and look at something. A huge blue fish was staring at him with beady eyes. Somehow, if such a thing was possible, the animal looked as submissive as all heck. Don pointed at the sign next to the tank. "It says here 'when there aren't any males around, the Napoleon wrasse can change sex, but only from female to male.' It's the opposite for you. You go male to female."

The wrasse's puffy lips made him look as if he'd done as many blowjobs as I had last night. I glanced warily at Gabriel, remembering his derogatory comments about men in drag, but he didn't catch on. Don gave a loud snort and headed for the exit. Gabriel scrambled to catch up. As they left, I gazed at Don's ass, recalling once again what it felt like having his cock wedged down my throat. The big blue fish lazily flicked its tail, heading up to the top of the tank as if to say, "The main man has left, no one left to interest me, buddy." Damn, even the fish were bowing and scraping. I hurried out after my companions.

Thankfully, I managed to get my way when it came to choosing where to eat. Gabriel was all for going to Macca's, but I insisted on going to the Brewhouse restaurant nearby. It had changed hands since I was last there, and I wanted to see if the beer was as good.

Gabriel screwed up his face at the word *beer*, but Don shed his polite facade and for once became animated. It turned out that we shared a passion for boutique amber ales.

Being the designated driver, Gabriel wasn't allowed to drink alcohol, but he didn't seem too fazed by that restriction and was content to guzzle glass after glass of cola.

When the waiter arrived to take our order, I was very proud of my deadpan expression as I queried whether they had any battered angelfish. The poor guy actually went and asked his boss, returning moments later with an, "I'm afraid not."

Don kicked my leg under the table.

The temperature was in the midthirties, so the first glass hardly hit the sides. By the time Don and I had sampled some of their famous pale ales and demolished a plate of oysters each, we were both nicely relaxed. It was hard not to be. The open-air setting, good food, and beer worked their own brand of magic. For once, smiles crinkled the corner of Don's eyes as we argued about which country made the best brew.

Gabriel fiddled with his phone, taking photos whenever he was bored. That's how he managed to fluke a priceless shot of Don with his moustache covered in a thick layer of foam after switching to Fat Jack's Stout.

Don chuckled when I offered to lick him clean. I leaned in close and raised my glass in salute as Gabriel took another picture. That one was also a keeper. I made sure he sent them to both of us.

Despite my annoyance at Gabriel's continued attempts to hijack his idol's attention, at least Don had stopped moping about Alex, and I hadn't thought about Julius for all of an hour.

Perhaps the location's stark contrast to the horror of the morning's news contributed to my mood. Certainly, the sight of all the tourists wandering along the waterfront with their souvenirs and ice creams was so normal that the concept of men wearing collars and begging to be beaten seemed as unreal as the bizarre fish we'd seen.

Unfortunately, the mellow mood dissipated as Gabriel grew progressively bolder, pressing for details about how things were done in the States, quoting something he'd read on Fetlife about a group being *Guardians of the Old Way*.

"Take what you read online with a huge spoon of salt, boy. Steer clear of the bullshit."

"But, Sir, shouldn't we be following the teaching of the Old Guard?"

"*I* respect their rules and traditions," Don said. "But most kinky gay men have never heard of them, or don't give a shit. Change is inevitable, and in the age of the Internet, it's happening. Fast." Don didn't sound too bitter about the fact. He was a realist.

From the stars in Gabriel's eyes, he was as enraptured by the romance of a bygone era as Julius had been. I found myself wishing that some of the old protocols *were* still in place, like asking permission before speaking. Of course, Don could always impose that restriction if Gabriel ever got on his nerves like he was getting on mine. Perhaps I should drop a hint.

Things took a turn for the worse when the waiter brought us our main course. Don had barely taken a few mouthfuls when Gabriel started asking him whether he currently had a slave. I could tell that the young man was angling to see if there was an opening for him.

Don kept avoiding answering the question.

I sympathized. It had probably been years since prospective candidates sought him out. Only a slight tightening at the corner of his mouth betrayed his discomfort until Gabriel said, "But, Sir, someone like you deserves to be served faithfully. Surely it would be an honor and a privilege for a submissive...."

At that, Don wiped his mouth and stood abruptly. His lips were a ghastly shade of white when he checked his watch ostentatiously. "It's getting late. I better go."

I gave a dismissive wave, as if his departure had been planned all along. "Yeah, you go do your shopping. I'll pay."

Don's hands trembled as he slid his chair into place. "Thanks, er... Gabriel and Steve. I'll see you at the Paradiso." He gave me a wry, twisted smile of gratitude and left before Gabriel had a chance to take in what was happening.

As he hurried away, the young man turned to me. "What did I say? What's wrong?" His voice broke in anguish. Don had disguised his inner turmoil well, but his abrupt departure needed some sort of explanation. Without going into too many details, I explained to Gabriel that Don's last slave had died recently, and the subject was too painful for him to discuss.

"Oh, the poor man."

Yeah, I felt sorry for Don too. I'd run, but I hadn't hooked up with someone else. For months after, I couldn't even let another guy touch me. What would it be like for Don? From the sound of things, Julius and Alex had fucked around without his knowledge, let alone his permission, so the truth must have come as a huge shock.

Gabriel started to get up. "What should I do? Run after him and apologize?"

I restrained him, saying, "No, that's the last thing he wants. Just respect his space."

If anything, Don had grown more wonderful in the young man's esteem. As far as Gabriel was concerned, losing a lover only added to his mystique.

"I didn't know." He nearly wailed the words.

"He'll understand. Don't worry."

"I've always wanted to be a slave, and I was hoping he could give me some pointers. All the Doms I've talked to aren't interested, saying I need more experience, but how can I get experience, if no one will give me a chance?"

"Listen, mate, I know it all sounds very glamorous, but, believe me, that's the last thing you want to be doing."

"How would you know?"

I picked up the knife, tempted to emulate Don's knife-throwing episode from this morning. "Never mind."

"Did you…? Are you…? Is he…?" Gabriel's eyes grew round as he stared at me as if such a concept was totally foreign to him.

"Are you asking whether Don fucked me last night? The answer is no." I didn't equate a hand job with fucking, so I actually told the truth.

"But you said you didn't know him." The kid was persistent, if nothing else.

"Turned out we had a mutual… acquaintance."

"Oh."

I could tell Gabriel wanted to know more. Bad luck. He wasn't going to get the tragic tale of Alex and Julius from me. Not today. "I'll be staying with him for a while." That was one way to explain our complicated entanglement and all Gabriel needed to know for now.

"Sorry, I guess it's none of my business."

"Nah, I guess after what I said last night, you were a tad confused." Confused? Yeah, given I was still having difficulty getting my head around everything, I didn't blame him. "Lunch is on me, by the way, as thanks for your help. Now let's go get my gear."

Gabriel was silent as we walked across Pyrmont Bridge, both of us enjoying the warmth of the spring sunshine. I'd missed this aspect of Sydney; there was nothing like it anywhere else in the world. Such a great combination of good weather and gorgeous scenery, and the people weren't bad either. Maybe it was the beer, or perhaps the sun shining off the water. Either way, I let all the crap that had been keeping me on edge since returning to Australia empty out of my mind. That's when I identified the strange feeling inside. All day, I'd felt different but couldn't work out why. Now I knew. That deep-down feeling of dread was absent. Not so much fear of Julius as a person, but fear of losing my freedom again.

CHAPTER
✚✚✚
ELEVEN

For What It's Worth

SO MUCH for a leisurely afternoon spent fucking. Gabriel was only interested in trying to pump me about Don and whether I'd ever been into leather. Talk about a pushy bottom. I managed to deflect his questions by keeping him amused. Seeing there was no rush to check out of the hotel, we did the usual touristy things, visiting the Maritime Museum and having a couple of battles of skirmish at M9.

Gabriel seemed so young. Immature. After vacating the room and loading all my gear in his car, I asked him outright, "How old *are* you?"

"Twenty-three."

I'd been nineteen when I met Julius. Impressionable. Naive. Trusting. Finding it hard to believe this godlike man was interested in me. After we'd been together a couple of years, Julius wanted to add a bit of kink. Inevitably, that led to the porn videos and imported magazines. At first, I'd been a willing participant. Who doesn't enjoy adding spice to a relationship? Unfortunately, just like with chili, you become accustomed to the taste, needing more and more to gain the same effect. Before we knew it, we were deep into BDSM. Floggers, whips, gags, the whole kit and caboodle. Being an actor at heart, I played my part as his submissive with gay abandon. Of course, Julius lapped it up, enjoying the feeling of power. For me, the by-product, mind-blowing sex, made it worthwhile. Or it did until he collared me as his slave on a twenty-four-seven basis.

85

"Don't rush things," I warned Gabriel. "You're just a kid."

A brief spark of anger flashed across my companion's face. "That's what everyone says. I'm scared that if I ask Master D, he'll say the same thing. Maybe he'll listen to you."

Yeah, right. The guy hadn't had much experience with guys who thrived on being in control, had he? "Why do you think anything I say would have any influence over him? I only met the man yesterday."

"I still get the feeling he'd respect your opinion." Gabriel didn't elaborate, keeping his gaze fixed on the road. I'd met his type before. On the surface they appear to be quiet, gentle, the sensitive type, but inside lurks a streak of rebelliousness people don't suspect.

"Look, I'm sorry. I'd like to be able to help, but, as I said, I hardly know him."

"You don't have to say much. Tell him I'm mature for my age."

Yeah? This from a guy who didn't stop giggling when we played laser tag, hiding behind the scenery and popping up to shoot when I came past. Every instinct inside me rebelled. "Are you sure you want to get involved? It isn't easy. I'm not even sure it's healthy. You're handing a lot of power over to someone. You have to trust that they know what they're doing."

"Master D would."

Judging by the glow in the young man's eyes, Don had passed every test with flying colors. And this was before the man had laid a finger on him, let alone a flogger. If Gabriel had a pain kink, he'd be addicted before he knew it. "How can you know that? You've only just met him."

"It was the way he ran the scene last night. He knew what he was doing."

"How would *you* know if you've never done it?"

"I've watched fetish flicks."

I gave a quick snort of disgust. "The actual physical contact and their reaction may be real, but the rest? The verbal abuse? They're playacting."

"You can still see the difference, though. Some of them, the best ones, care about the submissive and work to bring out the best in him."

"Yeah, some actors are better than others. Listen, kid, that's a dangerous road to wander down. Been there. Done that." *Wear the scars to prove it.*

"I knew you had."

Damn, I should have kept my mouth shut. Arguing with a guy like him was pointless. Once they have their heart set on something, they won't listen to reason.

At the next set of traffic signals, Gabriel turned to me with a triumphant grin on his face. "When I first met you, I knew you were into BDSM."

What the fuck? I hadn't worn a scrap of leather last night. "How? Because of the tat?"

"No, there's something about the way you carry yourself. Guys who are into BDSM have a certain kind of confidence."

Yeah, the cock ring of confidence. "Cockiness, you mean?"

"Maybe that's it." He shrugged. "Whatever it is, I wish I had it."

Physically, I might come across that way. Mentally, not so much. Gabriel seemed to think it was all so simple. Judging by the happy smile on his face, he didn't have a fucking clue what he was getting into. "It's not only about dealing or putting up with pain."

"I'm not stupid. I know it's all about mastery and submission. Serving them."

"Well, if you really want to serve, get a job at Subway." I stared out the window. From his frigid silence, I could tell I'd shocked the bejesus out of him. Good. Hopefully, he'd stop bugging me now.

We didn't speak again until we reached the Hotel Paradiso. By daylight, it looked seedier than it had the night before. Wind gusts whistled up through the narrow laneway, lifting a couple of stray leaflets and flattening them against the chipped concrete. I picked them up: advertising flyers for the previous evening. Seeing the photo of me as Stevie Tricks reminded me what I had come for. Gabriel's obsession with leather had made me forget.

I tightened my fist and lobbed the crumpled pages into the nearest garbage bin. Why couldn't I put my rubbishy past behind me as easily? No matter what I did, reminders kept sneaking past my defenses, threatening my newfound freedom. But I had to stop them. I was a free spirit now. A gypsy. Not tied to anything or anyone. The sooner I got my own set of wheels, the better. Shame about my bike.

Oh well, time to buy a car. Being dependent on other people sucked big time. Another thing to add to my to-do list. I couldn't wait for Monday to come around. "I won't be long. I've just gotta fetch some things. Here, buy yourself a drink while you're waiting." I tried to press some money into Gabriel's hands, but he put them in the air and looked mortally offended by my gesture.

Good one, Steve, I thought as I bounded up the stairs. *Way to win friends and influence people.* I shrugged. The sooner Gabriel drove us home and I waved him good-bye, the better. He did *not* need to be drawn into the M/s morass.

Someone had tidied the room. My Stevie frocks were hanging in their protective coverings, and all my makeup and gear had been stashed in their respective containers. Even the rhinestone earrings were wrapped in a tissue.

I slung the garments over my shoulder, tucked the wig boxes under my arm, and grabbed the handle of the little wheelie bag, feeling too much like a friggin' air hostess for comfort. It was a miracle I managed to make it to the top of the stairs without tripping over something. The previous evening when I had been carried down slung over Jeff's back like a sack of potatoes, I had noted how narrow the staircase was. At the halfway landing, where the stairs reversed direction before continuing down, my head had clunked against the wall. These old buildings were real firetraps. The mental cash register in my head *kachinged* as I added a few more thousand to poor Fred's renovation bill.

There was no way I could navigate down safely, carrying all this junk.

Fred was chatting to someone at the bottom of the stairs. In my best Stevie Trick's voice, I called out, "Hey, honey, can you give me a hand with these frocks before I drop everything?"

Instead of Fred's bulk appearing, I was surprised to see a trim figure in an expensive-looking charcoal suit head up toward me. When he arrived, Don extracted the coat hangers from my nerveless clasp and set off again without uttering a word. I blinked a couple of times and eventually remembered to shut my mouth. Damn, the man looked good dressed up. All the discomfort he'd displayed at lunch had evaporated, and his usual swagger was back. Now if Gabriel had been referring to *Don*'s confidence, he would have been spot on target.

"Wait." I raced down after him, my wheelie bag banging on each step as I made my descent. I'd been going so fast, I barreled into him when he stopped at the halfway point and turned to face me. My hands were full, so I had no way of preventing the collision, but he absorbed the impact with only a slight rock backward before regaining control of his feet. Extending his free hand, he steadied me until I proved I was in no danger of falling.

Heat radiated off him, bringing with it his unmistakable scent. Nice.

"New suit?"

His soft brown eyes twinkled. Standing in such close proximity, I could see them clearly, something I had deliberately avoided until now. No way did I want to fall under their spell. "You approve?" His voice reminded me of melted butter. All warm and golden.

My mouth went dry as his breath dusted my face. I wasn't used to being this close to someone as short as I was. In England, I'd been with lots of different guys, but most of them had been taller, and height difference doesn't matter as much if you're horizontal or on your knees.

I swallowed. Parts of me definitely approved. Don had draped my frocks over one shoulder, and the hand holding the hangers was at shoulder height, accentuating the broadness of his chest, bringing the rest of his body into focus.

I let my gaze wander over all the important parts. "Nice... er... cut."

He chuckled. "Well, you invited me to a wedding, and I didn't have a thing to wear."

"It looks expensive." It also made me want to peel him out of it and fuck him on the spot. Luckily, he couldn't read minds, or could he?

"Some asshole ordered it and never came back. The tailor was so thrilled at being able to offload it, that he gave it to me at a good price. He said they don't have many clients my size and shape."

I bit my tongue, trying to avoid congratulating him on both aspects. The guy had a big enough ego already. I dragged my gaze back up and found he was amused about something. He'd probably never seen me tongue-tied before. I swallowed. "The HOGs will cancel your membership if you're spotted riding a Harley in a suit."

"That's why I came in with you and Gabriel." He grinned and set off downstairs again.

I closed the extension and picked up my case by the handle this time, making sure it didn't bump on the way down. "You didn't need to buy something just for the wedding."

Don waited for me at the bottom. "I also have an appointment with the bank manager next week and need to look the part."

"Why are you going to the bank?" The words were out before I could stop them, but he didn't seem to mind my asking a personal question.

"Now you're back, I can reassure them the sale of the house will be happening sooner rather than later. Hopefully, the bank will give me an extended line of credit for the hotel renovations until the house sale goes through."

My throat suddenly felt dry. I swallowed and glanced across to where Fred and Gabriel were discussing some sort of cocktail he was mixing. "Hotel? I thought Fred bought this place?" Was I getting all my wires crossed? "Are you and Fred…?"

"No." Don placed his hand on my shoulder. "He's my manager." A slight flush ran over his face. "The hotel is another thing I can thank Julius for."

"Shit." I hadn't meant to say the word out loud, but somehow it escaped. I sat on the steps and clutched my wig boxes to my chest. Gradually, the world stopped spinning and Don's words registered again.

"Part of the reason Julius came to the States was to see how our gay bars and leather clubs operated. He wanted input based on our knowledge of what worked and what didn't. He told us about the perfect venue he'd found: a run-down hotel at the Cross that he wanted to purchase with the money he'd inherited from his grandmother."

That I could believe. One of Julius's greatest ambitions had been to visit the DC Eagle and be invited to attend Inferno.

The full extent of Don's words took a moment to sink in. "Do you mean to say you own this club and have half shares in my house without having to pay a cent? I've still got fifteen years of mortgage repayments ahead of me."

"Hey." Don seemed affronted by my accusation. "I sank everything I owned to pay for half of this place. Julius couldn't afford the full amount, so he suggested we buy in with him."

"But, why come here? Sydney is a heck of a long way from the States."

"But that was the point. Alex thought it was a great idea. He kept harping on how sick he was of the cold." Don placed one foot on the step beside me and leaned in closer so his voice didn't carry. "And of course, at that stage, I didn't know they were fooling around behind my back, and everything Alexander wanted, he got." Don shrugged and looked away as if embarrassed to admit he could feel the emotion for a slave.

"Okay, I get that Julius might have been able to persuade Alex, but why would *you* want to come here?"

"Much the same reason. My landscaping business normally slows during winter, and the economy wasn't helping, so when my major competitor offered to buy me out, I jumped at the chance."

I could imagine Don moving heaven and earth to achieve his aims, but red tape was notoriously difficult to cut. "How did you manage to organize everything so quickly?"

Don shrugged. "Alex knew someone in immigration who helped us. They were taking the Harley out for a final spin before packing it up for shipping."

And were killed. My brain added the words Don couldn't bear to say.

I took in the outdated decor and worn carpet. Run-down was putting it nicely. The hotel would probably be more of a drain on his resources than anything. "So now you're the proud owner of this dump." I waved my hand around derisively.

Don gave a curt nod. "I have some cash put aside, but not enough to finance running operations or pay for renovations. Things will be easier once probate is finalized, but, the rate things are going, it will be a while before everything gets settled." The sideways glance showed me a man with a heap of financial worries. "That's why I need to sell the house as quickly as possible."

My house. No wonder he was so keen to get rid of it.

Talk about conflicting loyalties. It also explained why Fred had been a bit vague about Julius when I talked to him. He assumed I knew he was dead and was wondering why I hadn't mentioned it. "You knew who I was all along. Didn't you?"

Don didn't deny my accusation.

"Why was it so necessary to get me here last night?" How much had been a setup from the start? Had Fred rigged the time on the blowjob, for example?

"Theoretically, I could just sell my share, but it's unlikely I'd find a buyer for half a house, so I was hoping to gain your consent to put the entire property on the market."

Back to square one. If I had known what was in the envelopes, would I have done anything differently? Not returned to Australia, that's for sure.

CHAPTER
+++
TWELVE

Sorcerer

GABRIEL and Fred approached. The former's gaze darted between the two of us, no doubt trying to work out what was going on. Good luck, mate. I was having trouble too. Somehow, I'd stepped onto one of those moving sidewalks, and it was carrying me along in the wrong direction. Fast. The news Don was desperate to sell the house was good, right?

"What are they?" Gabriel pointed to the frocks in Don's care and the unmistakable shape of hat boxes in my hands. The red dress was a dead giveaway. A flush of anger crossed his face. "You're the drag queen from last night."

What could I say? If I'd had my wig on, I would have curtseyed, but Gabriel wouldn't have appreciated the gesture.

"You'd never believe Steve could look so sweet and innocent when he wants to." Don's drawled reply broke the awkward silence.

"But didn't you mind him making fun of you on stage?" Gabriel stood, hands on hips, every muscle quivering with indignation.

"It was all an act, boy. It needs more than a bit of fly shit to make me wince."

Don had deliberately phrased his response to imply he had been the one doing the acting. But I hadn't been imagining things. He'd been angry last night. At Stevie Tricks the performer or Steven Stanhope the dishonorable slave?

Gabriel and I conducted our silent staring match for a while. Eventually, Don gave a snort and headed to the door. "Are you two coming? We need to visit a supermarket and get some food. And if it's okay with you, Gabriel, while we have the car, we should pick up painting gear. There's only so much I can carry on the bike."

After a smiling nod from Gabriel, Don led the way outside. The young man followed in his wake like an eager, obedient puppy.

Before I left, I handed Fred some cash and asked him to pass it on to whoever had tidied up my gear. Someday soon, I needed to have a word with my old *friend*. A serious word. First task would be to rip him a new one for not warning me what was going on. Then I needed to find out his angle on things. Not for one moment did I think Don had lied, but I wanted to find out what Fred thought of his boss. I wasn't sure what to make of the American. My body was definitely interested, even if my brain wasn't. But even that was changing. Unlike Julius, Don didn't hide his hurts and failings, or maybe I was simply able to read him better.

Of course, I was relegated to the backseat. Don might have forgiven me for my performance, but Gabriel definitely hadn't. He muttered a few crude expletives as he hung up the dresses on the suit hook.

I ignored his taunts. Last night I'd been prepared to put an end to my drag career, but now I was having doubts. Stevie Tricks didn't have hassles with houses, loans, commitments. The Past.

After a garbled apology for upsetting him at lunchtime, Gabriel tentatively resumed his earlier attempts to gain Don's interest, stressing he wasn't aiming to become *his* slave, more seeking advice on the best way to attract a Master in general. "What are they looking for?" he asked. "Proper respect? Obedience?"

"All of those things, plus a desire to learn."

I stared out the window, trying to tune out their conversation. *Way to kill my good mood, Gabriel.* I only paid attention again when my name was mentioned.

"Steve thinks I'm too young."

"Well, you are," I said to Gabriel. Then I added for Don's benefit, "Gabriel needs to learn to stand on his own feet before he starts kneeling for someone else."

Don twisted in his seat to look at me. "And you don't think the person he is submitting to can help him find his feet?"

"From what I've seen, they look plenty big enough already. He just needs to learn to use them properly."

Gabriel gave a huff of exasperation. "You're not helping, Steve."

"I never agreed to help you. I think you're making a huge mistake."

Gabriel started to speak, but Don placed a hand on his knee, giving him a quick shake of the head. "Why?" he asked me.

Why? Because he might end up in the same shit creek I'd been in. "Because he needs to learn to make up his own mind. Being told what to do is for kids."

"Interesting. Go on."

"But, Sir—"

Don cut in, "Stop interrupting, Gabriel. I want to hear Steve's reasons."

I bit the inside of my lip. If it had been only me and Don, I would have told him to bugger off and stop pushing me, but now, for Gabriel's sake, I had to open up. "As soon as they put a collar on you, it's like your brain isn't wanted anymore. Isn't worth anything. Every time you make a suggestion or express a different opinion you'll get shouted down. Even in bed, you won't be able to initiate any action. Do you have any friggin' idea how frustrating that can be?"

"But some people like being dominated in bed." Gabriel seemed to be having difficulty concentrating on the conversation and driving at the same time. He gave a quick glance at the man beside him, and his contribution was rewarded by another pat on the leg.

The puppy-dog analogy held true. I sighed. "Yeah, I'll admit that can be hot as hell, but sometimes it would be nice to be the one in control."

"Control is important to you." Don's softly spoken words were a statement of fact.

"Try losing it sometime and see how *you* feel," I retorted.

Gabriel's voice broke the uneasy silence. "Most subs need to give up control because the rest of the time they have too much. Isn't that what happens? The corporation manager who needs to submit to a Master because they expend all their self on being responsible for the actions of other people."

"Exactly," I pointed out, trying not to sound too smug. "So, how does that fit into where you're coming from? You're a uni student who lives at home. You don't need to lose control, you need to gain it. You said so yourself."

"But from what I've heard, you give up control and enslave yourself because you must. Because nothing else gives you the same high." This time, Gabriel didn't sound so sure of himself. Maybe I was getting somewhere.

"And what if you do? You see, that's the problem. Afterward, everything else tastes like cardboard. It's an addiction as bad as heroin and all that other shit. Once you get into leather and start down the slippery path of kinky slavery, you'll be agreeing to do anything they tell you, just to get that buzz again." My mother had been particularly critical of that aspect.

"BDSM, leather, and slavery don't have to be bedfellows. In fact, they rarely are," Don contributed quietly.

Maybe so, but that rare combination was what attracted Julius—the ultimate expression of a scene that he'd read about in books. "Well, as far as I'm concerned, the last one should be outlawed." I gave an ironic snort. "Oh, that's right. It was. A long time ago." Rhiannon had particularly enjoyed pointing that out.

Gabriel ignored me and directed his next remark to Don, as if he was answering a question in an exam. "I read somewhere that it's the giving away of yourself, your volition—the total belonging that matters."

"Bullshit!" I interjected when Don bestowed an A+ rating smile on him. "You're a person, not an animal. You don't *belong* to anyone. You come into this world alone, and you'll leave it alone."

"That's a sad existence in between," Gabriel said and exchanged a smile with the man seated beside him as if they shared some sort of secret.

I fumed inwardly. Don might not have been impressed by Gabriel's blatant flattery at the aquarium, but he appreciated the young man's sincere interest in a subject so dear to his heart. "At least I know I won't be betrayed by anybody."

"With the right person, it would work," Gabriel asserted. Again that shy sideways smile, seeking a seal of approval.

I stared bleakly out the window, nausea churning in my guts. How could I argue against that degree of enthusiasm?

Movement made me glance their way in time to see Don face front again.

"Look out." His voice rose sharply.

Gabriel's inattention resulted in a near collision with a car coming through a *Give Way* sign without stopping.

"Sorry, Sir."

"Let's leave this discussion for another time."

"Promise?" Even I would have found it impossible to refuse the plea in the gaze Gabriel directed at the leather man.

"This topic is definitely not finished with, boy. You can rest assured of that." He patted Gabriel's leg when he made the statement, but he was looking at me.

Double damn.

"Now, where's your equivalent to Home Depot?"

By the time we left the nearest Bunnings, Don was carrying enough paint to do the whole interior of the house. Antique white. Boring as hell. I loaded in all the other things we'd need: sugar soap, gap filler, cleaning sponges, brushes, and rollers. Gabriel's small car groaned under the weight.

"We'll eat before we go back to the house."

At times, Don's instinct to take control amused me. Other times, it didn't. In this case, there were a couple of restaurants nearby, so the idea was a good one. That was until Gabriel brought up the subject of leather again.

"Steve said you have to trust someone before you agree to submit to them."

With just a quick nod, Don paused in midchew and directed one of those meaningful looks at me across the table. I felt like poking my tongue out at him.

Gabriel carried on speaking, oblivious of our interaction. "But if they never get the chance to know each other better, how can a slave and Master discover whether this level of trust is possible?"

"Good point, boy."

Gabriel's smug smile made the steak I was chewing taste as bad as leather. Suspiciously, I checked the remaining meat on my plate, wondering whether they'd actually served me some out of spite. "I bet you wouldn't last a week." As soon as the words were out of my mouth, I wished I could take them back. Damn. Now I'd put one foot in, I might as well insert the other. "There's a huge difference between submitting to someone in a scene and being a slave twenty-four-seven. Very few people are cut out for that level of commitment. It's fucking hard."

"That's one of the things you should negotiate first. I've been studying the subject."

"Since when has BDSM 101 been a uni elective?"

"It's not, but there's loads of information out there."

"Yeah, well, avoid romance novels. They get it all wrong."

"I haven't been reading those sort of books." Gabriel looked affronted by my accusation. "Only the serious ones."

Yeah, right. Julius had read them too, and every time he found something new, he kept pushing me to accept more. *Let's take it to the next level* he used to say, as if the grades of commitment along the Master/slave continuum were a natural progression, like adding more weights at the gym or accepting a few more minutes of flogging. My therapist was old school, seeing BDSM as a psychiatric disorder, so she wasn't interested in discussing the psychology behind the different aspects. It was only after I stopped going to counseling and did my own research that I realized the ability to submit had more to do with a person's personality than anything. "It's still theory, though. Until you try it, you won't know what you can stand."

98

"Precisely."

No wonder I never made the debating team at school. Gabriel gave the leather man seated next to him a smug look. Don wasn't looking at him, though, he was studying me again. I should give him a microscope for Christmas. I returned his gaze as calmly as I could, my heart beating a rapid tattoo against my ribs. Eyeballing a Master still felt strange. It wasn't until I broke eye contact and fiddled with the food on my plate that he said, "Gabriel, why don't you come and stay with us for a while?"

"Just what we need," I drawled. "A slave to help us with the painting."

"No, Gabriel's right. He needs to learn about BDSM and submission from people who have been or are still in the scene."

Yeah, well I know what I would be saying to him. Warn him off for his own good.

"Gee, thanks. I've got some uni exams next week, but I'll be finished by Friday."

Gabriel's artless announcement was met by stunned silence. "Why didn't you mention them earlier, boy? Shouldn't you be home studying?"

"It's only Compu...." Gabriel blushed as he caught the don't-argue-with-me expression in Don's eyes and cut off his excuse. "Yes, Sir."

If I had needed any more proof that Don was used to giving orders, our next stop off at the supermarket removed any doubt. As we navigated the aisles together, he reminded me of a general preparing for battle, dismissing any opposition and ignoring his aides' advice. Mind you, "battle" was probably too strong a word. More like minor skirmishes. Gabriel's suggestion to stock up on Coca Cola in readiness for his visit was met by an emphatic, "No."

The pout looked kinda cute. Any minute now, I expected Don to utter the dreaded words: *Do it to please me, boy.*

"Yeah," I whispered in his ear when Don wasn't looking. "Removal of choice is easy when you feel it is the right thing to do, but it's amazing how difficult it can be when really important issues are at stake, like what to drink." I don't know why Gabriel gave me the finger. It was true!

Don only tried the paternalistic Dom act on me once, suggesting we didn't need a tub of Cookies 'N Cream ice cream. A quick "fuck off" saw him back off after giving me another of those long, penetrating stares.

Apart from the frustration the American obviously felt at not finding any of his favorite brands or foods, he didn't do too badly. Of course, I added Vegemite and a few other Aussie staples. Hopefully, I could con him into slathering a thick layer of the black gunk on his toast one morning before Gabriel was around to spoil my fun.

When we finished taking everything upstairs, Gabriel adopted the traditional submissive's pose: hands behind his back, head bowed. "Will that be all, Sir?"

"Yes, thank you. I'll see you at the Paradiso on Friday evening. Until then, I want you to concentrate on your studies."

"Yes, Sir."

"Thank God for that," I said as the security gate closed behind him. "I think I would have puked if I had to listen to any more '*Yes, Sir. No, Sir. Three bags full, Sir.*'"

Don stared at me in confusion. "I thought Gabriel was a friend of yours."

"Met him for the first time yesterday, Sunshine. But I've got news for you. He's already got one *Daddy*; he doesn't need another one." I went upstairs and started unpacking the groceries. Damn. While we'd been relaxing and drinking our beers, I'd almost come to like the man. Shame he was into leather.

"Gabriel will be fine."

I started and nearly dropped the bag of flour I'd been transferring to a screw-top container. "I hope so. Nothing I said would make any difference, though, would it?"

"Not in this case. He's tough underneath that fragile exterior."

I bumped the bag on the edge of the container, sending a puff of white cloud into the air. "How the fuck have you managed to deduce this after only a few hours of contact? You guys are all the same. You bloody think you know everything. Do you know what Gabriel really needs? He needs to travel, go overseas and see the world. That will give him the confidence and maturity he needs, not obeying all your petty demands."

"Julius did a real number on you. Didn't he?"

My hand shook so hard I dropped the bag on the bench, spilling flour everywhere. Anger flooded my voice. "Let's leave him out of this, shall we? My reaction would be the same no matter who the fucking Master is." I clutched the edge of the countertop, trying to regain control. "Gabriel's your typical North Shore, middle-class, overprotected kid. He probably doesn't go anywhere without asking for Mummy and Daddy's permission. He needs to get out and learn to stand on his own two feet before his freedom is taken from him again."

"What if I said, 'submission can set you free'?"

"I'd say choose another fucking Hallmark card! Shouldn't there be doves flying around with leaves clutched in their beaks when you make statements like that?"

No sooner had I finished speaking than Don nudged me aside and started to clean up the mess I'd made. My hands were still covered in white powder.

A sudden memory surfaced, of Julius being furious because I'd dropped a bag of sugar on the floor. Nothing was ever accidental. There was always a suggestion I'd acted purely to annoy him. My hands started shaking. I ran into the bathroom and stared at my tear-stained reflection in the mirror. The therapist had spent ages talking me through recalled incidents like these, putting them into perspective. She might not have understood kink, but she certainly helped me regain my sense of self-worth, reassuring me that I wasn't a total fuck-up.

The trouble was that now I had to stop judging people against Julius. Despite our argument, Don hadn't been angry with me. He'd simply gone on with the job that needed to be done.

By the time I calmed down and washed all the evidence off my face, the groceries were stashed in the cupboards, and the door to his bedroom was shut.

CHAPTER
✝✝✝
THIRTEEN

I Can't Wait

THE earliest appointment I could get with my lawyer ended up being on Friday afternoon. Until then, I had to trust that Don had told me the truth about the will.

"Where do you want to start?"

Don's question startled me. I'd been standing in the entrance to the living room, lost in a myriad of memories. The previous owners had used the large north-facing suntrap to practice their yoga in, but instead of doing downward dogs and saluting the sun, Julius thought it would be amusing to display some old whips and floggers—our method for reaching Nirvana. Much as I hated to admit it, bondage and discipline *had* helped me reach those levels. At least for a while.

Taking a deep breath, I turned to face the leather man. Last night, after Gabriel left, we'd headed off to our respective bedrooms. This morning, we'd settled into a kind of truce, sharing a common purpose: fix up the house so that we could get top dollar at auction. "Let's start by getting rid of all this junk," I muttered.

After a quick glance at me, Don strode over to the far wall and removed a six-foot bullwhip. His lips twisted as he ran his fingers along its length, no doubt noticing the way the loosely woven leather curled up at the edges. "Junk is the right word. Did you ever use this?"

I snorted. Unable to make the damn thing crack, Julius had given up in disgust, blaming the low ceilings. He hadn't been amused, either, when I suggested he try it outside.

"Give us a break. We bought that for our first-ever kink party." Julius had also framed the rest of my outfit—cock cage, studded leather cuffs, and play collar. Scattered around the room were other toys we'd either grown tired of or never used.

Don threw the whip into a packing box, where it was soon joined by other souvenirs of my sordid past.

A queer feeling of calm settled on me as he smoothed down the packing tape, sealing away my memories forever. When he'd finished, Don sat back on his heels, staring up at me in confusion. "Julius mentioned needing my help with his dungeon, but I imagined something more elaborate."

Please don't mention the "D" word. I shivered. Best to leave *that* sleeping dog lie. "Well, I'm the one needing your help now, Sunshine. Grab the other end of this sofa."

The damn thing weighed a ton, and it took ages for us to maneuver the three-seater out of the room and down the narrow staircase.

After clearing the rest of the furniture out, we shifted the exercise equipment and boxes of stereo gear into Don's office. "If we paint in here last," he said, patting the seat of the bike once it was in place, "I can go over paperwork while I work out." Glancing across at the window, he added, "At least I've got a good view if I get bored. Or should I say *when* I get bored." He gave me a wry grin.

Should I tell him that you get sick of staring at the ocean after a while? I smoothed my fingers over the faint gouge marks in the woodwork and wondered how long Julius had taken to repair the window frame after I left. The glass had broken easily enough, but removing the jagged edges so I wouldn't cut myself on the way out had taken some well-directed blows from the thick chains he usually used to bind me to the bed. Who knows why he didn't attach them that evening. He must have thought I was too sore to move. Lucky the neighbors didn't live close or they would have heard me howling in a mix of rage and frustration as every swing of the heavy metal links pulled at the lash marks on my back. The tears that fell that night weren't only from the pain—more from regret that I couldn't be the obedient slave he wanted me to be.

And all because I didn't clean his fucking boots properly.

Don's quiet voice hauled me back from a memory that still haunted my dreams. "Feel free to come in and use the bike whenever you want."

Free. I turned away from the evidence of a night I was still trying to forget and headed for the door. "No thanks, Sunshine. I only ride bikes that go somewhere." And mine was nowhere to be seen. "Let's get cracking. The sooner we get the rest of the stuff downstairs, the sooner we can start painting." *And the sooner I can get the fuck outta here.*

Don shrugged and followed me to the room with the built-in bookcases. We both picked up as much as we could carry and headed off to the garage.

Cradling a box under each arm, I paused at the top of the stairs, watching Don's stocky figure precede me. I felt like I'd known him forever, but how long had it been in reality? A couple of days. I didn't get the feeling the leather man was any happier about the way things had turned out than I was. But he was one of those practical people who saw what needed to be done and did it, making the most of a bad situation.

His calmness was rubbing off on me, preventing me from freaking out at being back where I had vowed never to be again.

But what would he have done if I *hadn't* returned to Australia? Most likely squatted here while all the legal issues got sorted. Anyway, who was going to object? Julius's parents lived in Melbourne, so they might not even know he was living in their late son's house. In our house.

Don raised his eyebrows when he came back up and found me blocking his way. "Anything wrong?" he asked and smiled.

White teeth glistened under the dark bristles of his moustache.

I'd never kissed a guy with a long mo before. What would it be like? Soft? Prickly? My cock jumped and started to thicken in my constricting jeans as we stood with our faces so close his breath warmed my skin. I licked my bottom lip. Why the fuck did Don have to be into leather? At another time and in another place I could have seriously gone for him.

He raised an eyebrow, and I was tempted to check his crotch to see if the feelings were mutual, but what if they weren't? Nah, too embarrassing. I kept my gaze up and turned sideways so he could pass.

As he drew level, Don reached out, cupping my growing erection. I clung harder to the boxes under my arms, making sure they didn't fall. My breath shortened to little more than gasps as heat rushed to my groin.

Don leaned closer, and his warm breath brushed my ear. "It's a shame you've got your own clothes now. I miss seeing you tenting out my boxers. Are you always this horny?"

"Only for you, Sunshine." I tried to sound like my usual snarky self but failed miserably.

Don chuckled and gave my bulge a squeeze before letting go.

My knees shook as I staggered down the stairs. I dumped the boxes and reached in to adjust myself. Damn the man. He hadn't seemed in the least bit affected.

Glancing around, I forced myself to calm down, noting all the things that should act as a warning not to submit to temptation. The dents on the garage door did the trick. By the time Don returned with another load, I was fully under control. Avoiding his eyes, I went back upstairs.

Don let out a sigh as I brushed past him but didn't make any other comment.

By the time we finished carting everything downstairs, the garage was filled to overflowing.

"Do you have Goodwill shops here?" Don asked as he cleared some space for the final load.

I snorted. "The Salvos and Vinnies would turn up their noses at this heap of shit. Most of it was here when we bought the house. We can hire a skip if you like."

Don surveyed the crowded garage. "I'll see if Fred knows anyone with a truck."

He disappeared upstairs as I finished stacking the last box of porn magazines. Moments later, he reappeared with a broad grin covering his face. "Good news and bad news. Two of the bouncers are renting a house not far from here, and they have a truck. They'll take anything they can use and dump the rest."

"And the bad news?"

"The guy who was supposed to work the bar this afternoon quit without giving notice." Don gave me one of his trademark piercing stares. "I told Fred I'd go in and help. Will you be okay on your own?"

On my own? Here? Again? I nearly laughed, but that would be a mistake. I was already having trouble keeping a lid on the mild case of hysteria bubbling under the surface. "I'll be fine as long as you leave me the remotes. Then I can get out of the garage if I need to."

Don frowned, his confusion evident. "No, I meant that I promised to help with the painting. I don't like leaving you in the lurch."

Oh. "You can go. I'll be fine." At least he had the courtesy to check.

The weird thing was that I *would* be okay. Life now seemed so simple and clear. Like looking through a telescope instead of viewing the world through a kaleidoscope and seeing only fractured specks of color.

I had one goal now: fix the house so I could leave.

After each scrub down with sugar soap, the freshly cleaned paint made the house seem so much brighter. Then, as I gradually covered the drab beige with a couple of coats of white, the house started to feel like it was jumping with energy.

I worked like a demon over the next few days.

Don accused me of getting high on the paint fumes. Maybe I was, but for once I felt happy as I cleaned and painted, playing music nonstop, singing Stevie songs.

Don did his fair share and always apologized when he had to fill in at the Paradiso. They still hadn't found a replacement barman. Each night, before he left, he told me to ease off. "I know you want to get out of here," he said, "but there's no sense in busting your gut. Gabriel can help when he comes next week."

That comment only made me work harder. This was *my* house, or at least half of it was. Gradually, any qualms I had about being left alone vanished. As long as I wasn't trapped here, there was no need to panic.

By the time Wednesday came around, we'd managed to finish the living room, the hallway, and the first bedroom. Since that episode on the stairs, Don had kept his hands to himself, but that didn't stop me from being turned on by his bare chest and snug-fitting jeans that left nothing to the imagination.

To disguise the way my body kept reacting whenever he was around, I took to wearing a tight jockstrap under my bike-fixing overalls. Paint splatters were now interspersed between the grease stains. I bent over to put them on. Phew. The weather had been steadily growing hotter as summer approached, and I'd been sweating like a pig. Some guys worked hard to smell funky, but I'd never found BO sexy. I checked to see if I had anything else clean. Nope.

I stripped everything off and bundled up all my clothes. By the sound of whirring bike wheels, Don was still in his office. Clutching the dirty washing to my chest, I opened the door and poked my head inside. "I'm putting a load in the machine. Need any done?"

Don glanced up from whatever he was reading. "Thanks. There's a pile of stuff in the bedroom."

His bedroom. Julius's bedroom. Once, it was *our* bedroom, but as we were sucked into the leather vortex, my lover had introduced all these arbitrary boundaries.

I'd protested, of course, but Julius convinced me that these restrictions were expressions of my love and willingness to serve. At first, it seemed a small price to pay, because he sensed my desire for not only pain, but also for the sexual thrill accompanying it. He played on my need like a maestro, manipulating me into thinking he was the only person who could help me reach those heights. Subservience to him was the price. The way he put it sounded kinky, but after a while, the kink factor lessened and all the mastery bullshit took over.

Rationally, I knew those rules no longer applied, but I still couldn't go in there.

Biting my lip, I stared at the drops of sweat clinging to hairs on Don's chest. What would he say if I offered to lick them off? And while I was there, I could give his nipples a working over. They sure looked like they could do with some attention. I groaned in frustration. Even that wasn't enough incentive to make me step inside. "Um, could you get them for me? My arms are full." I stepped back when Don grunted and went to fetch his washing.

Instead of dumping his collection on top of mine and returning to his office, he went into the laundry and dropped his dirty clothes into the machine.

Damn. If I followed his example, he'd see that I was sporting another fucking erection. Maybe taking everything off was a bad idea. "I can do the washing," I assured him. "You must have stacks to do." Don's desk was always covered in bits of paper.

"No sweat. I need a break, anyway. I never realized how much fucking bookwork was involved in running a hotel. Bloody BAS, as Fred would say."

I snorted, hugging my dirty washing tighter against my body. *Think about the GST, Julia Gillard... anything.* "Can I help?" I asked. Although I was good with figures, Julius never wanted my input on anything to do with money. He was the Master. The one in control.

Don smiled. "Nah, I feel bad enough leaving you to do most of the painting. Did you want to sort these out first?" He started to take the pile of clothes from my hands but stopped when he realized I was naked. He stepped closer, reached behind me, and palmed my butt.

Fuck. My hands were trapped again. I squirmed in frustration as he manipulated my bare ass. The grin he gave me was pure devil. "Shy? Steve? I pegged you for someone who liked flaunting his body." He tightened his grip. "Relax. I never fuck unwilling subs."

"I am not a fucking sub," I ground out through clenched teeth.

"I notice you didn't admit to the unwilling bit." Don laughed. "But it's a real shame to hide this delicious ass." Leaving one hand squeezing my butt, he moved the other to my cock, working the loose skin back and forth over my swelling shaft. My erection grew so hard and the skin so tight, his hand just rocked in place. Hot breath tickled my ear as he whispered, "You seem a tad desperate. When did you last come?"

I closed my eyes and moaned under his two-handed onslaught. One of the reasons I kept painting long after he left each night was to physically exhaust myself so that I would sleep better. The jerk-off option still wasn't working. Some long-established house rules were proving impossible to break.

Don leaned in closer, pressing his body tight against mine.

If I'd really wanted to, I could have told him to stop or broken free. Normally, any suggestion of restriction of freedom saw me scrambling for the door. But the sheer domesticity of the surroundings and the reassurance of familiar clothes clutched against my body must have stopped me from panicking. I moaned as the tip of his finger passed the opening. What would sex with Don be like? The man oozed dominance. Nothing overt. None of the posturing some leather men seemed to think was necessary, imitating jack-booted Nazis. When we'd stood close on the stairs, I'd been tempted to lean against him. And then to push and feel him resist. See how far I could go. Giving into the urge, I leaned forward.

Not a muscle moved. Shit. Now I'd lost contact with his questing finger. I arched back. A weird growling sound came from deep in his throat as his oscillating hand tightened. The growl turned into words. "That's right. Come for me, Steve."

I shuddered and shook as wave after wave of sensation flooded through my cock, erupting in spurts that sank into the clothes. Depleted of all energy, I let my head sink onto Don's shoulder, gasping for breath. He held me until the shakes subsided. "That's a good boy."

CHAPTER
FOURTEEN

Enchanted

BOY!

A shudder of a different kind ran through me. I straightened, giving Don a glare.

He laughed and slapped my butt before heading for the door.

I am not your boy. Your slave. Expected to submit to your every whim.

I threw all my clothes on top of his in the washer. Too bad if the colors ran. It would serve him right. As soon as my hands were free, I slammed the door behind him. A yellow garment hanging on the back interrupted my hissy fit.

From the front, the apron looked like a frock: big yellow and white checks cinched in with a bow at the waist and sporting a large lace ruffle around the hem. Being backless meant my ass was easily accessible, and that was all Julius ever cared about. Mind you, when he was in a playful mood, he managed to do some interesting things with the sash. Life here hadn't been all bad.

By the time I reached the kitchen, Don was already there, spreading some Vegemite and cream cheese on a bagel. Even slathering the vile stuff on thick for him one day hadn't worked. He simply licked his lips and wanted more. The man seemed impervious to all my attempts to bait him. His hide must be as thick as a rhinoceros. He raised one eyebrow when he saw me. "I see the Domestic Goddess has arisen."

"Thank your lucky stars it's not my Inner Goddess. She wouldn't approve of you."

Don nearly split his sides laughing. When he managed to calm himself, he said, "Well, Goddess, whatever type you are, any chance of a cup of coffee? I'm getting withdrawal symptoms."

"It's about time you learned how to make it yourself, Sunshine. I am not your slave."

All traces of amusement fled from his eyes. I could have kicked myself for reminding him about Alex. Me and my big mouth.

Don watched in silence as I made his coffee and one for myself. He still seemed upset when he took his mug outside to watch a couple of hang gliders who had launched themselves from the nearby lookout.

"Have you ever done that?" he asked as I came alongside him.

"Nope. Have you?"

He shook his head. "It looks dangerous."

"So is riding a motorcycle."

"Yeah, I guess you're right." Don took a sip and glanced around. "We need to do something about the yard before all these dandelions go to seed."

A simple garden ran along the edge of the cliff, with a dense stand of bamboo marking the southern boundary. Dotted around the yard were a few scraggly shrubs, badly in need of pruning. I sighed. Looking after the yard had been another one of my jobs. Julius hated getting dirt under his fingernails. Grease from the bikes was bad enough. "Not our problem. The next owners can worry about that."

"But from a resale point of view, fixing up the grounds is as important as fixing up the house. Shame there isn't any gardening equipment."

"This needs more than a mow, Sunshine. It needs a Backyard Blitz."

"That's what I did for a living, sweetie."

Oh, that's right. Don had mentioned having a landscaping business in the States. "At least you're the same size as Jamie Drury. Were you a Chippendale too?"

Don gave my ass a sharp slap.

"Ouch!" Definitely better than the hairbrush. I rubbed the stinging surface. You'd think by Don's sudden descent into playfulness that he'd been the one who'd just come, but maybe he was starting to read *me* better, getting a kick out of manipulating me. "Wasn't there a mower in the garage?"

"Not that I could see."

I shrugged. "It's probably in the garden shed."

"What shed?" Don stared around in bemusement. "I've seen no sign of one."

"Well, that's not what it was used for originally. The real estate agent called it a meditation room."

"Where the fuck is it?" Don set his cup on the garden table and put his hands on his hips, staring around as if expecting the shed to materialize out of thin air like the TARDIS.

I smiled to myself. The property had a lot of mysteries. At least this was one I could gladly share. "Got your keys with you?"

Don jogged inside to get them while I walked over to the bamboo. At this end of the property, the land curved around, dropping steeply into a water-eroded gully. The far side belonged to the national park. The only live thing I'd ever seen in there were deer, and they couldn't gain access, thanks to the six-foot-high fence topped with bird spikes that ran around the boundary. No way in and no way out from that direction, especially if you feared the return of a furious Master at any moment. Over the edge of the cliff was another matter.

From a distance, the bamboo looked like one complete line. It wasn't until you got closer that you realized there was actually a path angling through it.

"Stupid landscaping choice," Don commented as he broke off some shoots that were encroaching onto the roughly paved area. As we exited the dense stand, he stared in amazement at the natural watercourse. "Why the fuck would anyone want to hide this?"

I had a morbid fascination to see whether the area had changed much since I left. Had Julius ever discovered my escape route?

Don glanced over at the cascade of water tumbling to the valley floor below. "Wow, that drop must be at least fifty feet."

"Possibly more." The low-growing plant with its branches dangling over the edge was still there. My savior.

"Are you okay? You've gone pale."

Damn, did the man see everything? "Scared of heights." Hopefully, he'd buy that furphy. He'd never believe the real reason. Seeing the steep drop in daylight made me wonder how I'd plucked up enough courage to throw my backpack down and follow it soon after. The roar of the returning Harley had proved enough incentive. "Did you bring Julius's keys?"

"Yeah, but what did you need...." Don stopped in surprise when he saw the wall set into the side of the overhanging cliff. "Wow, is that a door?"

"Yep." Someone had painted the timber so it matched the surrounding orange-and-yellow sandstone. "It's pretty obvious close up, but from the other side of the creek, it looks like part of the landscape." I lifted the padlock to insert the key. The lock had rusted, and it took a few goes before I managed to open it and pull back the bolt.

Don's expression of amazement grew as he followed me inside. Boy, if he thought this was good, what would he think of... no, better not mention that other hidden beauty. "Officially, this doesn't exist, because the previous owners built it without planning permission." A typical example of their aversion to rules. To make the area habitable, the hippies had constructed a wall to house the door and inserted another, which consisted mainly of slatted glass windows, facing the sea.

"Great, the mower *is* here."

Don disappeared, lugging it up the steep path. Before too long, he was back to check out the makeshift structure.

The room wasn't large. Roughly twelve feet long and eight feet deep. The ceiling height varied in places because of the way the wind had scoured out the soft sandstone. The previous owners weren't the first people to use the natural formation for shelter. Dark smudges on the rock face suggested fires had been lit here by the local aborigines. It must have been a great home for them despite being exposed to the elements on two sides. Now, it was weatherproof.

"This place is amazing. I can't believe Julius was merely using it for storage."

I could understand Don's enthusiasm. I'd seen the room's beauty, but Julius had turned up his nose at the absence of a proper ceiling, floor, and walls on all sides. According to him, mankind had evolved, and only savages lived in caves. "You do realize that we'll have to restore the natural rock overhang before we can put the house on the market." I picked up the can of mower fuel and shook it. Damn. Empty.

Don was busy dragging a smelly old futon outside. He stopped and let the thin mattress go. The material almost disintegrated as it fell to the ground. "Why would we have to demolish this?"

"Council won't give us a building certificate because it's not on the approved plans. That's one of the reasons we got the place so cheap." *One* of them…. The other was the reason I had to leave as soon as possible. "Can't stay here all day, Sunshine. I have walls to paint. Real ones."

"Okay. I'll be up soon. Most of this stuff is useless." Don kicked the hedge trimmer and garden edger. "I'll add it to the pile the boys are coming to collect tomorrow."

He started sorting through the gear.

I left him to it and went back to my painting.

By the time Don came to help me, I'd finished the ceiling of the next room and started on the walls. The property had originally been built as a bed-and-breakfast during the Sixties. Now the place could be advertised as having five bedrooms and three bathrooms. Perfect for a large family.

But, paradoxically, I was beginning to think that as long as I retained a share in something solid, something real, the time I spent here wasn't entirely wasted. Selling up would mean I had to start all over again. Oh well. At least I had some alternatives.

Left to my own devices while Julius was at his crummy job, working for an insurance company, I'd learned the magic of equity warrants, discovering I had a real talent for day-trading: betting on a trend, testing my limits, and seeing if I could stand the pain without flinching.

If playing the stock market didn't work out, I could always go back to my old job—working in a bank. But when we signed Master/slave contracts on our fourth anniversary, Julius made me quit, saying it was his role to pay all the bills.

In the end, it was lucky that I had managed to squirrel away a decent profit, because when I left, two years later, Julius threatened to challenge the fifty-fifty split on the grounds he'd been paying my share of the mortgage. All I had to do was come back, he said, and all would be forgiven. He'd been surprised when the required amount arrived in the next mail. I think he assumed my family must have helped, but I had never asked them for money and never would.

Speaking of family, it was time I paid my mother and sister a visit. I'd stick this out for a couple more days, then see what my lawyer had to say on Friday.

Gabriel could paint Don's office and Julius's bedroom. I wouldn't be able to.

CHAPTER
✚✚✚
FIFTEEN

Bella Donna

THAT night, I fell asleep before Don came back from the hotel. When he returned, the familiar roar of the Harley rang an alarm bell in my brain. One that used to warn me my Master was back, expecting to be taken care of after a hard day at the office. I turned over and buried my head under the pillow. No, this man wasn't my Master. The tread on the stairs was different. He didn't bang doors, not caring if he woke me. In fact, I hadn't been permitted to sleep while Julius was awake. My job had been to tend to his needs. Whatever they were.

The soft creak of floorboards and the rush of running water echoed through the house. Then silence.

I tried jerking myself off so I could get back to sleep, but every time I got close, my hand would freeze, and the familiar sense of guilt returned. Fuck it. If I couldn't get myself off, perhaps I could give Don a blowjob.

Dragging the quilt around my shoulders, I went to check if he was awake.

At the doorway, I paused, wondering if he would kick me out if I went inside. Then I remembered the look in his eyes when he jerked me off.

Judging by the steady rise and fall of his chest, he seemed to be asleep. He certainly wasn't reacting to my presence. But you never knew with Don. The man reminded me of one of those large cats that

116

likes to pretend it's asleep but, when you least expect it, opens its eyes and fixes you with its inscrutable gaze.

Maybe I could lie beside him and tend to him in the morning.

He stirred slightly and turned over. Good. Now that his back was facing me, I could creep in unseen. I'd done that to Julius once. Shortly after he'd started imposing his stupid rules. He'd been livid when he woke up.

A hundred whacks with the hairbrush later, I had learned my lesson.

From then on, if I pissed him off, or if he deemed I had not been sufficiently subservient, he would chain me to my bed. If he was only mildly annoyed with me, I was told to sleep on the floor, but if I was in his good books, I was invited to share his bed.

Well, Don hadn't issued an invitation, and even if he did, the chances of my being able to accept it were remote at best. The room held too many memories.

Returning to my own bed seemed like accepting defeat. I lay on the floor and curled up into a ball, just outside his bedroom door. Knowing that someone was close was enough to help me sleep.

THE roar of the Harley brought me to my feet.

Outside, the sun was shining brightly. Shit. Don must have woken early and gone back to the Paradiso. He said he was giving Fred the day off. How embarrassing. What had he thought of my weird behavior when he stepped over me?

I stretched, trying to ease out all the cricks in my back. I hadn't slept on the floor since I left. If I ever discovered which fucking book that stupid concept was in, I'd burn the bloody thing.

Don had left a note in the kitchen. *Don't worry about cooking dinner. I'll buy something on the way home. I should be back by seven. Tell Samu and Buka to wait for me.*

For a Master, Don was definitely not the hard-nosed, keep-the-slave-in-the-dark kind. He was almost treating me like an equal. Wonders will never cease.

I'd nearly finished painting the third room when a horn sounded, signaling the arrival of the truck. I wrapped the roller in plastic and went downstairs to let them in.

Two Pacific Islanders smiled shyly.

I snorted. These were the "boys" from the hotel. Both were well over six feet tall and made the rugby players I'd met seem puny.

"Be my guest," I said, pointing to the assorted mess. Added to the furniture that had been removed from upstairs, there were now rusty barbecues and all the unwanted gardening gear that Don had carted up from the meditation room. "Just leave the mower, any bike stuff, and those books over there." I pointed to the stacked boxes.

Leaving them to it, I went back to my painting, but the guys kept interrupting me, asking questions, wanting to ensure they didn't take anything they shouldn't. Consequently, I hadn't finished by the time I heard the roar of the returning Harley.

Moments later, Don came in, carefully avoiding the wet paint.

"You're early," I said, wiping an itchy nose on my shoulder. "I hope you ordered enough for six. Those guys are huge."

"Yeah, but don't let their size fool you. They wouldn't hurt a fly."

"Unless it bit them first."

Don laughed. "True." He wandered around the room, inspecting what I'd been doing. "It's looking good."

"Yeah, I've only got the windows to finish. They always take longer than expected."

Don pulled a piece of paper out of his jacket pocket. "This came in the mail today." He handed me a slightly crumpled envelope.

I put the brush down and opened the back flap. Inside were two invitations and the details for Marty and Sara's wedding. The ceremony was at five, and the reception wasn't due to start until the formal photos had been taken. She wanted me to sing "Sara" after the food and speeches, probably around nine. A layout of the function center was included, plus they had some bedrooms available for guests. One of them was being set aside for me. Little Miss Efficient. Marty was definitely in good hands.

"Thanks. Can you put these somewhere safe?"

Don took the envelope out of my hand. "Come and have something to eat."

"Can't stop now. I'm nearly finished."

"Okay, but don't take too long or there'll be nothing left."

The smell of spicy curries spurred me on.

By the time I joined them, the table was covered with an assortment of plastic containers. Half the contents were gone, and, judging by the satisfied expressions on the men's faces, they were enjoying the meal.

"The park rangers reckon there are about four thousand now," one of the Islanders commented before shoveling a spoonful of rice into his mouth. I still hadn't worked out which was Samu and which was Buka.

"Four thousand what?" I asked, pulling up a chair and joining them.

"Deer."

While I concentrated on eating, the two men described how some local residents had objected to the annual culling. Then they moved on to filling him in on the last big fire that burnt out most of the park ten years ago, leaving areas with nothing but ash and blackened tree trunks.

"You would never know from looking at it now," Don remarked.

Vegetation recovers if the roots are still viable. So do people.

After scraping up the last bit of curry with my naan, I headed down to the garage, wanting to check whether the Islanders had left anything behind. Their idea of what was worth keeping differed from mine.

Everything was strewn around in a jumbled mess. Now that the tall cupboards were gone, I realized they'd been hiding a pile of stuff covered by a big tarpaulin. Before I could see what was underneath, I had to move all the other shit out of the way.

Some thumping noises came from upstairs, followed by the sound of laughter and heavy footfalls as Don and the two men came downstairs.

"What's under there?" I asked, pointing to the mysterious shape in the corner.

"More bikes. You told us to leave stuff like that alone."

Could one of them be my BMW? I started working quicker now, spurred on by hope.

After they left, Don said, "Do you want any help?"

"No, I'll be fine." He looked exhausted.

"Okay, it must be my turn to wash up, anyway."

"Hey, that doesn't count. All you have to do is throw everything into a garbage bag."

"I know." Don grinned and headed back upstairs. Shortly afterward, classical music filtered down from the stereo in his office. Probably suited his mood. How had his interview at the bank gone? Not that I'd ever ask him. His business was none of my business, but I noticed he wasn't smiling much. Money worries? Or was he still grieving for his lost lover?

I listened to the haunting music for a while, torn between going to join him and seeing whether that weird shape was what I thought it was. Some of the lumps could have been handlebars, but the shape was all wrong. A new tune came on, livelier this time. Damn. He didn't need me to cheer him up. I shoved the heavy boxes of books and useable garden gear aside. In my haste, I even bruised my shins, lugging the old Harleys out of the way. By the time I peeled back the heavy gray plastic, my hands were shaking.

There, beside the detached sidecar, was my R1200C Cruiser.

I nearly cried. My pride and joy looked more like a neglected puppy in the pound. But in its case, instead of dull fur, the chrome had a coating on it. Dust and something else. Paint? Oil?

It looked like it hadn't been used since I left four years ago. A faint slosh was the only result when I shook the bike from side to side, checking whether there was any fuel left. Shit. The tank was probably full of rust. I'd have to take it off and clean it before I could refill it.

The battery was also as dead as a dodo. But who cared?

I sank back on my heels and drank in the beauty of my dearest possession. No matter what condition the BMW was in, it was still mine, my ticket to freedom, but any hope of escaping from this house had evaporated along with the fuel in the gas tank. It would take days to get it roadworthy again.

I wheeled the bike into the center of the garage. To add to my problems, the rubber in the tires had hardened after flattening under the bike's weight. I would need to buy new ones.

Everything I'd shifted lay in a clutter on the floor. Damn, now there wasn't enough space to work on my bike. Stifling a groan, I sorted and stacked everything into neat piles.

CHAPTER
┼┼┼
SIXTEEN

Dreams

"TIME for bed." Not a suggestion. An order.

Don was standing at the base of the stairs, watching me. How long had he been there?

I wiped the dust and crap off my hands and stretched all the cricks out of my spine.

"What time is it?"

"Midnight."

We'd finished eating around nine o'clock; no wonder I was exhausted. I nodded wearily and followed Don up the steps. At the top, when I started heading to my room, he took my arm and steered me in the opposite direction, ushering me into the main bathroom. I plonked my butt on the toilet seat. "Hey, I've got a weird feeling of déjà vu about all this."

Don turned to leave.

"What? Aren't you going to undress me again? Soap me up under the shower and give me a nice towel down afterward?"

"If you were my *boy* I might, but as you keep reminding me, you aren't." Don sounded as tired as I felt. For a second, my cock perked up at the thought of sharing a shower with him, but then it too decided sleep would be a better option.

I let the hot spray pound the back of my shoulders, easing my aching muscles.

"That's enough." Don waited in the open doorway, holding out a towel.

I gave a huge yawn and turned off the taps. He watched in silence as I wiped myself dry. "Enjoying the view?" I asked, trying out one of my sexy smiles on him.

He replied calmly, "Making sure you don't hit your head on the vanity when you collapse."

Yeah, right. The bulge in his jeans suggested otherwise.

We retraced our steps from the first night. I balked at the entrance to his bedroom, but this time I didn't go so far as to physically obstruct the doorway.

"It's just a bed and a room, Steven." Don brushed past me and got undressed.

I stood at the doorway, admiring his trim figure. His clothes hid his best features, a firm butt and well-proportioned muscles. His semi-erect, circumcised cock swayed provocatively as he unselfconsciously moved around the room, disposing of his clothes neatly. Julius would have left everything on the floor, expecting me to tidy up.

There was a clinical precision to Don's movements as he folded back the covers and lay down, leaving enough space for me beside him.

A wave of tiredness sucked away all my remaining energy in its wake. One tiny part questioned where I was, what I was doing, and why, but for once, the majority ruled. I meekly joined Don under the covers and lay on my back, studying the familiar patterns on the ceiling. The moon wasn't full, but it still shed enough light to cast shadows. While my body might be tired, my brain suddenly wasn't.

I was now in the room I'd been too scared to step inside the previous night. Not only *in* Julius's room, but lying in his bed. Somewhere I'd vowed never to be again.

Damn, Don was good. Without betraying what he was doing, he had made me extend my limits. He'd seen my fear and brought it into perspective. This was simply a bed. The place where you slept or had sex. Nothing more, nothing less. If, at times, bad things happened here, it wasn't the bed's fault—it was the fault of the perpetrator. Even the room was an innocent bystander.

He achieved all this without making an issue out of it or challenging me verbally in any way. I was tired. This bed was available. Case closed.

The expression on his face when he ordered me to stop working should have tipped me off. His simple but firm command. The tone of his voice. But he'd waited until I was at my most vulnerable—too tired to think about what I was doing or saying—then gave me exactly the right level of dominance. Not enough to alert me or make me suspicious of his motives, only enough to achieve the result he wanted. Then he led me here, as easily as if I'd been on a fucking lead.

Wow! I'd just been played. By a real pro.

But did he *want* to share his bed with me? Surely, every time he saw me, I must remind him of his lost lover. Taken from him by the man *I* loved. Had loved. No longer loved. Hearing how Julius hijacked his slave helped bury any lingering love that remained. Until then, I'd been making excuses for my ex's actions. Refusing to see the bastard beneath the godlike exterior.

That Julius hurt me was one thing. Hurting Don was inexcusable. The man hadn't deserved to be drawn into Julius's web. There might have only been a few glimpses, but judging by his reaction to Gabriel's comments, Alex's defection must have hurt Don deeply.

Beside me, his body was still tense. From bitter experience, I knew it was times like these, trying to get to sleep, memories returned with a vengeance.

As he lay on his side, facing the window, the curve of his back was tantalizingly close. I ran the tip of one finger up his spine, feeling every bump along the way.

He shivered.

With a quick flick, I threw off the light covering and levered myself up onto one elbow. Ah. Now I could see his face. Although his lids were nearly shut, the whites of his eyes gleamed, contrasting beautifully with the dark irises.

I fell into their depths, drawn by the hunger inside. No exasperated comment, no suggestion I return to my side of the bed and try to get some sleep. None of the impatience of the first evening. More importantly, no sign of protest when I urged him to lie flat so I could kneel above him. Had he been lying there? Thinking? Remembering?

Unbidden, Stevie's lyrics about dreams came into my head: dreams of loneliness and how they can drive you mad. I sang them to him.

Don's breath caught on the word "loss," and a single teardrop glinted at the corner of his eye. Had he ever allowed himself to mourn, to grieve?

I knew all about having and losing. Would it be crass to use sex to distract him from his grief? But where to start? Hardly visible in the surrounding fuzz were the two dark nipples I'd lusted after the other day.

A soft growl greeted my first kiss, growing deeper as the kiss became a lick on nubs now hardening against my tongue. Even a sharp nip, followed by a suck, didn't provoke any of the resistance he'd demonstrated so masterfully during our competition at the pub.

Making myself comfortable, I stretched out along his body, maximizing skin-to-skin contact, enjoying the feel of his chest hair mingling with mine. The other nipple proved even more responsive. I alternated between the two, wondering whether he had slept with anyone since Alex died.

Don's breathing became shallow, unsteady, hitching every now and then when I gave a tiny nip. Singing softly to myself, I brought my hands into play, alternating between light caresses and deft strokes, in a kind of dance.

As his breaths grew steadier and deeper, I switched my attention to his heaving chest, using my tongue to makes patterns in his salt-and-pepper pelt. A purr erupted. Nothing kittenish about it, more like a big cat having its head patted. But every now and then there was a hitch in the rhythm, a hint of lingering sadness.

According to Stevie, thunder only happens when it's raining. Our hearts were certainly thundering, but did tears count as rain? What if you couldn't see them?

Moving my mouth to his cock, I took in his hard length, letting it fill the void, losing myself, trying to suck out the grief inside.

Tonight, time was on my side. The longer this took, the better. Each lick, every suck, worked its own piece of magic, gradually obliterating thoughts, and with them, cancelling out the past. For both of us.

A gentle touch on my stubbly scalp made me wonder at first whether that ghostly hand was caressing me again. No, this one was real. I glanced up without relinquishing my task. For once, there was no penetrating calculation or even sadness in his eyes. Instead, his face was transformed by an expression of peace. Neither of us was complaining about the use of hands. No rules. No need for limitations. He'd managed to extend mine. The least I could do was thank him the best way I knew.

Smiling around the obtrusion in my mouth, I was astonished how much his face softened when he smiled back. For a second, I forgot to suck, captivated by the way every part of me responded to such a simple change of expression.

Before I became totally lost, I returned to my task. This time, I had no fear his cock might escape, so I varied my tactics, lavishing attention on his balls as well. The heavy ovals were definitely worthy of worship. As I rolled them around with my tongue, I kept on humming Stevie's song, keeping my crystal visions to myself, especially the one about wrapping myself around his dreams.

Don seemed to enjoy having his balls sucked; his responses grew louder and more ragged. When I decided he had nearly reached his limit, I returned my focus to the silkiness of his hard shaft, licking up and down his solid length before engulfing it once more.

Now the pressure was off, I quickly recaptured the magic we'd shared at the pub, and, once again, sucking his cock seemed the most natural thing in the world. My murmurs of contentment may have been muffled, but his long drawn-out growls of encouragement weren't. After a while, his legs started to shake.

I stroked my palms along the long muscles, soothing them.

Don let out a long, low moan. "Damn... you're good."

There had been a slight hesitation between the first two words, as if he'd been about to say *boy* and stopped himself just in time. I renewed my efforts, pouring my heart and soul into the task. His actions grew jerkier as he finally lost control and came.

Success was sweet. After swallowing every drop, I lapped at the softening length in my mouth. Instead of having a sense of victory because he'd come so quickly, I was sad. I would have liked to have kept going. Maybe I could get him hard again so he could fuck me. The penalty of losing the bet had been flirting at the edge of my brain whenever I thought about Don and sex in the same sentence, something that happened more often than I cared to admit.

"That's enough." Insistent hands under my shoulders forced me to stop. Reluctantly, I let his cock escape, managing to give the tip a quick kiss on the way out. Don pulled me up until our bodies were level. Then, after a quick glance at the satisfied expression on my face, he kissed me.

At first, the bristles of his moustache tickled, but I quickly became used to them as we explored each other's mouths. I'd seen the phrase *languishing kisses* before. Well, these were more *languid* as we sleepily kissed each other.

"Feeling better?" I murmured when we relaxed back on the bed, our foreheads touching, our breath mingling.

"Uh, huh. But you'll have to wait until morning," he murmured sleepily

I turned over, spooning in his embrace. I was hard. Had been since getting into bed. It was only when I started drifting off to sleep that I realized another cliché of submission had occurred. Denying the bottom release. Typical.

CHAPTER
+++
SEVENTEEN

Whole Lotta Trouble

"KO-*EL*... ko-*el*." The damn bird woke me again just before dawn. Already, the sky was tinged with subtle shades of pink, but the sun was too lazy to appear. "Ko-*el*... ko-*el*." The same fucking boring call over and over again. If there had been some sort of melody, I wouldn't have minded so much, but the sheer monotony was driving me bananas.

I studied the sleeping form of my companion. He'd turned over again while we slept, so now he was spooned in *my* embrace. The temptation to retrace the bumps on his spine with my finger was proving extremely hard to resist. I buried my head in the pillow.

He'd told me to *wait until morning,* but was that a promise or a command? Should I hang around and wait for him to wake up? Perhaps he simply didn't want me jacking off while he was trying to get to sleep. I was sure *my* sexual satisfaction ranked low on his list of priorities. He was a Master, after all.

Carefully, I edged out of bed and headed for the room I'd slept in previously. Any remaining trace of sleep vanished the instant I went inside. *Wow.* While I was busy down in the garage, Don must have enlisted Samu and Buka to help him rearrange everything.

All the furniture had been removed, with drop cloths spread around ready for painting. Well, that answered my question about which room to do next. It made sense. With Gabriel due to arrive soon, unless Don was into threesomes, one of us would need to sleep in here.

Until now, I had successfully blocked the practicalities of our sleeping arrangements from my brain.

But that put a completely different spin on why Don got me to sleep with him last night. Had it been purely for convenience instead of helping me overcome an irrational phobia?

My enthusiasm for renovating had waned, so I pulled on my overalls and headed for the garage. Sex had got me into trouble the first time. The temptation to stay in this house was simply that, a temptation. I had wheels now. I could make like a tree and leave. Become the gypsy I had always wanted to be.

Once I started working on my bike, I was so engrossed in trying to remove the gas tank I didn't realize Don had joined me until his moustache tickled my ear.

"You weren't there when I woke up."

Do I need permission to get out of bed? I started to protest, but then I caught a gleam of amusement in his eyes. Damn, I had missed a reciprocal BJ.

"Can I take a rain check?"

"Add it to the list. Now I owe you two blowjobs, but you owe me a fuck for losing the bet."

Damn, he hadn't forgotten either. My cock grew interested at the reminder. *Down, boy.* "Did you have a good sleep?"

"I did, thank you. What about you?"

"Yeah, until the bloody bird woke me up."

Our heads were nearly touching. Memories of last night's kisses returned. Lip-locking in bed, before and after sex, was one thing, but any signs of affection here would feel strange... wouldn't it? The temptation to find out was nearly killing me.

"How is it?" Don rested his hand on my bike.

From his expression, you'd think he was a doctor checking on the health of a patient, a live being. I knew how he felt. When I first bought the BMW, it had been an integral part of me. My baby. "It needs a lot of work. Not only to make it look good, but to get it working properly again."

Don studied the pieces I'd already dismantled. "You never cease to amaze me. I assumed you would have a Harley too."

"Couldn't afford one." I put down the Allen key and wiped my sweaty hands on a rag. "Anyway, I prefer this. It's light but powerful enough to have fun. Don't you find the Harley heavy?" As soon as I asked the question I realized how stupid it was. Don may not be much taller, but he was a ball of muscle. He could handle the extra hundred kilos, no problem.

He shrugged. "Suits me. Besides, it's good for long trips."

I patted the saddlebag. "So is this. Once I pack everything in here, the world is my oyster."

"You plan on going any place in particular?" Don didn't look at me as he spoke. There'd been a definite edge to his question, though. As if the answer mattered.

"Yeah. I owe my mother and sister a visit. I haven't seen them since I returned to Australia. Then I'll go whichever way the wind blows."

Don straightened and gave me a nod of approval. "I'm glad you've got ABS fitted."

"They're standard brakes on the BMW. Didn't your Harley have them?"

"No." A flash of pain crossed his face.

Ouch. Would a better braking system have prevented the accident?

An uncomfortable silence descended as Don began to investigate the rest of the gear in the garage. I picked up the Allen key and went back to my task.

When he came to the sidecar, he stopped. "This looks in good shape."

"It should be. Julius bought it in a fundraising auction, and we never got around to using it. From the looks of things, he hasn't used it since I left, but it fits his Harley just fine."

After checking there wasn't anything else hidden by the tarpaulin, Don turned his attention to the back wall. At the closed door, he paused in his tracks and turned the handle.

A prickling sensation ran up and down my spine. I gripped the Allen key tighter. The bolt I was working on finally gave in. Wiping my sweaty palms on the rag, I stood up. Should I say something? As soon as Don mentioned selling the house, I was in two minds whether to tell him about what lay behind that door. In the end I decided not to. Some things are better left hidden.

My heart was in my mouth when he walked through the opening, but after a quick glance around, he came out again.

From where I was standing, all I could see were a bucket, mop, and a couple of brooms. Nothing else. A sigh of relief escaped. I crouched down and worked on my bike, hoping he wouldn't notice my trembling fingers.

"What's the matter, Steve?"

I glanced up and shrugged, as if I didn't understand what he was referring to. *Damn.* I kept forgetting he'd probably spent half his life watching for every flinch, any subtle sign something was wrong.

In two seconds, he had hold of my wrist.

I swallowed and pulled my hand away, but not before he detected my rapidly beating pulse. "You're terrified," he said, staring into my eyes.

Terrified? Wrong word, but I certainly wasn't calm. "Want some coffee, Sunshine?"

Before I could take a step, Don grabbed my shoulder, digging his fingers in. My knees started buckling. "Please, don't make me go in there." Already a spark had reignited in my stomach, and I didn't want it to get any stronger.

Don's grip loosened, but he still made sure I accompanied him when he opened the door again. "Did Julius lock you in here?" He gestured to the small ten-by-three-foot area.

I leaned against one of the bare plasterboard walls and let my head fall back. Laughter made tears stream from my eyes. "If he had, the most that could have troubled me were spiders. You want real trouble, try this on for size." I reached up. The concealed switch high in the architrave proved elusive for a few seconds, but eventually I found what I was looking for. I pressed it and stepped back, allowing Don to precede me through the gradually revealed opening. Once inside, I flicked a few switches so he could see everything, then I clasped my wrists behind me to prevent my hands shaking again. High above, a massive bank of red and blue LED lights gradually powered up. In another corner, a softer glow came from a smaller bank of fluorescents.

Don's face was a study in awe and bewilderment. "Fucking hell," he drawled as he stared around the room.

I snorted. "Not a bad description, actually. We should get it engraved on a shingle and hang it above the door." I didn't move from the entranceway. This time, I had the opposite problem. I *wanted* to go inside. Years of counseling and nagging from my mother about the evils of BDSM were proving little protection against the temptation contained within these four walls.

"So, this is what Julius was referring to when he mentioned a dungeon." Don turned on one of the taps and tracked the way the water ran over the sloped concrete before disappearing into a central drain. "Did you build all this yourselves?"

"Nope." I chuckled. "This is the main reason we got the place so cheap."

Don turned off the tap and came to stand beside me, shaking his head. "I don't get it."

"The former owners weren't completely legit."

That only confused him further. I took pity on him and explained, "The owners of the ashram were ex-hippies from Nimbin. According to police reports, they had a huge hydroponics lab set up in here. Hence the concrete floor and drain. After they were busted, the cops cleared everything out and destroyed the equipment. The guys claimed the marijuana was for their own use, saying it helped them achieve a blessed state easier. But who knows? The yoga retreat may have been a cover for their main money-spinner."

"Shit." Don set off across the room, counting his paces as he went. At the opposite wall, he turned toward me. "Must have been a big operation."

I shrugged. "Enough to earn them fifteen years in Long Bay. They had to sell the guest house to cover their legal bills plus pay a hefty fine. Julius heard about the property from a mate of his. No one else wanted it, so we made an offer."

The temptation to go inside was growing stronger by the minute.

"I wondered why such an average-looking building needed high fences and a security gate. I figured they must have been there to keep out intruders because of your isolated location." Don checked out the hidden switch in the access wall. "It's well hidden. I thought this section was simply a storeroom, and I've been in here a few times."

"Designed to fool casual visitors and the police. I gather the hippies pissed someone off, possibly a rival, who turned them in."

Don was grinning like a little kid as he tried out the different switches on the control board. I clenched my wrists harder. While it had been inaccessible because of the junk piled in front of the door, I'd been all right. But now it was open, memories of my time spent here came flooding back. Being transported out of my body by whips, ropes, and other toys. Losing all semblance of control. It wasn't the inanimate whip that made me leave, or the depth of the cuts it inflicted, more fear of the anger of the person who wielded it.

Once he'd tested the lights, Don turned his attention to the shelves stretching along the far wall. Piles of chains and hooks were stashed in neat bundles, some still in their wrapping.

"It's still not finished," I explained. Julius hadn't done much since I left. Figured. He might have been the brains of the outfit, the one who came up with all the bright ideas, but, in those days, I was the brawn. "Julius wanted to install an electronically operated sling, so he could move it around a track in the ceiling, but it's not easy to find tradesmen with the necessary skills and an open mind."

Don chuckled. "No matter. Places like this are a work in progress. Part of the fun is thinking up improvements or finding new things to add." Judging by the rapt expression on his face as he inspected the dungeon, Don was in seventh heaven. He tugged each of the restraints that had been bolted to the wall and felt the weight of the chains. Any lingering trace of tiredness from waking so early had vanished the moment he entered the room. Talk about a pig in mud. All his movements were quicker. Had more purpose in them.

I sighed. "Yeah, but what we did is amateurish. We made stacks of mistakes along the way. Unfortunately, no one's written *Dungeon Building for Dummies*. Julius read everything he could find on the subject, but he still had to rely on brief descriptions of what they'd done and pictures of the finished result. No instructions on the how or, more importantly, the why. Hence the need for your expertise."

A quick nod of comprehension followed as Don moved to the wall where I'd strategically placed hooks to display equipment. After a few minutes' contemplation, he lifted down a four-foot whip, tested its balance, and then dragged it along the floor a few times before letting it fly. Not hard enough to make a noise, just testing his boundaries, working out whether he had enough room to use it properly.

The answer was *yes*. I could vouch for that.

"Kangaroo hide." His comment was a statement, not a question. The man knew his craft and his tools.

"Yeah, Skippy leather is great. Light yet strong, a real beauty." Now I had my hands locked behind my back as securely as if I had a fucking chain wrapped around them. Trust Don to pick my favorite. He gave his hand a quick flick.

The resulting crack echoed around the room, magnifying it to perfection. A shudder ran through me as keenly as if the end had connected with my skin. That sound never failed to make me hard.

Don had been watching me the whole time, so he didn't miss my reaction. He coiled the strands and tapped the handle on his palm. "From your obvious reluctance to enter, I assumed you hated S and M."

I gave a loud snort. "Well, you thought wrong, Sunshine. It's not the kink I couldn't cope with."

Don returned my stare, as if trying to read what was going on in my mind. "When Julius told me about you, I imagined someone who couldn't cope with the pain of being punished." Don still held the whip in one hand, tapping it against the palm of the other. The tension in his body seemed as coiled as the strands, though I could never imagine him wielding it in anger.

"Listen, mate. If I hadn't made a vow never to get involved in S and M again, I'd show you how much pain I can stand. But that wasn't the point. Do you know why he punished me so severely? Not because of his fucking boots, not even because of the fucking door, but because I wanted to leave him."

The whip paused in its movement. "He said you signed an agreement, submitting to him completely and agreeing to stay—until 'death do us part' were the words he said you both used."

"Yeah, just like a fucking marriage ceremony. And I treated it as such, putting up with the crap for as long as I could. But he changed. I changed. Not our minds, but our personalities."

"According to him, you took off his collar because you refused to submit to his authority."

As far as Julius was concerned, once I accepted his collar and agreed to be his slave, I needed his permission to leave. A vivid recollection hit, of tears streaming down my face when I finally removed the damn thing. *Collar. Submission. Authority.* A wave of revulsion swept over me, replacing the pain. "Authority? Yeah, well as far as I'm concerned, all that Master/slave stuff is bullshit. Things were fine until we went down that road."

"So, you ran."

"*Ran?*" I snorted in disgust. "Yeah, I guess you might call it running. Breaking out of a first-floor window in the dead of night. Then having no way to get back inside to access the gate controls or collect my bike, so I was forced to escape via the cliff face you admired the other day." My heart was beating as frantically as it did that fateful evening. "Oh, I forgot." I gave a soft laugh. "After that, I had to jog through the railway cutting at the bottom, hoping like hell I reached the other end before the next train to Wollongong did."

And made it with only minutes to spare. A cold sweat broke out at the recollection of catching the train at the next station and sitting in the corner of the carriage, curled into a tight ball, nursing my hands and wincing every time I moved because of the deep welts. "You know what's funny?" I chuckled sarcastically. "Adding security to keep potential thieves from a million-dollar crop works just as effectively as a prison for those locked inside without a key."

Don didn't seem to find it funny at all. "Why didn't you ask to be released?"

"What makes you think I didn't?" Long pent-up frustration made my voice crack. "I did. Time and time again." Biting my lip, I tried to stifle the tears that threatened to spill. When I finally reached my family, they couldn't understand why I hadn't left sooner. Deep down, I suspect Julius didn't believe anyone would ever *want* to leave him. Certainly not someone who loved him. Once I had myself back under control, I continued, "I'd given my word, so I put up with the Master/slave bullshit for as long as I could, hoping Julius would eventually get bored and our relationship could revert to the way it was when we first hooked up. Happy. Normal. I even tried to be what he wanted me to be, but when he resorted to using the whip for punishment and wielded it in anger, not to get us both off, that's when I, as you so sweetly put it, ran."

"Fuck!" Don's normal cool, calm composure shattered for a second, to be replaced by pure fury. I was wrong. He did look as if he wanted to hit something.

I snorted and emphasized my derision with a dismissive flick of the wrist, indicating a room I remembered with conflicting emotions. Pain and pleasure inextricably entwined like the long strands of the implement he was holding. "But now, you can see why selling this place may not be as easy as you thought. We'll have to dismantle the dungeon too."

Don replaced the whip, caressing the surface first. "I definitely need to rethink this."

I stood aside as he preceded me through the opening, noting the considering look he shot my way as he went past. Once he was clear, I flicked the switch, shutting off my view of the beautiful collection we'd accumulated.

CHAPTER
✚✚✚
EIGHTEEN

Sometimes It's a Bitch

I DIDN'T get any more work done on the bike, but Don helped paint the last bedroom, so we were finished in time for him to give me a lift into town for the appointment with my lawyer.

After it finished, I decided to walk back to the hotel. I needed to think about what I was going to do before I saw Don again. Irving Schofield's words reverberated through my skull as I made my way through the botanic gardens. *There could be grounds to challenge the will.*

Irving was an old flame of my mother who had kept in touch over the years. When I left Julius, she asked for his help.

While I sat in his plush office, too stunned by the concept to think, Irving went through all the different avenues available. Julius's lawyer had provided him with a copy of the new will. I recognized the signature, so there was no doubt of its authenticity. Then he asked whether I thought Don or Alex had forced Julius in some way. I laughed. No one could ever force Julius to do anything. But even the suggestion that Don may have colluded with Alex filled me with revulsion. I'd known the guy for less than a week, but already I knew the unlikelihood of that happening. And from what I'd heard of Alex, while he may have wanted the will rewritten, there would never be any element of force about it.

According to Irving, another option would be to contest the will on the grounds of being unfair. Dates would be important. The terms of the original will. Documents surrounding the purchase of the house. Proof of how long we'd lived together. Letters Julius had sent, begging me to return. The news I had binned them only caused a moment's hesitation. Mr. Schofield was of the opinion that, because Alex and Don were married and still living together at the time of the accident, there could be no suggestion Alex and Julius were in a de facto relationship.

Mr. Schofield couldn't understand why Alex, a guy who had absolutely no connection to Julius, should benefit from his will. Especially as he felt I had a greater claim to the money.

That meant I had to reveal their affair. Mr. Schofield raised his eyebrows and asked the obvious question, "How long would Julius have been able to hide this from Don? It wouldn't have been easy, making use of the man as a mentor while fucking his lover."

I shrugged and replied, "That was Julius all over. I don't think he would have thought that far ahead. Once Don's money was committed to the project, Julius couldn't have given a hoot. He was a man of the moment and liked the challenge of working things out at the last minute. He'd ignore everything that didn't suit his carefully planned scenario."

The discussion explained one thing: Don's continued wariness toward me. Irving had informed Don's lawyer that a challenge may be issued, hence the delay to probate.

"Think about it," he said. "You don't need to make a decision immediately. Next week should be fine."

By the time I reached the art gallery, the flying foxes were already en-route to their feeding grounds. I headed toward Mrs. Macquarie's chair and sat on the historic sandstone seat, watching the boats on the harbor as night descended. My cell rang a couple of times, but I ignored it. The caller ID told me it was Don. Then a message arrived, asking if I was okay. I sent him a text, saying I would see him later. He wouldn't be able to leave the Paradiso for a few hours, anyway. In reply, I received a brief "See you then."

Were his actions simply designed to make me sympathetic toward him? How much had been genuine? I'd possibly misread his motives last night. Was everything fake?

Sure, I felt sorry for him. Sorry that he was stuck in a strange country. Sorry that his money was tied up without a safe word to gain freedom. Sorry also that his little slut of a boyfriend fell for the same bastard I did.

Mr. Schofield didn't share my sympathies. The only person he cared about was me. He knew of the months I'd spent seeing a psychiatrist, getting my head back together. In his off-the-record opinion, Julius owed me big time.

He even intimated if I didn't challenge the will, Julius's family might put in a claim. All my hackles rose at that prospect. Because he didn't want to lose favored-son status, Julius never admitted he was gay. He merely told them to back off when they suggested he settle down with a nice girl. Who knows what they thought of me? The live-in help who did all the cooking and cleaning. A quasi butler. That they could accept. His parents didn't need the money. Don and I did.

The stone under my butt grew cold as it lost the sun's heat. Although I still hadn't made up my mind about what to do, it was time to go. I headed back up to the Cross via Woolloomooloo, dodging the homeless men with their blankets and mattresses set up in the shelter of the overhead railway line. Home may be where the heart is, but when push comes to a shove, it's better to have a roof over your head where you can feel safe.

When I entered the Paradiso, Don was sitting on a barstool, chatting to a few patrons. He had changed into full leather gear, looking once more like he'd stepped off an old calendar. Everything about his posture was so upright, so correct. The mere thought he'd ever do something underhanded, like wheedle his way into my affection, made me feel sick. I stayed just inside the door, watching him.

As well as paying attention to his companions, he was using his vantage point to keep an eye on the kitchen, the bar, the patrons in the other part of the pub—the consummate ringmaster. But never once did he glance in my direction. His shoulders looked tense, and his lack of eye contact was deliberate. He knew I was there. Was he afraid? Apprehensive? I didn't know him well enough to be sure. Now I was the one trying to work out what was going through *his* mind.

The door behind me opened, and I stood aside to let the person enter. *Damn.* It was Gabriel. I'd forgotten about him.

Because I was partially hidden by the open door, Gabriel didn't see me, but I could see how his face lit up when he spied Don. As soon as he reached his side, the young man sank to his knees. Someone had been practicing. He slid to the floor as gracefully as if he'd been doing it for years, not days.

Don automatically smiled at the gesture, but this expression didn't linger long. His eyes met mine, and the smile disappeared.

I couldn't get over the power I had over the man. One word to Mr. Schofield could make or break him financially. Things would be tough enough, but I had the chance to make his life a nightmare.

All sorts of mad alternatives flew around my brain as we stared at each other. In one lifetime, I could picture myself doing another runner, fleeing outside to seek shelter in the homeless men's hostel. It wasn't my problem. Let Mr. Schofield sort out the mess. In another scenario, I was the spurned suitor, jealously ensuring Don didn't get a penny from Julius's will, spending years fighting him in court, growing progressively more bitter as the litigation proceeded. In another vision, held only for a second, I knelt alongside Gabriel and offered my submission. All options were possible. Which to choose?

Damn, making decisions was such a bitch.

Gabriel turned to see what Don was looking at. I pushed myself away from the wall and walked toward them. "How did your exams go?" I kept my voice as neutral as possible, taking care to hide my irrational jealousy. I'd forgotten how good-looking he was.

"Fine."

As Don and I returned to our staring contest, Gabriel's gaze flickered between us. Now was neither the time nor the place to talk.

"Are we eating here or back at the house?" I managed to keep my voice impassive, hiding the conflicted emotions inside. I didn't want to study them too closely.

"Which would you prefer?" Don asked quietly.

A question, not a command. I'd put some steaks into a honey-soy marinade before we left, and there were definitely enough salad veggies in the crisper. I stared around the hotel, noting once again the outmoded furnishing and fixtures. "Can we go home?"

Outside, the awkwardness continued. Was I going in the car with Gabriel or riding with Don again? I hesitated, but Don merely handed me the second helmet. For a second, I nearly refused, but then I would have had to travel with Gabriel. No way.

The ride back to the house was a stark contrast to our first trip. This time, as we covered familiar territory, I had no problem hanging onto Don's waist. His scent and the general feel of him were starting to penetrate my defenses. Simply because he was so different from Julius. At the turn off to the house, I wanted to suggest we keep going. He wasn't the type to shirk his responsibilities, though.

Before we went upstairs, Don retrieved the spare remotes for both the garage and gate and pressed them into my hands. "I never want you to feel trapped here again."

I stared at him as he curled my fingers around the controllers. What was he saying? Was he referring to my physical presence in the house, or suggesting he didn't want me to feel trapped by ownership issues? The arrival of Gabriel's car prevented me from finding out. I headed upstairs and started dinner while Don showed Gabriel the dungeon.

After we finished, they complimented me on the steak and pasta salad. Thankfully, someone appreciated my cooking. Every bite tasted like ash in my mouth. During the meal, the discussion revolved around what the different apparatus in the dungeon were for.

Don deflected any queries from Gabriel that I avoided answering.

Julius would have ripped me a new one for sulking. But I wasn't. I simply felt like a third wheel. A flat one at that.

After dinner, I headed down to the garage. As soon as I left, the mood upstairs lifted. Gabriel's voice drifted down the stairwell, sounding much more animated.

I stared at the bright, shiny Harley standing next to my half-disassembled BMW. While mine might not be able to go anywhere, Julius's bike could. Don had left the key in the ignition. The temptation to take off took hold. I dragged the remotes out of my pocket. The garage door rose smoothly on its tracks. Outside, the security gate slowly swung inward.

I wheeled Julius's bike around so it lined up with the opening, sat on the seat, and stared out into the blackness. Nothing was stopping me. No gates. No bars. No locked doors. I could almost feel the wind whipping through my hair. I rubbed a rueful hand over my shaved scalp. No, some things had changed irrevocably. The simple, uncomplicated man I'd been before I completely enslaved myself to Julius was gone. Upstairs, the man who had taken his place, in the house, in his bed, was now training another young man to be *his* slave. Could I stand by and watch?

A car drove past, its headlights momentarily illuminating the outside world: grass, trees and, what was more important, the dark-gray strip of bitumen that extended all the way around Australia, through bustling mega-cities, small country towns, coastal plains, the dry outback, ending in desert. This was one road I could take. The safe road.

As the sound of the passing engine faded in the distance, I turned the key and planted my foot down.

CHAPTER
+++
NINETEEN

If Anyone Falls

IT TOOK me a few minutes to get used to the weight of the Harley again. But then the sensation of being in control blocked out every thought as I rode through the night.

Heading north along the highway, I retraced the route I'd already travelled twice that day. The need for speed was an itch needing to be scratched, as if, somehow, I could outrun all the shit in my life, all the decisions I had to make. A few trucks passing in the opposite direction flicked to high beam: the standard warning of a police radar unit. I wasn't wearing a helmet, and my wallet and phone were lying on the small table at the top of the stairs. *Damn.* The last thing I needed was to incur a fine.

Ahead, the Waterfall entrance to Royal National Park came into view. I slowed down to take the sharp turn and swung off to avoid the cops.

At night, the tall eucalypts standing like sentinels on each side of the narrow road reminded me of crowds lining the route of a procession. In the still evening air, the moon glinted off their silvery-gray foliage, giving them a ghostly presence.

I drew in a deep breath, drinking in the familiar scent of the Australian bush. There was something about riding through the empty blackness that suited my mood. No streetlights, nothing except me and the wind blowing in my face.

The speedometer gradually crept up as the thrill of cornering took hold.

Shortly after arriving in England, I'd bought a secondhand Kawasaki.

Concerned about my ability to handle black ice and the wet conditions, my mother had insisted I take an advanced skills course. Now, as I negotiated the twists and turns, I practiced the things I'd learned at the Mallory Circuit, using gears to decelerate into each tight curve, counter-steering to get the line right, feeling the tires grab extra traction as I accelerated again.

Unfortunately, the Harley didn't handle nearly as well, and it took me a few corners to get it right. I couldn't wait to get into the saddle again and try the technique out on my BMW.

After a while, I stopped thinking as the moves came naturally. That was probably what saved me. A dark shape blundered out of the trees and stopped dead center of the road.

Shit.

The red glow of its eyes caught the beam of my headlight as the startled animal stared around in amazement.

Without thinking, I applied gentle pressure to the handlebars and turned toward the deer for a second rather than wildly swerving to avoid it. Thankfully, the bitumen was dry and clear of leaves. The bike did a perfect reverse *S,* almost jumping to one side, and I was past the animal before it had the chance to move again. Strictly speaking, there was no way I should have made the Electra Glide respond like a sports bike, but for some reason it did. Otherwise, I would never have been able to keep the fucker upright.

The shakes started in my ankles and worked their way up through my knees. I managed to make it to the now-deserted lookout at Stanwell Tops, but I half fell off as I dismounted, then crouched down until my legs stopped wobbling.

They say your life flashes before you in the instant before death. Mine seemed to be on a time delay. Now the images came in quick succession. Car trips with my mother and sister in the Dandenongs; Rhiannon puking in the gutter when she got carsick; my first push bike, skateboard, broken collarbone, trail bike, broken arm; getting my license; buying my first motor bike; riding through the night with Don after learning I'd never see Julius again. The image of my dead lover standing in this precise spot when we took the Harley for its first spin. A ghost, beckoning me to join him.

Pulling myself upright, I looked over the edge. Below me, the lights of the coastal towns spread like a string of pearls between the black of the ocean and the dark hulk of the escarpment. This was the perfect place to do a Thelma and Louise and discover if the Harley could grow wings like a bat out of hell.

But judging by the way I'd instinctively avoided the deer, if dying was what one part of me wanted, the rest wanted to survive. Anyway, my death wouldn't make it any easier for Don. It would only give him more mess to clear up. He had given me the remotes, perhaps even left the keys in the ignition on purpose, sensing I needed to feel I wasn't a prisoner anymore. Not physically, anyway. He was getting to know me too well.

In contrast, I knew next to nothing about him. I knew his age, where he came from, and the fact he was into leather. I knew he liked listening to opera, but he also liked Bruce Springsteen. I knew he was like a bear with a sore head until he had his morning cup of coffee. I also knew I could make him feel good when I gave him a BJ. But I certainly didn't know his fears and his fantasies. It wasn't only my life at stake here; it was his future.

Gabriel wasn't the only one who needed to get to know the man better and discover if he could be trusted. But now Gabriel might be getting to know Don too well. Were they already fucking in Julius's bed? Or should I say Don's bed?

Staring into the distance, I tracked the lights back along the cliff top until I worked out which house was ours. Both levels were lit up. Someone was still awake. I dusted off my hands and remounted the Harley.

A crouched figure rose to greet me as I coasted to a halt in front of the garage. Don was wearing *my* overalls. So much for my fears about what he'd been up to in my absence. While waiting for my return, he must have been working on my BMW, separating the gas tank into its different components, and judging by the crud on the ground, he'd also flushed it out with soapy water. I started to thank him, but then I saw his face. To say he was furious was an understatement. Fucking livid was a better description. A vein pulsed in his temple, and his hand shook as he held the bike steady while I dismounted.

"Don't you ever go out again without wearing your helmet." He banged his fist on the top luggage case where they were stored. "Why do you think Alex and Julius were killed so easily? Julius wouldn't have survived, but Alex might have."

My first impulse was to get angry and tell Don to fuck off. He didn't own me. But he had a point. When I left, that inner fear nobody cared whether I lived or died *had* been at the back of my mind, but the scare with the deer proved *I* cared, even if no one else did. Don leaned in closer. I glanced up and immediately wished I hadn't. For someone who usually looked so in control of himself, I would never have imagined him revealing such raw emotion.

"Promise?" he asked quietly.

I nodded and backed it up with a verbal affirmation. "Yes."

He let out a long breath, but the tension didn't vanish from his posture as his voice dropped to a dull murmur. "I didn't even know they'd taken my bike. The first inkling I had that there was a problem was when the police knocked on the door, wanting to know if I knew a Julius Foster and an Alexander Carter. I never want to go through that again." His face had gone pale at the memory.

Shit. One question was answered. His fears. I swallowed. "I'm sorry. I should have asked your permission first."

"No." He yelled the word at me. "That's not what I'm getting at." He pinched the bridge of his nose. "Look at you. You're not dressed to ride. What if you took a tumble? Leather isn't only a fashion statement. In those clothes, you'd rip your skin off. You've got protective gear. Wear it." He ran his hand through his hair. "I have no doubt you have the skills. You're not stupid. If you didn't, you wouldn't have taken the bike. I can trust you that much, can't I?"

"Yes." I was surprised I didn't have any inclination to add the word Sir, though it would have been natural in other circumstances.

This wasn't a jawing from a superior, or even a Master. This was a plea from a friend. A very tired, very worried friend.

"Where did you go?"

"Royal National Park."

He sighed. "Last night, Buka said that, because of the deer, nobody in their right mind rides through there after dark. Not unless they have a death wish." Don leaned over the bike and gathered the front of my T-shirt up in his big fist, drawing me toward him. "Do you have a death wish, Steven Lindsey Stanhope?"

"No." I muttered my reply and repeated my response more forcefully when it looked like he didn't believe me. "No, I don't want to die."

"Good. Because I don't think I could stand it if you did." He rubbed the back of one grease-stained hand along the edge of my jaw. I moaned under the gentleness of his touch. So unexpected. Then his lips met mine. Only for a second, but that was perhaps the sweetest second I'd ever had in my whole life. All the worries about whether he was faking an interest in me disappeared. No one was that good an actor.

Together, we wheeled the bike into the garage and locked up for the night. A quick glance assured me Gabriel wasn't sleeping in our room.

"Shower before bed?" I suggested.

Don nodded and didn't object when I helped him undress. He stood under the warm spray, braced against the tiles, hanging onto them for support as much as anything. The water seemed to revive him. I squirted some glycerin and sorbolene cream onto a big sea sponge and massaged his back muscles. Damn, the man was strong. No wonder he had no trouble with the Harley. When I switched to his front, Don grabbed my wrist, pulled me closer, and kissed me again. This time, there was more desperation than affection in the act, taking not giving, as if he was trying to suck the life out of me.

I let him. It must have worked. With every passing second, his vitality returned.

Don's shift from passive to aggressive happened suddenly. A switch flipped. Our mouths never broke contact as he propped one of my legs out of the way so he could work on my butt. Using another squirt of the soap substitute as a lubricant, he loosened me up while I encased both our cocks in my hands, letting them slide together. When he figured I was ready, Don turned me around so I stood spread-eagled against the wall, my outstretched hands where his had been only moments before. Despite the water splashing down our bodies, I could still feel the heat in him, the tension. His erection poked into me as if it had a life of its own. My cock was squashed against the tiles. Damn, it felt good.

Even better was the feel of his moustache on my neck as his questing lips worked their way around to my ear. "Please tell me you have a condom handy."

I shook my head, ready to say forget it, but before I had the chance to speak, Don grabbed my wrist in one hand, a towel in the other, and headed for the bedroom. I barely managed to turn the water off before we left.

Without bothering to dry either of us off, he threw the towel on the bed and pushed me on top of it.

"Turn over." The command came through gritted teeth as he grabbed a condom from the drawer and ripped it open. I lay on my front, palming my cock frantically. I wanted him in me. Now. After a quick slather of lube, he obliged. Damn, he was big. Despite his prepping, the initial pain was excruciating, but once he was sheathed inside, he stopped moving.

"Shh."

At first, I thought he was telling me to be quiet so we wouldn't disturb Gabriel. Then he gently stroked the wet skin on my shoulder, soothing the trembles like a rider would settle a startled horse.

I wasn't upset. I must have been waiting for this, wanting it on some subconscious level. Needing someone to take complete mastery of me. Not using ropes or any other means of constraint, simply an incredible sense of wanting me, or at least wanting someone alive. "Fuck me now. Not next week, damn you," I begged as my body submitted to him.

The gentle stroking ceased, to be replaced by a firm grip on my shoulders.

I arched my spine, thrusting back against him, taking him deeper. "Please."

"Yes."

The fucking was fast and furious. We'd been circling around each other for days, the blowjobs only adding to the sexual chemistry that had been present from the start. Not that either of us would admit it, both too constrained by the past and memories of ex-lovers. I didn't know whether Don thought of Alex as we fucked, but he obliterated my memories of Julius as easily as the wind blew away dandelion seeds. No cheesy porn dialogue, instead he assaulted me with his body: his hands, his mouth, his cock, his hips. Every part made their presence felt. All the time, he growled like a tiger. But that was the wrong way around. *I* was the tiger. Yet, from the sounds he made, you'd think he was.

"Fuck, yeah." I came first, my hand pressing out spurts into the towel.

Don growled louder. His entire body jerked as he filled the condom. Afterward, he kept thrusting into me as if he didn't want to finish. I wasn't complaining. My heart was still exceeding the speed limit.

Eventually, he pulled out, stripped off the condom, and chucked it on the floor. The damp towel followed soon after. Then he turned me over and peered down into my face, his lips only inches above mine. "Promise?"

My affirmative reply was swallowed by a kiss.

This time, I had no more energy left to give, and, after a few minutes, we curled up, ready for sleep.

As I lay, entrapped by his circling arm, I wondered what would have happened if our lovers had worn helmets and Alex had survived. If I didn't challenge the will, he'd now own Julius's share of this house and the hotel. Would Don have forgiven his cheating slave? Either way, I certainly wouldn't be where I was now. It was hard not to feel happy.

Sleep claimed me quickly, and in the morning, I still felt on top of the world.

Don's face was turned toward the window. Was he awake? If not, he would be soon. Moving as stealthily as possible, I squirmed down and gently pried his ass cheeks apart

He tensed for a second.

I took a deep breath, waiting to see what he would do. His distinctive smell of overnight sweat and funk filled my nostrils, making me hornier. After a contented sigh, he settled himself more comfortably on the bed, spreading his legs to allow me easier access to lick his hole. No, definitely not objecting.

After a few minutes, he angled himself so he could jerk off at the same time. "Fuck, yeah." The gravelly voiced growl was cut off as I buried my tongue inside. Being able to reduce a man like Don to incoherence was a heady experience.

We tried to keep the noise down, but Don's growls grew in intensity, and I wasn't exactly a silent slurper. The more enthusiastic I became, the more Don seemed to like it. His hand flew in time with my tongue plunging inside. His hips bucked against my hands as I pinned him down. The intensity of his contractions as he came nearly made me come myself. I groaned and stopped licking long enough to watch the creamy spurts land in his cupped palm.

Damn, that was so good. I could feel it as if it was my own climax. I returned to gently lapping at his ass while his body gradually lost its tension. As soon as he was fully relaxed, I spooned against his back and whispered in his ear, "Am I forgiven now?"

Amusement lurked in his eyes as he turned to face me, bringing his come-smeared hand to my mouth…. He knew exactly how much I wanted it. I licked his palm clean, humming contentedly against his rough skin. As soon as I finished, he grabbed my chin and forced me to look into his eyes. There was no hint of amusement present now. "I meant what I said to you last night."

He'd said a few things. Promising me he'd never trap me here. Making *me* promise to never ride without a helmet. He'd also said he couldn't bear it if I died.

I was too scared to ask which one he was referring to.

Don's eyes drooped shut as he drifted back to sleep. He was pushing himself too hard. He'd looked exhausted last night and the previous evening when he handed me the invitation.

Shit. The wedding. I'd never performed "Sara" in public before and didn't have a suitable version of the song.

Taking care not to disturb Don, I rolled out of bed, pulled on my jeans, and headed for his office. At the door, I paused for a second, surveying the room I had come to hate, but the morning sun shone in, chasing away all reminders that it had once been my prison.

I fired up Don's computer, got onto the Internet, and soon found what I wanted: a recording made in Stevie's days with Fleetwood Mac. Unfortunately, a wedding audience was totally different from a stage. I didn't know the exact layout of the room, but if it was anything like other receptions I'd been to, a big clear dance area would separate the wedding party from the guests. Virtually theatre in the round. There would be no props, no band or back-up dancers to provide a distraction. The official Fleetwood Mac version with all its singers and different instruments would sound weird. Me and my big mouth. In theory, it sounded like a good idea; in practice it promised to be a total disaster.

"What are you doing?"

I turned to face a yawning, bare-chested Gabriel.

"I've been asked to perform as Stevie Tricks at a wedding reception."

"When?" His brow narrowed as he added suspiciously, "Is Don going to be involved?"

"No, wh...." I suddenly cottoned on to why he was eyeing me so warily. "No, I promise. He's not going to be involved in any shape or form."

Gabriel stared at me for a few more seconds, his lips pressed tightly together.

"Cross my heart and hope to die," I added and grinned.

"That's all right, then." As if I needed his permission. "What's wrong?"

I outlined my problem, and he caught on pretty quickly. "There must be other versions of the song. Let's check YouTube."

After listening to the first version all the way through. Gabriel rolled his eyes and said, "Great choice for a wedding song."

He had a point. "Sara wants me to perform it in memory of her dead mother. She'd been named after the song. In a way, it is a tribute to her."

Gabriel took my place at the desk and began scrolling through all the related videos of Stevie's performances. As he did, I peered over his shoulder. Now he was satisfied I wasn't going to make fun of his hero, he was happy to throw himself into the task, bookmarking the different clips, listening to them for a few minutes, then passing onto the next. I left him to it and studied his bare shoulders instead, checking out the tattooed angel he'd shown me a glimpse of the night we met.

Outspread wings spanned his shoulders, stretching down to below his shoulder blades. The details of the pinions were missing, but you could envisage what they would look like when complete. In the center, with his arms held stiffly out, apparently struggling to keep the weighty wings aloft, was the naked torso of a man. Long hair obscured the features of his bowed head. The artist was every bit as good as the guy in England who had done mine.

I traced the outline with the tip of my finger. "This is beautiful."

"They're both beautiful." A deeper voice broke in as Don entered the room.

I hadn't realized he was up, let alone known he'd been making coffee. He placed three mugs on the desk and came around to stand beside us, resting his hand briefly on Gabriel's shoulder when he started to get up. "No, don't move. I want to look at both of you."

I stood still as Don took his time inspecting the artwork of the two animals gracing my back. I couldn't stop the shiver that ran through me when he traced his fingers over the raised stripes of the snarling tiger. His words might be impersonal, but his touch had the usual reaction. My cock thickened in interest.

"Are either of you aware how revealing these tattoos are? How much they tell me about who you are?"

I swallowed. I knew what I wanted mine to say, but I wasn't too sure how another person would interpret it. To me, Gabriel's angel depicted a man burdened by the weight of the world, or of being good, at least. What sort of cares would a young boy his age know?

Don rested his hand on my back. Heat burned into my skin, sending more blood rushing downward. He seemed oblivious of my reaction as he said, "What are you doing?"

As Gabriel explained my predicament, visions of the previous night lingered in my mind. I jumped when Don suddenly said, "Go back."

Gabriel clicked on the previous track.

"Yes, that one."

The stage was dark. A single spotlight shone down on Stevie's head as she started singing. This was one of her later solo concerts. She'd lost her fey youthfulness but still looked fantastic. Her distinctive voice had deepened with age, and the words seemed to have a lot more meaning, especially when she sang about the way love had gone.

Don moved his hand away, and it felt like my anchor had disappeared. *Drowning in the sea of love.* I took a deep breath.

"Okay, no twirls, no lace. Wear the black outfit you did your blowjobs in."

"The chiffon is torn in a few places. I'll need to get it fixed first."

He nodded. A trifling detail. "We'll have you seated on a chair, sitting side on, as if you're alone somewhere, singing your heart out, mourning a lost love. In this case, a mother losing her daughter and vice versa."

Don didn't blink when he returned my stare, but I could feel the undercurrents passing between us. *Lost love indeed.* Who was he thinking about? Alex?

I shoved that thought to the back of my brain and considered Don's suggestion. No, it was more than that. His plan. His concept about how things should be done. Let's face it, the man probably spent most of his time conjuring up scenes. At least, doing it his way, the song would be homage to Sara, almost like her mother was singing it to her. Hopefully, that would counteract any suggestion that the couple might split up as the lyrics suggested. Don had seen it all so clearly, made up his mind in an instant.

Cheers from the live audience in the video helped me break eye contact. "I'd like to use it," I said regretfully to Gabriel, "but there's applause at the beginning, plus a few catcalls halfway through when she does some dance moves."

"I can fix that." Gabriel grinned at me. "I'll run it through some audio-editing software. There are programs for cleaning things up, as long as you know what the different spikes in the soundtrack represent."

"No hurry," Don said. "There are still a couple of weeks before the wedding. Let's see what you're like at cooking first."

It was frustrating watching Don teach Gabriel how to cook. This was *my* kitchen. I put on the apron as a silent protest. Don raised his eyebrows when he saw me but made no comment. He'd been quiet all morning. I'd caught him glancing at me every now and then, as if unsure of himself. Unsure of me. The will. He needed a decision.

Damn. After last night, I was even more uncertain about what I should do.

Over breakfast, I made a special effort to be nice, praising Gabriel's cooking and insisting that, "No, poached eggs should be a bit watery. And super crispy bacon is my favorite."

Don wasn't fooled for a second. He kept glaring at me whenever Gabriel wasn't looking, and my shins would have been black and blue if he could have reached them. He did surprise me, though, when he asked Gabriel if he could borrow the Corolla.

"Sure. Where do you wanna go?"

"Fairlight. I promised my grandmother's sister I'd come and see her, but I haven't had a chance ever since I arrived."

Great Aunt Mildred who had sent Don the boxers. I vaguely recalled him telling the rugby players that one of his grandfathers had met his wife up at the Cross when he was here on R&R. A young war bride.

"Fine." Gabriel shrugged. "I'm happy to drive you anywhere."

"No, thanks. I'd prefer to go by myself."

We both waited for Don to give more details, like why he wasn't riding his bike.

When none were forthcoming, Gabriel added, "But you're not used to driving on the other side of the road."

Oops, kid, first rule—never question your Master's abilities.

Don raised his eyebrows. "I've been riding the Harley around for weeks, and I *can* drive a car, if that's what you're worried about."

Gabriel grew all flustered. "No, no. I'm sure you're okay. But wouldn't you like me to go with you? Fairlight is way over on the other side of town. You might get lost."

"You've got a GPS, haven't you?"

"Yeah, but I wouldn't mind driving you. I can wait in the car."

Don gave a dismissive flick of his wrist. "No, this will give you some time with Steve. He can tell you what it's like submitting."

Gabriel looked downright appalled.

Damn cheek. If it hadn't been for me, he wouldn't even be here. I counted to ten and started again as the steam still threatened to come out my ears.

"But what will I do all day?" Gabriel sounded more like a whiny brat than a guy who fancied himself ready to be a slave.

I kept my mouth shut tight.

"Do? Whatever Steve tells you." Don sounded surprised he would ask.

Yes!

Gabriel took one look at me and swallowed.

CHAPTER
TWENTY

Fall From Grace

BEFORE he left, Don bailed me up against the garage door, shoving his groin tight against mine. "Be good," he muttered.

I stared back with wide-eyed innocence, wishing my body didn't respond so enthusiastically to this little display of aggression. "Who, *moi*?" I put my palm to my throat in mock horror that anyone should dare to think otherwise.

"Don't be too rough on the boy."

Boy? I smiled sweetly. "I'll be the very picture of gentility."

Don twisted my head slightly, then back the other way. Probably trying to see if I was lying out the side of my mouth. "Why do I get this feeling you're up to something?"

I rolled my eyes and shoved my hard-on against his. "I'm only up for you, big boy."

He gripped me tighter and gave my butt a slap. "Behave."

I leaned forward and gave him a slow tongue kiss. At first, he seemed reluctant or maybe just surprised, but then he gave back as good as he got. Damn, the man had a wicked mouth. I licked my lips when he sauntered to the car, admiring the way his suit showed off his broad shoulders. In a high-pitched voice, I called out, "Give my love to Aunty Mildred, Sunshine."

When he turned around, I gave him a jaunty wave. The pink washing-up gloves and yellow apron certainly added the wifey touch.

After he drove off, I muttered to Gabriel, "Pick your safe word," and returned to the task I'd been doing before Don left, clearing up the mess in the kitchen.

The young man bounded up the stairs behind me. "What safe word? He said you weren't to be rough." Gabriel's posture screamed how much he hated being left behind. So did I, but I was more curious about why Don wore his new suit and what prompted all those sideways glances when he thought I wasn't watching. Didn't his aunt know he was gay? Was that why he didn't want either of us around?

If Gabriel hadn't given me such a hard time about what I was wearing, I probably wouldn't have let that good ol' Trojan virus kick back in.

"I can't understand why you wear dresses and things." Gabriel gave the flounce a derisive flick. "Just looking at drag queens makes my stomach turn." He walked away before I could tip a pan of sudsy water over his head. He seemed oblivious to my reaction as he continued, "I think it demeans the gay community when men call each other girls."

I waved the sudsy pan at him, wishing I could give him a whack over the butt with it instead. "Have I ever asked you to refer to me as a female or called you girl?"

"No," he admitted grudgingly. "But if you *do* refer to me as *girl*, I'll whip your ass."

"You and whose army?"

Gabriel smirked and settled himself on the stool. "Look out. You're dripping water all over the floor."

I stared at him. Was he riling me deliberately? Usually, I would have been amused, but he picked a bad topic to get me revved about. "If it wasn't for the Stonewall queens you wouldn't be out and proud now."

"Don would never wear anything remotely feminine."

"Maybe not him, but I've seen some real butch guys get into drag. Anyway, it only goes to show what an ignorant little shit you are if you think all drag queens are the same." I pulled out the plug and washed the suds down the drain.

"Well, I think it's stupid."

Wiping my hands on the apron, I sauntered toward him, putting a wiggle into my walk. Too bad I didn't have my heels on. "Not as stupid as agreeing to be someone's slave."

"Yeah, well, I've read my history, but today's generation is different. You've got to get with the times, old man."

"Old man." I snorted. "Having good manners and being courteous is one of the first rules you need to learn if you want to be a slave." I started ticking them off on my fingers. "No lies. No egos. You have to have integrity, be reliable, trustworthy, responsible, and be willing to serve. Can you do all that?"

"Just try me."

Try him? Did that classify as permission? "You really think you have what it takes to be a slave, or do you simply want to submit for a scene?"

"A slave." Gabriel shifted uncomfortably and raised his chin, sulkily returning my gaze. My fingers itched to wipe the expression off his face. "I can take anything you dish out."

Bingo! "You're on. Say *Drag Queens Rule* if you want me to stop at any time." I tweaked his chin. "You're lucky you're getting that. Most slaves in twenty-four-seven relationships don't get safe words, but seeing as you're a beginner, I'll make an allowance for you." Once I signed the contract, I had lost that option.

"It won't matter. I won't need to use it," Gabriel muttered defiantly.

That's what I had thought at the start, especially as I hadn't needed to use it while we were just indulging in kinky play. *Right, buster, time for your lesson.* "Finish clearing up. I'm going to get changed. By the time I come back, be ready to tell me what you want from this week."

As I got dressed, I grinned wryly to myself. You'd think, to make my point, I'd be putting him through what Julius had done to me. But that wouldn't work. Gabriel had to discover for himself that being a slave was stupid, and this was my last chance to show him.

By the time I finished applying my makeup, Gabriel had resorted to playing Angry Birds on his iPhone. I put on the black chiffon, jagged tears and all, but instead of emulating Stevie, my lipstick was a garish shade of red, way outside my normal lip line. My eyebrows arched up toward my forehead, and I had so much eyeliner on, it looked like one of my ancestors had been a panda. I didn't bother wearing a wig.

Gabriel's jaw dropped when he saw me.

"What's the matter, dahl?" I hiccupped, pretending I was drunk, and gestured for him to get up. I simply wanted to sit on the chair, but he misunderstood, scrambling to his feet and sinking to his knees before casting a wary glance upward.

If one of the aims was to keep the submissive unsettled, so far so good. Before sitting down, I corrected his posture, making him kneel straighter. "Much better. You stoop too much. You're tall. Be proud of the fact." Placing the things I'd gathered within easy reach, I crossed my legs and pulled up my skirt to crotch level, displaying the tops of my black mesh stockings. "Go on."

Gabriel leaned forward with a ghastly expression on his face.

I knocked him back with my curled fan. "I don't want you to suck my dick, you idiot."

"But you said, 'go on'."

Should I punish him for not calling me *Sir*? Nah, I hated the word with a passion. Rolling my eyes, I added waspishly, "Think, *boy*. What did I ask you to do?" I could almost see the gears grinding behind those beautiful blue eyes.

"Oh. You wanted to know what my expectations were?"

"What you *want* from the week." I tapped my fan impatiently, like Don did with his whip.

"I thought I'd get to walk around naked with chains around my ankles."

The usual shit. I raised one eyebrow and tapped my knee with the fan again.

"Then there would be sensory deprivation? Blindfold? Earplugs? Things like that?"

His voice rose at the end of each word, making them into questions. Unsure. Waiting for approval. Nasty habit. "And?"

"Um, lots of kneeling?"

"And…." Another tap of the fan.

He gulped. "I thought Don might show me what it's like to be spanked."

"Hm." Judging by the redness of his face, Gabriel hoped sex would follow. "And what would be the point of all that?"

"Point?"

"Yeah." I leaned back and steepled my fingers, enjoying his obvious discomfort. "Why the chains, the kneeling, the nudity, etcetera?"

"I don't know. It's what slaves do, isn't it? Tradition?"

"Fuck tradition. I believe in practical." Much as I wouldn't mind staring at his bare butt all day, I didn't want him to get sunburned. I handed over the bundle we'd found left behind by the former owners.

"What's this?"

You'd think from Gabriel's appalled expression, I'd handed him a snake. "Don't worry. They won't bite."

He shook out the garments. "I'm not wearing a dress. And… a scarf?" He brandished a long piece of material.

"Wrong. It's traditional garb for men in India. You said you like tradition. Take off all your clothes first."

Gabriel eyed me warily but did as he was told.

Instead of folding the dhoti over to keep it on his hips, I cheated by making a small knot at the waist.

Gabriel didn't like my reaching between his legs and dragging up the material. "It's a fucking nappy."

I tweaked his balls on the way through. "First word's right. You can fuck in it quite easily. But it won't absorb any piss." Julius had made me wear it in a few scenes. Maybe that's where I'd realized I liked dressing up and becoming someone else.

"You know what I mean," Gabriel muttered sulkily.

Oh, the boy was just begging for a spanking. I arranged the folds of material front and back, giving him a smack on the butt when I finished. Then I slid the kurta over his head. "Orange doesn't suit you, but that's probably why no one else wanted it. You look like you belong to the Hare Krishna."

"It's all hot and prickly."

I clasped my hands together, beaming at his scowling face like a mother gazing at her little boy all dressed up for the kindergarten hat parade. "What was the next thing you wanted?" I hit myself upside the head. "That's right, chains. What did you want them for?"

"For?" Gabriel stopped trying to work out what to do with his half-hard dick and looked up in bewilderment. "So I can't escape?"

"But if you're a willing slave, you don't want to run away."

"Is it because the weight is a constant reminder you belong to someone?"

I stared back at him. Both answers were true, but as far as I was concerned, his last answer was too close for comfort. "What else?"

He shrugged. "Symbolism for the fact you have relinquished your freedom?"

"Ah, now you're getting warmer." I locked a thin silver bracelet around each ankle and threaded an even finer necklace between the two. Once it was fastened, he would need to shuffle to get anywhere.

He gave the chain a gentle tug. "I could snap this in one second."

I smiled. "Smart boy. But that would mean breaking your shackles, wouldn't it? I thought you wanted to be chained up."

Gabriel glared at me.

"Don't worry. You'll be conscious of the weight, or should I say, the lack of it. It's a constant reminder to be careful."

He started to kneel again in front of the chair. I tugged at his arm.

"See, that's another stupid aspect of being a fucking slave. Kneeling for hours on end while someone reads the paper or does their own work. What a bloody pointless waste of time." Using my most imperious voice, I snapped my fingers and headed off downstairs. "Come on, *boy*. I have a task for you."

Gabriel took a few minutes to negotiate the steps, going down sideways so he wouldn't snap the delicate chain. While he was busy doing that, I collected everything we needed from the garage and led the way outside. By the time he arrived, his face was bright crimson. I gave him an encouraging smile. "In case you forgot, the safe words are *Drag Queens Rule*."

He scowled at me. "What do you want me to do?"

"Well, now, if this was a traditional scene, I'd have an array of shoes and boots that needed cleaning. That's what all the books have. Right?"

He glanced around but couldn't see any. I stuck out my foot. "But seeing I'm wearing strappy sandals, that would be too easy. I suppose I could fetch Don's motorcycle boots for you to slobber over."

Gabriel's face perked up at the suggestion, but I shook my head. "A quick coating of Kiwi boot polish will be fine." I waved away his appalled reaction.

"I wouldn't mind cleaning his Harley. It looks dirty."

"I know you wouldn't. But that's the point. Slaves are traditionally given meaningless tasks or things they hate doing." At least I had been. "Here, use this." I handed him the weeder. "Dig up those weeds." I waited a second before saying, "Please." For someone who was craving being given commands, making it into a request would really give him the shits.

"Huh?" He stared around at the lawn. Some dandelions had already gone to seed, their fluffy white heads ready to be blown away by the next gust of wind.

I grabbed the weeder from his loose grasp and demonstrated what I meant. "See, you have to get down far enough to dig up the root. It's no good simply lopping off the top with the mower. They'll only grow again." I handed him the tool.

He bent over and poked at the next one.

"Harder. Put some beef behind it." I tweaked his ass with the folded fan.

Gabriel yelped and rubbed his butt. At most, it might have felt like an insect bite.

"Don't bend over. You'll get a sore back. Kneel."

After a quick glare, Gabriel sank to his knees. "This is fucking pointless. I didn't come here to do the bloody gardening."

"It's not pointless! You're kneeling in chains and serving me. In one fell swoop, I've fulfilled most of your fantasies." What a shame he didn't appreciate my sense of humor. I gave him a bag to put all the weeds in and returned to the garage to check out what else Don had done to my bike. As well as cleaning out the gas tank, he'd removed the battery and placed it on the charger. Damn. In some ways, he was making it easier for me to leave and in others, harder.

I stared out into the garden. Though it was only November, the day promised to be a scorcher. Gabriel's hair was already stuck to his forehead. I went back upstairs to collect a broad-brimmed straw hat left behind by the previous owners. The colorful scarves I tied to the headband made it look really cute.

Gabriel didn't agree. He complained when I placed it on his head. "I don't need that."

Clasping my hands together, I summoned up a suitably gushing attitude. "Masters are supposed to take care of their slaves." I sighed and caressed his cheek. "We wouldn't want your white skin going pink now, would we, *boy*? Not this bit anyway. Down here is another matter." I gave his butt a playful pat. "Oh, I nearly forgot. Here's a cushion for your knees. They must be getting sore by now." I noticed he didn't complain when I gave him a piece of foam. I wasn't being a total bitch. I knew how hard the fucking ground could get when you had to kneel out there for hours on end. "And finally, you wanted some sensory deprivation. Here you go." I showed him the MP3 player and earpieces I'd brought with me. "What would you like to listen to?" I tried not to smile. It wasn't easy. He should have known it was a trick question.

"Let me guess. You're going to play Stevie Nicks songs, *ad nauseam*."

"Oh, you bitch." I gave his butt another tap with my fan. "You could get into big trouble for giving sass. The correct response is *Whatever pleases you, Master*." I put the earpieces into his ears. "Now, see how deprived your senses feel after listening to Barry Manilow nonstop for the next two hours." I pressed the button on the MP3 player before strapping it to his arm. Gabriel poked his tongue out at me.

"Three!" I chortled. He stared at me uncomprehendingly. "You don't think those taps with my fan were punishment, do you?" He rolled his eyes. "Ooh, that makes four." I laughed and trotted back inside the garage.

As soon as I was out of sight, I doffed the frock and started working on my bike again. First off, I tipped a small amount of petrol from a jerry can into the gas tank and swirled it around before emptying it into a basin. Don had done a good job last night. The fuel came out free of rust particles and other cruddy sediment. Next thing was to change the oil. The bolt was stuck on tight, but I eventually managed to loosen the plug enough to start the draining process. I put a collection tray underneath and let gravity do its work.

The next stage would get messy. Before I got too dirty, I went outside to check up on Gabriel. He must have been hot in all that gear, but at least he wasn't sunburned. He'd managed to remove a fair portion of the weeds, shuffling around, taking care not to break the slim chain. As soon as he saw me, Gabriel gave a snort. "What are you doing now? Channeling *Rocky Horror*?"

I glanced down. Clad in only black panties, a matching corset, mesh stockings, and heels, there was definitely an element of Frank-N-Furter in my attire. Hm. Maybe I should buy a black wig to complete the picture. "No. Just a good Master, checking on his slave."

"Well, thanks to you, I'm getting fucking blisters." Gabriel held out his right hand, showing a red patch on his palm. "You could have given me some gardening gloves."

"Hang on, sweetie." I rushed into the house and came back with his phone, a long pair of pink evening gloves, and a bottle of water. I handed him his phone first.

"What's this for?"

"You were complaining about your sore hands. Phone someone who cares."

He stuck out his tongue again.

164

"Five." I handed him the gloves.

"You don't expect me to wear those, do you?"

I shrugged. "Suit yourself. They're more than I ever got."

After handing me back the phone, he grudgingly put them on. While I had the opportunity, I took a photo of him in his all his gear and e-mailed it to myself. I knew he'd delete it as soon as he got the chance. Last, I gave him the bottle of water. That, he did thank me for.

Once he was settled again, I returned to the garage. This time, I managed to remove the oil filter and grease the O-rings and gasket, but then I discovered the oilcan was nearly empty. Damn. Before going any further, I'd need to buy some. Should I wait until Don came back with the Corolla? I sighed. No, the sidecar was the way to go, but it was filthy.

After rescuing the can of Mr. Sheen that Don had taken back upstairs, I started cleaning the chrome until it shone like new. Then it took me another hour to clean all the dead insects off Julius's bike.

Gabriel still hadn't finished pulling all the weeds, but he'd done most of the yard. I was actually quite impressed. The chain was intact, but his earpieces were dangling around his neck. Cheeky sod. Oh well, we all had our limits. Guess being forced to listen to Barry Manilow nonstop was one of his.

"What a good boy," I said, unclipping the chain between his legs. "As a reward, I'm taking you to lunch."

"Dressed like this?"

He really, really shouldn't tempt me. A picture formed in my head of a bald Tim Curry riding the bike while Gabriel, dressed in orange with his pink gloved hand holding onto his hat, occupied the sidecar. Nah, adding public humiliation to the mix might be a step too far, even for me. "Have a shower and get into your normal clothes. We don't want to scare the local yokels."

He gave a sigh of relief.

"But first, I have to deal out your promised punishment."

"You wouldn't."

"Oh, yes, I would. What's the matter, Gabriel, scared?"

"Of you? No!"

A battle of wills ensued. The funny thing was, I'd never had much faith in pecking orders, but it seems they do exist. I might not be a Master, but I was stronger than Gabriel, and he knew it. With a resigned shrug, he followed me back inside.

Tying him up with Stevie's scarves was fun. I didn't pull them tight, and it was more like being wrapped in swaddling clothes than real bondage. However, I did make sure his bare butt was accessible.

He yelped loud enough when I gave him the required number of swats with the spatula. "Now you've had your bondage and discipline. Everything your heart desired. Still not going to admit that drag queens rule?" Sweet sarcasm dripped from every word.

Gabriel poked out his tongue again. Not that he had much else he could move. I did have a lot of scarves.

I gave him the last flick. "Have I convinced you yet that becoming someone's slave is a load of bullshit?"

"No." He glared at me. "You shouldn't make fun of something that should be treated with respect."

Oh well, I tried. He'd already demonstrated Stubbornness was his middle name. But I did get the lawn weeded.

We changed into suitable gear and used the Harley to pick up fuel for the mower and as many parts for the bike as I could carry. Gabriel sat in the sidecar on the way to Engadine, and as a reward—or was it a bribe?—I let him have Coke with his burger for lunch. On the way home, he rode behind me because the sidecar was full of the things I'd bought to get my bike roadworthy again.

By the time we got back, Gabriel seemed to have forgotten the morning's session, not complaining once when I asked him to mow the lawn while I prepared a lamb roast for dinner.

CHAPTER
✝✝✝
TWENTY-ONE

Doing the Best I Can

BOY, did Gabriel lap up the praise for a job well done when Don arrived home.

Shame he didn't appreciate that if I hadn't ordered him to remove the weeds, it wouldn't have looked nearly as good.

While we were eating, I asked Don how the visit to his great aunt had gone.

He laughed. "Turned out there was a good reason she never married. An interest in leather runs in the family."

"You're kidding."

"Nope, but in her case it was bike leather. Her parents—my great-grandparents—were strict. They only had the two children. My grandmother escaped by marrying my grandfather. Mildred rebelled by going out with a member of the local motorcycle gang. When he died in an accident, she refused to marry anyone else. She wants me to bring the sidecar over one day and take her for a ride."

For a second, I grew excited at the prospect. Then the truth hit me. I would probably be gone by then. The reality of leaving had never struck me so forcibly. I sat there, shoving peas around my plate. No one spoke for a while.

"What's the house like?" Gabriel broke the awkward silence. "Fairlight's an exclusive suburb; some of those old houses are huge."

Don seemed surprised by Gabriel's interest in real estate. Obviously he hadn't discovered that, to a Sydneysider, where you lived was the first and most important question people asked. Location. Location. Location.

"Does it have a water view?" I added. "That's the main thing."

"There's a house between her and the waterfront, but you can still see the Heads and watch the ferries come into Manly wharf."

Gabriel whistled. "Wow, must be worth a fortune."

A strange expression washed over Don's face, almost embarrassment.

"Does she know you're gay?" I asked.

"She does now." He shrugged. "For someone her age, she's very supportive. After her parents died, she converted the house into four flats. One is occupied by two elderly bachelors who pretend to be just friends, but she reckons they're more like an old married couple. Always bickering."

I laughed, but inside I envied them. It would be better than growing old alone.

"They keep an eye on her, feeding her cat when she's not there. Collecting her mail." Don's moustache quivered in amusement. "But she thinks it's a hoot that, whenever she puts out clothes for a charity pickup, a number of dresses are missing by the time the collectors arrive."

I found that funny, even if Gabriel didn't.

After clearing up, Don suggested Gabriel wait in the dungeon, as they needed to discuss what he wanted to get out of the week.

"Ooh, we've already been through all that," I teased as I hung up the frilly apron.

Gabriel gave me the finger before he left. No doubt he'd soon be filing a complaint about my bitchy behavior.

"What was all that about?" Don fixed me with one of his penetrating stares.

I shrugged. "You told me to show Gabriel what being a slave was like."

"Oh?" Don raised his eyebrows but didn't push me for more information.

I headed into the garden and drank in the smell of the newly mown grass. The yard looked totally different now. Much more presentable. Ready to be sold.

Once I tuned out the background buzz of the cicadas and crickets, nothing else disturbed the silence. If I hadn't known better, I would have sworn I was alone until a mosquito buzzed around my ears. Damn. That sound was as unwelcome as any evidence of Don and Gabriel being involved in a scene. I didn't want to go inside again, and I was too tired to take the bike out. If I needed to think about my future, I could always use the meditation room. That's what it had been designed for.

There wasn't any electricity, but a row of scented candles stood on a narrow shelf. I lit them all. The meager flames threw long shadows onto the rough multicolored sandstone.

Wow, now that Don had cleared everything out, the room looked much bigger.

I placed my palms against the cool surface of the slatted windows. Outside, the mozzies buzzed against the barrier, but in here I was protected. Safe.

With the candlelight behind me, the dirty panes acted like a mirror. Staring back at me was a ghost of myself imposed upon an expanse of ocean bathed in moonlight.

Ever since I'd seen Mr. Schofield, I'd been keeping myself busy, delaying the decision. But I couldn't hold out any longer. *Should I challenge the will or not?* Don needed to know. I needed to know. I asked my ghostly reflection for advice.

If you fight the new version in court and make life difficult for him, you can kiss good-bye to any more sex with the man.

But do I want more? My ass gave a sharp twinge, reminding me that the previous night's sex fell on the raw and brutal side. I groaned and adjusted my jeans. *Who am I kidding? Of course I want more. More sex, at any rate.* Picturing Don switching gears from passive participant in the shower to aggressive dominant in bed was enough to get me hard again.

Stop thinking with your cock, Steven Lindsey Stanhope! Sex with Julius was great too, and look where that led you! And just what were you trying to prove by pulling that stunt today? Warning Gabriel off BDSM or warning him off your territory?

Damn guilty conscience. But even if I didn't challenge the will and kept Don happy, could I risk hanging around? I didn't want to start down that slippery slope with another lover.

Start? You're well on the way to tumbling down! Admit it; you're falling for the man.

No, I'm not! Or was I? Lately, I'd been getting turned on just thinking about him or listening to his gravelly voice. *It's not love. I'm just lonely. Sex starved!*

If an apparition could snort, mine just did. *Just as well you don't want to be in love with him. After today's performance with Gabriel, you've probably stuffed your chances in that regard, big time. But that still doesn't solve your problem about what to do with the will.*

Making decisions was such a bitch. Especially ones affecting my future. Resting my forehead against the window, I breathed in deeply and let the sweet scents of the candles chase my tormentor away.

THE sound of the opening door and familiar footsteps alerted me to Don's presence. I kept my eyes closed, unwilling to face him.

"Here you are. I've been looking for you everywhere." A gloved hand rested on my shoulder. I checked out Don's reflection in the glass. At some stage he had obviously changed for a formal scene. His harness adorned his bare chest, and he was wearing his leather pants. A sick feeling entered my gut. Envy? Jealousy? Dread? Or a mix of all three?

This time there wasn't any pressure in Don's touch, more a connection being forged, transmitting energy. I shifted my focus to the distance, looking past our reflected images, unwilling to face the severity in his gaze.

"Gabriel told me what happened while I was gone."

What could I say? Utter an apology for making fun of something so important to him? Give him an explanation? I snorted. "Yeah, I'm sure he did. Little shit." He had probably hoped that I would get a spanking. The hard kind, not the prelude-to-a-fuck kind.

Don gave a brief huff of a laugh. "He's young. He'll get over it. And I did tell you to give him feedback on what it's like submitting."

"Well, you know what they say. Show is better than tell." That earned me another chuckle. As we stood near the window, admiring the view, our bodies were close enough to provide warmth without touching. Instead of the censure I'd been expecting, there was an easy companionship. I twisted my head to look at him. "It's funny. I've been hiding away in here, expecting you to be mad at me, and you're not. Why?"

He shrugged. "I *was* angry initially, and then I thought about it. You may not have meant to, but you managed to break the ice and got Gabriel thinking and talking about why he was here. You know, I meant it when I said we should take the opportunity to get to know each other. Find out whether he's ready to submit or if I'm ready to take on the role of a Master again."

Not be a Master? Even now Don's posture oozed dominance, his stance as correct and stiff as I'd ever seen it. "Bullshit. You were born to be a Master. It's a wonder your mother didn't dress you in leather nappies." Damn, why did he have to look so hot in all his leather gear? I faced the window again to hide my body's vote of appreciation.

"Yeah, right." Don leaned closer, his moustache tickling the back of my head. The hand on my shoulder tightened, and his voice grew serious again. "But it's true. Ever since Alex died, I've felt adrift. Unsure. The last thing a Master can afford to be."

"Unsure? That doesn't sound like you."

"No, I know. And that's what's worrying me. But everything happened so fast. Before the accident happened, I'd been busy sorting the business out and packing up the house, getting ready to move to another country. Then until he died, I sat with Alex day in and day out. And after that the funeral…."

I could picture Don sitting by the hospital bed. Stiff and upright in an uncomfortable chair. Grief etching deeper lines into his face. Torn between love for his slave and anguish at his betrayal. I'd thought my pain at leaving Julius had been bad, but that must have been horrendous. "It must have been a difficult time."

The hand on my shoulder tensed. Yeah, that was probably an understatement. The silence grew, but it didn't feel uncomfortable. The soft glow provided by the flickering candles added a touch of intimacy that would have been spoiled by the glare of electric lights.

"Didn't you have anyone to help you?" I finally ventured to ask when the grip on my shoulder relaxed.

Don let out a deep sigh. "Normally, I had a great network of support back in the States. Vince, one of my mentors, offered to come, but he was busy looking after some brat called Jason that he's been saddled with. But in the end, it was easier to submerge myself in the details so that I didn't have time to think."

It can't have been easy, coming to live in a strange land. "Surely you must have been tempted to stay in America and sort out everything from there."

"Yeah, but once I'd made that commitment, I felt I had to follow it through. It seemed an opportunity for a new life. I know that if I'd stayed, everything would have been a constant reminder of what I'd had and what I'd lost."

"In the stillness of remembering what you had and what you lost." I said the words rather than sang them.

"Huh?"

I chuckled. Poor Don, no wonder he was confused. "Just quoting one of Stevie's songs. If you listen to her lyrics, you'll realize that she's had her ups and downs, but her love for music pulled her through. It was her salvation, the one constant she could rely on."

"Yeah, it certainly helps if you have something or someone you can rely on. Speaking of which, until he died, I never appreciated how much my boy did. Paid the bills. Looked after me. In some ways, I had become dependent on him. Maybe, deep down, he sensed that and was seeking someone stronger."

Stronger? Julius? My ex might have been taller, but the figure reflected in the dusty glass looked like he grew out of the solid rock. I turned to face the original so I could obtain a clearer view. "You never sound bitter when discussing Alex. Weren't you angry with him?"

"No, not with Alex. My pride was hurt, but I would never have made Alex stay with me against his will. I should have sensed his need for something I wasn't giving him. That's why I'm wondering whether I still have what it takes to be an effective Master or even if I want to be." Don let out a deep sigh.

"That would be a shame. As I said, you're a natural." Much as it hurt me to admit it.

"Thanks for the vote of confidence, but even Masters aren't infallible."

"It takes a big man to admit he's not."

Don gave a dry chuckle and squeezed my shoulder. "Thanks for listening. I've missed being able to chat to someone who is not an employee or a patron at the hotel."

"My pleasure." It was strange to see him admitting a need, and I had just added to his woes. "I know you say I helped, but I really shouldn't have given Gabriel such a hard time today."

Don laughed. This time the unfettered sound reverberated around the confined space. "Strange as it may seem, your display helped me remember what appealed to me about BDSM in the first place. Gabriel's confused garble about the way you made a mockery of bondage and discipline helped me look beyond the trappings. By the time I finished explaining it all to him, I recalled the total buzz I get out of being in control of someone else and loving the extra power their capitulation gives me."

Oh, good one, Steve. You just made the man more determined to stay involved. I relaxed back against the glass and gave an ironic laugh. "Glad to be of assistance."

Don studied me for a moment, then removed his glove and rubbed my forehead. Seemed some of the dirt from the window had stuck. His action had been so casual, so matter of fact, I wasn't sure he was conscious of doing it. I stayed still and waited as he wiped his hand, replaced his glove, and smiled. "Gabriel kept ranting on about how you had no respect for people who were happy being subservient. That your contempt ruined everything for him, and it wasn't fair. Blah, blah, blah. The usual diatribe of a self-centered youth who only sees the world as it relates to him."

I gave a loud snort. "Well, he's right, isn't he? I hate the Master/slave bullshit."

Don shook his head slowly. "That's what I thought at first. But now, I think that's part of the armor plating you hide behind. Deep down, I suspect you understand the ethos behind the exchange of power, but you don't want to admit it. It's not disrespect for the concept that makes you reject the scene so forcibly, but a lack of respect for the man who claimed to be your Master."

There were too many elements of truth in that last sentence. All I could do was pick up on one word and repeat it. "Respect."

"Yes. Respect has to be at the heart of everything." Don was studying me closely now, not like an insect, but more as if he was trying to tell me something. Convey some meaning his words barely touched on. "It's weird. We may never admit it, but even when dealing out our most humiliating treatment, in our hearts we admire anyone who takes our crap without complaining. So the respect is mutual."

Mutual respect. In my case, the more I submitted to Julius, the less respect he showed me, even while demanding more submission and respect, as proof of my love.

Don brushed something off my cheek with his gloved hand.

Before the single tear became a cascade, I took refuge in facing the window again.

Don gripped my shoulder, tighter than before, but I didn't dare look into the dusty glass to see the pity in his eyes. It was bad enough hearing it in his voice. "You haven't told me much, but I'm gradually getting a picture of what life must have been like for you here. Trapped, isolated, and deprived." He gave a soft chuckle. "I had to laugh when Gabriel told me all the details of what you did today. As he raved on, I translated them to the opposite, and pictured you out in the yard, exposed to the elements, kneeling with nothing to do, bored shitless and in pain." He paused. "You were, weren't you?'

174

I nodded at his reflection.

"And yet you stayed."

I swallowed and nodded again.

"With a man and in a scene you no longer respected?"

Wasn't there some sort of cultural significance to three nods? Three strikes and you're out. Jesus being betrayed by Peter three times. At my third nod of assent, Don finally found my limit. I started crying. No sound, simply a steady stream.

Don started massaging my shoulders. "It was Aunt Mildred who gave me my answer."

"Your great aunt?" The flow ceased as suddenly as if the tap had been turned off. Shock does that. I turned to face him. "You didn't discuss me with her, did you?"

Don gave one of his lopsided grins, and his brown eyes warmed to molten chocolate. "Actually, I did. We got talking about where I was staying, and before I knew it, I told her everything."

"What did she say?"

"That you would have stayed with Julius out of love, not out of respect, and it demonstrated how much love you are capable of giving to the right man."

The right man who wasn't involved in leather. When it all came down to it, that basic difference would always prevent any chance of the two of us having a long-term relationship. "She sounds like a great lady."

He nodded. "She is. I'm glad I went. My grandmother had often spoken about her beloved sister who never forgot a birthday or Christmas."

Before today, we'd never had a chance to discuss our families—the people who were important to us. "I'm glad you've got someone living locally, even if she is elderly."

"Yeah," he drawled, and his face started glowing as if all his Christmases and birthdays had come at once. "Turned out the visit proved profitable in more ways than one." He waited, drawing out the surprise. "I didn't want to discuss it in front of Gabriel, but he's gone to bed."

Part of me wanted to know what sort of scene they'd done, but I didn't have the guts to ask. Anyway, what happened in the dungeon should stay in the dungeon. It was none of my business.

"Well, go on. Tell me." I smiled. Don looked like a kid who'd been given the toy gun he'd always wanted or, in his case, a whip.

"One of the reasons for my visit was to ask if she would act as guarantor for a bank loan to tide me over until the house is sold. She went one better. Not only did she agree to that, but as I'm her only relative, she offered to buy your share of this house. Amassing prime real estate is almost a hobby for her, and when I described where the house was, and the view, she figured the place would be a good investment."

CHAPTER
+++
TWENTY-TWO

If You Ever Did Believe

CHILLS swept through my body, starting at my toes, travelling in successive waves, each stronger than the first. "Buy me out? You mean, instead of selling the house, you want to *stay* here?"

Don nodded. "As soon as I saw the dungeon, I realized this was what I've always wanted. Don't get me wrong. The Paradiso"—he gave a dismissive wave of his hand—"is fine. But leather bars are dicey propositions, and there's limited room for growth. This place has tons of potential to earn extra income. People can pay to stay here for a few nights, allowing me to introduce them to leather in controlled circumstances. There won't be any extraneous noises from patrons who aren't interested in what's going on, and they won't have to drive anywhere afterward. It's perfect." There was a note of reverence in Don's voice. Then he must have sensed the turmoil raging inside me because his enthusiasm dimmed. "Of course I need to get the place valued so I can work out what your half is worth, and if you challenge the will, it will be harder, but I'll manage somehow. That way you can leave as soon as you like."

I slumped against the glass and hoped, belatedly, it would hold my weight. Nothing else seemed to be keeping me upright. "You *want* me to leave?"

"No, of course I don't." Don took a deep breath. "But you said you *wanted* to leave, and I won't keep you here against your will, especially if you aren't a hundred percent behind the concept of what I want to do."

Earlier, I'd found it difficult to cope with Don being in the dungeon with Gabriel. How could I stay here and watch him indulge in a kink denied to me? "I suppose you're right." I turned back to the window and stared out to sea. The wind had dropped completely, and the only thing disrupting the moon's reflection were dark shadows of ore carriers lined up ready to enter port. Silently, they waited. Predators ready to pounce.

Don moved around to stand beside me, studying my profile. He couldn't have failed to see how upset I was. All his joy at imparting the news vanished. "What's wrong, Steve? I thought you'd be happy."

I remained silent, chewing on my lip. He grabbed my elbow roughly, turning me to face him. "Damn it, man. How can I know what you're thinking if you don't tell me? You hide everything and never let on how you feel."

"*Feel?*" How could I tell him how I felt when I didn't know myself? I tore my arm from his grasp and began pacing around the small enclosure. "It's difficult to explain. At first, I'd been able to cope with the idea of selling the house, figuring once everything was dismantled and sold I could move on because nothing remained to remind me of what happened here. But now… I don't *know*…. This place…." I waved my arm around. "Not this room, the house… the yard… everything holds memories. Not only horrible ones, there were good ones too."

A flash of irritation washed over Don's face. "Sit down. I feel like I'm at a tennis match with you going backward and forward." He indicated the bare bench that was still waiting for another cushion to replace the moldy futon. "Okay, tell me about some of the good memories. Why did you stay so long?"

I sat and hugged my knees.

Don folded his arms tightly across his chest in a typical square-shouldered Dominant's pose. He wasn't going anywhere until I answered his question.

Checking out his boots was easier than meeting his gaze. In the flickering candlelight, their gloss didn't seem so overwhelmingly bright.

Imagining the repetitive task of polishing them helped clear my head enough to think. Spit… rub. Spit… rub. *Why* didn't *I leave earlier?* Spit… rub….

I smiled as one of the happier memories rose to the surface. "You should have seen us when we finally got the keys. We stood inside the gate, gazing at the house—*our* house—and Julius put his arms around me. After a while, he rested his chin on my head, promising that it would be *our* castle. No one would ever be able to take it from us. Then we behaved like two little kids, running around, touching everything." I chuckled as I remembered something I'd forgotten. "Julius even pissed in every corner of the yard, like a dog marking his territory."

No response from Don. I glanced up. Every muscle of his body seemed rigid, taut. He certainly didn't seem to be sharing my enthusiasm. "We *were* happy," I reassured him. "And we would *still* have been happy if it hadn't been for his bloody obsession with leather." My voice broke on the last word, and I started shivering.

"Shit. It always comes back to that." Don sat beside me, wrapping me in his warm embrace. Whatever he'd been doing in the dungeon had worked up a sweat. He smelled all man. "I know it's hard to believe, but not all leather men are the same." A deep sigh escaped, caressing my skin like a gentle kiss.

Twisting in his arms, not far enough to break free, just increasing the distance between us, I made a show of rubbing my neck where the skin still tingled from the contact. "You really should shave that bloody thing off. It tickles."

"What tickles?"

"Your moustache. Get rid of it." I gave him a cheeky grin. "Unless you're thinking of joining a Village People tribute band."

Don smiled briefly before his serious expression returned. "Humor. Your favorite form of defense. Anything to avoid thinking or talking about the subject." His lips twisted into an ironic grimace. "Okay. You hate leather. I get that. Especially after what happened with Julius. Yet, when I first entered the dungeon and saw those empty pieces of equipment, in my imagination, the chains weren't hanging loosely against the wall. They were bound to cuffs at your wrists or anchoring your feet. I could picture you straining against those bonds like a captive tiger, testing their strength while waiting for my whip. Not fighting to get free but impatient to welcome it."

The picture Don painted burst into life. I had always seen everything from my perspective, never from that of another person. A lump formed in the back of my throat, gagging me as effectively as a piece of rubber. He might have seen an image of me, dancing at the end of his whip, but all I could see was him wielding the instrument. Sweat pouring off his body. The muscles of his brawny arms popping with the effort. The physical side of BDSM required strength and stamina. Something Don had in spades. "There are some aspects I really miss." I shivered again, from need more than the cold.

Don pulled me back into his embrace, rubbing my arms, calming me. Leaning in closer, he whispered into my ear like a lover sharing a secret. "One day, when you're ready, I'd like to try out different things and see how you react. Would you like that?"

No! Yes! Then I wouldn't have to leave this house, my home. I squirmed in his arms, trying to bring as much of my body into contact as possible. "Maybe."

Warm lips pressed against the side of my head. "If I did, I would have to trust you to be honest and tell me exactly how you feel. I'm not a mind reader." He slid his hands down my arms and grasped my wrists tightly, lifting them from my sides.

The feel of being embraced by his leather sent sparks of electricity shooting up my spine, radiating out to each limb. My heart sped up, like an out-of-control train, until I could almost hear it pumping in my ears. Paradoxically, the thoughts churning through my brain settled into a simpler rhythm. Don's grip tightened, and a knot deep inside me unraveled, allowing the rope tethering my body from the inside to slip from its moorings. My cock filled. *No! This is wrong. Sick.* I twisted my hands to break free.

Don released me immediately. One gloved finger touched my face, forcing me to turn and look at him. The other hand rested on my erection. He whistled softly through his teeth. "Hmm, so bondage still turns you on."

"Of course it does. How do you think I got into this fucking mess in the first place?" I spat out the words, angered by my body's betrayal.

"Okay, I used to get off on being tied up. What does that prove? I'm sick."

"*No!*" I winced at the anger in Don's reaction. He lowered his voice to a more reassuring level. "Is that what your therapist told you? That you were sick because you liked being tied up when you have sex?"

I swallowed, trying to find that anchor again. "Yeah."

"Fuck that. Getting off on kink doesn't mean you're sick. What *is* sick is having a major part of who you are at war with the rest. She should have encouraged you to embrace that aspect of your personality just like you embraced the fact that you're gay."

The man in front of me had obviously come to terms with his kink. A memory surfaced of sitting in the waiting room and leafing through brochures on *Healthy Minds* and *12 Steps to Overcoming Addiction*. "My therapist described BDSM as a form of addiction."

Don scowled. "That's how they used to view it. The current theory is that it's not unhealthy as long as it's consensual. Yours obviously wasn't."

"But it can still be addictive. She said the only solution was to give it up completely."

"Bullshit! Eating chocolate can be addictive too. Abstinence is unnecessary if you deal with the underlying problem that causes you to overindulge in the first place." Don reached for my wrists again, holding them looser this time, his massaging thumbs weaving their special brand of magic. In a gentler voice, he added, "Isn't it about time you stopped blaming BDSM for all your problems?"

He hadn't been speaking loudly, but the words seemed to reverberate around the small enclosure. "What do you mean?" I asked hesitantly.

"It's like blaming alcohol or drugs for breaking up a marriage. The abuse of the substance is not the cause, it's the symptom."

Silence fell as I acknowledged the truth of his words. Even when we were together, I was blaming BDSM instead of looking at the situation honestly. Now it felt like a crutch had been taken away from me. Every instinct rebelled, wanting to hang on, but Don's confidence oozed out, engulfing me in its embrace as surely as rope, allowing me to stay upright. "How can you be so sure? Of this? Of everything?"

Don gripped my wrists tighter. "Okay, I may not have formal academic training, but I've attended conferences, workshops, and read as much as I can about the psychology behind BDSM. I bet I have a better concept of your problem than your therapist did."

"I wouldn't have dared to come back to Australia if she hadn't fixed me up."

"Fixed you up?" He snorted. "From what I can gather, Julius injured you mentally as well as physically. But once you escaped from his influence, of course you improved. Now you should be fine."

I'd never heard him sound so sure of himself, so positive he was correct. Was he right? "My therapist said that the scars will remain forever. What makes *you* think different, Sunshine?"

"I've seen enough to give me a fair idea of who you are. Your therapist fixed you to a certain level, and you needed that. But for the rest? One by one, you're confronting situations that were limiting you, and by doing so, you're proving you are strong enough to deal with them. I believe you shouldn't deny yourself something you once enjoyed just because you had a bad experience with it. It's like denying yourself chocolate bars because one of them was out of date and made you sick."

Oh, the temptation. "Sounds good in theory, but what about in practice?"

Don laughed softly. "You sound like Vince, the guy who introduced me to leather. He maintains that nothing beats gut feeling."

I broke away from Don's clasp and rubbed my own wrist. The man had an uncanny ability to make my insides squirm whenever he touched me.

"Why don't we try some bondage, and you tell me to stop if it's too much?" He raised an eyebrow, challenging me.

Could I? "What if you trigger something, making me worse?" Echoes of screams as I begged Julius to let me go plucked at my mind like mosquitoes buzzing against the glass. Hope battled with panic. Julius was gone, I reminded myself. I was free.

A soft twinkle lifted the corners of Don's eyes, luring me into their depths, offering the chance to join him in that most basic form of kink. "I'll monitor your reactions the whole time. Observe every twitch, gauge every breath, listen to the tone of each whimper."

Whimper? "I don't whimper."

Don smiled and grasped my wrists again, lighter this time, massaging my pulse with his thumb. "Oh, believe me. You will."

Hope won. "Okay, let's see how good you are, *Master* D!"

CHAPTER
TWENTY-THREE

How Still My Love

A SIGH of relief escaped when he led me upstairs. For some reason, I thought he meant to take me straight into the dungeon.

In the bedroom, Don shed all his clothes, repeating the same tendency to be neat I'd witnessed previously. He didn't expect a slave to follow around, picking up after him. Wearing only a pair of dark-blue boxers, he left the room, presumably to lock up for the night.

I put on his Aussie boxers and cleaned my teeth, taking my time, wondering whether I'd made a huge mistake. The sarcastic voice inside my head certainly thought so.

Finally, Don came into the bathroom and stood behind me, checking my reflection in the mirror. He must have sensed my apprehension. "Stop worrying, Steve. Remember, when I start something, you'll be in control the whole time. Any time you want me to stop, just say so. And if I think you're having difficulties, I'll put an end to proceedings whether you like it or not." He pressed his lips against the mouth of the snarling tiger on my back.

I spun around to face him. Concentrating on his brown eyes was much easier than witnessing the reflected version of the vulnerability in my own.

"Is that right?" I tried to sound cocky, but I had difficulty summoning my typical smartassed confidence when I wasn't in drag.

Don took my hand, led me into the bedroom, and eased me down onto my back. Then he placed his mouth right next to my ear. "There are times when I'll ignore you and times I won't. But any time we're having sex or doing something physical, you only have to say one word, and I'll stop. Understand?"

"Echidna," I muttered.

"Hmm." He eased his body away. "And what the fuck is an echidna?"

"It's…."

He ran his palm over my chest, down over the tented fabric of my boxers.

Yeah. "Like a…." Words proved difficult to find. "A porcupine, only bigger."

"Prickly, huh? Suits your personality."

Don's hand kept working its magic, playing with my tackle. He didn't seem to be in a rush to start anything. Maybe he didn't mean tonight. Perhaps he was planning to take me into the dungeon in the morning. I relaxed back into the mattress, content to surrender to his touch.

"I wonder what Aunty Mildred would say if she could see you wearing these." Don cupped his hand around the bottom of my balls, bringing the whole package up so it strained against the satiny material.

"Ugh. Remember to thank her for them, next time you see her."

"Will do."

"But if you keep doing *that*, I won't last five minutes."

"What? This?" He brought his mouth down and worked his way along the length of my cock, sucking through the material.

I arched back. The moist heat of his mouth through the satin nearly brought me to a climax then and there. "Yeah," I moaned in appreciation.

"You're that easy, are you?" Don teased, mouthing my cock through the fabric again.

"Mate, you have no idea. Once you get your mouth on my dick, I'm a goner."

"I bet you could last longer if you wanted to."

Not if last night was any indication. "Nope, five minutes, max."

"Let's be fair and make it thirty. I like the parallel."

He was joking, wasn't he? "You have this weird fascination for taking bets. Must be your Aussie heritage." My eyes rolled back as he gave my shaft a long, firm stroke. This was nothing like his previous rough hand job; this was perfection. "Okay, but what do I get if *I* win?"

"You get to fuck me."

I scrambled up onto my elbows and stared down at him. He gave me a seductive smile from under his eyelashes. Damn the man. I tried to remind myself I didn't like his moustache. It tickled. Made him look ridiculously out of fashion, but the only thing agreeing with this sentiment was my brain, and even that was having an argument with itself. "And... what... if you win?" I managed to grind out.

"You don't get to fuck me, but I get to fuck you."

"Again?" *What sort of penalty was that?*

"Yep."

My vision blurred. Every particle of my being seemed to be floating above the bed like a helium balloon; the only thing preventing me from drifting free was my brain. Forming sentences became an effort. "The other bet... I would have won... if that guy... hadn't interrupted."

"Correct." Don gave my shaft another stroke.

"But... why the money shot?" He returned to mouthing me through soaked material. Boy, talk about good. I was having trouble thinking, let alone speaking. "That was no way... to treat a... lady."

Don pulled back, and our gazes met. "I couldn't help myself. Like you said, I'd have come earlier if that jackass had kept quiet. You have a very talented mouth."

So did he.

Shit, all this conversation was distracting me. Or was that his plan? Draw the time out, so he would win. "You're not supposed to be talking," I reminded him.

He grinned. "Okay, but you can't use your hands either."

While he'd paused to speak to me, I'd given my cock a quick swipe to ease the pressure. I studied Don warily, but he'd gone back to lapping at the hard edge of my shaft, chasing it around inside my boxers. Come was already churning in my balls. Who cared? I wouldn't last long either way. "Fair enough, but to make sure I don't use my hands, I'll hang onto this." I grabbed the railings of the bed behind me. A quick memory surfaced of being chained in this position for hours at a time. The recollection vanished as quickly as it came when Don resumed sucking. Bliss. I relaxed and lost myself in the moment.

He stopped again.

"What the fuck is wrong now?"

Don sighed. "Let's see if I've got this right. You don't let go of the end of the bed, and I don't talk. Correct?"

I nodded.

"And if you don't come within half an hour, I win."

Huh? Somewhere along the way, the logic had been twisted, but I was too far gone to think straight. "Yeah, something like that."

Don continued speaking while rubbing his thumb up and down the material, using just enough pressure to move the skin on my cock. His voice was devoid of emotion, matter-of-fact, as if he were discussing which type of bread to buy. "But I can use *my* hands, because this is the opposite of the BJ in the Paradiso, isn't it? The aim is for *you* to come as quickly as possible." Without waiting for an answer, he pulled my boxers down so the waistband was lodged under my balls, bringing them up, ready for his attention. A featherlight touch of his tongue sent me arching off the bed again.

Don sat back on his haunches and grinned. "You let go."

"Of course I fucking let go. I nearly came."

Don slid off the bed and returned with the blue silk tie he'd worn to visit Aunt Mildred. "I won't do it up tight, but it might help you to hang on."

At least it would be more comfortable than bloody chains. "All right." I eyed him warily as he gave the tie a single twist around my wrists before attaching it to the brass railing. Could this be Don's solution? Test me out first with some playful kink. The sort even vanilla lovers do. I gave the tie a tentative tug.

"It's a quick-release knot. I can have it undone in a second."

Stop worrying. The bonds are a reminder, not a restraint. "Okay."

"Good. Remember, you can tell me to stop whenever you like."

Yep, we were definitely in a scene, but Don was disguising it as fun to distract me. Oh, what the heck? I should just lie back and enjoy it.

Don fondled my balls, weighing them in his hands. "Hmm, nice. I wonder how big they are compared to the eggs that fucking bird lays."

My eyes rolled back into my head. "We agreed.... Ugh.... No talking."

"We haven't started yet."

My knees jerked up as his touch became a tad firmer and more insistent. He pushed my leg back down. "Hm, I better restrain these as well."

Fuck it, I was nearly there again. I took a deep breath. Could I cope with more restrictions? It wouldn't be for long. I could do this. My body used to love being bound even if my brain didn't. "Do your worst, but untie me the minute I come. Got it?"

Don's smile disappeared, and there was no playfulness in his voice when he replied, "I promise," but immediately, the grin returned.

After glancing around the room, he crossed to the cupboard and pulled out a couple of terry-toweling bathrobes. Once my boxers were off, he looped the ties around each ankle before fastening them to the posts at the foot of the bed. I could still slide my feet along and escape if necessary. Good.

A drop of precome slid onto my stomach. In a way, Don was playing into my hands. Everything he'd done so far was working in my favor. Already, my cock was so hard a few seconds in his mouth would get me off. I stared at him. What else was going through his devious mind? "No cock and ball torture," I demanded.

"Wouldn't dream of it." Don eyed the jerk my cock gave with a raised eyebrow. "Another time, maybe," he muttered. He laughed when my cock twitched again.

"No cheating by walking away and leaving me here for half an hour." Like Julius would have, simply because he could.

Don's smile vanished. "Either my mouth or my hand will be on your cock at all times."

Another drop of liquid slid into my navel to be promptly lapped up. My back arched as I reacted to his touch. Damn, I loved it when he did that. Although they were loose, the restraints served their purpose, keeping me helpless. I moaned.

Don laughed, his white teeth gleaming. Without saying another word, he leaned down and started licking my slit, extracting all the come that hadn't dripped off.

My moans grew louder as he worked his way lower, taking my cock into his mouth bit by bit. My leg trembled. Immediately, the suction ceased, and the only contact was a slow lick up and down with just the tip of his tongue.

Fuck. Once again, Don had picked the exact moment to stop. Did I have traffic lights on my head or something? If so, they must have been stuck on bloody orange.

Another hard suck nearly made me come, and then another. I groaned. The man was a master of edge-play… *Master*…. Oh, damn. I shouldn't have thought of that word. No matter how much being bound turned me on, that was what it all came down to in the end, wasn't it? Ownership. Control. Manipulating how much I could move. Restricting my freedom.

Ghostly screams echoed in my head, rattling my brain, bringing with them memories of being chained to the bed for hours, sometimes for days on end, lying in my own piss.

Even worse, Julius beating me after a violent fucking when crap had dribbled out and stained the sheets. I jerked my leg restlessly. The rope tightened. Blood pounded through my veins as I tried to escape.

"*Noooo!*"

CHAPTER
+++
TWENTY-FOUR

Stop Dragging My Heart Around

THROUGH the jumbled nightmare of images and sounds from my past, I heard a quiet but firm voice saying, "Stop panicking, Steve. I'm releasing you now."

Putrid bile surged up from my gut. "Need to...."

"I know." Just as I started to heave, miraculously, I was free.

I swung my legs over the edge of the bed and buried my head in my hands. My fingertips tingled as if someone was sticking needles into them. Vaguely, I became aware of a bathrobe being draped over my shoulders and someone sitting next to me, hugging the scratchy material close but, thankfully, not too close.

Still, the shakes continued. My teeth were now chattering like castanets, and breathing became difficult. This wasn't a nightmare; I was really here. Back where so much shit had gone down. I shut my eyes to divorce myself from the reality of my surroundings. A man was talking to me, but his words made no impression or sense.

Gradually the calm, even tones penetrated the mess in my mind. Don's American accent helped. "You're okay, Steven. Breathe deeply. In.... Out."

This might be the same place, but it was a different time, a different man. A feeling of *déjà vu* descended. My skin felt as cold and clammy as it had been on the night we met.

Don didn't restrain me as I scrambled off the bed. Sliding my hands into the robe's sleeves, I staggered into the bathroom. Thank God someone had purchased more mouthwash. I swilled some around and spat into the sink, gripping the porcelain edge with white-knuckled tension. A few more deep breaths and I was able to look at myself in the mirror. Bad idea. Splashing warm water on my face removed some of the chill but didn't do much for the ice inside. I accepted Don's proffered towel without comment. The contrast between the sexual high I'd been drifting on and the sudden descent into darkness had startled him as much as it had me. I pulled the open edges of the robe together. No fucking belt. Oh, that's right. They were the bloody problem in the first place. A shudder ran down my spine.

"Aargh," I yelled, venting my frustration. "Go away." When would I ever be free of these damn fears?

"I'm not going anywhere."

"No! Not you." I grabbed Don's arm. He didn't show any signs of moving, but I'd never been so grateful for the solidity of his presence, reminding me of the here and now. "These bloody memories. I want to be able to do these things, but I… just… can't…."

Don rested his hand on my shoulder, pressing hard enough to anchor me. "So I gather. Don't worry. I have you now."

I rubbed my wrists, trying to erase the memories the bonds had triggered. Fortunately, the restraints hadn't been tight enough to leave a mark. Nothing external, anyway.

After a couple of minutes, Don took my hand. "Come on. We can't stay in here all night."

Shuffling along the corridor under Don's guidance, I felt like a hospital patient, except for the fact that I wasn't wearing slippers. Gabriel was standing outside our room, his face nearly as white as mine.

"Need any help?" he asked.

"No, but thanks anyway." Don waved Gabriel away. "I'll be able to manage."

With a tentative smile in my direction, Gabriel disappeared into his room.

191

I thought we were going into our bedroom, but Don placed his hand on the small of my back, guiding me into the kitchen.

Pulling the robe around me, I sat on a stool and watched as Don dragged all the ingredients out of the cupboard and made me a hot chocolate. Somewhere along the way, he had put on the other dressing gown. What a pair we made. Sexy, *not*.

"Thanks." I accepted the mug from his hands and took a sip. He must have ladled in at least three spoonfuls of sugar. "Trying to sweeten me up, Sunshine?"

Don gave a wry grin and perched on the stool beside me. "It'll warm you up. Plus it's the best thing for shock."

Shock. Yeah. That was one word for it. "Sorry. I don't know why I reacted like that."

After taking a long sip from his mug, Don rested his hand on my thigh, giving it a small squeeze. "I'm the one who should be apologizing. It looks like whatever treatment you underwent placed a scab over the problem, but, deep down, there must be festering remnants."

"But I knew I had nothing to fear from you."

"Not the point. The trouble is that when scenes become intense, your unconscious mind can take over, allowing suppressed fears to escape." Don took a deep breath. "No, I fucked up, big time, Steve. I should have made sure you were truly ready."

The poor guy looked nearly as shaken as I felt. "It's not your fault. Everything was going so well, and after what you said, I thought it was worth taking a chance." I tightened the robe around me. At least Don's thigh pressing against mine felt warm.

"Is there anything you should be taking? Valium? An antidepressant?"

"The doctor tried me on a few things, but nothing actually prevented them." I shrugged. "For some reason, they don't work for me."

Don let out a deep sigh. "I can't believe you didn't tell me that you get panic attacks. Is there anything else you failed to mention? Epilepsy? Migraines?"

"No."

Don's fingers shook as he rubbed them through his hair. "I'm too used to dealing with people in the scene. I should have checked that there were no medical problems. I'm slipping."

It hurt to see him so upset. "I haven't had an episode in ages."

Neither of us spoke as we drank our chocolates. Don seemed preoccupied by something. Eventually, he placed his empty mug down and wrapped his hand around my wrist, checking my pulse rate. It was back to normal. "What I can't understand is why you agreed to be tied up if bondage freaks you out so much?"

Because I want to see if I can become involved in the scene again! Then I wouldn't have to leave. The silly thing was that, now I was out of the bedroom, my fears seemed irrational. Don wasn't Julius. "It wasn't the *feeling* of being bound, more the other shit. Worry about being left alone. Not being able to move." I mumbled the words into my mug, trying to hide the lump in my throat. "Sorry for flipping out on you like that."

"No. My fault. I didn't realize how badly you would react."

"Yeah, well, I didn't think. I guess my cock was ruling my head."

"Bullshit. That's half your problem. You never *stop* thinking. I tried to keep your mind focused on other things, and for a while there I thought you were enjoying it. But something happened, and you lost it."

Lost it. Lost him. I took another sip. How the fuck did Don manage to break down so many of the barriers I'd erected against men in leather? He wasn't that good looking. He wasn't tall or even my type, yet part of me ached at my inability to let go and surrender to him.

"You're doing it now."

I glanced up and caught a look of exasperation crossing his face.

"Doing what?"

"Your brain is churning with thoughts, but they can't get out, or you won't let them."

For good reason, Sunshine. "Why should I?"

"Because by sharing your thoughts, you might actually avoid getting into sticky situations."

"Are you saying I should have talked to Julius more?"

"Yes. Of course you should have. But let's leave Julius out of this for the moment."

I snorted at hearing my own statement reflected back at me but remained silent.

"If you don't let me know what you're thinking, how am I going to understand what your problem is?"

Problem? Falling for him was my problem. "What if I'm keeping my lips zipped because I don't want to expose the weakness inside?"

Don's eyebrows rose in astonishment. "Weak? Who's weak? You're certainly not. Being submissive doesn't equate with being weak. Far from it. It takes a lot of guts to give up control." His thumb started massaging my wrist, soothing the panic that had begun to escalate. "You're not weak, Steve," he repeated more softly. "Think of it as turning over your strength, your power, in exchange for the feeling of happiness and security that can be achieved in return. The more you can give, the more you should get back in an equal trade."

I sighed and shut my eyes, imagining that hand caressing skin he'd set on fire. Flogger? Crop? His palm? I'd let him use any. All. And if I did, how much could I get back in return? Happiness? Ecstasy? Don was waiting for me to *share my thoughts*. Shit, this was much worse than the whip. "Do you know what scares the fucking shit out of me?" I opened my eyes, but unshed tears made my vision blurry. "The thought that if I ever got over my fears and ventured back into the BDSM scene, I would be making the same damn mistake."

The gentle massage ceased, but Don didn't let go. Between his hand on my wrist and the other loosely resting on my thigh, I felt bound to him tighter than ropes. I stared blearily at the two points of contact and wondered why that thought didn't freak me out.

Don's quiet question startled me out of my contemplation. "Is that how you see what happened with Julius? A mistake?"

I stared at him in horror. "Of course it was. The biggest bloody mistake of my life."

Don's expression hadn't changed since we'd started talking. I detected concern in his eyes but no trace of condemnation. He heaved a deep sigh. "Yet you are the man you are now because of that so-called mistake."

"Sorry, Sunshine, you've lost me there."

"Nobody should have to put up with a lifetime of being held against their wish, but by refusing to succumb to his abusive treatment, you became strong, like a sword does when it's tempered by fire. In the process, you learned a lot about yourself and about others. I admit I didn't know you before you met Julius or what you were like with him, but the man I'm getting to know harbors a lot of compassion." Don gripped my thigh tighter. "Even if he does try to hide it under a tough, shiny exterior."

"Yes, *Doctor.*"

A tiny shake of his head was the only reaction. No smile. No frown. Had I overstepped the boundary again? Me and my sass.

Gripping the front of my robe, Don pulled me closer and kissed me.

Wow. That was sure different from the hairbrush. The last remaining niggling fears fled from my brain. By the time Don released me, my pulse was beating too rapidly again, but in a good way. "You should bottle those kisses. You'd make a fortune."

The smile warmed his eyes. "How do you feel now?"

"Much better, thank you, nurse."

"Do you want another hot chocolate?"

"How about a good fuck? That works just as well, and it's much kinder on my waistline."

Don chuckled. "You and your shiny armor."

When it came time to get into the bed, I couldn't.

I stood staring at the crumpled sheets. Don came up behind me, his moustache nuzzling the back of my neck as he guided me forward until my knees touched the mattress. "I could bend you over and fuck you here, but you'd be much more comfortable lying down." He snaked his hand under the opening of my robe, easing it off my shoulders. "On your front."

I did as I was told and didn't move while Don knelt above me, kneading my shoulders. Okay, a massage would work too. After a few minutes, all the tension drained from my body, leaving me a boneless wreck in its wake.

A wet tongue traced down the curve of the dragon's tail, followed by the swirl made by the two bodies, ending with the tiger's tail at the apex of my butt.

I groaned.

Don's finger followed the path lower, easing my ass cheeks apart. Cool moisture replaced the finger as his tongue took over again, licking around my hole before forcing its way inside.

Thank God he wasn't in a hurry. By the time Don started to add a finger into the mix, opening me up gradually, I was ready to go again. Taking some of the weight onto my elbows to grant him better access, I arched my back and silently begged him to fuck me.

A couple of slaps on each butt cheek had my cock dripping precome onto the bed. My final moaned plea of "Fuck me, damn you" was answered by a quick application of lube and the unmistakable sound of a condom wrapper being opened. I groaned as his sheathed cock slipped inside, but this time there was no pain.

Last night the urge to possess had taken precedence, but I'd been wondering what Don would be like when he took his time fucking. Some things were worth waiting for.

Since I'd left Julius, a couple of random fucks had hit the *not bad* mark, but they varied a lot. Some were aggressive, and you felt like they had something to prove, with lots of slaps on the ass and "Fuck, yeahs." Others were silent, so deeply lost in their own headspace, you wondered whether they were even aware of whose hole they were fucking.

Don was different again.

He never actually said words, but with his succession of growls—never grunts—it was like being in bed with a tiger. Each snarl matched the intensity of his movements. He worked my ass like he owned it, and every time he pulled back, I clenched my muscles in appreciation, not wanting him to escape. That only earned me a deeper response and faster fucking. Pretty soon, it was me voicing my approval of what he was doing. He'd wanted me to be honest and tell him how I felt. I'm not sure what I was babbling; I just let him know whenever he touched that magic point inside. As soon as I did, all his attention switched to there, and after a while, I wished I hadn't, as he hit the spot over and over again.

Tingles started in my toes, and it wasn't chills swirling around my body but little spasms of energy. I collapsed onto one elbow and frantically tugged at my cock.

"Now."

One word. That was all I was waiting for. Everything went off as we both came, like those pyrotechnics on New Year's Eve when five different kinds of fireworks explode at different heights all at the same time. One massive *kaboom*.

"Shh."

Maybe I screamed. My throat sure felt like I had, but I didn't recall making a sound.

After cleaning up, Don took care of me as if we'd finished a heavy scene, holding me in his arms, soothing me, praising me for doing so well. My skin wasn't red raw from a beating, but my heart certainly was.

CHAPTER
✛✛✛
TWENTY-FIVE

Outside the Rain

WHEN I woke, the first thing I became aware of was the steady thrum of rain against the windowpane. The view might be spectacular, but the big drawback of living in such an exposed position was southerly gales bringing half the ocean with them.

I lay sprawled out, almost covering Don, my head on his chest.

Hot chocolate and pre-sleep sex had done the trick, as had the proximity of his warm body. I glanced up to see if he was awake. He was, and something was annoying him. His brows were drawn together, giving him an expression as dark as the sky outside. "What's wrong?" I drew away slightly. "Am I squashing you?"

"No." He gave me a brief hug, drawing me closer. "I was just thinking."

"About what?"

"Julius."

I leaned up on one elbow so I could see him better. "Anything specific?"

"How my opinion of him has changed over time."

"And…." I prompted. It was strange, seeing him so upset about something.

Don gave a squeeze of reassurance, as if appreciating my concern. "When we met, my initial reaction was sympathy. Hearing tales of his slave who didn't cut it because he was weak. A coward. But then I met *you*, and nothing added up. Even when you wear a dress, you're strong. Fearless." Don sighed. "That made me question my feelings toward the man. After learning of the accident, I was angry at first because he took Alex out on the Harley without permission, but I figured he'd paid the ultimate price. Then after hearing of their affair, I was more concerned about my failure to meet Alex's needs than pissed off at the man who caused his death." Don paused and gave a snort of disgust. "Now, seeing you too afraid to enter a dungeon you obviously love and then panicking last night, it's lucky Julius is dead, or I might be tempted to kill him myself." His mouth closed into a thin white line.

"Why?" The intensity of his glare surprised me. He usually managed to keep a tight rein on his emotions.

"Because of the damage he did to you."

I flinched at the venom in Don's voice but relaxed as he drew me back into a close embrace, his fingers tracing the raised scars left by Julius's whip. The tattoo hid them effectively. Saved awkward questions when I went swimming.

His anger disappeared, to be replaced by a gravelly rumble. "I'm not just referring to the psychological damage. Scars like these are meant to be worn with pride, not hidden. That alone should have told me everything I needed to know."

I remained silent, content to let his caress cleanse away the hurt.

After a while, he said, "What shits me is that I didn't realize what Julius was really like. He must have been on his best behavior around me."

Yeah, but whenever he had Alex to himself, Julius would have undermined Don's authority every chance he got. I didn't want to remind Don of Alex, though, so I kept my suspicions to myself. "The therapist said that, from what I told her, Julius must have had a narcissistic personality."

"Could be. There's no denying the fact that certain personality types are drawn to BDSM. That's why it's important to control the scene or at least have people around who can keep an eye on things." Don flipped me over so he could see what he was doing. I'd never had anyone pay so much attention to my tattoo before. You'd think he was the tattoo artist himself, recreating every line, paying attention to detail. Warm breath caressed my back as he murmured, half to himself, "It's strange. Tigers and whips always remind me of those old-fashioned ring circuses. Terrible things. At least humans have a choice whether they submit or not. You *are* a tiger, but Julius cut the tendons at the back of your knees. Yes, you could snarl and bare your teeth, but you couldn't fight back. I think Julius feared you would leave him. That's why he collared you. Not because you both got off on the relationship."

Don pulled me up level, allowing me to see the raw emotion in his face and witness the truth of his words as he continued, "That's why I can never forgive him. His selfishness and stupidity stopped you from enjoying what should be a rich and rewarding experience for both parties: the kink, the mastery, the full experience of leather."

The unspoken message was: "any chance of being involved with him." I couldn't imagine Don having a lover who didn't participate at that level. The watery gloom seemed to creep inside.

For a moment, I thought Don was going to kiss me again, but instead, a veil fell over his eyes—sternness replacing sympathy. Almost brusquely, he rolled out of bed, saying, "Where's that boy? He should be up by now."

I knew the man well enough to understand he was upset but hiding it under typical Master behavior.

"Any chance of a cup of coffee, Sunshine?" I could fake a 'tude with the best of them.

Don turned and scowled at me for a second, then seemed to calm down. "Okay. I suppose you want frothy stuff on top."

"Yes, please, *Sir*." I drawled the last word and blew him my best Stevie air kiss.

After he left, I lay back in the bed thinking about what he'd said. In a weird way, instead of hating Julius, I was starting to pity him. He would have been devastated to lose the respect of someone like Don. But last night's disastrous experiment proved one thing: having to witness Don and Gabriel in action would only emphasize what I was missing.

Missing? Steven Lindsey Stanhope, the sooner you stop thinking with your cock, the better.

Shit! My ghostly twin from the meditation room must have snuck inside when I wasn't looking. But he was right. I had to leave before I reached the end of the slippery slope. Don's words, and the way he'd made love to me last night, meant I was nearly there.

Judging by the gurgling noises, he had finally worked out how to use the cappuccino machine. I breathed in, sucking the welcome aroma deep into my lungs. It was as good as a vitamin shot.

I didn't follow him into the kitchen immediately. I hadn't heard any voices, but that didn't mean Gabriel wasn't in there. After last night's fiasco, I'd been dreading having to meet the pity in the young man's eyes. He wasn't a bad kid, really. He deserved to be taught by someone who knew what he was doing. I might have hated being a slave, but that didn't mean I should prevent Gabriel from becoming one. I just didn't want to watch Don collar him.

When I arrived, Don was alone, reading the *Herald*.

"Where's Gabriel?" I asked.

"Researching a discussion on Fetlife about Consent and Non-Consent in a Power Exchange."

He should have consulted me. I was an expert on the subject.

Don put down the paper and pushed over a packet with grease stains on the outside. "He went out earlier and bought a newspaper and croissants. Want one?"

"Thanks." I chewed the buttery pastry, gaining an instant energy hit. The coffee helped too. I took a deep breath. Damn, this was difficult. "I've been thinking."

I waited, expecting a reaction, but Don kept his attention glued to whatever he was reading—the weather page, by the look of it.

The food turned into a solid ball as I swallowed. The words were proving harder to say than I would have imagined. "I need to leave here."

"Yup." Don's gaze didn't shift from the paper.

"After last night, you *still* want me to go?" I swung around on the stool, ready to storm out of the room. It was one thing for me to *decide* to leave, but another for him to *want* me to. That hurt.

Before I could get far, Don's hand shot out, trapping my wrist. Shit. I knew he was strong but not that strong.

"Sit."

He'd never used that tone of voice on me before. There was no way I could disobey. I sank back onto the stool and glared at him. He was upset, but I didn't think he was actually angry. At least not with me.

"I don't *want* you to leave, but I think you *should*. At least for a while."

"Why?" I knew why I had to go, but I was curious why he wanted me out of the way. Did he want time alone with Gabriel? The thought of the two of them together made me want to puke.

He took a deep breath, and his moustache quivered with the exhalation. "Forget all that crap last night. You still have to decide what you want to do about the will and the house."

Oh, right. The will. I'd been trying *not* to think about that. Don hadn't released his grip, but the tension slackened. I could have broken free if I wanted to, but I didn't want to break the connection.

"If you stay here, I will always wonder whether I influenced you too much. Sex can be a powerful motivator."

"We don't have to…."

Don's eyebrows rose. I looked down. Shit. Hard dicks don't lie. He let go of my wrist and rubbed my thigh, smiling into my eyes, teasing me. "It's not a question of having to; it's a question of us both always wanting to."

I started to make a smartass comment about speaking for himself, but stopped. *See, he thinks you've been thinking with your cock too!* Damn it, the man was right as usual. "How long do you want me to go for?"

Don didn't answer immediately, making a big production of sweeping up the pastry crumbs into a pile. "As long as it takes. You spoke once about how Gabriel should leave home and make his own choices. I think you need to do the same. Whatever your decision is, it needs to be one you've made yourself. Without me influencing you in any way."

Rain pelted horizontally against the glass. I had wet weather gear, but the saddlebags on the bike weren't a hundred percent waterproof. "I can't leave until my bike is fixed."

"Correct." Don flicked the paper with his finger. "The rain is supposed to clear by tonight. Tomorrow should be sunny. If we work on the bike together, it should be ready by then."

I smiled inside. One part of Don would always want to be the man in charge.

The only problem was, now I knew I was leaving, every instinct inside rebelled at the thought. "Whatever you say, *Master*."

Don whacked me over the knuckles with the rolled-up newspaper.

AS SOON as he finished breakfast, Don borrowed Gabriel's car but didn't tell me where he was going. I started working on the disassembled BMW and was soon surrounded by more bits and pieces. Hopefully, by the time I finished, there wouldn't be any screws left over.

Not long after Don left, Gabriel came down to watch me. He didn't seem at ease in my company, and I wondered how much he'd heard last night. His bedroom was next to the kitchen, and the walls weren't exactly soundproof.

I was replacing the hoses on the coolant tank when Don returned with two new tires for the BMW.

"Wow, thanks." I'd been wondering how I was going to get them. "But I don't have that much cash on me. I'll give you what I have and send you the rest." I clambered to my feet, ready to head upstairs to get my wallet.

Don grabbed my arm. "Consider it a gift." He didn't say so, but I got the impression this was some sort of apology for last night. "Anyway, I'll sleep better knowing that you have a decent set of wheels under you."

"No way. You're not made of money. Give me your bank details so I can transfer the money into your account." A staring match erupted, but Don wasn't responsible for me or for last night's fiasco.

"Stubborn mule."

"Hee haw."

Don snorted. "We'll sort out who pays for what later. In the meantime, fixing the bike is top priority. I'm going to get changed. Try not to wreck anything before I get back."

"Yeah, slip into something more comfortable. You'd look cute in a black negligee."

"Not as good as you."

As he left to go upstairs, I noticed Gabriel grinning.

"What are you laughing at?"

"You two crack me up."

Don's return prevented me from putting the kid in a headlock and teaching him to respect his elders.

Thirty minutes spent listening to us rave about metric versus imperial screws and bolts and which wrenches were best proved to be Gabriel's limit. He yawned ostentatiously. "I'm going to play a computer game."

Don gave him a dirty look. "This isn't an all-expenses-paid holiday, boy. If you've finished checking those discussions on Master and slave relationships, you can hook up the stereo system and the television to the PC. All the gear is stacked in those boxes in the library."

"Yes, Sir…. Sorry, Sir." Gabriel accepted the rebuke and scurried upstairs.

Instead of cringing at the formal mode of address, I accepted the words for what they were, an acknowledgement of their respective positions. Neither term would ever apply to me.

A comfortable silence descended, broken only by the predictable "ouchs" and "damns" as we scraped knuckles, struggling with tight bolts.

It didn't take long to recognize an expert. Compared to him, Julius and I were rank amateurs. "How come you know so much about BMWs? Most Harley riders tend to think anything else barely qualifies as a motorcycle."

Don tightened the screws on the reservoir after flushing and bleeding the brakes. "Dad owned a garage, so I grew up among all sorts of bikes in his workshop." Don held out his hands, turning them over, showing me the scars on his palms and rubbing at his grease-stained fingernails. "Over the years, I must have used bucket-loads of orange degreaser, and as for my nails, at times I feel like a fucking manicurist."

"As long as you don't fuck a manicurist, *dahling*. Unless he's male, of course."

We concentrated on our own tasks, and apart from the odd request to pass the screwdriver, or getting a second opinion on things he wasn't familiar with, we worked in silence until Gabriel brought down a couple of beers and some salad rolls for lunch.

The alcohol must have loosened my tongue, because after we finished eating and Gabriel disappeared upstairs again, I found myself telling Don about the different times Julius and I had worked on our bikes together. That, in turn, prompted a tale about how he and Julius had wrenched on Don's bike back in the States, comparing modifications and boasting about which was best. He'd been staring at Julius's Harley as he told me the tale. The make and model might be the same, but it would never be as good as the one he'd owned.

"Yeah," I said. "Only people who have owned bikes know how attached you get."

Don started and blinked. "It's like a third person died that day. And I can't get rid of this stupid guilt trip that my bike let them down at a critical moment."

I grabbed his hand, crushing it in both of mine. "Don't you dare think like that. Julius was a good rider, but so many factors could have contributed to the accident. It wasn't his bike, so he wouldn't have been as aware of its quirks. He might have been showing off to Alex. And as you said, they weren't wearing helmets." A shadow still lingered in Don's eyes. Damn, I wasn't the only one haunted by ghosts. "Hey," I said to change the subject. "Whadda ya think of the German skullcap helmets that are all the rage?"

The bleak expression vanished, to be replaced by one of disgust. "Best use of them would be as a pisspot."

I laughed.

Don stroked a grease-stained finger around the edge of my mouth.

"Not as good as lippy, *dahl*." I pretended to lick the gunk off. "Does it come in caramel flavor too?"

A slight smirk was the only response I got. Don's voice sank to a reflective murmur as he continued to trace a pattern around the edge of my lips. "Maybe I went overboard this morning, saying I wanted to wring Julius's neck for hurting you." He sighed and gave an ironic laugh. "Nah, the thing that pisses me off is that he also robbed me of the ability to beat the shit out of you and fuck you afterward."

Any sane person would cringe at the idea, but part of me wanted the same thing. Ached for it. "If Julius hadn't taken the bike out that day, we wouldn't be talking here now."

"True." Don leaned in and pressed his lips against mine, his tongue demanding entry. As soon as I capitulated, he drew back and sighed. "I suppose I should be thankful for that."

"Do you still miss him?"

"Who? Alex?"

"Yeah."

"I probably always will. Not only did I love him, but no matter how long it lasts, a genuine Master/slave bond doesn't end when someone dies or leaves. There will always be a gap that can only be filled by that person and their own unique brand of submission."

I didn't say anything and went back to tapping the dirt out of the air filter. I couldn't identify with that statement because, in truth, neither Julius nor I ever fulfilled those roles. Not in the true meaning of the words. "Did Alex ever say why he hooked up with Julius?"

"He said he got bored."

Bored? I glanced up at the bitter undertone threading through Don's words.

"I'd been busy at work, trying to make ends meet, accepting landscaping contracts that were on the other side of town, which meant I was often on the road early and wouldn't arrive back until late at night. Alex was left alone a lot, so when Julius needed a place to stay for a few months, I thought he'd be good company."

"You make Alex sound like a fucking pet that needed minding." I couldn't help the spark of jealousy arising. As long as I had freedom of movement, I used to love being by myself while Julius went to his day job. "If he hated being left behind, why didn't he go out on the job with you?"

"Live-in Master/slave arrangements are hard enough to handle. Having Alex as part of my work crew as well would have been impossible."

I tried to picture how a Joe Blow off the street would react. "I suppose you're right. Time-wise, which came first? Your involvement in the S and M leather scene or marriage?"

Don winced when I used the other M word. "S and M. I was dead set against making our Master/slave relationship twenty-four-seven, but Alex kept pestering me to try, and I'd thought we'd succeeded." He let out a deep sigh. "I suppose there's a bit of an actor in all of us if we want to make a relationship work."

"What I find really weird is that Alex doesn't sound the type to be unfaithful."

"In all honesty, I don't think he saw it that way. We needed a change of some sort. Things weren't looking rosy on the business front, and Alex saw this as an opportunity for me as much as for him. I think he had some starry-eyed notion that, when we got to Australia, we could have some kind of threesome, with him serving us both."

"You and Julius living in the same house? You gotta be kidding."

"Why? We got on okay while he was staying with us."

"Only because he was on his best behavior. Come on, tell the truth. Would it have worked?"

Don gave a wry smile. "I doubt it. Two slaves can serve one master, but I've never heard of one slave with two Dominants unless the latter are lovers. Too much competition."

Competition? Julius wouldn't have regarded Don as a threat, simply because he picked up after himself and didn't expect anyone to kowtow to him. "Anyway...." I added, remembering Gabriel's presence in the house, "threesomes never work. Someone always feels left out." I dropped the conversation like a hot potato.

By the time we finished changing the tires, greasing chains, lubing cables, and even replacing the fork oil, my BMW sounded as good as new.

"Yay." We exchanged high fives as the familiar roar reverberated around the garage. Outside, the rain was still falling steadily, so Don wouldn't let me do more than a slow circle around the yard. Everything seemed to be fine.

When I dismounted, it was difficult to keep my tears from showing. "Thank you. I'd never have been able to do all that by myself."

"You're welcome." Don wiped his hands on a rag. "I better check on the boy and make sure he hasn't got his wires crossed."

I scrubbed my face with the back of my hand and took a deep breath. "You could stay and help me clean it, *dahling*."

Don grinned and rubbed more dirt onto my face. "Wouldn't dream of depriving you of the pleasure, *sweetie*."

His delivery would have done a drag queen proud.

I didn't mind being left alone to do the task. It gave me a chance to check the bike over closely and make sure everything was functioning perfectly. It also gave me time to think about another difference between the two men.

Julius believed a slave had no skills or ideas to contribute, whereas Don didn't feel it lessened his position to delegate tasks he knew I could do better. And that didn't mean merely cleaning the bike. Don didn't expect me to wait on him hand and foot, but neither did he treat me like a useless plaything. Paradoxically, that only made him stronger in my eyes. Leaving was proving to be more difficult than I ever dreamed it would be.

Most of the dirt from the bike seemed to have transferred itself onto my skin. After clearing up downstairs, I had a quick shower and went to see what the other two were doing.

CHAPTER
+++
TWENTY-SIX

Ghosts

IN MY absence, the library had been transformed into an entertainment area. The large flat-screen TV and sundry set-top boxes graced one wall, while the stereo equipment and surround-sound speakers were now interspersed between the empty bookcases. To reduce clutter, cables had been fed through camouflaged holes in the separating walls. Gabriel was busy connecting everything up to the computer in the office.

Sitting cross-legged on the floor with my back to the shelves, I watched Don sort through the boxes of books that had been stashed in the garage while we painted. There was purpose in every move he made, dusting each copy before deciding where to put it. The Koel was taking over the nest.

"I gather Julius took doing-it-by-the-book to extremes." Don extracted Julius's cherished copy of *Mr. Benson* and placed it alongside other classics. He seemed bemused by the extent of Julius's collection, mostly titles from the seventies, imported from overseas, as they weren't available in bookshops here.

"Are you saying they're wrong?"

"No, but *Mr. Benson* was never meant to be taken literally. The writings of Bean, Baldwin, and Magister are reliable, but they have to be understood in the context of what was going on in the scene at the time." Don sighed. "The world was a different place back then." He

209

picked up a copy of *Carried Away*. "Perhaps Julius should have read this book more closely. The characters discuss how difficult it is to keep up a Master and slave relationship twenty-four-seven."

"Well, why did you do it with Alex?"

Don flushed. "I figured that because I was aware of the dangers, I'd be able to avoid them." He handed me the copy. "Sometimes we only see what we want to see."

I studied the drawing on the cover and snorted to myself. Don was the spitting image of the leather-clad Master. But that wasn't what he'd been referring to. "Julius was a great one for selective reading too." I sighed and handed him the book. "He was more interested in what slaves should be like than how *he* was supposed to behave. Every time I disagreed with him, I wasn't showing sufficient respect. And he hit the roof if I thought one of his commands was funny or gave him a bit of sass. I think that's what drew me into drag. I loved the irreverence, their ability to take the piss without fear of reprisal."

"Yet you chose to portray a singer not noted for her aggression."

I shrugged. "My choice was based more on what I looked like when dressed for the part. I don't have the height to carry off the glamour queen roles. Plus, the flowing dresses and sleeves hide my tattoos."

Don leaned back against the shelves, tapping the book against his palm, much like he did when carrying his whip. "So, let me get this straight," he said, his gaze fixed on mine, refusing to let me retreat now we'd reached another level of understanding. "You and Julius were fine together when it was just BDSM?"

Bittersweet memories flooded back, bringing a lump to my throat. "Yeah. Being tied up and fucked was a real turn-on. I loved the flogger and even the whip, but then Julius started pushing me more and more, trying to mold me into something *he* wanted. That's when it all started to unravel. We were like two gamblers who thought that because we'd poured so much money into the pokies we only needed a little more and then we'd hit the jackpot, but the goal was always just out of reach. Our scenes would be proceeding well, and then, wham, we'd lose the plot. Either I'd lose my concentration and start thinking about what to cook for dinner, or Julius would get bored."

Don stacked all the Larry Townsend books together. "Your main problem was that you were trying to live up to someone else's ideals instead of doing what comes naturally. Lots of gay and straight couples make the same mistake and end up being miserable as hell. Who cares what your relationship is like? As long as it works."

Tell me about it! "All I know is that we were fine until he started introducing Master and slave into the mix."

"Master and slave?" Don slammed another book into place with a vicious shove. "Not all those relationships are bad. You seem to be hung up on the words themselves, but they're only labels. Before Alex and I got together, I would take on anyone who was prepared to accept whatever I wanted to dish out. Or whatever I felt they needed. I didn't care what they called themselves: Top, bottom, switch, whatever. My only stipulation was that they had to consent to me treating them however I wanted. If they didn't want to come back for more, I counted that as a failure on my part. Call me a greenie if you like; I believe in recycling, not discarding. The most important thing was that we *both* got off on the interaction. What's between our legs told us if it was working or not."

The conviction in Don's voice made my cock stand up and take notice. I hunkered down, lost in my memories, lamenting the might-have-beens.

After a while, he asked quietly, "Why didn't you bail earlier if you didn't enjoy submitting to Julius?"

Good question. The trouble was I'd never been able to pinpoint the exact time when everything changed. When fun turned to fear. My therapist hadn't understood my answer when she asked the same question.

The absence of sound made me glance up. Don had stopped sorting the books and was waiting for my reply. Maybe he *would* understand. He'd sold his business and moved to another country to make his slave happy. "Faced with a choice of splitting up or acting the role, which would you choose? I tried to be what Julius wanted. I could see how much it meant to him, and...." I shrugged. What could I say? "I loved the guy. Simple as that. I would have done anything for him, but I was always so tired. No matter how much I gave, it was never

211

enough." My voice sank to no more than a whisper. "He made me feel such a failure."

Don rested his hand on my shoulder, comforting me as my calm threatened to break. "Handing over all your power to someone else is a rare gift. You were always going to feel resentful if you had to give up something you value—your freedom—and received nothing of equal or greater value in return. It didn't help that you weren't honest about your needs, so they were never going to be met."

Hearing the truth hurt as much as a single-tail whip. I couldn't meet his gaze. The sympathy in Don's voice was bad enough. *Honesty.* That was one point where he agreed with my therapist. Was I being honest now? I'd told Don I wanted to leave as soon as the rain stopped, but all the time I was hoping he'd ask me to stay.

The door to the library opened.

For once, I was happy to see Gabriel. This conversation was simply making me realize what I'd missed out on.

"I've finished setting up the network and loaded Skype. Now you can chat to your friends in the States." The young man's face brimmed with enthusiasm, which made me suddenly feel old. "Wow, look at all those books." He stared around in amazement. Bypassing the well-thumbed porn magazines, he headed straight for the bookcase and took down title after title. I met Don's gaze and raised my eyebrows.

"Boy, although we're not in a formal relationship, is that the correct way to enter a room?" Don drew himself up. The cloak of Mastery settled onto his shoulders.

With his face aflame, Gabriel hastily replaced the books and stood quietly, head bowed respectfully, hands clasped behind his back.

I sighed and rose to my feet. As I shut the door behind me, I heard Don say, "This room is off limits unless I give you permission to enter. Do you understand, boy?"

"Yes, Sir."

THE rest of that day would always remain in my memory as surreal. Don tried not to take on the role of decision-maker, but he couldn't help himself, supervising every aspect of my trip. He'd even purchased a map when he bought the tires. Once he knew the route I'd be taking, he plotted how far I could get on each tank of gas and where I should stay for the night. Possibly, it was his way of doing the trip with me.

When it was finally time for bed, Don made love to me so tenderly I nearly cried.

In the middle of the night, the damn Koel started up again. I lay there for a while, listening to its call and wondering whether I'd miss it too.

CHAPTER
+++
TWENTY-SEVEN

Gypsy

"HAVE you got everything?"

"Yes, *Daddy*." I gave Don a smirk. "Stop nagging. I feel like a kid going off to boarding school." I'd eventually managed to grab a few hours of sleep, but, two cups of coffee later, I still wasn't firing on all cylinders. Don had tried to make me eat breakfast, but I'd refused, figuring I could get something on the way. Besides, I was getting hot because I was wearing my leathers.

The saddlebags were jammed full. Working out what to take and what to leave behind had been a challenge. The more I took, the worse my fuel consumption would be. The problem was that I didn't know how long I'd be gone. Days? Weeks? Years?

I swung my leg over the seat and straddled the BMW. The bike felt a lot heavier, but still not as heavy as the Harley.

"Wait a sec." Don disappeared upstairs.

Gabriel passed him on the way down. I grinned at the young man's serious expression. "Cheer up, kid. I thought you'd be happy to see the back of me."

"Not really. Now I'll have to do all the cooking." Gabriel gave a wry smile.

"Try not to wreck all the saucepans."

"I've only burnt something once!"

"Yeah, I know." I'd spent some time teaching him the basics. "And don't forget to wear the apron. You gotta look the part."

Gabriel's sour expression made me laugh. He stood there for a while, scuffing his foot on the ground. Why did I suddenly have a weird lump in my throat? I should be happy to see the last of Gabriel, shouldn't I? "You'll be fine," I assured him. "It's simple. Just do whatever Don tells you. And be honest. Talk to him if something is bothering you." I was good at dishing out advice, not so good at following it.

Gabriel did an exaggerated eye roll. "Then I'll get a half-hour discussion on why it's important to take things slowly at the start. Sometimes I wish he wouldn't pussyfoot around so much. I can take it."

"Careful. You don't want a reputation as a pushy bottom. He's probably demonstrating who is in charge."

"Oh." His face brightened as if a light bulb went on inside. "I hadn't thought of that."

I sighed. The kid still didn't seem happy, but I couldn't say anything else as the clunk of boot heels announced Don's return. Before he came into view, I added quickly, "Look after Don. Sometimes he pushes himself too hard."

This time Gabriel looked me fair and square in the eye. "Okay."

I started to put on my helmet but stopped when Don appeared in full leather gear.

Don grabbed his helmet. "Amuse yourself in the library for a couple of hours, boy. I'm going with Steve for a bit to make sure the bike is working perfectly."

I sat, too stunned to move for a second; then my heart took off like a rocket. *Yes!* But apart from the thrill of being able to ride with him, his suggestion made sense. The problem was that the highway south wouldn't be much of a real road test. We needed somewhere to check the brakes and steering. "How about we begin with a circuit through National Park?" That took me in the opposite direction from my ultimate destination, but I would welcome any delay to our inevitable parting.

"Sounds like a plan." Don gestured for me to go first.

Thanks to the recent downpour, the traffic on the tourist drive was virtually nonexistent. I took it easy to start with, leaning the bike lightly from side to side to wear some of the newness off the tires. Even if I'd wanted to push the speed, I couldn't. Sodden leaves and water seeping across the road made the hairpin bends tricky.

As soon as he was satisfied my bike didn't have any problems, Don began to enjoy himself, pulling out to pass, then dropping back to give me the lead again, giving me a thumbs-up grin each time.

The BMW handled like a dream, almost as if it could read my thoughts, responding like a long-term lover. Every minute of work we'd spent on it had been worthwhile. Gradually, my speed crept up to the maximum, but when I came to the spot where I narrowly avoided hitting the deer, Don beeped his horn and gestured to a nearby clearing.

After pulling over, I placed my helmet on the seat and crossed to where he was straddling his bike, staring back down the road.

"What's up?"

He dismounted so we stood toe to toe. "Why did you slow down?"

"What do you mean?" I hadn't applied the brakes or anything, more an instinctive wariness the deer might still be around.

"I've spent eighteen years watching out for cars that might kill me. Did you think I'd miss noticing a change in your body language?"

Damn. Forget being a Master. The man must have a PhD in observation.

Don gave an exasperated sigh as I confessed to how close I'd come to collecting a deer. When I finished my tale, he pinched the bridge of his nose and took another deep breath. "You weren't going to tell me, were you?"

I shook my head and remained silent. My knees felt as shaky as they had back then.

Don dragged his fingers through his hair. "I don't know whether to hug you in relief or spank you for not mentioning it."

I would have taken either option as long as it didn't involve a fucking hairbrush.

Don rested his gloved hand on my shoulder.

I felt like rubbing my cheek against his fingers like a cat, but he had grown distant again. Impersonal. Like we were two friendly acquaintances. Nothing more.

"Oh, what the heck." Don's sudden tight hug affected me more than a kiss would have. For once, I felt he was hanging onto me more than the other way around.

A car drove by, forcing us to separate. "Promise me you'll keep in touch. Text a photo of the scenery. Anything. Just so I know you're okay."

I knew how he felt. After one of my cousins died in a road accident, it took ages for my aunt to stop worrying whenever her other kids went out in a car. She used to say that unless you've experienced that dreaded "knock on the door" you can never understand what families go through. Don probably felt the same.

He seemed more relaxed as he remounted his bike and drew alongside, as if finally reconciled to the fact I was going. Don's reasons for putting distance between us while I thought about my future made sense, but that didn't make leaving any easier.

After all we'd been through in the last few days, a simple hug on the side of the road seemed the wrong way to part. And too soon. "If you've still got time, why don't we head across the new Coalcliff bridge and check out my favorite café on the beach at Thirroul?"

Don didn't take much persuading.

Thanks to the sun breaking through, the road dried quickly. For the next half hour, it was just the two of us, travelling like I'd always wanted. Free as a bird.

Over a midmorning BLT, Don grilled me about my family and what I did before I met Julius and after I left him. He was surprised when I told him about my success as a share trader. He gripped my hand under the table. "Too bad we didn't meet in different circumstances."

Perhaps we should have gone somewhere less public to talk. But if we had, we would have only ended up fucking again. Already, I had to restrain myself from climbing across the table, straddling his lap, and kissing him. Memories kept flitting through my mind at the most inappropriate moments. It didn't help when Don opened his mouth extra wide to slip a chip inside, or the look on his face when I slowly licked the froth off the bottom of my spoon. The other customers probably wondered why two men who hadn't been talking suddenly burst out laughing.

My watch beeped, signaling midday. Don sighed. "Time to go. Gabriel and I are on bar duty tonight, and you won't make Eden if you don't leave now."

"Okay, but I need to go to the gents first." I paid the bill and asked the waiter for the key to the restroom. As soon as I stepped inside, Don slipped in behind me and kicked the door shut. He didn't bother trying to peel me out of my leathers, just pulled down the zip and delved inside my Lycra bike shorts. "Tight."

"Understatement of the century, I thought I was going to explode in there."

"You better come quickly for me, then." He knelt at my feet.

Oh fuck… Don may have been on his knees, but there was nothing submissive in his actions. He had total control of my body at all times.

I didn't know where to put my hands. Touching his head was out of the question. I could only rest them on his shoulders, more for support than anything. My legs started shaking as he expertly drew me into his mouth. Damn. Simply the sight of Don with his face pressed to my groin was enough. No sooner did my cock hit the back of his throat than liquid heat flowed through me as my body jerked uncontrollably. "*Fuuuuuuuuuck.*"

Don came to his feet, a smug smile shining out of his eyes. Forget about thirty minutes; that was more like thirty seconds. He kissed me before swallowing, passing my semen back to me. I was still coming down as I accepted his gift.

"That was fucking awesome." I clung to him as he carefully packed away my tackle and pulled up the zip. I took a deep breath and let out a long sigh. Eventually my brain caught up with my body. "You?"

Don shook his head and kissed me on the forehead. "Something to remember me by."

We were finished and cleaned up in less than five minutes. If I had a glazed look in my eyes when I returned the key, the guy didn't comment.

Right up to the time he left, Don kept issuing instructions. "Never assume other drivers have any brains. Expect the idiots to turn in your path." Nothing I didn't already know and practice habitually. I filed his advice alongside earlier remarks about not taking any risks. No speeding. No drinking. The instinct to take care of someone ran bone deep, and Alex's death only made him worry more.

"People can cut in front of you in life too. Prevent you from being who you are meant to be. Julius may have shackled you with ropes and chains, but society's demand to conform can be just as restricting." He gave an ironic laugh. "Oh, listen to me. I sound like my mother." He glanced around to make sure we were alone before giving me a final, furtive kiss.

"Take care," he said, stroking my bottom lip afterward.

The feel of his moustache brushing against my skin lingered long after I watched him ride out of sight. Every particle of my being wanted to follow him. It took me ages to turn my brain in the opposite direction and get moving.

I was already behind schedule. My ultimate goal was Sorrento at the bottom of the Mornington Peninsula. I could shorten the trip by cutting across to the Hume Highway, but instead, I kept to the route Don had planned. At least the coastal highway would provide me with stacks of opportunities to take a break, walk along the waterfront, and stretch my legs.

At every stop, I took a photo on my phone and sent it to Don.

Without fail, a message came back almost instantly: "Thanks." That was it. No words of affection, not even a smiley.

In the UK, I'd done the London to Brighton run a few times, but the distances were nothing compared to this. I'd forgotten how huge Australia was. As the towns sped by, I tried to delve inward and think about life, the universe, and everything, but instead, the sheer thrill of being on my beloved bike again took precedence.

By the time I arrived in Eden, all the motels were sporting *No Vacancy* signs. My fault for setting off so late, but I didn't begrudge one minute spent with Don.

What to do? Backtracking was out of the question. I could have camped on the side of the road somewhere, but rain clouds had been gathering all afternoon, and I hadn't brought a tent. There weren't many options ahead. Only Mallacoota, a small holiday town on the coast, just over the Victorian border.

After refilling the tank and having a bite to eat, I pushed on. The journey only took an hour, but by the time I pulled into the caravan park, I was stuffed. I'd been on the road for six hours, covering over five hundred kilometers. Luckily, an on-site van was available.

As the sun sank through the narrow gap between the cloud bank and the horizon, red rays bathed the bottom of the dark mass with a pink tinge. At the water's edge, a fisherman was filleting fish and throwing the scraps to the gathered pelicans, who were demanding to be fed.

I took a couple of great photos and sent them off, then barely mustered up enough energy to have a shower and crash on the bed. I lay there, waiting for the beep signaling a return message, but sleep claimed me first.

In the morning, there was still no response from Don. Strange.

It *had* rained overnight, but a wind had sprung up while I slept, driving the clouds away. A definite plus. After wiping the bike down with one of the towels provided, I swallowed a revolting cup of the free instant coffee and devoured all the cellophane-wrapped biscuits.

By the time I went to the office to check out, it was already nine o'clock. "You caught me just in time," the attendant said as I handed her the key. "I have to go to the bank."

Still nothing from Don. I took another photo, adding a message to get his sorry ass out of bed. As I pressed *Send*, I noticed a small sign saying "Queued for Sending" above the previous message. Crap. No mobile reception. I should have thought of that. The campground was in the middle of nowhere.

What to do now?

There was a public call box near the office, but the handpiece was dangling uselessly by a partially severed cord. Jogging along the water's edge made no difference to the number of bars showing. *Great. That's what you get when you buy a phone plan designed for city living.* I checked around, but no hills or towers signaled an area with better reception.

What would Don be thinking? Would he worry? I shoved my cell in my jacket pocket. According to the map, Cann River was the next town—an hour's journey. Fuel wasn't the problem. Time was.

I felt the telltale vibration when I reached the highway, but there were no safe stopping places. Damn. Imagining how Don would have responded kept my insides churning until I reached the entrance to a fire trail. All his message said was "This sorry ass hasn't been in bed."

I punched in the number, and the man himself answered almost immediately with a gruffly barked, "What happened?"

As I apologized and explained about the lack of mobile reception, his occasional grunts of response were the only indication he was listening. The din of passing cars and trucks made conversation difficult. At one stage, a large group of bikes thundered by, adding to the confusion.

I'd expected to be ripped a new one for not letting him know that my plans had changed, but instead Don seemed distant, remote, as if I'd already been put out of his mind. One day on the road and that was it? I was about to hang up when he said quietly, "Keep in touch."

I stared at the phone after he cut the connection. He might be able to keep me out of his mind, but he hadn't left mine for a second.

This *was* what being a gypsy was all about, wasn't it? The freedom to go wherever I pleased and do whatever I wanted? Why then this sudden urge to head home immediately?

No, I hadn't come this far simply to give in and go back.

The roar of engines approaching from the Cann River direction made me look up. A couple of bikes slowed and pulled into the clearing.

One of the guys removed his helmet and said, "We didn't see you until we'd gone past. Are you okay?"

I stashed my cell away. "Fine, thanks. Just making a phone call." The guy who'd spoken gave me an appraising look that I returned with interest.

In some ways, he reminded me of a young Julius: tall, tanned, good looking, though his shoulder-length blond hair had been squashed by the full-face helmet.

His mate turned his Suzuki around, ready to set off.

Before he left, the blond said, "We're having a bite to eat at the Cann River pub. Wanna join us?"

I nodded, and they waited while I replaced my gloves and helmet. By the time we got going again, the rest of the group was nearly out of sight.

As we entered the historic hotel, the sound of talking and laughter spilled out the door. It turned out they were on their way to the Phillip Island Circuit where the Eight Hours Endurance Championship was being held. They'd assumed from my bike and racing leathers that I was heading there and wondered if I was having mechanical problems.

"Thanks for stopping." No wonder there were no rooms free in Eden. I'd seen a number of bikes parked outside the motels.

"No worries, mate. Code of the Road and all that."

Kieran, the guy who'd come back to make sure I was okay, was definitely giving me the eye. I revised my earlier opinion. Physically, he may resemble Julius, but this guy was *genuinely* interested in other people and friendly. My therapist had pointed out the difference. "Watch how others react," she used to say. "With a narcissistic person, there is often someone in the group who sees beyond the charm." She was right. In Julius's case, they were the ones he would shit talk behind their back.

"Hey, Steve, why don't you come too?" Kieran's invitation was endorsed by some of the other guys. We'd spent the last hour arguing about whether the Suzukis were beatable.

"Thanks, but I promised my family I'd be there by this evening."

"What about after? I've got a week off work," Kieran asked quietly.

"Sure. Here's my contact details." The usual exchange of cell phones took place.

As I tucked mine away, a couple of the guys kidded Kieran about making sure he wore a *helmet* whenever he went for a *ride*.

The sly winks that accompanied the jibe told me they knew he was gay, but their shared interest in bikes overcame any differences that might have occurred otherwise.

I was sorry to have to leave, but after demolishing a traditional pub breakfast of sausage, bacon, eggs, fried tomato, plus an overlarge serving of potato wedges, I made my apologies, thanked Kieran again for stopping, and went on my way.

CHAPTER
✝✝✝
TWENTY-EIGHT

Maybe Love Will Make You Change Your Mind

THE rest of the trip proved uneventful. The wind picked up, increasing fuel consumption, but the towns were closer together, so refueling was never a hassle. I made Sorrento before nightfall.

My reception was as I expected: the prodigal son finally returning home. My mother may not have prepared the traditional fattened calf, but her slow-roasted lamb and Moroccan couscous came a close second.

"What have you done to your hair?" Rhiannon shrieked, rubbing my shaven scalp.

"At least it's not purple." I pulled her hair affectionately. She'd gone Goth since I last saw her. She looked good, but the color must have made her stick out like a sore thumb in a holiday town like Sorrento. Seemed the spark of rebelliousness didn't begin and end with me.

Her new boyfriend, Evan, joined us for dinner. Currently, he was employed as a lifeguard at Sorrento's back beach on the ocean side of town. The rest of the time, he worked as a groundskeeper at one of the resorts. Talk about as different as chalk and cheese: the sun-bronzed Aussie who spent all day outdoors, and my sister who rarely saw daylight, thanks to her job in the local library.

Next morning, I'd barely finished eating breakfast when my mother asked me to go through some boxes she had kept for me. "Tell me what can be chucked out."

She sat on the bed as I removed the packing tape and sorted through the contents.

In one was my much-loved Mick Doohan helmet. In those days, I'd lived and breathed bike racing, and he'd been one of my idols.

"You could sell that on eBay," my mother commented. "It's in pretty good shape."

"What? Part with this? I bought it with my first pay packet." The red, white, and blue helmet went into the keeper pile. "Anyway, it's always handy to have a spare in case I want to take a passenger for a ride." As I laid it down, I noticed that to save space, something had been stuffed inside. "What's this?" I pulled out the furry thing and laughed. "Hey! You didn't need to keep Little Ted." One eye was missing, and half of its hand had been chewed off. I threw it onto the discard pile.

"No, you don't." Mum scrambled off the bed, rescued the bedraggled plush toy, and hugged it to her breast. "You slept with this every night from the day you were born until you were ten." Turning it around, she planted a kiss on its nose. "Woe betide me if it fell out of your cot in the middle of the night."

I tried to grab it back. "Give me a break. I'm nearly thirty. That was a long time ago."

"No." She held it out of my reach. "This reminds me of how loyal and stubborn you were. You never wanted to replace it with something new."

Seemed I'd always had a tendency to cling on to people and things long after they should have been discarded. "Time he was given a decent burial." I grabbed Little Ted and ran outside before she could stop me.

After two days of nonstop bike riding, I needed to stretch my legs. A walk would be good. I stared at the mangy plush toy in my hand. Try as I might, I couldn't throw Little Ted in the garbage. He needed something more fitting. Hoping my mother wouldn't find it, I stashed the memento of my past into one of the bike panniers.

It didn't take me long to reach the town center. Nothing had changed. It rarely did in places like this—one of the reasons I'd left. Sydney seemed exotic and dangerous. A challenge.

People nodded when I walked past, but I didn't recognize anyone. The nearby wine-growing area had become popular, bringing an influx of tourists.

When I arrived at the water's edge, the car ferry was leaving, bound for Queenscliff on the opposite side of the bay. Thanks to the narrow strip of land that almost closed off the port, the only waves lapping the sand came from the big boat's wake. Totally different from the raging surf that battered the ocean side of the promontory.

There was an incredible contrast between the two waterways: one calm, one dangerous. I much preferred the wild side.

My mother was clearing out more cupboards when I got back.

"How about we visit some of the wineries?" I suggested.

Her face brightened. "Why not? I haven't been there for ages."

"I'll drive your car. That way you can drink as much as you like."

"No. Let's take your bike. Much more fun."

Because of my promise to Don, I was reduced to swilling and spitting, but after the first few cellar doors, I didn't bother and instead watched my mother enjoy herself. This outing was about reestablishing connections, not buying wine.

We ended up having lunch at Vines of Red Hill.

After filling me in on her current job working in the local real estate office, my mother took a long sip of her Pinot gris and eyed me over the rim of the glass. "Irving is still waiting for your decision about challenging the will."

I sighed. The food had lost its flavor. "Hasn't he heard of client confidentiality?"

"You have to make up your mind soon. Otherwise that man will inherit Julius's money."

"That man has a name: Donato Rossi."

She flicked my comment off with a twist of her wrist. "Whatever. Although I hated Julius, you did live together for six years. You deserve it."

Seeing Don had sent me away to reach a verdict without feeling pressured, the last thing I had expected was to be ambushed by my mother the day after I arrived. "Stop nagging. I'll make a decision when I'm good and ready." My voice had risen along with my temper, but luckily none of the other diners seemed to notice.

"I just want the best for my boy."

Boy! I laughed at the irony. My mother was like a lioness when it came to protecting her cubs. After my escape, she'd taken me in without question. No recrimination, at least not until my wounds had healed. She'd wanted to press charges, but Julius would have just waved our signed agreement in the judge's face. I didn't want to go that far. Her strength and belief in me were more important than dragging all my sordid kinks through court. I think that's why she hated BDSM. "I'm sorry. I know you do. It's just…." I sighed and rubbed the back of my neck. "This concept of deserving something really sticks in my craw."

"Well, what are you going to do?"

"I don't know. It's complicated."

"No, it's not. Challenge the will. It won't cost you anything unless you win."

"And what if I *do* win? Legal challenges cost a bomb, and the money is all tied up in the two properties."

"Sell the hotel to pay Irving."

"Can't. Don still owns half of it."

"Get him to buy you out."

"What with? He's got all his money tied up in the venture." Don's aunt might be prepared to buy my half of a house, but she probably wouldn't have enough money to buy out my portion of a licensed hotel. I hadn't asked Don how much he paid, but the place must be worth well over a million.

My mother chewed thoughtfully on a piece of bread. Working in real estate made her very aware of the value of property. "If you win, the house will belong to you. Sell that."

Sell the house? Wasn't that where all this started? "Given today's market, once I pay off the balance of the loan and my legal bills, there still wouldn't be enough to buy Don's share of the hotel." I paused and took a deep breath, trying to calm myself. "Anyway, what would I want with a fucking leather bar?" I must have spoken too loudly. One of the other patrons gave me a sideways look.

If I bought Don out, he could go back to the States, but I didn't want to investigate that option too closely.

"Haven't you any money of your own?"

I stabbed at the tablecloth with my butter knife, wondering how long it took to learn how to throw knives like Don could. "With what I've saved, I suppose I could pay most of my legal bills and get a personal loan for the rest. At least I wouldn't have to sell anything then." The only problem with that solution was then neither of us would have any money to do anything. "Don't forget that Don would still own half the hotel, and I don't fancy having to be in business with someone after costing them a heap of dough."

"Well, what happens if you *don't* challenge the will?"

Stay with Don and be forever tempted to join him in what he loves doing. "His aunt has offered to buy me out."

"What aunt?"

That meant I had to explain about Don's Great Aunt Mildred.

My mother poured herself another glass of wine. All the different alternatives were making my head spin. I eyed my mother's Pinot gris. Maybe one glass? No. I'd promised.

"I guess it's your decision." From the curl of her lips, she definitely wouldn't be happy with my refusal to challenge. "Remember you can always live here."

Ouch. No. "Thanks for the offer, but I'm not sure if I could put up with the winters."

I didn't know what my mother's blood pressure was like, but her skin was definitely flushed, or maybe that was the wine speaking. Don was right. Obligations to family could trap me as securely as Julius's chains.

"You make everything sound so complicated." She picked up her napkin and threaded it through her fingers. "Damn. This has left me with a sour taste in my mouth." Her finger went up to call over the hovering waiter. "Could you please bring the dessert menu? I need something sweet."

After ordering, she swirled her wine around in the glass and stared into its depths. "It's all Julius's fault," she muttered.

"Well, no matter how much you hated him, he didn't deserve to die. No one does."

"No." She brushed my remarks away with another wave of her hand. "But by the time you left, you thought you weren't worth anything. That's what I objected to. He brainwashed you into thinking you were lucky to have him when the reverse was actually true. He drained you of all your energy and confidence. He was like a parasite."

"I let him be one."

"See. You give in too easily and allow people to walk all over you. Now you're doing the same with this American, Donato, or whatever his name is. I get the feeling you're trying to protect him instead of looking out for number one. Are you sure he's worth it?"

Yes. "He's nothing like Julius."

"What's he like, then?"

"He's different." How to explain a man as complicated as Don to my mother? "For starters, he controls his temper much better than Julius ever did." Memories came back about the different episodes when I'd stirred him up or other people had made him mad. "In fact, the only times I've ever seen him angry are when he's cross at himself or when I told him how Julius had hurt me." Once, I'd likened Don to a bulldog, a scrapper, while Julius had been a thoroughbred. My analogy still rang true, but in Don's case, there was a different kind of class. Integrity. He treated everyone he met with unfailing civility and respect, both to their face and when they weren't around. He made me feel as if I was important, too—a heady experience when you're used to being treated as nothing.

"Have you got a photo?"

I flicked through the gallery on my phone until I found the one I liked best: Don with his foam-covered moustache at the aquarium. My mother perused the image for a second and then glanced at the next photo—the one Gabriel had taken of the two of us laughing at the camera, our glasses raised.

After she handed the mobile back, I found it difficult to put my phone away. Other than the simple messages in reply to the "Wish you were here" photos, Don hadn't contacted me. Were he and Gabriel too involved in their explorations of leather? *No.* I had to stop thinking like that. I had to be happy that both of them were getting what they wanted. Didn't stop me from missing him, though. Big time. I checked the photo of the two of us together and smiled.

"You're in love with him," she said quietly. I'd never heard her sound so sad.

"No. I'm not!" I protested, but I'd never been good at lying.

Judging by her expression, she'd need two helpings of dessert to make her feel better.

"We're just good friends," I assured her. Given his coolness since I left, he must have simply seen me as a convenient fuck. But that was okay. This love business was a pain in the ass anyway. I'd survived breaking up with Julius, and I hadn't known Don for anywhere near as long.

My mother shook her head and continued to sip her wine. I could tell a battle was raging between her preconceptions and the possibility she was wrong. I didn't try to influence her. If I did, her prejudice against Don would only increase. We were too alike for comfort.

Having polished off the whole bottle of wine by herself, my mother was quite tipsy by the time we finished dessert. That was probably what got her talking about the man who had fathered me, something she'd never done before. He'd been a friend from university, and one night, when they were high on wine and weed, they'd had sex without a condom.

"One time! That's all it took." Her voice betrayed her disbelief.

"What did you do?" I asked.

230

"Got married, tried to settle down. Except he wasn't ready. He left three years later, saying he had too much living to do, and I haven't seen or heard from him since."

"Bastard."

"He was young, and so was I. Nineteen." She grabbed my wrist tightly and leaned closer so only I could hear. "But the scary thing is that, if I'd known he was going to leave, I would have had an abortion. Then you would never have been born." Tears formed at the corners of her eyes. "You're probably wondering why I'm telling you all this."

I nodded uncomfortably.

Her grip tightened. "Because, afterward, I decided that things happen for a reason. Even those that, at the time, smell like the biggest pile of shit in the universe. I'm glad I had you. Never doubt for one minute that you're special and worth a hundred of all those motherfuckers out there."

I twisted my hand to make her let go. "Well, if things happen for a reason, maybe the fact that Alex died *after* Julius means that Don *should* benefit from the will."

My mother winced as if I had hit her. "Should you decide that way, you have to promise me something."

"What?" I asked warily.

"Whatever you do, don't go back into all that slave and Master bullshit."

Once, I'd tried to explain that leather wasn't only whips and chains, but my mother couldn't understand the kink, let alone the other aspects. "Please, Steve," she urged. "I'm begging you. When you came to stay with us after leaving Julius, your spirit was broken. You were a shell of the person you are now. I couldn't bear to see you so degraded again." Her voice had risen, and, once again, tears threatened to spill from her eyes.

"Okay, I promise I will never call another man my Master."

A clunk sounded in my brain, reminding me of a heavy jail door closing. Hopefully, I was on the right side. Whichever that was.

CHAPTER
+++
TWENTY-NINE

Rhiannon

THAT night, I lay in bed thinking about the promise I'd made to my mother. *Never call another man my Master.* A few years ago, I'd made the same vow to myself, but saying it out loud to someone else made it more final. Like locking away the kinky part of myself for good. Exactly the opposite of what Don had told me to do. But Don was born to be a Master, and Masters need slaves. Well, no matter how much I loved him, it looked like that slave wasn't going to be me. Curiously, instead of feeling upset, I finally felt completely free.

Free to consider what to do about the will without putting myself into the equation. It was no longer a question of how it would affect me, but what was the right thing to do by Don. The facts were simple. I'd left. Julius had made a new will and died before Alex. Simple. Things happen for a reason. Maybe Don was meant to come to Australia?

A phone call was all it would take to let him know of my decision not to challenge the will. But then, because of his strict sense of honor, he might think he owed me something. A house. A home. While he continued to be involved in the scene? Anything but that.

Once all the legal work got sorted, I should tell him to accept his aunt's offer. Then he could pack up the rest of my gear and courier it here. In the meantime, I should stay as far from temptation as possible. Go strictly vanilla.

Stroking my cock, I thought back to all the guys I'd hooked up with in the UK. The trouble was that none of them had given me that heart-racing buzz of danger and excitement I got whenever Don was around, as I wondered what he was going to do next, knowing that whatever it was would be good. In bed and out of bed, he functioned beautifully in all gears: hard, soft, tender, or rough.

My hand flew as memories returned. Away from the house and its old rules, even thinking about sex with Don could get me off: his growls, the way he commandeered every thought, every action. Damn it, the man had sure revved my engines.

I wiped away the sticky mess and turned over, but the mattress felt uncomfortable, wrong. Being back in my childhood room with all the echoes of my past was constricting me as securely as chains. I burrowed my head into the pillow, trying to hold back the tears.

In the morning, I contacted Mr. Schofield.

He accepted my decision, though he didn't agree. "We stood a good chance of at least ensuring you inherited some of his estate. And you shouldn't have been worried about my fee."

My mother must have already told him about our conversation at the winery. "I appreciate that you're trying to look out for me, but I've made up my mind."

His sigh could be heard down the line. "Your call, but if you sell your share of the house to that relative of his, a fair valuation in the current market isn't going to net you anywhere near what you invested." *Uh-oh.* My mother had obviously also spilled the beans about Don and his aunt. They must be closer than I realized. Time to get my own lawyer.

"I don't care." Funnily enough, I didn't. Losing the link to Don would hurt much more.

He sighed again. "I'll let his lawyer know that probate can go ahead. Don't do anything about the house until that's settled."

"Okay." Instead of feeling happy about my decision, a solid lump formed somewhere near my breastbone. One thing for certain, if I wasn't prepared to become part of Don's scene, I had to find somewhere else to live. Someone else to love. I couldn't put my life on hold forever. I had to move on, but this time, I resolved to take it slow. Get to know the guy first. Don't jump straight into bed with him. That had been my track record to date, and look where it got me. Two broken hearts.

Later that morning, a text arrived from Kieran. "Still interested in getting together"

I contacted him back, saying, "Sure where do u wanna go"

His enthusiastic response came immediately. He'd never been down this way, so he was keen to see as much as possible.

I suggested he meet me in Sorrento. Now that Rhiannon was living with her boyfriend, my mother had a spare room.

She was ecstatic. Anyone but *that guy who is into leather*.

When I opened the door to let Kieran in, I was reminded of his resemblance to Julius. Maybe that's what was making me cautious and preventing me from getting too excited.

What to do? Where to go? Ever since arriving, I'd toyed with the idea of catching the ferry to the opposite side of the bay and following the coast to the Twelve Apostles. I would have preferred going with Don, but that was impossible now.

My mother had a go at me for leaving again so soon after arriving, but I suspect she was secretly pleased, especially as she warmed to Kieran immediately.

Even Rhiannon liked him when she heard he was a board rider, extracting from him a promise to stay for a couple of days when we got back, so he could go surfing with her boyfriend.

Next morning, after a quick ferry trip, we headed west along the Ocean Road. The weather was kind, and we put in good time, enjoying the spectacular views of the limestone cliffs and the contrasting fern-lined gullies. I took a couple of photos, one with Kieran in it to give Don an idea of how big the ferns were. I sent them on and received the usual response. "Thanks."

That night, when we booked into a motel, I pleaded tiredness when Kieran showed an interest in taking our relationship further. It wasn't only due to my decision to take things slow. The urge simply wasn't there. Sure, I liked the guy, but there was definitely no spark.

Nothing like the current that had started flowing through me after that first night with Don. The one that made me feel alive again.

Far from being hurt by my lack of interest, Kieran didn't seem to mind. I think, like me, he was happy to share the trip with someone.

Instead of returning via the same route, we headed back along the main highway and spent a couple of nights sampling the Melbourne gay nightlife. A real eye-opener.

Kieran seemed amused by the way I dragged him around to so many different places. "Why don't we have one of these in Sydney?" he commented when we went to The Laird. "Not just gay-friendly but for gay men only?"

Checking around, I discovered the hotel had managed to convince the licensing board that they had valid reasons for exemption from the anti-discrimination laws.

I could see both sides of the problem. Lots of girls preferred gay venues because they could have a good time and perv on guys as much as they liked without being hit on by fuckwits who only wanted to score. But a lot of gay men wanted their own space.

Times were tough. Recently, Sydney had lost a few popular iconic gay nightspots. Ken's, the infamous sauna in Kensington, had recently closed down. Manacle was gone. Finding the perfect mix was proving elusive. Pity Don wasn't with me. He would have been fascinated by the possibilities.

No one I spoke to had ever heard of the Hotel Paradiso.

I took stacks of photos and sent them back. Even if I wasn't going to be involved, I didn't want Don to fail. He would need all the help he could get to make the place a success.

When we returned to Sorrento, my mother seemed keen to get all the gossip. I could tell she was busting to ask me about Kieran. *Was he the one?* After I got sick of avoiding her hints, I told her to give it a rest. I wasn't ready to settle down. It was too soon.

I think she thought I was referring to Julius, but instead I was still mourning the fact I could see no way of being involved with a man who was totally immersed in leather.

On Friday, after she finished work, Rhiannon invited us to the beach, offering to lend Kieran Evan's board, as his lifeguard patrol didn't finish until six.

Although, at low tide, the rips and rocks made swimming hazardous, my sister and I had both learned to swim in the surf as kids. The guys on duty did a fabulous job, only opening the beach when it was safe and making sure the flags were in the best position.

I spread my towel on the sand next to Rhiannon and watched Kieran paddle out beyond the break. Despite the heat, she was still wearing shorts and a boob-tube top. No bikini for her. She'd never be a surfie chick.

We'd already caught up on most of the normal things siblings chatted about, skating around anything that might be painful. I think she was happy having her brother back. In Rhi's eyes, I'd been "gone" a lot longer than the four years that I'd been overseas. "I like your boyfriend," she said.

I chuckled. "Kieran's not my boyfriend."

My sister seemed confused by my comment. "Well, he should be. He's nice."

"We're friends. That's all. He's never seen this part of the world, so I'm showing him around. No big deal."

"Why can't you fall in love with someone like him?"

Because I'm already in love with someone else. The weird thing was that Kieran would make the perfect vanilla boyfriend. Kind. Thoughtful. "Love doesn't work like that." I glanced across at the tower where her boyfriend was checking on the board riders through his binoculars. "Anyway, what about you and Evan?"

"What about us?" Rhi ran her fingers through the sand.

"Why are you in love with Evan? You're not into board-riding or any of the things he's interested in."

She grimaced. "That's what most of my friends say." Her fingers dug deeper into the sand, and she flicked a heap up into the air before continuing. "He never harasses me about spending all my time reading, and I like watching him surf."

"Don't you get bored?"

"No." She shook her head emphatically. "He likes taking his board out after patrol finishes. Sometimes, he's by himself, especially if the surf isn't running. I come down and read, checking on him every now and then. If he gets into difficulty…." She held up her mobile. "I can call for help. But if I was into surfing, I'd be tempted to join him, and then we both might get into trouble."

Her reasons made a lot of sense. "So you're actually acting as a sort of lifeguard."

She laughed. "I suppose I am in a way. Just like he has to stay out of the water to keep an eye on the swimmers." She shrugged again. "What can I say? It works."

Don had said something like that. *Who cares what your relationship is like? As long as it works.* "I'm happy for you."

I studied Evan as he whistled to some swimmers, warning them that they were drifting too close to the virtual boundary marking the edge of the rip. He could rescue them if necessary, but it was better to make sure they never got into trouble.

My heart beat faster as I considered the situation from a different angle. To be a lifeguard, you needed to be an experienced surfer. BDSM could be as bad as a rip, sweeping you up with its all-consuming power, taking you out of your depth before you knew it. Don wasn't a novice, but he could still use someone *on the beach* keeping an eye on him. If I wanted a place in his life, was that the solution? Stay out of the water, as it were, and make sure he was okay? But how to broach the subject?

The arrival of a cold, wet, but happy Kieran put an end to any chance of doing something immediately.

As soon as Evan finished duty, we all went for a ride along the road leading to the end of the promontory. First off, I showed Kieran the notorious beach where one of our prime ministers drowned or was taken by a shark, and then we stopped at the old fortifications on Cheviot Hill.

My three companions explored the tunnels, poking their hands through the barred windows, pretending they were prisoners. They kept egging me on to join them, but the dark enclosed spaces brought back too many memories. Instead, I took photos and sent them on to Don.

Once more, the only reply I got was "Thanks."

Texts were no good. I wanted to talk to him, see what he thought of my idea, but just as I went to dial his number, Rhiannon came to join me, hugging her arms around her chest and shivering. "I'm cold."

"Hang on." I went to the bike and pulled out my leather jacket. As I did, something fell to the ground. I picked it up. My old teddy bear.

"Isn't that Little Ted?" Rhi took the coat from my hands and put it on. "What's he doing out here?"

"I want to give him a decent burial."

Rhiannon laughed. "Sure you don't want to keep him? He's cute in a zombieish sort of way." She staggered back to rejoin the others, doing a passable zombie impression.

Tears of affection came into my eyes as I watched my sister leave. Years ago, she'd been my lifeguard, alerting me to my own danger. I dug into one of the panniers and pulled out a trench digger. One of those never-leave-home-without-it implements that most bikers carried.

Don had sent me away to give me enough distance to think about the will. But it also helped me see BDSM and its trappings more clearly. The bars and darkness were symbolic, not the intent. That lay in the hearts of the people involved.

As I entered the underground tunnel, Don's words about being strong and expanding my limits came to mind. I had a choice. Now it was time to make the most of this freedom.

The walls pressed in on me from all sides, but I clenched the spade tighter and kept going until I emerged at the other end in an open courtyard. Most of the ground was covered in cement, but small patches of dirt and low-growing weeds provided exactly what I needed for Little Ted's final resting place.

Carefully, I pulled the weeds aside, taking care not to disturb the roots, and dug a hole in the underlying soil. It didn't need to be deep.

A curious peace fell over me as I laid my old toy in the shallow depression. In one way, I was sad at losing a childhood companion, but in another I was getting closure.

Rhi came back with Evan and Kieran as I finished patting down the dirt and replacing the natural covering.

They laughed when I told them what I'd been doing and insisted on saying a little prayer. Then they left me alone to *pay my respects in private*, as they jokingly said.

My sight blurred as I gazed at the newly dug area. I'd done a good job in hiding the evidence. Hopefully, Little Ted's final resting place would remain intact. There was a lot more in that grave than a bedraggled old bear. Alongside him were the ghosts of my former self and Julius, bound together in the warped version of BDSM we'd created.

The trouble was, I'd never been able to say good-bye to my lover or grieve his death.

Who knew where his ashes lay? His parents would never let me get anywhere near them, that's for sure. But it wasn't only the bad memories of Julius that got interred; I buried the good ones also. Like when we first met—at a bike race, funnily enough. We'd ended up in the john at the same time and done the stereotypical sideways glances. He'd caught me looking and teased me unmercifully about it forever after.

Don had mentioned feeling that he had failed Alex by not being what he needed.

In the same way, I must not have been what Julius needed. People change, people grow. Sometimes in the same direction, but more often than not, apart. Over time, Julius had become less sure of himself, while my confidence grew. Instead of seeing him for who he really was, I had clung to the ideal, the memory of what had been.

Don was right. Julius had feared he was losing me, or at least losing my respect, so he tried to bind me to him with physical ties. But he didn't need to. I loved him so much that I was prepared to overlook the flaws in his personality. I would have been much better off recognizing those flaws and accepting them.

And what of Alex? Did he sense Julius's need for someone to worship him? Unconditionally? If so, I hope that they found happiness in the short time they had together.

I smiled as an image flashed into the foreground. The first time I saw Don. His physical strength so obviously on display as he tapped his whip against his shiny leather boots.

I hadn't liked him when we first met, or at least I'd been suspicious of his motives, so I'd studied him carefully. Inspected each action, looking for character flaws that didn't exist. Sure, he was far from perfect, but aren't we all?

In his case, my early preconceptions proved to be wrong. What I initially took for arrogance, I recognized later to be a mix of surefire confidence and humility. He knew what he wanted, but he wasn't prepared to walk over other people to get there.

The man cared for other people and wasn't averse to fixing up their messes when he had to. Stubborn, but only because of his deep instinct for what was wrong and what was right, and being prepared to move mountains to achieve the latter.

My mother didn't think he deserved to inherit the property, but to me, it was just recompense for Julius ruining his life.

Fate had decreed that Alex died after Julius, not at the same time. Then fate gave him another bonus, a fairy godmother who arrived out of the blue, waving her magic wand and offering to help him out financially. A perfect example of good karma if ever there was one.

My mother believed things happen for a reason.

So did I.

Don may not love me like I loved him, but that didn't matter. I wanted to be close to him. Needed to be close to him. Even if only as friends who shared a passionate interest. That would have to be enough. As long as I could convince him that he needed his own personal lifeguard.

I missed him. Since leaving him, I felt I was merely filling in time, drifting. Ten days seemed more like ten months, and every minute apart was like a minute wasted.

Sure, it had been good catching up with Rhiannon and my mother, but I didn't belong here. Not that they didn't love me, but my family didn't *need* me. Don did. He needed my help around the house, at the Paradiso, and to make sure he didn't drown in the sea of BDSM like I nearly did.

Life wasn't going to be easy. It wasn't meant to be. But if there was any possibility of the hotel becoming a success, I shouldn't stand in his way, especially if I could be by his side when he did it.

Hopefully, he would see things my way.

CHAPTER
THIRTY

Sara

IT WAS dark by the time we arrived back at my mother's house. Before I had a chance to call Don, my cell phone rang. My heart started racing as soon as I realized who it was.

"Did you remember to contact Sara?" Don didn't even bother to greet me.

"Sara?" My brain was so busy registering how pissed off he sounded that his words took a while to register.

"Yes, Sara. The wedding is tomorrow night."

Oh, shit. I'd promised to perform as Stevie Tricks. She must be freaking out. "Sorry, I forgot."

"I'll let her know you can't make it and say you had a family commitment."

"No," I butted in hurriedly. "You don't have to lie for me. I'm coming back anyway. I was just about to ring and let you know."

"Oh." Silence on the end of the line.

Did that mean he didn't want me around at all? The sooner I got there, the better. "If I leave now, I can be in Sydney by morning. The trip up the Hume Highway is much quicker."

"It's still over six hundred miles, and I have enough to worry about without imagining you out there by yourself, dodging trucks all night." He still didn't sound convinced.

Kieran was in the shower. He'd already told me he had to be back at work on Monday. "I won't be alone. A friend will be travelling with me."

Don didn't answer immediately, and when he did, his voice was quieter, but still determined. "It doesn't make any difference."

But I could tell that it did. "Look. I promised Sara that I would be there, and I don't break my promises." *And simply hearing your voice makes me want to leave this minute.* "If we head out first thing in the morning, I can be there before the reception starts. She doesn't need me to perform until nine."

"What about makeup? Your costume? Unless you exceed the speed limit, you won't make it in time."

"Theoretically, it's possible, and I promise I'll be careful. Okay?"

A grunt was the only response.

My brain started ticking off everything I would need. *Music.* "Is Gabriel still around?"

"Yes." One word that covered a defensive position, six feet thick.

Confirmation the young man was still on the scene should have worried me, but strangely, it didn't. My jealousy had disappeared as soon as I realized there *was* a place for me in Don's life, even if he didn't know it yet. "Did he get round to fixing the song?"

"Yes." Don sighed, sounding as if the weight of the world hung on his shoulders. What the fuck had been going on in my absence? Finally, he took a deep breath and said quietly, "If you're that desperate to strut your stuff, we can bring everything to the reception place. Meet us there." He sounded as if he couldn't think of anything worse.

"Great."

The phrase, "*Stubborn bastard*," just made it through before he hung up.

"Love you too, Sunshine," I said to the blank screen.

Was it my imminent return or the journey itself that was bugging him? The distance wouldn't be a concern, but he might be worrying that I would ride carelessly in my haste. Fat chance. On the way south, I hugged the verge on curves when the middle of the road was the better line. Julius's accident must have weighed heavily on my mind.

Happily, Kieran fell in with my plan. Of course, then I had to tell him all about Don and my drag act. It was midnight by the time I got to bed, but I managed to get some sleep before we left. At dawn my mother and Rhiannon saw me off, making me promise to ride carefully and keep in touch. I texted Don before we left to confirm I was on my way.

A stiff southerly sped us along. We pushed the speed limit whenever we could, eating up the fuel, but I only had to switch to my reserve tank once.

Kieran peeled off at King Georges Road with a blast of his horn and a wave. We'd already planned to meet up again. He was an electrician by trade, so I had asked him to come and give us a quote on wiring the meditation room. I loved candles, but only for decoration.

By the time I dismounted at the reception center, I was bouncing off the walls. Either from the caffeine tablets I'd been consuming or the anticipation of seeing Don again.

The car park was almost empty. Good, the guests hadn't arrived yet. Don must have heard the bike. He checked his watch as he came down the steps to greet me. "Nine and a half hours. If you were my boy, I'd spank the living daylights out of you."

He was wearing his nice suit, but the pose he adopted—arms crossed, legs shoulder-width apart—was pure leather. Damn, he looked good. But then I got past the exterior and studied his face. No, he looked tired... and pissed off with me. Again. "Nice seeing you too, Sunshine." I blew him an air kiss. No cinematic slow-mo clinches or signs he was glad to see me. Speaking of boys…. "Where's Gabriel?"

"In the changing room." Don tossed his head in the general direction without breaking eye contact. "Looking after all your gear."

"Okaaaay…." Don's attitude was so different. An unscalable fence had sprung up between us, but this time he wasn't handing me the remotes. "Where should I leave the bike?"

"Next to Gabriel's car." Without uncrossing his arms, Don turned to stare in the direction of a jacaranda tree in full bloom. Shit. The purple flowers would stick to the hot engine. Oh, well, the bike would need a good clean tomorrow anyway.

Don was still waiting for me when I came back. "I'll tell Sara you're here. She's been worried that you wouldn't make it in time."

"Should I go and see her?"

"No need. I have to speak to the photographer about something anyway. Gabriel will give you a hand. There's a corridor leading off from where all the tables are set up. He's in the second room on the left."

Without waiting for my reply, he turned on his heel and went back inside.

I followed like a suitably chastened puppy.

At the rear of the dining room, an Asian dude with a long ponytail was setting up a follow spotlight. Don spoke a few words to him, then headed out into the garden.

Through the floor-to-ceiling windows, I could see the wedding party posing for photos. When he saw Don, Marty glanced over at me and said something to Sara. She looked surprised at first, then gave me a cheery wave, probably wondering how someone like me could ever look like a female. *The magic of makeup, dahling.*

The Chinese guy, or he could have been Korean, scanned me from head to toe before giving a slight chuckle. "Don tells me you'll be performing later. He's asked me to do some mood lighting." Another American, from the sound of things. I wondered if he was a friend of Don's.

"Hi, I'm Steve." I held out my hand, and he shook it.

"Daniel Ho, but you can call me Danny." He gestured out to the garden where a big, bald guy was moving the wedding party into their respective positions. "The photographer is my boyfriend, Nathaniel Taylor."

Ah, good, we weren't the only gay guys around. In his bright orange vest and faded jeans, Danny reminded me of one of the tropical fish we'd seen at the aquarium. Restless energy flowed through him. Nerves or excitement? "Taylor?" The name sounded familiar, but I couldn't place it.

Danny came to my aid. "Nat's won stacks of awards for his photos. He doesn't normally do weddings, but Rob asked him to."

Rob. I checked out the wedding party again. Sure enough, the big rugby player who had given me such a hard time at the buck's night was standing next to Marty. I recognized a couple of other guys I'd sucked off. It was strange seeing them in formal attire. "I better get ready."

"Happy tucking, dahling." Danny's sultry drawl took me by surprise. As did his wink.

I checked him out again. With his long hair, from the back he might be mistaken for a girl, but there was nothing soft about him. I snorted to myself. Who was I to talk? You didn't have to look feminine to do drag. I was a walking, talking illustration.

Following Don's instructions, I found the room set aside for me.

Dressed casually in loose-fitting board shorts and with only one button of his shirt fastened, Gabriel winced when he turned to greet me. "Thank God you're here."

I removed my boots and peeled off the dusty leathers, then chucked everything onto the floor. The sweat-soaked T-shirt and Lycra shorts clung to me like a second skin. Shower and shave were first on the agenda. I glanced across at Gabriel. He still looked uncomfortable. "What's wrong? Why aren't you dressed for the wedding?"

Gabriel twisted his shoulders awkwardly. "I'm too sore to wear a suit."

My stomach lurched as the words sank in. "Show me." If Don had cut Gabriel badly, I'd wring his neck. So much for taking a few days to get to know the young man.

Gabriel winced as he tried to take off his shirt, so I helped.

His back was a dull shade of crimson, the result of repeated lashings from a flogger. Two long, dark welts showed he'd also been whipped. "Ouch." I sympathized with him. "When did Don do these?" No sign of bruising.

"This morning." Gabriel smiled ruefully. "He rubbed some salve in after. That helped."

I sat on the bed, considering the implications. No leather adorned his neck. Not even a gold chain. "What is it between you and Don? Is he going to collar you?"

"No." Gabriel shook his head vigorously. "He said he's happy to introduce people like me to the scene, but he doesn't want another long-term slave."

A wave of relief made me feel giddy. *So much for not feeling jealous!* "I suppose he's still not over Alex."

"It's not that. He reckons he's learned his lesson. Trying to dictate to someone what to do day in, day out is impossible when you're up to your neck solving staffing issues or worrying why the order is late."

Tasks someone else could easily take care of. Should take care of. What the fuck was Fred doing? Don needed a proper manager. "Yeah, it's not easy being a twenty-four-seven Master unless you're super rich and living in the lap of luxury on a tropical island."

Gabriel laughed, but he still didn't look comfortable.

"Are you sure you don't want me to rub in something? I've got some Papaw ointment in my bag."

"I'm okay. Really I am. Don didn't want to use the whip, but I begged him to."

"Why?" I studied Gabriel more closely. He'd changed. The eager puppy dog had gone. There were signs of maturity. Despite the tenderness in his back, he stood up straighter than when I first met him. "Curiosity killed the cat, you know."

Gabriel snorted. "He'd already used the flogger on me earlier in the week to show me what it was like. But he was so uptight, I sensed he needed something more to distract him."

Judging by the cool reception I'd received, Don was still on edge. "Okay, he may have been mad at me for coming back for the wedding, but he knows better than to take his anger out on you." My reassurance to my mother that Don could control his temper crashed in smithereens at my feet.

"He never went beyond what I could stand."

"Are you sure? Were you honest with him?"

Gabriel gave me a quick grin. "Does telling him that it fucking well hurt count?"

I laughed. If Don had been expecting a meekly submissive *thank you*, he would have been sorely disappointed. "Did you enjoy it?"

"The flogging was okay." Gabriel shrugged and winced again as the gesture pulled at the wounds on his back. He'd learn not to do that too often. "The whip was a bit much. I guess I'm not a pain junky. Don reckons it won't hurt as much tomorrow, but I rang my parents and told them I'd be staying for a few more days. I hope you don't mind?"

"Mind? Me? Why should I?"

"You guys probably want some time alone."

That had been the plan. I'd been going to offer my services, hoping he would accept them out of friendship if not love, but now I was wondering if I'd been deluding myself. Perhaps coming back was a bad idea. I gazed at the young man as he shifted uncomfortably from foot to foot, glancing up every now and then to check my reaction. "Give me another look."

The red welts bisected the tattooed angel wings perfectly, almost like red strokes across signs, negating the symbol within. But why? Was their placement deliberate? A message for Gabriel that he wasn't an angel and shouldn't aspire to be? Or stating that Don wasn't an angel? Or both?

My initial gut reaction faded as I admired the clinical precision. The blows were the work of an artist.

I hadn't expected such an immediate test of my resolve to be an onlooker without participating. Was I disturbed by the flogging or jealous? Funnily enough, neither. More concerned that Don had acted while upset. That was a big no-no. "I feel responsible in a way, because I insisted on coming back for the wedding. He's still leery about accidents."

"No!" Gabriel winced as he drew the shirt on properly this time, fastening three buttons. "Gee, you can be dense sometimes. It wasn't only that. He was upset because he gave you space to make up your mind, and you immediately hooked up with someone else."

Huh? "Who?"

"That guy you went sightseeing with. He said he looks like Julius."

"Kieran was just a guy I travelled with."

Gabriel's look of disgust made me squirm. "What did you expect Don to think? Especially with all the pictures of the pubs you went to.

He assumed you must be out partying. Oh, and the night your text didn't arrive…." Gabriel shook his head. "I had to stop him from calling the police. He was convinced you were lying on the side of the road somewhere."

"Why didn't he say something?"

"He didn't want how he felt about you to influence your decision."

How he felt about me. "He used those exact words?"

"Yeah."

My heart started beating so wildly I couldn't speak.

Gabriel grinned slyly. "After the first few nights of putting up with him moping around the house and threatening to buy a shotgun to kill the bloody Koel, I said if he wouldn't tell me what was going on, he needed to talk to someone else. So, in the early hours of the morning, when he couldn't sleep, he Skyped a guy he knew in the States. Someone called Vince."

"And you listened in?"

Gabriel nodded sheepishly. "Sometimes I couldn't sleep either, and you know what the house is like at night—quiet as a graveyard. Mostly they chatted about the Paradiso and his plans, but they also discussed self-esteem, ego, Don's needs."

Speaking of needs. "Did you… he…?" As soon as the words left my mouth, I burst out laughing, remembering Gabriel asking me the same question the day after we met.

"Once."

My laughter died, and I felt as if he'd socked me in the stomach.

Gabriel noticed my reaction and grew defensive. "It was your fault."

"*My* fault?"

"Yeah. The night you sent him the photo of that guy, he drank half a bottle of Scotch."

Fuck. I racked my brain but couldn't recall Don having more than a couple of beers or the occasional glass of wine to be sociable.

"I rolled him into bed and held him and things went from there." Gabriel blushed. "More of a sympathy fuck than anything."

My jealousy vanished in an instant. At least someone had been there to take care of him. "How did you like his growling?"

Gabriel stared at me as if I was crazy. "He didn't make a sound. I don't think either of us really enjoyed it."

I wasn't sure what to make of that revelation. *Should I feel relieved or not?*

Cars started pulling into the car park. Shit, much as I would have liked to explore how much Don had missed me, I had a performance to prepare for. I dashed into the bathroom and had a quick shower and shave. This was one of those occasions when I was glad I wasn't one of those drag queens who wore revealing outfits. I'd done that once, but the embarrassment of having to ask the attendant whether the pantyhose were sheer to the waist turned me off doing that too often. Silently, I blessed Stevie for wearing clothes that floated loosely around her. "Have you got the music?"

Gabriel was fiddling with the controls of the MP3 player.

"Yeah, I'll take this outside when you're ready to perform. I've already checked how to link it up to their sound system."

"Can you put it on while I get ready? I need to get my timing right."

"Sure."

I turned down the volume until it was barely audible and sang along as I smoothed on the first layer of foundation. Usually it took me over an hour to do my makeup and another twenty minutes to put on my body. Tonight, I managed to complete the first part of my task in half that time. Gabriel had done a fabulous editing job. The music was crystal clear and the audience applause barely noticeable. "Great job, mate. Thanks."

Gabriel did one of his exaggerated eye rolls. "Don made me redo it until it was perfect. He's a real perfectionist."

"I could imagine." I'd watched him paint. He was one of those people who could do edges without having to use masking tape.

"Are you going to sing along with the music?" Gabriel sounded curious.

I chuckled. "Nah. The audience doesn't want to hear *me* singing. They want Stevie."

"Why not? You've got a good voice, and it doesn't sound that different."

"I'm fine on the low notes, but Stevie's singing sounds so natural, so unforced, that you don't realize she's got a pretty impressive range. I'll stick to the impersonation, thanks."

The face gazing out of the mirror was no longer mine. Dark kohl rimmed my eyes, making them appear huge. False eyelashes added to the illusion. Layers of foundation and heaps of blush had changed the contours of my face.

All the time, Gabriel had been watching me. Finally, he spoke. "Why do you do drag? Did you dress up as a kid?"

"No, but I used to watch my mother getting ready to go on a date and found the whole process fascinating." That was after her second husband died, when Rhi was still a baby and she had hopes of finding another husband.

"Well, what made you get into it?"

"While I was in London, I became friends with an Aussie who was into drag. One day, for a lark, he made me up, and that, as the saying goes, was that."

Gabriel looked bemused as I strapped on my foam tits. "Stevie hasn't got big boobs."

"Now she does." I'd been to one of her recent concerts. "Plus, it's expected, dahl."

After pulling on my third pair of tights, I worked my balls up into their snug cavity and forced my cock back. A few pairs of undies ensured it stayed in place. I didn't bother taping, but I found early on in my career that if I didn't tuck, it was too easy to forget and drop out of character. Anyway, I'd have been roasted on a spit by my fellow artists if they discovered I hadn't.

"Doesn't that hurt?" Gabriel had been watching quietly while I worked, more intrigued than disgusted. That was a nice change.

"Not as much as being flogged by a whip."

He laughed. "Good point."

251

"It's more uncomfortable than anything. You get used to it after a while."

"Like bondage."

Silence fell, and all of a sudden I became aware of the clatter and noises coming from the other room. "What do you mean?"

"Don hogtied me one day. Trussed me like a chicken in record time."

A shudder of revulsion ran through me. "How did you like it?"

He grinned. "The ropes bit into my muscles at first, but I gradually got used to them. He left me like that for so long, I fell asleep."

I looked across, alarmed at this news. "Did he walk away and leave you?"

"No, he was with me the whole time, working on things in the dungeon, checking up on me at regular intervals, wetting my lips, making sure the rope didn't chafe. He talked to me a lot, explaining the principles of bondage, but after a while the words became a blur, and I zoned out."

"So, you enjoyed that part of the week?"

Gabriel came around to stand beside me. "Don't get me wrong. I enjoyed *all* of it. Don's great. He knows his stuff, and he's a fantastic teacher."

I fumbled with the catches of my corset. I couldn't look at Gabriel; otherwise he would have seen the jealousy in my eyes.

"Do you want some help?"

I stared up in amazement. "This from a guy who thinks drag is the pits?"

Gabriel blushed. "Don explained that, in some ways, leather is similar. Wearing specific clothes to create an effect. He said there's a lot of discipline involved in drag. Rules to conform to. Procedures to follow." Gabriel hooked me up. "Almost a brotherhood."

"Sisterhood, sweetie." I knew what he meant. With only a few words, the Asian guy outside had announced his membership of the club as effectively as pins or badges on a vest.

252

Lastly, I slipped into the black chiffon outfit they'd brought. Don must have had it mended and dry-cleaned. Did the guy ever stop thinking about other people? No wonder he looked so tired.

"Sounds like you had a busy week." I smoothed the dress over my fake hips and stared out at the car park. "What else did you get up to?"

"We finished the painting yesterday. Don's got this photographer coming tomorrow to take some promotional shots for a flyer he wants to make. He's furnished the rooms upstairs so that people can stay overnight."

"You talk too much, boy."

I swung around at the sound of Don's curt reprimand. I'd never seen him so pissed off. If he'd had his whip, I'm sure he would have been tapping it against his boot.

"He's been telling me about the work you've been doing. No harm in that."

"I expressly told him not to."

Ouch. I glanced at Gabriel, who, instead of blushing guiltily and looking down at his feet, was meeting Don's gaze. His face was flushed, though, and he'd bite through his bottom lip if he chewed on it any harder.

"Sorry, Sir, but I felt Steve should know."

Don used his foot to slam the door behind him, cutting off all sound from outside. "Did you? Care to tell me why?"

"It's his house."

Paradoxically, at that point, Stevie was singing about her loved one building his house and calling her home. I turned off the MP3 player and slid into my stilettos. Seemed like the boy had learned a lot about our situation in my absence. Had Don told him, or had he overheard him talking to his colleague back home? "Don owns half of it," I said quietly. Don still looked as if he wanted to put Gabriel across his knee and spank him. "I sent word to Mr. Schofield that I'm not challenging the will."

"I know. My lawyer told me he'd received a letter from him." Don didn't seem overjoyed. In fact, if anything, he looked sad.

Gabriel shuffled uncomfortably from foot to foot. "I'll get the music ready." He straightened his clothes and edged past Don, letting in the noise from the reception on his way out. They were up to the speeches. I was on next. Nerves started fluttering in my stomach. Because of the performance or the expression on Don's face?

His temper had vanished as quickly as it erupted. Once, he had studied me like some sort of strange insect, but now there was sadness in his gaze. He needed someone around to snap him out of those moments of funk. Unfortunately, all my lighthearted quips refused to come to my aid.

Facing the mirror, I settled the blonde wig on my head, anchoring it down to make sure it wouldn't move. All I had time for was a quick teasing fluff to make it look natural.

Lastly, I drew on my gloves.

Outside, the clatter of people eating and chattering died down. My performance was due to start at any minute.

Don held the door open for me. "It's time."

Yes, it is.

He led me along the corridor, resting his hand on the small of my back, but his face showed no indication he was doing any more than politely guiding a female he had just met.

When we entered the darkened room, the only light came from candles flickering in the middle of the tables. An expectant hush fell. People craned around in their chairs, trying to see who had arrived, but all their attention switched back to the opposite side of the dance floor when the master of ceremonies started speaking. "Ladies and gentlemen, tonight, our special guest, Stevie, would like to dedicate this song to the bride, Sara, in memory of her late mother!"

If anything, the audience grew quieter. When the first notes of the organ started, all eyes were still on the spot-lit man. A few cheers erupted when they recognized the opening notes, and then a purple spotlight shone down on me from above as I mimed the words. Danny had concentrated the light, leaving all but my face in shadow.

The moment I started performing, all my worries vanished, and I entered my own special subspace where nothing mattered except the song. Stevie Nicks deserved no less. In a way, she was my Mistress, and I served her to the best of my ability, having no trouble emulating her performance as I sang about drowning in a sea of love.

When I came to the part about meeting my match, the bridal couple rose from their chairs and made their way onto the dance floor. The bright spotlight changed color and switched from me to illuminate them as they began dancing. At that particular point on the video, the audience had started applauding when Stevie did a little dance during the instrumental section.

Right on cue, as if a prompter held up an applause card, the wedding guests started clapping and cheering, drowning out anything Gabriel hadn't been able to eliminate. I caught sight of Don watching from the sideline. Although he wasn't smiling, I could tell that he was satisfied with the outcome. Exactly as he had planned it.

When the song ended, Marty thanked me repeatedly, and Sara gave me a big smoochy kiss. "I just wish Mum could have been here. She would have loved it."

"You're welcome, honey. I'm sure she's with you in spirit."

After I posed with the happy couple for a few photographs, Don approached me. I was still giddy with my after-performance buzz, but the seriousness of his expression sobered me instantly. "Thanks for all your help with the music. It worked brilliantly."

From the coolness of his reaction, you'd think we were strangers. "You performed well. Would you like a drink?"

I smiled at him. "I'd kill for a beer, Sunshine."

A weird expression crossed his face. Pain? Anger? "Not while you're riding. I'll see what I can get." He went off to find a waiter.

Moments later, Gabriel brought me a glass of orange juice. Then he disappeared, saying he needed to rescue his gear. Don wasn't anywhere to be seen.

I threaded my way around the edge of the dance floor. A few guests wanted their picture taken with Stevie Tricks, but I didn't hang around too long. All the guys I'd sucked off during the buck's night were present, deliberately avoiding eye contact. The WAGs on their arms wouldn't appreciate my presence if they knew how I'd met Marty.

Glass in hand, I wandered outside onto a balcony. The light from inside didn't penetrate far, and most of the area was bathed in darkness. Only a red glow followed by a distinctive smell betrayed someone's presence. The sudden increase in illumination allowed me to recognize who was there. Rob. No sign of any companion.

Closing the gap between us, I gestured at what he was smoking. "Celebratory cigar?"

He snorted, rested his elbows on the balcony railing, and muttered, "Hardly." The tip glowed red as he drew in another long pull. "Congratulations on your performance, by the way. You had a few of them fooled for a while."

I rested my hand on his arm. I'd been pleasantly surprised by Sara. She wasn't the typical beautiful bimbo who usually paired up with Aussie sportsmen. Not that she didn't look good, she did, but there was a down-to-earth friendliness that set her apart from most of the other WAGs. "Sara seems a nice girl. She'll be good for Marty."

Anger infused Rob's face as he turned toward me. For a second, I was scared he might retaliate physically, but he merely took a deep breath and muttered, "I hope you're right. Nothing could have come from it, anyway."

Well, his response answered one question. Rob was happy to admit to me that he was gay. Given the degree of homophobia in the sporting world, it would take a brave man with a lot of balls to come out.

Each no doubt lost in his thoughts about love, we shared a companionable silence, the tip of his cigar flaring brightly every few seconds.

The door to the balcony opened, and a curvaceous blonde in a short, figure-hugging gold dress stepped outside. "Rob, the photographer wants to take a few more shots of the wedding party." No friendliness in her tone, more impatience, if anything. A flash of light sparkled off a large diamond on her ring finger. Without waiting for an acknowledgement, she went back inside. I caught a grimace of distaste on Rob's face before he turned and stubbed out his cigar in one of the potted plants.

Heck, I thought my life was complicated. Obviously, I wasn't the only one.

Before he could leave, the door opened again. This time, Don and Gabriel emerged. Don strolled over to us, giving a nod of greeting to Rob before addressing me quietly. "Gabriel's collected his gear. We're going now."

"Okay."

He paused for a second, as if he was going to say something else, then turned on his heel and went inside.

There was no point in staying. The men I'd met during the buck's night weren't my friends and never would be. They'd happily use my mouth in private but wouldn't want a thing to do with me in public. While the photographer and his boyfriend looked like nice guys, they were too busy to chat. Even Rob had other duties to attend to.

I held out my hand, expecting Rob to shake it. Instead, he raised it to his mouth and brushed the back with his lips. Coming from such a rough-looking man, the gesture took me by surprise. "Thank you," he said.

For understanding and not teasing him about it? "Yeah, see you around."

As I went down the corridor to get changed, Gabriel's car pulled out of the car park.

Fuck. They'd gone without me.

CHAPTER
┼┼┼
THIRTY-ONE

Love's a Hard Game to Play

AS THE Corolla's taillights disappeared from sight, my world felt like it was falling apart. Even when faced with Don's frigid politeness and the continued presence of Gabriel on the scene, I'd managed to keep a lid on my emotions and pretended I had everything under control. Except I was wrong.

No matter how Don felt about me when I left, the situation had obviously changed. He may not rant and rave like Julius, but he must be furious with me. Or if not angry, disappointed. Much worse.

Had there been an element of trying to make him jealous when I sent that photo of Kieran? Maybe I *was* subconsciously trying to provoke a reaction from him other than "nice" and the simple "thanks." Damn. Didn't the guy realize how much I missed him?

Okay, I screwed up, but once we were back at the house I would be able to explain everything. Except I hadn't brought the remotes, and the gates would be locked.

A hand came to rest on my shoulder. "Is everything okay?"

No, of course it isn't fucking okay. I turned to find Danny eyeing me in concern. "Just trying to work out how I'm going to get all my drag gear back to the house."

"Aren't you with Don?" Danny glanced around.

"Yeah, he must have forgotten that I couldn't carry everything on my bike." Except Don never forgot anything.

The big photographer approached, beckoning to my companion. "Danny, can you come now? Everyone is ready for the final group picture."

"Look, I gotta go. Nat needs me." Danny patted my arm reassuringly. "Leave your gear with ours. We're doing a photo shoot at your place tomorrow. We can bring it with us."

"Thanks."

Danny joined his boyfriend. After a quick discussion, he adjusted one of the lights while Nat arranged the group, ready for their photo. The two men seemed to have made a success of living and working together. I envied them.

I returned to the change room and slowly removed my Stevie Tricks persona, thinking about the evening and everything Gabriel had said. Why *had* Don gone without me? Apparently he'd been upset when he thought I'd hooked up with Kieran. Had he been jealous that I was talking to Rob?

No, I would have picked up those vibes in an instant. So, why had he left so suddenly?

Fuck it. I wouldn't get any answers to my questions here.

Most of my under gear was too smelly, so I just wore my Lycra shorts under my leathers. After packing up all the drag clothes, I stashed the suitcases where Danny said. He gave me the thumbs-up sign but didn't leave his task.

More questions and doubts raced through my mind as I negotiated the city streets. Gabriel said Don had missed me, but would he accept me back into his life?

The first glimpse of the imposing brick fence sent my pulse racing. Not from fear, more from a recognition that this was where I belonged. Now to convince Don. But if everything was locked up, how would I get in? The only option would be to lean the bike against the gate to gain enough height to haul myself over the top. At least that section was lower and wasn't lined with spikes.

Slowing the bike to a crawl, I approached the entrance and let out a relieved sigh. The gate was wide open.

He wasn't completely shutting me out.

I cut the engine and surveyed the exterior. All the lights were off in the upstairs windows, and although the door was open, the garage itself was in darkness. No overall-clad figure was waiting to greet me this time. Was everyone asleep? In which bed? To avoid waking them, I dismounted and wheeled the BMW inside.

As I removed my helmet and gloves, I realized a thin sliver was glowing at the base of the door in the middle of the far wall. Someone was in the dungeon.

Cautiously, I went inside.

With helmet and gloves still gripped in one hand, I stared, transfixed by the scene before me. This was the dungeon Julius had dreamed of building. The sling was now suspended from the ceiling along with our collection of toys, giving the place a suitably phallic feel. Even the Saint Andrews Cross from the hotel had been relocated here. A faint snore alerted me that the room was not empty.

Partially hidden by a screen, Don lay sprawled in a leather chair I'd never seen before. The low padded seat looked perfect for all sorts of things: spanking, getting a blowjob from someone kneeling at your feet. So many possibilities.

Clad only in his favorite pair of jeans, he must have been cleaning the flogger he'd used on Gabriel that afternoon. The long strands were draped across his lap while a tub of saddle soap sat on the floor beside his feet.

Dogs wag their tail the moment they see their masters. Don may not be my Master, but my cock certainly jumped to attention as I gazed at him. Why was I so attracted to the man? No one would ever call him handsome. At least not by modern standards. But deep inside, every part of my being said this man was right for me. If I hadn't been so tired, I would have jumped him then and there and smothered him in kisses. Who cared why he had left me behind? The gate had been open. That meant a lot.

But now the dragon was back in his lair, guarding his pile of treasure. In his case, a sleeping dragon.

Operating the Paradiso wouldn't be easy. From the sound of things, he'd been finishing off the house renovations while I was gone, plus the stress of having to look after Gabriel's needs, obviously to the detriment of his own. He looked as if he didn't have a scrap of energy left.

Should I wake him and send him off to bed? Sometimes it was difficult settling again after being dragged out of a deep sleep.

Hot chocolate would help.

Trying not to disturb him, I quietly retreated into the garage, stripped off my leathers, and dumped them on the floor. Wearing only my Lycra undershorts, I tiptoed upstairs.

My hands shook as I heated the milk and stirred in the cocoa. With a mug in each hand, I ventured downstairs. How was the dragon going to react when I nudged him awake? Would he breathe flames? I was walking slowly because I didn't want to spill anything, right?

Nah, you're scared stiff. Admit it!

The rhythmic slap of hand on leather greeted me when I made it safely to the entrance. Despite my efforts not to disturb him, Don must have heard me in the kitchen. He didn't take his eyes off his task as I entered the dungeon. "What are you doing up, boy? I told you to go to bed."

"How many times do I have to tell you that I am not your boy?"

Don stared at me in amazement as I walked toward him. "I didn't hear the bike."

"You were asleep, Sunshine." I handed him the mug. "I thought you might like a nightcap before going to bed. You can't stay in that chair all night. You'll get a stiff neck."

"Yes, Mom." He checked the contents and sniffed.

"Do you want something stronger? I haven't added any scotch, but I can if you like."

Don's gaze flickered up to my face, then down. The problem with standing in front of a seated man was that my crotch was now at his eye level. He couldn't fail to notice the evidence of my arousal. Lycra didn't hide anything.

"Has that boy been talking?" he asked gruffly, taking a cautious sip.

"You mean Gabriel?" I smiled sweetly. "He may have mentioned you had a drink or two. It's okay. I don't mark levels on the bottles in this establishment, though you might want to do it at the hotel. You can't trust the staff, you know."

"Still wearing your shiny armor, I see."

"Comes with the goods. Gotta problem with that?"

Don took another sip and smiled faintly while doing another full-body scan. "No."

I collected one of the cushions from a pile on the shelf and dropped it next to his chair. Sighing, I sat down, leaned back, and sipped my drink. The silence stretched on, but neither of us seemed inclined to end it. I could get used to this.

Eventually, Don placed the empty mug on the floor beside me and resumed his cleaning. The pain at seeing the car drive out of the parking lot returned. "Why did you leave me stranded at the reception place?"

Don laid the flogger down and rubbed his hand over my scalp. This simple form of intimate contact felt as reassuring as a kiss. I almost purred under the contact. He let out a long sigh before he began speaking. "When you sent word that you weren't challenging the will, I expected you to return immediately, but when you didn't, and started sending all those photos, I figured you'd decided not to come back at all." The stroking stopped, and he removed his hand.

I squirmed closer, hoping he would touch me again, but he didn't. I twisted around to face him. "I told you I was coming back."

"Yeah, but I assumed that was just because of your promise to Sara." His face betrayed some of the pain my thoughtlessness must have cost him.

"Kieran is just a guy I met. We're not involved in any way."

"I didn't know that until Gabriel told me in the car."

"I'm sorry if I gave you that impression." If anything, that made him look even sadder.

"Why did you?"

"I don't know." I paused for a second and muttered, "I guess, in a way, I wanted to see if I could make you jealous."

"You succeeded."

If he had been my Master, Don would have given me whatever punishment he deemed suitable for sending the photo of Kieran without any explanation. Then that would be that. The matter would be forgotten. The transgression forgiven.

On the surface, vanilla might seem easier, but knowing my actions had upset Don caused me a different kind of pain. It hurt me to think that I had hurt him.

I shuffled around until the cushion was between his feet and sat cross-legged, facing him. Don spread his knees apart, allowing me to get closer. Ah, that was better. Now I could see his eyes. The chocolate had revived him, but he still looked tired.

"Thanks for not shutting me out," I whispered.

Weariness turned his voice into rough gravel. "That gate has been open every night you've been gone. I wanted you to come back, but I had to make sure it was what *you* wanted." He took a deep breath. "Why *did* you stay away so long?"

I told him of my promise to my mother.

He chuckled quietly when I finished, more ironic than happy. "So, in the end I made you leave so as not to influence you, and your mother did instead."

"Maybe I need being told what to do."

Don raised his eyebrows.

I laughed. "Okay, maybe not."

He smiled at my admission.

"But deep down I was always trying to find some solution that wouldn't hurt you. Possibly, there is a part of me that always needs permission or at least acceptance from the ones I love." I rubbed my cheek against his knee like a cat does when it conveys the same emotion to its owner.

Don tilted my head so he could see me. "After you left, I realized that if it came to a toss-up between the house and you, you would win hands down every time. I missed you."

"Missed you too." We smiled at each other. That's all we needed to say. Those three words conveyed as much as undying words of devotion ever would.

"But will you be able to live here?" He stroked the top of my head, but this time I could see the love and concern while he caressed me.

"I couldn't live anywhere else." Exist, maybe. Not live. "Gabriel told me you're ready to take in guests."

Sparks of energy flickered in Don's eyes. "Yeah. It's all coming together. Places like these are rare. People need a space to explore their kink safely, and not only guys into leather."

I nodded and made sure I kept a straight face. "I gather you're planning on doing some filming. You should shave your hair into a mohawk like Tony Buff and get in touch with Dawson the Dyson. Fetish porn is a big money-spinner."

Don gave me a sharp clip on the side of my head. "Nat and Danny are simply coming to take photos for promotional flyers and a website."

"Ouch!" I rubbed my ear ruefully. At least his smile had returned. "Yeah, they're bringing my Stevie gear."

Don chuckled. "You remind me of a cat, the way you always fall on your feet." The smile faded. "But seriously, are you sure you're going to be able to live here and not be involved?"

"Yeah. Funnily enough, it was my sister, Rhiannon, who showed me the solution. She watches while her boyfriend goes surfing. In the same way, it will help you to have support from someone *outside* the culture who understands what you're trying to do without needing to be told."

Don nodded. "I must admit that being in control twenty-four-seven is exhausting, especially if your workplace is your home. It will be good to have someone around who has my back." He sighed and closed his eyes before letting his head collapse against the headrest.

Some tension still lingered in his body, though. I knew the perfect solution for that. "Now we've got all the serious stuff out of the way, may I please suck your cock, Sir?"

Don opened one eye to see if I was serious. I was. Sort of. "I doubt I've got enough energy to do anything," he muttered.

"Relax, I'll look after you." Don didn't object, so I knelt up and undid his jeans. He wasn't exactly unwilling as he squirmed around to make my job easier. His cock was at half-mast as it flopped out into my hand. I cradled it in my palm and glanced up. Don's eyes were like slits, barely open, but I had no doubt that he was watching me. I blew him my best air kiss and got to work.

I was right—the chair was at a perfect height. I settled down and concentrated on my task. It didn't take me long to get him fully hard.

Don moaned appreciatively as I brought him to the brink time and time again. As I did, I sang one of Stevie's songs under my breath. "Ooh, baby, ooh, baby, ooh." He liked that. I'm not sure how many times I took him to the edge before he finally came, but it could have been seventeen.

"I'm glad you're back," he murmured before sleep finally claimed him.

Licking my lips, savoring the last drops, I sank back on my heels and rested my head against his knee. Finally, I had a place in the world where I belonged. I was home.

CHAPTER
THIRTY-TWO

Secret Love

"YOU were right—I did get a sore neck." Don gently shifted my head as I came out of a deep sleep. He tucked himself away and stretched, straightening out his cricks.

"What's the time?" I murmured drowsily.

Don checked his watch. "Nearly five."

I glanced around, taking in more of the improvements he'd made. Little touches that would make the dungeon more practical. "You've been busy."

"Yeah, but you haven't seen the best bit yet." Don held out his hand to lift me to my feet and steered me outside.

"Where are we going?"

"You'll see." The smile he gave me was one he reserved for special occasions.

Instead of leading me upstairs, Don guided me into the meditation room. The sky was just starting to lighten. Now and then a bird called out, announcing the start of a new day, but nothing else disturbed the peace and quiet.

He'd painted the walls, purchased new cushions, and placed rugs on the floor. Working his way around, Don lit the candles. "All we need now is electricity."

"Kieran's a sparky."

"Kieran?"

"The guy in the photo."

Don groaned and buried his head in my neck. "Don't remind me. You're mine."

"Am I? You haven't even kissed me since I got back."

"Come here."

Who could refuse an order like that? Seconds later, our lips mashed together, teeth clashing at first. Then I gave in and let him take control, allowing him full access to me—my mouth, heck, even my heart. He'd earned it.

Still, the intensity continued, I broke away and took a deep breath. His kiss had sucked all the oxygen from my lungs, zapping any remaining strength.

Don backed me against the windows and resumed his kiss, attacking my neck this time. Though I could now breathe easier, forming words was a struggle. I turned to stare out to sea. If the wall gave way there was a sheer drop below. "Careful, I don't know how secure this thing is."

That made Don pause. He stopped and cupped my chin, forcing me to face him. "While you were gone, a friend of Fred's who is a structural engineer came to check the place out. He said this room was fine as long as we drilled extra holes into the rock, top and bottom, so the walls could be attached more securely."

I glanced around, and, sure enough, large bolt heads proved his words.

Don grasped my head in both hands and groaned. "When will you learn to trust me? Don't you think I would have taken that into consideration? I look after those I care for."

Damn. I'd hurt him again. He hadn't released me, though. His hands still cradled my face. I licked the rough skin on his palm. I hated witnessing the pain I'd caused. "I'm sorry."

He forced me to look at him again. "I'm not going to lie and profess undying love. I'm not sure I'll ever be able to lower my defenses enough to feel that way again. But know this: each day you were gone was torture, and not only from the fear you might have an accident, or even the money angle. When you sent that photo, I tried telling myself I was glad you'd found someone else and were having fun. You deserve to be happy. But I couldn't get rid of this weird feeling of loss." He gave a wry grin. "Weird, seeing how you've been a thorn in my side ever since we met."

A big admission for a man protected by the toughness of leather. "Sorry for being such a pain." I gave a rueful grin.

The faintest glimmer of a smile appeared, banishing the bleakness. "You and your shiny armor." Don gave a soft chuckle. "When we first met, I thought you were an obnoxious ass, but then I saw the grit and determination as you refused to be cowed or beaten. In your case, not by whips or chains, but by life itself. You *are* a tiger. I've told you that before. When will you start to believe me?" As he spoke, Don caressed my jawline. His thumbs sent goose bumps cascading over my skin.

"Are you sure you want to live with a thorn in your side?" I asked warily.

Don knew me well enough by now to understand what I was saying. *Can I be me, or do I have to change?*

"No doubt I'll be rolling my eyes when you sing while you cook, clad only in your frilly apron, but you do provide balance in my life. Your thorniness will quickly deflate any sense of superiority I might have."

"Ooh, but you *are* superior." I thrust my groin forward to show him what I meant.

Don didn't retreat, not one inch. If anything, he pressed his body closer to mine, trapping me harder against the window frame. All trace of amusement vanished. "I'm serious, Steve. A lot of people are drawn to BDSM because in the safety of a scene they can admit to desires and emotions they feel uncomfortable expressing otherwise. If you stay here as a bystander, I won't be able to use traditional methods to break down the barriers you erect, so you're going to have to do that yourself. In other words, I'm going to have to rely on you to be totally honest with me and communicate your needs and wants. Can you do that?"

I brought my hands up to his chest, threading my fingers through his pelt, and found his nipples. Damn the man for reading me so well. I caressed the soft nubs with my thumbs, making them hard. "You want me to communicate my needs…." I pretended to think for a moment. "How about, 'I want you to fuck me now.' Is that what you mean?"

"No." Don scanned my face for a long moment.

I returned his scrutiny, not concentrating on the surface of his eyes, or dwelling on their brownness, or the way they reflected every change in his mood, but instead delving inside, trying to reach his soul. *Honesty.* He deserved that. I took a deep breath and swallowed. "I'm sorry. I'll try to be less of an uncommunicative brat."

Don's grip on my chin grew tighter, and the glimmer of a smile returned. "See, that wasn't too hard." He kissed me again, gently to start with but then deepening the pressure as all the blood started racing again. He pulled back and released me. "Speaking of hard…."

A tortoise woven out of cane, sitting beside the candles, proved to be the hiding place for strips of condoms and lube.

"Expecting someone?"

That jibe drew another flash of exasperation. I kicked myself for once again letting my insecurity surface.

"'Hoping' might be a better word." He used his teeth to rip a condom from the strip and threw the remainder on the rug. Leaving the foil clenched between his teeth, he unbuttoned his jeans. All the time his eyes were fixed on mine, sending their own command. *Strip.*

My hands were shaking as I tried to comply. The only problem was I couldn't take my eyes off him, and my erection was straining the Lycra, pulling it tight. Damn, where were Aunt Mildred's boxers when I needed them?

After he released his own cock, his low growl of impatience only made my fingers more useless. Don ended up having to finish the job for me.

"Turn and face the window."

Kicking the abandoned shorts aside, I followed his direction, shivering with anticipation as he moved in close behind me. Once again, it was as if a switch had been flipped. Placing my hands on the window, he muttered fiercely, "Don't move."

How could I when he had me trapped against his chest with one arm while the other worked its way all over my body? Reasserting ownership, leaving his mark, if not physically, at least reminding me my skin was his to touch, his to hold, his to do whatever he liked with. At times, his touch was a caress, at others a pinch or a tweak, until I was writhing in his warm embrace.

Then the growls started in earnest, but now they were interspersed with words: "My tiger," "Stay with me," "Mine," and one time, "Need you," all whispered into my ear as Don slicked up his fingers and worked on my butt, getting me ready.

He didn't say the word I most wanted to hear, but that didn't mean I couldn't say it, at least to myself. *Love the way you touch me. Love the way you need me. Love the way you want me to stay.*

Don closed his eyes when he slammed his cock home. I knew he did, because the windows did their magic trick again, working as a mirror, reflecting our faces. I didn't close my eyes. Couldn't. Loved watching Don as he thrust deep inside me, again and again, claiming a little more with each stroke, pushing me closer and closer to the edge. I was trapped by his left arm, kept immobile by his strength. Then his other hand found my cock, hard and leaking as his shaft stroked my gland. He gripped my cock tight and used it to force my body back against his, increasing the pressure.

Thud, thud, thud. His hips snapped back and forth like a pile driver, hammering home his dominance.

The restriction should have worried me, made me panic. Instead each stroke pounded at my fears, driving them away. Without using any artificial restraints, Don had captured my body, my heart, and my soul.

His movements became erratic as his hand sped on my cock.

Words seemed to come from nowhere. "Please," and then, "I want." What did I want? More. But could I stand any more of this? Already my heart felt like it was beating so hard it was in danger of escaping. Did I need bolts to keep it down, or could I let it fly?

Once, under the ministrations of Julius's whip, he'd got the intensity just right, bringing me close, then backing off until I was screaming for more. Finally, he had tipped me into that subspace where he could do whatever he liked, and I would accept it.

Don may not have used a whip or a cane, but his cock achieved the same result. Nirvana. With one final thrust, he buried himself to the hilt and shook as he came, muffling any words he might have said by latching on to the skin of my neck in a ferocious bite.

Come spurted from my shaft in long, creamy pulses, spraying his hand and the window. I managed to restrict myself to one word, "Love." Thankfully, the final "*you*" was trapped by teeth-clenched lips.

We staggered to the cushion-covered bench and collapsed. Finally, we were able to muster up enough energy to attend to the usual post-sex chores.

Afterward, Don's moustache tickled, as it always did, when he kissed my neck.

No words of love had been spoken, by Don at least. Possibly none ever would be. He still hadn't fully opened up his heart, but he smoothed his palm over every inch of my naked body that he could reach, claiming ownership of it, just as Julius and I had claimed ownership of this property soon after we bought it.

I couldn't think of a better location for make-up sex. The cushions covering the natural stone bench and rugs on the floor made the basic room a comfortable bolt-hole, even if it would never be perfect. Every time it rained, moisture would still seep through the stone in places. Geckos and skinks would find their way inside, and the slatted glass windows would be a bugger to clean.

I sighed and settled back into his embrace. "I'm so glad you've restored this room to what it used to be like."

Don nuzzled my neck. "My gift for you. I want this to be your special place."

"I don't have anything to give you in return." A gesture like that needed something meaningful. "Wait a minute. Yes I do." I ran outside.

Lifting up a branch of the straggly plant that grew in the crevice near the door, I tore off one of the toothbrush-shaped red flowers and presented it to him. "Not exactly a rose, but just as precious to me."

Don accepted my gift, looking rather bemused. "What is it?"

"Some sort of grevillea. I looked it up when I got to England."

"And this is precious to you, why?"

I let the long branch drop back over the edge. "This was the closest thing I could get to bedsheets when I escaped that night." I avoided looking at Don as I told him how I'd thrown down my backpack and used the plant to work my way over the edge before grabbing onto the different ferns and plants growing in the cracks to slow my descent as I slid down the sheer rock face, ripping my fingertips to shreds in the process.

"Fuck." Don stared at the flower in his hand and took a deep breath, obviously shaken by the risk I'd taken.

"Hey." I put my arm around his waist and hugged him. "At the time, I kept thinking of all these escape movies: Steve McQueen jumping the fence on his bike, prisoners scrambling over the top of barbed wire. They're scared, but those endorphins drive them on. No half measures if you want to succeed."

"That's my tiger."

Arms around each other, we strolled back to the house.

CHAPTER
+++
THIRTY-THREE

Trouble in Shangri-La

SURPRISE, surprise. Gabriel had finally mastered the art of making an omelet. "Hmm, it's good," I said with my mouth half full. "But why aren't you wearing the apron?"

He blew me a raspberry.

"Children!" Don's voice may have suggested he was annoyed, but I noticed the edge of his eyes crinkling. He seemed almost smug this morning. Well, I suppose he should be. He was the laird of all he surveyed and had two people running around, ready to carry out his every wish.

After breakfast, he took me on a tour to show off the rest of the renovations. He and Gabriel had certainly been busy in my absence. Not only were Don's room and the office now sporting fresh coats of paint, but he'd bought new furniture for the other bedrooms. "Everything looks great." It did.

He hadn't spent a fortune, but the stark burnished wood and multiple touches of black leather transformed the house from a run-down hippy guest house into a gentleman's retreat. A kinky gentleman's retreat.

"Where the heck did you find the bed heads?" They certainly hadn't come from some crummy secondhand furniture store.

Don gave me one of his biggest shit-eating grins. "Back home, one of my landscaping clients wanted to get rid of their old-fashioned gates and fencing, and I discovered that wrought iron is great for bondage. Sydney has a great selection in the renovation shops. All you need is someone who can weld, and one of Fred's friends is...."

"A welder." I wasn't the only one who always landed on his feet like a cat.

Midmorning, Nat and Danny arrived with my gear and were clearly impressed by everything they saw. I tagged along as Don showed them around the garden, explaining his landscaping plans. Not for resale, but to make the place appealing for guests who wanted to indulge in their kink alfresco. For starters, he wanted to create secluded sections where the hang gliders wouldn't be able to see into the shelters he was describing. When we came to the bamboo, I expected him to say something about the meditation room, but when I started to mention its existence, he put his finger to his lips.

After lunch, they lugged an assortment of paraphernalia into the dungeon to start filming while I settled down to clean all the bugs and dirt off my bike.

Both the dungeon door and the one in the back wall were closed, so I worked in silence.

A faint buzzing, repeated at regular intervals, broke my concentration. At first, I thought it must have come from their equipment, but then I realized it was coming from upstairs. I went to investigate and discovered Gabriel's cell phone almost jumping off the table. An SMS was displayed on the screen. "Please call me. It's urgent. Mum."

Normally, I wouldn't have interrupted them, but she'd been trying to contact Gabriel for a while.

I cautiously opened the dungeon door. Gabriel was bundled up in ropes as securely as a pig ready for roasting. I averted my eyes and addressed Don. "Gabriel's mother is trying to contact him. She says it's urgent. Should I say he's tied up at the moment and take a message?"

A look of exasperation crossed Don's face, but he quickly released the knots.

Once he was free, Gabriel took the phone outside to get a better reception.

While he was gone, everyone stood around gazing at each other as if wondering what to do next. Don didn't seem to want to look me in the eye. The amazing thing was that seeing Gabriel in bondage hadn't freaked me out. Perhaps because it was happening to someone else. Anyway, it was daylight now, and there were other people around. Part of my previous fear had been linked to the night and being left alone.

"Do you want to see what we've filmed so far?" Nat Taylor gestured to Don to look at the screen. I wandered across to speak to Danny.

"How's it going?" I asked him.

"Not bad. The overhead lighting's too harsh, and it's casting shadows, so we're trying to fix that." He glanced over to where Don and Nat had their heads together, studying the camera. Danny added quietly, "Personally, I think the main problem is that Don is finding it difficult to relax enough to make it seem real."

Gabriel ran back into the room, tears streaming from his eyes.

"What's wrong?" I think we all asked the same question at the same time.

"Dad's had a stroke. He's in intensive care at St. Vincent's."

Don led Gabriel over to the chair and forced him to sit down. "Take a deep breath. Getting into a panic won't solve anything."

Gabriel buried his head in hands, his shoulders shaking with the strength of his sobs. No matter how much Don tried to reassure him that some people make good recovery from strokes, Gabriel kept crying. I half expected Don to get angry. Julius would have snapped after a couple of minutes.

Danny, of all people, came across and started talking to the distraught young man. He spoke too softly for any of us to hear, but his words had the desired effect. Gabriel took a deep breath and stood up again, wringing his hands and chewing on his lip. "I'm sorry. It came as such a shock. He's only in his sixties and keeps so fit."

"Would you like me to drive you to the hospital?" Don asked.

"No!" Gabriel obviously felt his response seemed curt. He blushed. "No, I already feel bad that I won't be able to help out today."

Don shook his head. "Don't worry about that. We'll do it another time. Come on. Let's get all your gear together." Gently taking Gabriel's arm, he led him out of the dungeon. "Entertain Danny and Nat for me, please, Steven."

Nathaniel Taylor was winding up Don's ropes, his gaze fixed on his boyfriend. Meanwhile, Danny was staring at me. What to do now? Don had given me an order, but he'd hidden a message in it. Steven. Not Steve or Stevie. Telling me to behave.

As if I'd get up to any mischief while he's gone.

"Was this your first experience of bondage, Nat?" I asked, trying to be polite. The way he was touching the ropes, you'd think they were alive.

"Actually, it's not."

Danny flushed at his comment.

Whoa, this looked interesting.

The tall Aussie came to stand behind me and draped a loop of rope over my shoulder. I had the distinct impression that he was more interested in Danny's reaction than mine.

Danny didn't appear to be concerned by the intimacy of his boyfriend's actions. "I'm not doing it, and that's that." He sounded more pissed off than anything.

I felt like I'd stumbled into the middle of a longstanding argument.

I turned my head and looked up at Nat. A wry grin twisted his lips as he caught the query in my eyes. "Danny and I went to see Hajime Kinoko perform recently in an old warehouse near Sydney Uni. He's a Japanese rope artist. Shinbari. Kinbaku." As Nat spoke, he expertly wrapped the rope around my wrists and twisted them behind my back before layering a series of ropes across my chest. I was so busy watching Danny's face that I didn't catch on to what Nat was doing until it was too late.

I waited for panic to flare up, but it didn't. Part of me seemed to be standing on a platform, looking down at the scene and objectively evaluating what was going on. Yes, a man was tying a rope around me, but it wasn't attached to anything. I could still run or call for help. But the urge to flee wasn't there. I was more interested in watching the interplay between Nat and Danny. Apparently, my therapist was right. She had told me that panic attacks came because I was fearing what *might* happen, instead of concentrating on the here and now.

Danny's attention was focused on his boyfriend. I'd never seen an Asian blush before, but his cheeks certainly darkened. "I don't mind you practicing on me," he said, "but I don't want to be photographed. Okay?"

From the way Nat threw the loops around me and the deftness of his knots, I could tell that he must have had *lots* of practice.

"But that's the whole point, honey. You look magnificent when I tie you up, and Don has offered us the use of this space and its suspension points." Without pausing, Nat indicated the spot where Gabriel had been hanging.

Once again, I waited for that sick churning in my gut, but all that surfaced was a concern that the beam would be strong enough. "Are you sure that's safe?"

"Don told me he had a structural engineer out to check it last week."

I should have realized that Don would be thorough once an expert was present.

Nat glanced around the room. "This would make a fantastic backdrop for a shoot with Danny, but he still can't be tempted."

Although Nat was trying to make it sound like fun, Danny's shyness was obviously an issue between the two of them. "Sounds fascinating," I prompted, eyeing Danny with interest. Until now, I'd thought he was the stereotypical Asian: cool, calm, and collected. But fire flashed in his eyes as his boyfriend continued to wrap the rope around me, jerking me about as he constructed the knots. I glanced down. My bike maintenance overalls bulged out in all the wrong places. "I think I'm wearing the wrong outfit, sweetie."

Nat laughed—a big guffaw coming from the depths of his stomach. "You're right. I should have made you strip first."

Danny didn't seem impressed by that remark. Maybe he wasn't cool about the way his boyfriend was touching me. I could imagine him as the subject. The pale rope would contrast beautifully with his darker skin and jet-black hair. "Leather bondage is usually quick and nasty," I commented wryly. "Tying someone up so you can fuck 'em."

Both men laughed at that. Nat added, "Yeah, but I like to think of this as gift wrapping." He turned me to face the door so he could work on the knots behind my back.

Don was standing there, his face a curious mix of anger and concern. "Are you okay?"

I gave him a quick nod.

Don's shoulders didn't relax as he scanned my face, searching for any sign that I needed rescuing, but once again, I marveled at my composure. Perhaps, last time, deep down, there'd been an underlying fear that I *had* to submit or I wouldn't be able to stay. Now, I was welcome whether or not I participated in the scene. Don wanted me. That made a huge difference. "Nat's been demonstrating macramé for dummies, or should I say on dummies." That drew another chuckle.

Don came closer and brushed his lips over mine. "Gift wrapped," he murmured in my ear. "I like that thought."

There must have been some suspicion of territorial encroachment because Nat started untying me as soon as Don appeared. When he finished, Don pulled me aside. "I can't leave you alone for five minutes without you getting into mischief. Are you sure you're okay?"

I rubbed my arms to get the circulation back. "Yeah, it was strange. Part of me was just waiting to freak out, but in the end, I was too interested in Danny's reactions to worry about myself."

Don looked intrigued, but now wasn't the time nor the place to discuss it. I leaned forward so my voice wouldn't carry. "Tell you later."

"Okay, but I don't think we'll push our luck any further today." With one arm looped casually over my shoulder, he turned to face the two men. "Sorry for wasting your time, boys. We can do the rest another day."

"Why can't Steve be the model? He's got a great face for photography."

Nat's comment drew another glare from Danny.

278

Don didn't seem too happy either. "Uh, no. I don't think that would be a good idea. You got off a few before Gabriel left, didn't you?"

"Yeah, but we've only got bondage shots. Didn't you want to do some with the floggers and the cross?"

"No!"

"Fine with me."

Our responses coincided.

A stubborn expression came over Don's face as he shook his head emphatically. I made the universal symbol for time-out and dragged him to one side.

"Why can't I do it? Time is money for these guys. It may be weeks before they can get here again." I gripped Don's arms tightly. I felt like shaking some sense into him, but he still wasn't budging. His lips formed into a thin line.

"What about your vow not to be involved?"

"I only said I wouldn't call anyone my Master. I'm not planning on making a habit of this, but you need someone now."

Don still didn't look convinced. He not only respected my decision to stay at arm's length, he was prepared to help me keep it. But today was different. He needed what I could provide. I chewed on my bottom lip, pondering what to do. Each year, to maintain his lifeguard qualification, Evan had to prove he was a competent swimmer and that he had mastered the latest first aid standards and rescue techniques. The analogy still rang true. "Look at it this way," I explained. "There may be times when you need a guinea pig for testing new equipment or just for practice. Wouldn't it be an advantage to have an experienced person around who can provide you with that service?"

"Yes," he drawled. "Your point being?"

"I wouldn't need to be totally immersed in the scene to fulfill that role, but I would need to get my feet wet now and then to remind me what the water feels like."

Don's brows narrowed as he finally caught on that I was placing flags on the sand, marking my limits. Eventually, he sighed. "You know that I've always wanted to beat the crap out of you in a scene so I could show you what a true Master is like, caring for you as much as demanding to be served. But not like this."

All that promise of power and aggression went straight to my cock. "Don't you want these photos done?"

"Yeah," Don muttered. "But we should have discussed this properly beforehand."

"So? Adapt. I'm not afraid of that level of involvement, Sunshine. Are you?"

Don's back straightened as he sensed a challenge.

Was this the spark that was lacking from the shots with Gabriel? Keeping my gaze locked on his darkening brown eyes, I slowly stripped out of my overalls. Underneath, I was only wearing a black jockstrap. One that barely contained my erection.

Don growled, and his nostrils flared.

Nat's whistle just made him growl louder.

As if on cue, Danny wheeled the Saint Andrew's Cross into position. He'd make a great stagehand. I sauntered across and leaned back against the wood, then grabbed the attachment points.

"That's enough," Don snapped.

Nat was already moving around, taking photos. "Testing the light," he muttered.

I think the big photographer thought Don's annoyance was directed at him, but I knew *I* was the real source of his frustration. Don was feeling manipulated, and he didn't like it one bit.

Lowering my voice, I tried to make it sound like a choice, not a challenge. "It's simple. You need a model for a flogging scene, and I'm offering you one."

Don's scowl lessened, but he still wasn't giving in. "In case it's escaped your attention, Gabriel was already marked, so we were going to pretend."

"Why can't you pretend with Steve?" Nat interjected.

Grasping my waist, Don spun me around to face the cross, and then he stepped away and ran his hands over my back. "Any idiot will know it's fake because this isn't red."

The roughness of Don's palm took all the strength out of my legs. I grabbed the supports and clung on for dear life as the soft caress affected me as much as a whiplash.

"I suppose we could always use makeup." Don's sigh suggested he was halfway to accepting my proposal.

I turned my head and snarled at him, "Over my dead body, Sunshine. Warm me up properly."

Don slapped my bare ass cheek. "I'm not tying you up, and that's that."

"You don't need to. I can hang on."

He let out a deep sigh. "I suppose that might work. One hand off means you want to talk. Two off means we stop. Like it or not."

"Sounds fine to me." I settled myself more comfortably against equipment I knew so well, yet every former encounter felt like it had happened to a different person. I loosened my grip, letting air pass between my palm and the support. Part of my brain was in the here and now while the rest already floated free. "Before we start, should I change into something more appealing? Some leather or lace, perhaps?"

"No." I hadn't realized Don was standing so close. He ran his hand over my bare ass.

I arched my back, pressing into his touch.

He seemed to like that. His touch grew firmer. "I like you the way you are. Raw. Natural. Perfect." Leaning in closer, he muttered in my ear before connecting with my bare butt with his open palm. "But damn, you deserve a spanking for forcing me into this."

I hung my head. Perversely, I was ashamed. Not because of the way I'd manipulated him, but because I wanted this so much. "I'm sorry."

Don growled again, but from annoyance this time. "Remember, being kinky is not a sin. Forget what your therapist said. Unless they've had firsthand experience, they don't know what the fuck they're talking about. Don't ever be ashamed of what we do." His hand caressed the spot before striking me again, harder this time. Heat blossomed. These were his marks—ones not in the script. Ones he needed to make to regain some sense of control.

Three, four, five.... Each blow went straight to my cock. My ass would be reddening nicely, but that wasn't all he needed for the photo. "Come on. What are you waiting for? Spanking is for boys. I'm a man."

"Argh," Don groaned and strode out of sight.

I glanced over my shoulder and saw him grab a flogger off the wall. Not the one he'd used on Gabriel, but a longer, thinner one. The strands danced as if they had a life of their own. This must be one that he'd brought with him from the States. His arm blurred as he tested its reach and chose his spot. "Face front," he barked.

The first blow stung more than I expected. Was I out of practice, or had Don meant to hurt me to test my resolve? I gripped the bar tighter and was astonished when he approached and ran his hand over the area he'd struck.

"Sorry, I didn't mean to hit you so hard." Don took a deep breath, his moustache tickling my neck as he nuzzled the skin. "This is fucking difficult. Part of me wants to let go because I know you can take it. I have to keep reminding myself this is all for show. A performance. No more."

"Don't hold back. You have to do what comes naturally or it won't look right."

Another sigh tickled my skin. "Okay, but remember you're in total control the whole time."

Yeah, all I have to do is let go. I gripped the wood tighter. It wouldn't be the pain that would make me quit, more the buildup of tension. Already the spring inside had started tightening in anticipation. Excitement and fear were also contributing. Not fear of being hurt or the memory of past encounters, but fear I would let Don down. "Go on."

A final rub over and Don disappeared again. A swish was the only warning I received as blow after blow rained down on me, much gentler than before. These were butterfly kisses, all the same weight and speed. Controlled to the last inch. Damn, I wished the place had mirrors or Nat had a video camera. I wanted to watch the expression on Don's face as he worked. Witness the light I knew would be shining in his eyes.

Approving noises from Nat told me that he was finally getting the shots he wanted. By the way he muttered "yes" and "more," you'd think Don was a runway model, strutting his stuff, not the master of his art, showing the world how it should be done.

My back burned. Every part had been touched at some stage by the leather, but if I was asked to say exactly where it hurt, I couldn't pinpoint a spot. It was more a general sensation of fire and aliveness. The spring inside tightened. How much further could it go?

"More," I bellowed.

My cry echoed from the ceiling, reverberating around the room.

"Yes." The simple response from Don was followed by an increase in intensity, giving me exactly what I wanted, what I needed. The room disappeared. We could have been stuck in the middle of the Simpson Desert for all I knew. The lights above were the hot sun beating down as everything around me dissolved into a haze, shimmered up like a mirage, and left the two of us as the only solid beings present.

I gripped the wood tighter and clenched my muscles. Each blow now seemed like a gift, a promise of more to come, a kiss.

Dimly, I heard Don speak. Something about how proud he was of his tiger.

Was he speaking to me? He must be. Who else was present?

A rough hand caressed my back. Adding heat, but cooling it at the same time. Exquisite agony. I trembled and nearly let go, not from the pain, but from the gentleness of Don's touch.

Then he pressed his body against mine, allowing me to feel his erection. His hand snuck around to grip my cock, which hadn't stopped straining against the thin material of my jockstrap. He let out a low growl when he realized how turned on I was.

"First time I saw you in here, I knew I could bring out the inner beast. Not leash him, but set him free."

The spring inside had melted in the heat of his embrace and was swirling around, molten lava waiting to erupt and spill that fire on the ground. Tears streamed down my face. There were too many to flick off as I usually did, so I tried to wipe them off with my shoulder. No way was I letting go. My hands were glued to the wood as surely as if they'd been bound on by multiple strands of rope.

I rested my head on my arm. Gradually, my sobs subsided. Don hadn't let go. The thudding in my ears also died down, leaving the room in silence except for the soft exhalation of Don's breath against my ear. His hold on me was as tight as my hold on the cross.

A long sigh of contentment escaped as I gradually came back to earth.

Glancing over my shoulder, I finally realized we were alone. "Where are the others?" I was too tired to remember their names.

Don chuckled and pushed his groin closer. "Upstairs fucking, I assume. They made some excuse about leaving us to it and mixing business with pleasure by taking some photos of the guestrooms."

I sniffed. "Thank God. Taking photos of guys with snotty noses is definitely not sexy."

Don chuckled, giving my neck another nuzzle. "Your resilience never ceases to amaze me. I don't think I've ever met anyone who bounces back as quickly as you do."

His heart was thudding against my back, but while most of my tension had gone, Don still seemed to be wound super tight. "Have you finished?"

"No."

I tensed at the terseness of his reply.

"I want to hear my tiger roar. One lash with the bullwhip. No more. Not as a punishment but as a statement." He drew back and ran his hand lightly over my flayed skin, teasing the nerve endings, adding oxygen to the mix, but it still didn't ignite.

I let my head fall forward, not in shame this time, but mesmerized by his voice as he continued, "I want you to think carefully before consenting to this, Steven. Both you and I know how much it will hurt, especially now that you've cooled down a bit. But you won't be doing it for me. You're doing it for yourself. Not in that condescending way that con artists or unscrupulous bastards make you choose between two options, both being bad for you. I'm offering you a real choice, giving you three options."

I nodded to show I understood what he was saying. "Go on."

"You saw the way I marked Gabriel. None of us are angels in society's eyes."

My hunch was correct. I nodded again to convey my understanding.

"Are you ashamed of being gay?"

I shook my head and grunted out a "No." Words of one syllable were all I could manage.

"Neither should you be ashamed of being kinky. It is not up to others to judge who we are and what we do. Nothing that is done in here with consent is anyone's business but our own. The choice of where I aim this last lash is yours alone. Through the tiger, denying who you are? If so, I'll respect your wishes even if I don't understand them. Through the dragon? A rejection of anyone having authority over you? Or would you rather have no lash?"

I snorted. This was as bad as a council election. "None of the above."

Don's hand paused. "What?"

Given a short respite, I managed to string words together. "Through the middle, where they're fighting each other."

A sharp intake of breath sounded extra loud against my ear. "Are you sure?"

"My hands are still here, aren't they?"

His footsteps receded.

I craned my head to see which whip he'd choose. Aah. My favorite.

Don flicked it back and forth a few times, reacquainting himself with its weight and flexibility. I wasn't the only one who was coming in cold. Normally, he would have had a chance to practice, to get his range right, but every second he delayed, the more I cooled down, ensuring the pain would be that much more intense.

The tears had dried on my face, but none of my fingers had unfurled from their positions.

A low, continuous growl started behind me as Don paced back and forth. He may have called me his tiger, but for now, he was the king of the jungle. The rumble grew in intensity, and then it stopped.

From then on, the only sound was the beating of my heart until Don cried out, "Now let me hear my tiger roar."

The blow came immediately. The searing blast of a volcano finally erupting, spewing up years of trapped fire. "*Aaargh!*" My cry dwarfed any I'd made previously. I couldn't see whether Don had hit the correct spot, but I didn't care. A curious calm descended.

For a while, I thought someone had placed a watch next to my ear, but then I realized that it was my heart, sending its message that I was alive and life was good.

Fingers prized at my hand, accompanied by soft words of encouragement. "It's over, Steve. You can let go now." Don twisted me around so I could fall into his embrace without hurting my back. He held me up as my knees threatened to collapse.

"Thank you."

"No, thank *you* for being willing to trust me. Anytime you want or need a scene, you have only to ask, and I won't even make it conditional on sex afterward."

"Was that a promise or a threat, Sunshine?"

A couple of tears shone at the edge of Don's eyes. Tears of pride. "My tiger," he said and kissed me.

EPILOGUE
+++

Leather and Lace

SOME idiot had stepped on Don's boot and left a scuff mark. The crowds had been heavier than I had anticipated.

"Stop fussing."

"You have to look perfect." I had bought him a new pair of studded engineer boots, and we didn't have time to undo the straps. Anyway, I'd have had a rat's chance of undoing them without ruining my false nails. I sank to the floor, spat on the toe, and gave the leather a few licks before polishing it with the end of my scarf.

This was a big night for Don. His coming out, as it were. His face was flushed by the time I finished, and he pulled me up. "Now your lipstick is smudged." He eased his finger over the edge of my mouth to rub off the excess.

Damn, I was tempted to smudge it further and give him a kiss. He looked so adorable when he got flustered.

I took his hand and pulled him to the door of the hotel bedroom. The same one I'd used twelve months ago to the day. Inside may have been the same, but outside there'd been lots of changes.

In the end, I'd used my savings to buy shares in the hotel, and Aunt Mildred had bought a share too. So now it was a three-way venture. Just as well, as renovations had proved more expensive than I had envisaged. The alterations were paying off, though. Having dance floors on two levels meant the Paradiso could offer different types of music. Downstairs, they played house music and there was a raw, grungy feel to the space, while upstairs, a Diva Dive with disco anthems from the Seventies and Eighties drew in a totally different crowd.

We'd learned early on it was much better to keep the two groups of people apart.

Special days were set aside, and too bad if they forgot to check their diary and turned up on the wrong one. Guys dressed in leather, wearing boots and not a skerrick of cologne got most put out when we had our "Open-Toes Mandatory" evenings. The girls liked coming, and gay guys who were into the music and didn't do drag found it a challenge to source sandals that looked halfway decent. We did set a "no socks" policy, though.

Some girls still tried to get in on our "Closed-Toe" nights, but so far we'd managed to convince them they really didn't want to be there. Most of them accepted our argument it was important to have a place where guys could feel comfortable.

Tonight, though, was a mixed bag, or at least no restrictions. That meant the entertainment had to be harmless, but as it was for a special occasion, no one seemed to mind.

Downstairs, the noise was reaching deafening proportions. I'd managed to hire a few of my favorite Aussie drag performers, and Amelia Airhead and Minnie Cooper were strutting their stuff. It was a shame I was missing it, but Nat and Danny were on hand to record the show.

A knock sounded at the door. I opened it to find a grinning Gabriel.

"When did you get back?"

"Flew in from Abu Dhabi this morning."

Being the first slave Don had ever taken on to train, the young man would always hold a special place in our hearts. He'd taken a gap year and spent the last six months seeing the world. While he was overseas, we'd kept in touch via Skype, and the other day he'd blithely informed Don that when he came back, he wanted to learn how to be a Master.

"You didn't tell us you were coming." Although I could hear the underlying strain, Don's voice still carried that stamp of authority.

"I wanted it to be a surprise, Sir. Wouldn't miss this for the world." Gabriel turned his head to the door, listening to someone's comment. "Fred wants to know if you're ready."

I glanced at Don. He'd relaxed a bit when he saw Gabriel, but his knuckles were still white as he gripped the handheld microphone.

Rolling my eyes, I gave a slight shake of my head, taking care not to dislodge my wig. "Give us a moment, hon. If there's a short break, the punters might buy more drinks."

As soon as the door closed, I turned Don to face me. "Are you going to be able to do this? If it's too much, I'll understand. We can just mime to the recording."

Don swallowed and took a deep breath, making his moustache quiver. I stroked it with my gloved hand. I was going to miss it. Over the last year, I'd grown used to the way it tickled my neck, but after the performance, he was shaving it off as his arse-about contribution to Movember, the fundraiser for prostate cancer and depression initiatives. Oh well, I supposed he could always grow another one.

The prospect of seeing the impossible happen had brought a lot of people out of the woodwork, wanting to see if Don would really do it. Twenty-five thousand dollars had already been pledged. A phenomenal figure. But once word got out that Don was shaving off his signature mo, the money started rolling in.

"It's weird. Get me up on stage with a whip, and I'm fine. But these things"—he grimaced at the microphone—"always freak me out."

"I know, Sunshine." I patted the back of his hand. "But it's good to stretch your limits sometimes." Fluttering my eyelashes, I added the phrase I used to dread, "Do it for me." The following air kiss was a nice touch, I thought. I squealed as his hand hovered dangerously close to my butt. "Careful, you might hurt yourself on the padding. Save it for later."

Laughing, I dragged him to the door, and we went downstairs.

The lights dimmed, and a spotlight followed as we approached the stage. I was wearing my best Stevie Tricks gown, a lace number we'd bought especially for the occasion. A long gold shawl was draped over my shoulders, covering my tattoos. Don looked magnificent in his full leather regalia.

The roar of the crowd surprised him. I don't think he appreciated how loved he was. Many people into BDSM had already benefitted from his instruction. On the rare nights when he did come to the hotel, I made sure he had nothing to do except sit on a stool at the bar and hold court for his adoring fans.

Hand in hand, we made our way through the crowds. When we finally made it onto the stage, Don gave my fingers a squeeze before letting go. He was still too nervous to smile.

On the contrary, I was able to give everyone a huge grin. This was the culmination of a year's work. Proof that leather and lace did mix.

For once, we were working with a live backing band. Thank God my husky voice wasn't a bad approximation of the real thing. As I sang the words about needing him to love me, they never seemed so true.

By the time Don's part came around, he'd found courage from somewhere and sang with confidence. He actually didn't have a bad voice. As the last notes faded, triggering enthusiastic applause, Don leaned in close and whispered, "I meant every word I said. Give to me your lace, and I'll give you my leather."

Oh, who cared if my lipstick got smudged? I kissed him in front of his fans, his friends, and his family. Aunt Mildred wasn't going to miss that night for anything.

And no, I still don't call him Master, but I acknowledge he is a great dungeon master, and while he may not call me his boy, I am very much his.

The snarling tiger and the flame-breathing dragon.

Unlike many authors, A.B. GAYLE hasn't been writing stories all her life. Instead she's been living life.

Her travels have taken her from the fjords of Norway to the southern tip of New Zealand. In between, she's worked in so many different towns she's lost count. She's shovelled shit in cow yards, mustered sheep, been polite to customers, and traded insults with politicians.

Bored with traditional romances, she discovered M/M romance, where the story is about life and all its complexities, not just the ring, the wedding, and the babies. When pressed she'll admit she loves reading and writing about men, because they can do all the things she would love to do but can't, simply because she's female. And if reading about one man is good, reading about two must be better! Right?

Now living in Sydney, Australia, A.B. finally has enough time to allow her real-life experiences to morph with her fertile imagination to create fiction which she hope her readers will enjoy.

Visit her website at http://www.abgayle.com.

Opposites Attract from A.B. GAYLE

RED + BLUE

A.B. GAYLE

http://www.dreamspinnerpress.com

Also from A.B. GAYLE

http://www.dreamspinnerpress.com

www.ingramcontent.com/pod-product-compliance
Lightning Source LLC
Chambersburg PA
CBHW070055030726
47506CB00002B/470